Love Me Today

A.L. Jackson
www.aljacksonauthor.com

Cover Design by RBA Designs
Editing by SS Stylistic Editing
Proofreading by Julia Griffis, The Romance Bibliophile
Formatting by Champagne Book Design

More from

A. L. Jackson

NEW YORK TIMES BESTSELLING AUTHOR

Love Me Today

NEW YORK TIMES BESTSELLING AUTHOR

A.L. JACKSON

Prologue

ENERGY CRACKLED THROUGH THE DIM-LIT HALL.

Tension binding the oxygen in attraction and need.

Every-fucking-thing I could no longer ignore as I stared at her where she hovered in front of her door.

"Caleb." My name barely hit the air.

At the sound of it, I broke.

I crossed the space. No restraint left.

My hand dove into her hair at the side of her head, and I curled the other around her waist and tugged her against me.

We collided in a torrent of greed.

Mouths and tongues and spirits that no longer knew how to exist without the other.

We spun, gripping at each other, desperate to erase every inch of space as I kissed her.

Kissed her with a madness that burned me to the soul.

This woman who'd scored herself into the places I wasn't supposed to let her go.

Because I knew what I brought into the lives of the people I cared about.

I knew the price they paid.

And I should have known what touching her would cost...

Chapter One

Paisley

LEAVE IT TO ME TO BE LATE, BUT IT COULDN'T BE HELPED. Gathering the straps of the reusable grocery bags, I slung them over my shoulder and shifted my cell to my other ear as I hustled out the automatic doors of the small grocery store.

"You know I don't have many details," I told my bestie Dakota as I jogged toward my old truck in the parking lot, my boots thudding hard on the pavement. I pinned my phone between my ear and shoulder so I could dig my keys from my bag. "You know Ryder got me the gig. Some cousin he doesn't know all that well has a little girl who got her first pony, and she needs to learn how to ride it. Easy peasy."

Extra cash in my pocket. Exactly what I needed.

"Are you sure you don't just want to come and work with me at the café? We're slammed this morning. I could really use the extra help."

A small chuckle got free. "Which is why you're wasting your time on the phone with me?"

"Hello, bestie duties. I needed to get the details before you run off to some rando stranger's house in the middle of nowhere. You haven't even talked to the guy. You could end up dead in a ditch somewhere. Buried in a shallow grave. Locked in an attic or basement with some freak telling you that you're his new pet."

I could physically feel Dakota shudder through the phone. She was so dramatic.

"You really should stop listening to true crime podcasts before you go to bed at night. Your paranoia is getting out of control. Besides, this is Ryder's cousin we're talking about. He isn't going to send me to some serial killer's house."

At least I hoped so because it was super odd this guy had only communicated through email, all formal and calling me Ms. Dae, referring to himself as Mr. Greyson as he gave me the precise time to show at his ranch.

What a weirdo.

As far as I knew, Ryder had spent summers with him growing up, but they hadn't seen that much of each other as adults, and the mysterious Mr. Greyson had moved into Time River about six months back. In all that time, I didn't think anyone had ever even met the guy, which considering the size of the town we lived in, that was on the questionable side.

He had to be some kind of recluse, I guessed.

"It's fine," I told her. "You know Ryder wouldn't lead me astray."

"Okay, just text me as soon as you're done. I want all the details. Or wait, come into the café so you can tell me face-to-face. Even better."

A giggle slipped up my throat. "You missed me while I was away, didn't you?"

"I won't even try to deny it. This town was boring as crap without you."

Regret pulled at my ribcage. The intense kind because you could never make up for time that had passed or the things you had missed. But I couldn't wallow in the mistakes that I had made, I could only make sure I never repeated them again.

"I promise you will be bored no more," I said like a solemn oath. "Mack's Friday night?"

These cowgirl boots were made for dancing, and I was about to set them free.

"Um, you could not keep me away. Kayden is having a sleepover at my mom's, and this girl is ready to get her party on."

Dakota's son was almost two. He'd been born while I'd been living in Arizona. It was just another thing I'd missed—being there when he was an infant, being there for my best friend.

"I can't wait," I told her. "I gotta run. I just picked up my grandpa's medication and need to drop it off at his house before I head out to this interview, and I'm wicked late already."

"Give your grandpa a hug for me."

"Will do. Talk to you soon, Doodle-Boo."

"Bye, Paisley-Cakes."

Ending the call, I yanked open the door to my old truck who I lovingly called *Maybe*.

Her hinges creaked in protest.

Yes, I'd named her. She'd been with me from the beginning, since I was sixteen and had scraped together enough money to buy her, and she'd been by my side through every escapade I'd embarked on ever since.

I tossed the grocery bags across the bench seat and hopped in, and I pushed myself up close to the steering wheel as I leaned in and stuffed the key into the ignition. I bounced as I gave it a little gas and cranked it over, coaxing her with sweet nothings. "That's it. We have this. It's you and me, Maybe. Don't let me down now."

She roared to life.

And I mean, roared, my old girl rumbling and chugging and vibrating like a raring beast. I caressed a hand over the weathered dash that sported a crack rivaling the Grand Canyon that ran from one side to the other, a perfect reflection of the one that ran across the windshield. "You're so good to me."

My phone pinged, and I glanced to the side where it was sitting on the seat.

Ryder: Don't be late.

I rolled my eyes. As if.

Okay. Fine. I was always late.

Ryder knew me well. And truth be told, I didn't want to make him look bad, so I pressed down on the brake as I shoved the gear into reverse.

Plus, I really needed this job. No, I really *wanted* this job.

I could feel the hope of it vibrating through my spirit, and I needed to get my butt in gear before I messed up this opportunity before it even started.

I glanced in the rearview mirror, squinting against the blinding rays of morning light that streaked in as the sun climbed into the endless expanse of blue Colorado sky.

All clear.

I gunned it out of the spot.

I jarred forward when Maybe banged into something from out of nowhere. The sound of grating metal was garbled by the screech that tore up my throat.

I rammed back on the brakes, holding tight to the steering wheel, blinking through the confusion, before my mind finally caught up to what had just happened.

"Crap," I grumbled under my breath, and I tossed it into park and hopped out. I absolutely didn't have time for this.

My boots hit the pavement, and I rounded the rear to find Maybe's tail-end banged up against the bumper of a shiny black Range Rover.

Just freaking awesome.

The SUV was halfway out of its spot, too, and appeared to have been pulling out to head the opposite direction. The two vehicles had made impact right in the middle of the aisle.

I knelt to inspect the spot where we'd collided.

Relief gusted.

There was only a small dent and a scratch on the Rover's bumper, and my truck didn't have any damage at all.

It didn't look bad. Nope, not too bad at all.

Except I was pretty sure the other driver might not agree when I felt the dark cloud descend from above.

Warily, I looked up, and my heart pitched in my chest.

I could barely make him out with the sunlight that blurred around him, the man a silhouette of darkness that towered two feet away. That didn't mean I couldn't feel the stone-cold eyes glaring down at me.

"Are you hurt?" His tone was completely at odds with the question.

"No. I'm fine." It came out shakier than I'd anticipated.

Air huffed from his nose, and his deep voice was a rumble of condescension as he looked at the damage on his bumper. "I guess it's too much to ask people to watch where they're going."

I pushed to standing, my words cracking with anger. "Excuse me? You ran into me."

Okay, we'd run into each other, but if he was going to be a jerk about it...

A displeasured scoff blew from his nose, and he stepped forward.

I really hoped my eyes hadn't actually popped out of my head when it brought him into view.

Bollocks and ballsacks.

I'd backed into an Abercrombie model.

Or maybe a Greek God reincarnated.

He glowered, his jaw and cheeks as hard as the icy blue eyes that seemed to glow from his ridiculous face. He was all sharp angles and polished stone, his lips so full and red that my tongue unconsciously stroked over mine.

Correction.

Fallen angel.

That's what he was.

A dark one who'd been booted right out of paradise for being a giant dick.

His brow lifted, his dark blond hair mostly short, cut close on the sides, but the longer pieces on top were pushed back, making him look fiercer.

My stomach twisted.

"I ran into you?" he challenged.

I crossed my arms over my chest. "Um, yes, you did. You're clearly farther out of your spot than I am. Besides, doesn't your fancy-ass car have some sort of warning system to keep you from crashing right into unsuspecting people?"

I flung a hand toward his showpiece, scowling hard to prove my point.

Annoyance had him readjusting the cuffs of his suit jacket.

His *suit* jacket.

Seriously, who was this guy and where did he come from? He was obviously lost. Men like him didn't belong in Time River, a spec of a small town in Nowhere, Colorado.

But he wouldn't be the first tourist to stray from the big city and onto our streets. Seeking the beauty of the plains set in a backdrop of breathtaking mountains and the gorgeous river that ran through. In the winter, the mountains would be covered by snow, but at this time of year, only the soaring peaks were painted white, the snow slowly melting as the fullness of the summer approached.

The irritation the man wore was almost palpable. "It warned me, but since you flew out of your spot without care in that monstrosity, there was no time to avert the accident."

Monstrosity?

"How dare you call Maybe a monstrosity." I set my hand on the tailgate like it could shield her from the slur.

Exasperation seemed to shake his head as he shifted a bit to the side, and he had the audacity to rake his teeth over that full bottom lip. He returned his potent gaze back to me, blowing out a sigh of resignation. "You know what, I don't have time for this."

"Like I do," I spat, trying to ignore the buzzy power radiating from him.

It wasn't like he was beefy or anything. Everything about him was lean and hewn, but I'd bet my ass everything under that suit was sculpted in strength. Deceptively smooth. He was the type of guy who would strike before a person even knew he was coming for them.

I propped my hands on my hips. "Do you want my insurance information or what? Or we can exchange numbers or whatever. You barely have a scratch on your car, but I'm sure you're going to want to get it fixed."

Like this guy would settle for anything less than perfection.

"No, I don't want your information. I'll handle it."

My mouth dropped open. I didn't know if I was offended or relieved. "I do have insurance, you know."

"Congrats, but I think I'll see to things for myself."

I blinked.

Congrats?

Without saying anything else, he turned on his heel and strode around the side of his car, taking that dark, broody, self-righteous ego with him.

I stood there gaping at his overpowering form as he slipped into the driver's seat, the man far too tall and powerful for anyone's good.

He didn't spare me a glance when he put the SUV into drive, his tires squealing as he peeled away.

"Grrr...what a freaking jerk," I shrieked. And still, I stood there staring as he took off onto Manchester, the main street that ran through Time River.

The second his SUV disappeared, I tore myself out of the trance he had me under and hightailed my ass back to the driver's side of my truck and climbed inside. I shoved it back into reverse the way I'd done before I'd been so rudely interrupted and finished pulling out of the spot, then I shifted into drive and gunned it.

Sorry Ryder, now I really was going to be late.

Chapter Two

Caleb

I STARED THROUGH THE REARVIEW MIRROR AT THE WOMAN WHO stood behind that thing that was, in fact, a monstrosity.

A faded yellow Chevy with a thick, cream-colored stripe surrounding the entire rusted, dinged-up body.

Not old enough to be considered a classic but run-down enough to know her life was in danger every time she got behind the wheel.

Everyone else's, too.

Maybe.

She'd fucking named it *Maybe.*

Who the hell named their car?

I couldn't stop from glaring as I took in her fading form when I got to the end of the parking lot and stopped at Manchester, the main drag that ran through Time River.

The woman looked like chaos standing there.

Chaos wearing boots and cut-off shorts and the tightest fucking tee I'd ever seen.

All tits and thick, toned thighs.

White, shiny, silvered hair billowed around her face, soft waves that rippled like the churning of the sea. It was so long it nearly touched her ass.

But it was that smart mouth that had me in a knot.

The girl a reckless riot where she stood at the back of her truck like it was my fault that she'd come whipping out of that spot without care. I'd already been fully out of the parking spot and putting my Rover into drive when she'd come barreling back from out of nowhere.

I raked the back of my hand over my mouth to clear the bad taste that lingered on my tongue, and I tore my gaze from her and turned it to the little girl strapped in her booster seat in the back.

Brown eyes wide and unsettled, her little fingers clutching the doll she had on her lap.

Worry tightened my heart into a fist.

"Are you sure you're okay?" I asked for the tenth time.

"Yes, I'm sure. I only heard a little bang, and only felt a little bump, but I didn't get broken." Her voice was soft yet tinkling, barely touching the air, timidness oozing out of every pore of her tiny body.

Pain stabbed me so deep I nearly buckled.

I hated that I didn't know how to break through, how to reach her, how to bring her out of this.

Hated that I couldn't fucking fix it, especially when I was the cause of it.

I swallowed it back and forced myself to keep it together, doing my best to keep the rigidness out of my voice. "Good. That's good. But I need you to tell me if you are ever hurt or feel bad. No matter what the situation is. Do you understand?"

I didn't so much ask her as tell her as I pulled out onto the street.

"Okay," she mumbled with the doll pressed to her face.

God, I was fucking this up. My teeth ground as an uncomfortable silence moved through the cab, then I nearly jolted when her tiny voice whispered, "Are you hurt?"

Regret pilfered through my nose. It probably hadn't helped that I'd snarled and snapped a slew of curses when the truck had rammed into us.

"I'm fine, Evelyn. I promise that I'm fine. You don't ever have to worry about me, okay?"

She was back to gnawing her bottom lip in uncertainty.

She clearly didn't believe me.

I wondered if she'd ever believe it of anyone.

"Let's just get back to the house, and you can get ready, okay?" As if that would fix everything.

"Okay." Her voice perked up a little at that.

My phone rang through the speakers, and my teeth gnashed again at the name that showed on the screen.

I was supposed to have heard from him two days ago.

Diverting the Bluetooth, I snapped up my cell and pressed it to my ear, my voice low and harsh because this wasn't a conversation Evelyn needed to hear. "Allen, what did you find?"

From the other end of the line, my private investigator cleared his throat. "I dug around on Tarek Paltrow, pushed some buttons. Gut tells me he was not responsible."

Goddamn it.

My hand tightened on the phone, rage clouding my sight.

"Are you sure?"

"Yes."

My teeth ground harder. I'd been through every one of our family's enemies. Sifted through every connection. Every deal gone bad, and we'd come up empty.

But someone had to be responsible, and it was my gut telling me it was Paltrow or someone associated to that family. No one hated me as much as them.

"This wasn't random," I gritted out.

"We are regrouping, going back to the beginning to see what we can find. And we will find something," he promised.

"I want the one responsible found, and I want him now."

"It's not that simple, Caleb. You know that."

"It is. Someone sought revenge on my family, and I want to know who it is," I grated, my voice low and barely controlled.

"I'm doing everything I can."

Frustration carved a canyon through my spirit. "I'll be in Seattle next week. I want every detail you have, a list of every fucking person my father was involved with. From the beginning."

Because apparently, if I wanted something done, I had to do it myself.

Chapter Three

Paisley

MAYBE BLEW A RUMBLY PATH UP THE TWO-LANE ROAD. I'D traveled about thirty miles out of town in the direction of Hutchins Ranch, and I was finally coming up on the turnoff. I glanced at the dial clock on the dash.

My stomach twisted.

Crap.

I was fifteen minutes late.

Not that I didn't already know I was going to be, but I guessed I'd been praying for some kind of osmosis or teleportation or maybe just a dose of good luck to get me here on time.

It wasn't like I was going to cut out going back by my grandpa's house before coming here. He was my priority, and he'd needed that prescription this morning and something to eat for lunch while I was away.

When I'd returned to Time River two months ago, I'd moved back in with him, needing a place to stay until I got back on my feet. He'd welcomed me, the way I knew he would, and I was grateful it gave me the chance to look out for him now that he was alone.

I wasn't about to neglect that responsibility this morning when the doctor's office had called and said he needed to up his heart medication.

Still, I was all sweaty and anxious.

This wasn't exactly the best first impression I could give.

Slowing, I eased Maybe onto the wide dirt drive that was marked with a big wooden sign overhead that read *Hutchins Ranch.*

I'd passed by the turnoff a thousand times, but I'd never actually been out onto the property. For at least a century, it had belonged to the Hutchins family. It had been passed down from generation to generation, but the last owner had had no children, and when she'd passed, it'd been put on the market.

And it was like a gazillion dollars. Apparently, Ryder's cousin was loaded.

The dirt road wound over the grassy plain, the green fields going on for miles, rolling out from all sides to touch the pines and evergreens that hugged the land in the distance. Blue sky ran forever, an endless expanse that burned with the white glow of the sun. Below, horses and cattle grazed in the fields.

It was so gorgeous my heart squeezed.

My insides glowed with anticipation, this excitement that spiked in my blood.

I hadn't worked with horses in…years.

For far too long.

Regret washed through me. It felt like everything I'd left behind was right here, teasing me, so close but out of reach.

I had the power to change that now, though, didn't I? So I bit it back and hauled butt up a hill, dust flying behind me as I raced to shave off a few seconds.

My breath caught all over again when I got to the top of the ridge and caught sight of the ranch tucked in the valley on the other side.

"Holy crap," I mumbled.

Outbuildings were situated on the property, barns and corrals and cabins all built on the breathtaking land, surrounded by those rolling fields and thickets of trees.

On the far north side, the river weaved its way through the property. Stoic oaks and rustic firs raced the edges of its path, as if they had chased it in a bid to catch up. Mountains capped with snow set it all in a glorious backdrop.

But what dropped my jaw was the cabin sprouting up from a copse of trees at the far side of the valley, about a hundred yards in front of the river.

Cabin schmabin.

I'd call that sucker a mansion.

At least three stories tall, its pitched roof crept out from the tops of the soaring trees. From this vantage, the trees camouflaged a lot of it, but I could make out enough to know it was all kinds of grandiose.

Stone and wood and totally imposing.

I'd heard this place was incredible, but I'd had no idea what that really meant.

Apprehension chugged in my blood. Somehow the sight of it made my tardiness feel ten times worse.

I swallowed it down because I didn't want to be some kind of weirdo who was stammering all over herself when I met my new boss.

Overimpressed.

That was so not me.

I'd just be myself. Show him that I was the most qualified to do the job. Wasn't that really what mattered?

He'd given me instructions to meet in front of the main barn. It couldn't be missed since it was just off the right side of the road that cut through the middle of the ranch. The barn was painted burgundy with white accents.

Corrals and pens surrounded it on each side.

It was ten times larger than any other building on the property.

I parked in front of it. Shutting off the engine, I scanned the area, wondering exactly where I was supposed to go.

The huge double-doors were open, revealing row after row of stables inside. A few men were rambling around, watering down horses and mucking stalls.

I climbed from my truck and poked my head through the doors. A guy who was probably too cute for his own good was closest. Tight denim jeans hugging his firm ass, dimples on his cheeks, and blond curls peeking out from under his cowboy hat.

"Excuse me," I called to him.

He finished tossing some hay into a bin before he turned my way. A grin sparked on his face. "What can I help you with, darlin'?"

His eyes took a slow perusal over me, riding from head to toe and back up again.

I was flattered and all, but I didn't have time for flirting.

"Do you know where I can find Mr. Greyson? I have an appointment with him at ten. I was supposed to meet him out here at the barn."

The dude cracked a smirk. "Hate to break it to you, but it's ten-fifteen. I'm thinkin' he's not gonna be impressed, though I can't say the same about myself."

His grin only grew as his eyes made another pass.

Frustration sailed through me, and I shifted on my boots.

"Damn it," I muttered under my breath.

I hated the idea of messing this thing up. Not only did I need the money…but the horses.

Disappointment flared, and I dropped my head.

"You supposed to teach the little one to ride?"

I perked up at that. "That's right."

He canted his head toward my left. "Filly is in the first corral on the north side. Can't miss her. Black Leopard Appaloosa. Beautiful as can be."

"Thank you," I wheezed in relief.

Grinning, he tipped down the brim of his hat. "Anytime, gorgeous. I'm Nate."

"Thanks, Nate. I'm Paisley, and I gotta run."

I pulled away from the open doors and walked around the corner of the building to the north side. It ran with a long row of covered exterior stalls, and there were two round pens to the left, plus a bunch of corrals extending beyond.

I immediately headed for the filly in the first stall. She was as beautiful as could be, just like Nate had said. Her coat was white and dappled with black dots, and her mane and tail were completely black.

My chest squeezed, affection pulsing through my blood.

When it came to horses, I believed in love at first sight.

Easing up to the wooden fence, I stepped onto the bottom rung so I could peer over the side. "Hey there, girl. You are something special, aren't you?"

She was grazing from a low bin filled with hay, and I leaned over the top rail so I could reach down and brush my fingers down the slope of her neck.

It was then I heard the low, quiet grumble stake through the air from behind. "You have to be fucking kidding me."

I whipped around, and my eyes went wide, shock tossing my mind into confusion.

It didn't take long to come to realization.

I really hated to agree with the asshole, but yeah, *you had to be fucking kidding me.*

No, no, no, this was not *the* Mr. Greyson.

He couldn't be.

But there was no mistaking the fact that the jerk from earlier stared back.

Okay.

Glared.

Glowered.

Whatever you wanted to call it.

All I knew was his icy blue eyes burned through me like daggers. Searing me to the depths. Somehow they narrowed even more as they moved from my face and down my spine, dragging farther in a slow slide of obnoxious observation.

His gloriously obscene face twisted into a disgusted sneer when his attention came to rest on my backside.

Right.

I was fully leaned over the top rail wearing my cut-off shorts. Believe me, they had completely earned their name.

My ass up in the air, so up front and center it might as well have been in a display case.

In my defense, it was going to be like a thousand degrees today, and I was supposed to be out working the horse, showing off my skills, wooing this elusive Mr. Greyson into hiring me for this sweet, easy gig.

It'd seemed like the right choice in attire at the time.

Clearly, I'd been mistaken.

On all accounts.

I mean, I'd imagined Ryder's cousin was going to have some kind of stick up his ass, but I sure as heck hadn't expected it to be stuffed so far up there it would never see the light of day.

And no, I'd definitely not imagined he'd look quite like this.

This guy was no rancher.

This...this...dark angel who oozed controlled wickedness soaked in a vat of arrogance.

Frustration threatened to roll up my throat on a groan, all mixed with this sticky awareness that covered my flesh. My throat suddenly felt a little too thick for comfort.

Crap, his glare only darkened as he took me in, gaping at him where I'd frozen perched ass-up on the fence.

Finally gathering my wits enough to move, I slowly twisted around and slipped off the fence. My boots hit the ground with a thud.

Icy eyes traced over me from the front, scorn flying from him, as if he were personally affronted by the sight of me.

Seriously, what had he expected? For me to show up in a pencil skirt and heels? Or maybe in a suit? You know, considering he was still wearing one. He'd at least had the sense to remove the jacket, and the sleeves of his white and blue striped button-down were rolled up his forearms. It exposed that sleek muscle I'd been sure had been hidden under that suit.

But what took me aback was his arms were covered in intricate black ink, indistinct faces and designs.

Heat flashed, sparks that raced across my skin.

I bit my lip to stave off the redness, the awkwardness, and I fumbled around in my head for a way to make this right.

I needed a redo.

A fresh start.

An eraser to completely scrub out the run-in from this morning.

That seemed the best course of action.

I pasted on a bright, inviting smile and stuck out my hand, my voice all kinds of chipper. "Hello, you must be Mr. Greyson. I'm Paisley Dae. It's so nice to meet you."

It was amazing that stony brow could curl at all, but against all odds, disbelief knitted his forehead. "You're going to stand there and act like we've never met."

It wasn't even a question.

It was a growl of judgement.

"Have we?" I feigned confusion.

His head swung to Maybe sitting in front of the barn before his attention swiveled back, a sound of irritation ripping off his tongue. "Just as I said this morning, I don't have time for this."

He started to turn on his heel like he was just going to walk away.

That time, it was my forehead that curled. "Time for what?"

"For you to play games. Acting innocent when you are the farthest from it."

Me, acting innocent?

I could only imagine the skeletons this guy had in his closet. He clearly needed to purchase a ten-thousand-acre ranch so he had a place to bury them all.

"What happened this morning was an accident, and I said I was sorry."

"You said you were sorry?" he said, so incredulous and rough, his voice as dark as the demons that played in his eyes.

Okay fine, I hadn't.

But whatever.

"I think we got off on the wrong foot, Mr. Greyson. Let's start ov—"

"I'll compensate you for the time it took you to come out here, but this is not going to work."

Wait.

Was he serious?

"You're just going to fire me...before I even start? I am the most qualified—"

Anger burst through his expression, so fierce it made me stumble backward into the fence. "I can't afford for someone as reckless as you to be on my ranch."

It took me a second to get my bearings before my tongue was lashing out its retaliation. "I'm not reckless. You're the one who backed into me. If anyone is reckless, it's you."

He scoffed. "That is absurd. And on top of it, you're late."

"Um, yeah, because you backed into me."

The challenge had him cocking his head. "Funny, I made it here on time."

What a freaking jerk—

The snippy retort froze on my tongue when I suddenly sensed the presence to the side. My attention jerked that way.

A tiny girl with a mess of long brown hair that whipped and blew in the breeze stood there. She wore a pink tee shirt and jeans and these pink cowgirl boots emblazoned with crystals.

She was slight, not plump and round like you'd expect a small child to be, almost too thin. Something about her was fragile, her giant brown eyes appearing too big for her face.

Reserved and unsure, she wrung her little hands in nervousness as she watched our encounter.

Poor kid, having a jerk for a dad like this.

Hopefully her mom didn't suck, too.

"Do I get to see Mazzy now?" she asked, her tone timid and shy. She barely peeked at the man who looked down at her in something that I had to process through.

My stomach fisted when I finally put my finger on it.

Fear.

I had to be imagining it.

Guys like him didn't fear. They incited it.

He blew out a harsh breath, roughing a hand over his lips like maybe he could rub off some of the snide.

Good luck with that.

"Evelyn, I thought you were with Ms. Sandberg? Where is she?" he asked.

Huh. He'd managed to keep the asshole out.

"I dunno. I wanted to see Mazzy, but I couldn't find her to ask her to come with me, but I saw you out here through the window, and it's past ten, so I get to see her, right?"

He moved and knelt in front of her, taking her by the forearm. "I'm afraid that isn't going to happen today."

It was more than disappointment that dampened her expression. She looked absolutely crushed.

The sight of it stung the back of my eyes.

"Can I at least pet her for one second?" she whispered, so sweet that I kind of wanted to punch this guy in the throat, drop him to his knees, so I could run over to her, sweep her into my arms, and give into this little girl's every whim.

"Please? I'll be so careful."

Reservation clenched his sharp jaw when he turned around to glare at me.

There was nothing to do but prop my hands on my hips and glare right back.

Defiance filled me to the brim, and I lifted my chin at him in a clear challenge, daring him to send me away when his poor little girl stood there silently begging to get to pet her horse.

I thought I could actually hear his teeth grinding as he stared at me, but I didn't back down, well not until the craggy voice came barging into our showdown.

"Evelyn, there you are. I told you not to leave the house without permission."

I looked into the distance to find *the* Ms. Sandberg scurrying our way.

This day just got worse and worse.

She'd been a substitute teacher in the Time River School District for my whole life, probably my parents', too. Let's just say we hadn't exactly hit it off when I was in kindergarten. The old hag hadn't hesitated to hold it against me.

Was she...Evelyn's nanny?

Revulsion crawled through me at the thought of it.

Gross.

He roughed a hand over the top of his head. "Evelyn, please go with Ms. Sandberg for a moment while I speak with Ms. Dae."

Warily, Evelyn looked between us before she slowly moved to the old lady who stood about thirty feet away, out of earshot unless we would have been shouting, but it didn't matter anyway because he strode back for me, grinding out beneath his breath, "Come with me," as he passed.

He stormed around the side of the barn, riddled with discontent when he tossed a look at me from over his shoulder when I didn't scramble along fast enough to keep up with him before he disappeared around the corner.

I followed, then gasped when I was suddenly snatched by the wrist, spun around, and pinned to the side of the barn.

My jaw dropped.

What the hell?

"I don't appreciate you manhandling me, Mr. Greyson." I jerked against his hold, refusing to evaluate exactly why my heart was thundering in my chest.

Why heat spread and my stomach twisted.

"And I don't appreciate you waltzing in here without care or concern or respect for other people's time or safety."

Safety?

He was concerned about safety when he looked like a fucking hazard?

Air puffed from my nose. "You think I don't care about your daughter's safety? You don't know the first thing about me."

For a fleeting second, he looked like he'd been punched in the gut before a grim darkness clouded his features, and his voice filled with spite. "I know you're reckless."

Offense shook my head. "If this is about our little fender bender this morning, you can get off your high horse because you were just as much at fault as I was. There was no neglect or disregard. I thought it was clear when I pulled out. But you know, if you need someone to blame it on, fine. I'll admit there was a glare from the sun in my rearview mirror. So maybe you were in a blind spot, or maybe I was blinded. Or maybe it was just a freaking accident. Whatever the case, it doesn't give you a pass to be a total jerk about it. So, I think I'll do us both a favor and leave."

I jerked my wrist out of his big mitt and wound myself out from under his ridiculously tall frame.

I wasn't about to put myself through this misery to earn a few bucks. My boots kicked up a dust storm as I beelined toward my truck.

From behind, he snatched my wrist again, stopping me in my tracks, voice so dark when he murmured, "Don't leave."

I'd do best to get out of there before it was too late, but I couldn't help but slowly turn around.

Something like regret and a plea spun through his expression.

What the hell was up with this guy? Talk about whiplash.

"Please."

"Let go of me."

I was surprised he complied.

I crossed my arms over my chest. "Tell me, why should I stay? Ten minutes ago, you were telling me this wasn't going to work out. I hate to agree with you, but I think you're right."

"Whatever you charge, I'll pay double." He was back to grinding out the words.

"What do you even care? Or do you just need someone else to pawn that little girl off to for a few hours of the day?"

Uh-oh.

Wrong thing to say.

He went from fallen angel to dark demon in a flash, flying in my face so fast I lost my breath. Blue flames burned hot in the depths of his eyes, those too full lips twisting in animosity as he angled in close to my face. "That *little girl* is the only fucking thing in this world I care about. Don't ever imply otherwise. Do you understand?"

My pulse thudded at a wild beat. Instinct told me to run, so why the hell was I still standing there? More concerning was why I was whispering, "I understand."

He edged back, his voice going smooth, pure business. "Do you wish to teach Evelyn to ride?"

After everything, I should tell him to shove it.

But I really wanted to work with horses.

"I do."

"You have one more chance. Don't mess it up. You've already disappointed me twice."

Unbelievable. I felt like a ping-pong ball with this guy.

"Well, Mr. Greyson, I will do my best not to fail you again," I bit out, my words holding just as much vitriol as his. Riddled with a challenge and firing with the same heat that was radiating from him.

He inhaled, his jaw rigid, before he shifted just to the side, as if he were gathering his thoughts.

He roughed those hands through his hair, and for the first time, a bit of vulnerability seeped into his tone.

"She is obsessed with that horse," he said, "but she doesn't have the first clue how to interact with it or take care of it. She remains timid, instinctively aware that horses can be dangerous, which I consider a plus. Her safety is my main priority. Introduce her to it today because she's been dying to pet it. After that, you can advance her as you see fit."

He gestured like he was giving me permission to return to the north side of the building, his voice cut in a warning when he said, "You will be careful with her, Ms. Dae."

A lump clogged my throat. "Of course."

Though apparently, I had no clue how to be careful with myself.

"Come with me."

Chapter Four

Caleb

I WASN'T SURE I'D EVER BEEN SO BACKED INTO A CORNER AS I was right then.

In a standoff with this riot of a girl, one who made me want to rage and rant and haul her impertinent ass off my ranch and dump her back in town where she belonged. It was up against the child who'd come out here with so much broken hope that it wouldn't allow me to take that action.

Last thing I could do was paint that disappointment on Evelyn's face. So I'd asked the woman to stay, even though it went against every fiber in my being to put my trust in Paisley Dae.

Trust her.

I didn't.

Not in the least.

But there I was, backed into a corner.

Trying to figure this bullshit out and knowing I wasn't equipped to do it.

I moved around the edge of the barn and searched for Evelyn. She sat beneath a tree on the rambling lawn that took up at least three acres in front of the house.

The child was patiently waiting for the answer to the one thing she had ever asked me for.

I strode that way with Paisley at my heel. Timid hope filled Evelyn's face as she watched us coming. I stopped two feet away, barely able to scrape the words free. "Evelyn, this is Ms. Dae. She is going to help you learn how to take care of your horse."

That hope flared and a shy smile took to her face as she looked at the woman who stood like a flame beside me. "Which day are you?" Evelyn asked. "Today is my favorite day because I get to pet Mazzy."

The woman giggled at my side. "Well, Ms. Dae is a different kind of a day."

Evelyn's shoulders went to her ears, and she swayed. "Well, I guess I like all the different days."

For a moment, Paisley just stared at her like she was caught up in the sweetness that was the child. I had to clear my throat to break her out of it, needing to get out of there before I got swept up, too.

"Enjoy your lesson, Evelyn."

I moved away from them but found I wasn't able to force myself back to my office in the house. The entire reason I'd hired Ms. Sandberg was so she could keep a watchful eye on Evelyn so I could continue to work.

But no.

I loitered, watching.

From afar, I watched as Paisley knelt in front of Evelyn, saying something to her that I couldn't hear. Evelyn gave her the slightest smile before she took the hand Paisley extended, unsure yet filled with her innocent faith that I couldn't fathom still remained.

How was it possible it wasn't completely tattered and torn? Shredded and mangled? Nonexistent?

I began to pace within the confines of that nonexistence, agitation a hurricane battering my insides. It was a wonder I was able to stop myself from barreling over to stop Paisley as she led Evelyn toward the corral.

Nothing about this felt safe. I'd brought Evelyn to Time River, to this ranch, thinking that's what it would be. Where it was secluded and sheltered. Hidden away from the rest of the world.

What I hadn't anticipated was Evelyn becoming obsessed with the horses. Like she was just going to stay in the house all fucking day and never venture out?

She'd actually come to me, which she never did, and asked if she could ride one. The next day, I'd purchased the Appaloosa filly, promised it would be the gentlest I could find, already tamed though young enough that Evelyn would be able to grow along with it.

Safest bet.

But right then this bullshit wasn't feeling all that safe.

Paisley talked to Evelyn nonstop as they walked together toward the stall. Paisley Dae all but skipped, reckless the way she was, no caution in her step. White waves cascaded down her back, glinting in the sunlight, her legs tanned and toned and exposed thanks to those fucking shorts she thought prudent to wear for an interview.

My cock jolted at the sight, the same way as it had when I'd walked up to find her bent over the corral fence.

Her ass was a round, ripe fruit begging to be bitten.

Or spanked.

A little punishment might do her well.

Digging into my pocket, I pulled out my phone because I needed a distraction. A place to direct this cagey rage still blustering through my blood at the nonsense this woman had already pulled.

Ryder answered on the second ring. "Caleb, man, how is it goin'?"

"I think you know exactly how it's going." I couldn't keep the accusation out of my voice.

When it came to Evelyn, Paisley Dae was everything I couldn't tolerate.

Uncontrolled and wild.

Reckless.

But still, I hadn't been able to let her walk away.

Ryder laughed the way he always did. Loud and free and like he didn't have a care to be counted. "Paisley is there? She's great, right? What did I tell you, brother?"

My attention traveled to where she was in front of the gate of the corral. Once again, she knelt in front of Evelyn, though this time she had her by the outside of the shoulders. Her stance serious, like whatever she was saying she was trying to emphasize to her.

My throat nearly closed off when she then situated Evelyn off to the side and stood to unlatch the gate.

I hated feeling out of control. Giving it to someone else.

"Is she really?" I asked in what amounted to a snarl because my cousin had a twisted sense of humor. "In one single morning, she's both ran into the back of my SUV and was fifteen minutes late."

Paisley led Mazzy out by the reins, and I watched like a hawk in case I had to dart across the space to get between Evelyn and the horse.

Ryder laughed a low sound. "That's all part of her appeal, man."

I wouldn't be giving her this chance if it hadn't been for him singing her praises. He'd told me I was a lucky bastard she had moved back into town because he didn't know of anyone better.

"Appeal?"

Irritation burned across my flesh as I watched the woman talking to Evelyn while she ran her hand down the white and black-dappled neck of the pony, giving some kind of instruction I couldn't hear.

"Her brilliance. Her smarts. Her skill and experience. Whatever you want to call it. It just can't be tamed or controlled the way you like to control those around you. She might do it her own way, but you won't find anyone in Time River who is going to take better care of both the horse and Evelyn. That little girl couldn't be in better hands."

"I'm not so sure about that."

"You need to lighten up, Caleb. Loosen the reins. Literally."

I all but growled.

He chuckled, though the amusement in his voice filtered out. "You know I wouldn't recommend someone being around Evelyn if I didn't implicitly trust them. And I trust her. You don't have anything to worry about."

I had plenty to worry about without having to worry about this woman, too.

"She screws up again, and she's out," I warned.

Paisley stretched out her hand and slowly guided her up to the horse. Evelyn reached out, her movements tentative as she brushed her little hand along the side of the horse's neck, touching it for the first time since it had arrived five days ago.

"Can you do me a favor and try not to be a total prick to her? Know that's your M.O., but Paisley-Cakes has been through her own shit. She doesn't need you ridin' her ass and making it worse."

Paisley-Cakes?

What did that even mean?

"I'll see what I can do," I gritted.

"Well doesn't that sound promising," he tossed back, dripping sarcasm. "You are nothing but a fuckin' ray of sunshine, Caleb Greyson."

I grunted.

"Just relax, man. It's all good. Try to chill and enjoy your ranch. You have some of the most beautiful property around, and you're over there wound so goddamn tight you can't enjoy it."

Enjoy it?

There was no enjoying anything until I buried this threat.

"Listen, I need to go. Swing by later?"

"Yeah," I told him.

"Cool." The line went dead.

Annoyance gusted, and I pressed the end of my phone against my forehead in hopes it would relieve the splitting headache that had formed.

Had to wonder if coming here hadn't been the biggest mistake I'd ever made.

Only I knew that wasn't the truth. Because I had a fucking lifetime of them, and one had destroyed everything.

Chapter Five

Paisley

I FLOPPED ONTO A CHAMPAGNE-COLORED VELVET STOOL AT THE high-top counter at Time River Market & Café, still reeling from the whiplash I'd sustained by being in the presence of one Mr. Greyson.

The café oozed both luxury and comfort.

The epitome of Dakota herself.

Trendy and eclectic with a country kick.

Growing up, it had been a regular greasy diner until Dakota had gotten her hands on it. She'd sectioned the large building into two rooms and had opened a country store in the front, but the real draw was the delicious café and bakery in the back.

I still didn't know how she'd pulled off its transition. Creating something that was both upscale yet downhome.

Booths ran the walls of the café on three sides. They were high-backed, gray wood with blue and cream-colored checked cushions, and each had a spray of cream-colored flowers in metal containers tucked against the wall.

The middle section was set with long tables, at least ten chairs on each side, which she'd meant to encourage random people to eat their meals together. In a small town such as this, you were likely to eat breakfast or lunch with a friend who happened to be in that day.

Or run into your biggest enemy.

Funny how I'd never even had one of those until today.

Lucky me.

When I came into the café, I preferred sitting here at the rustic bar, one half of it running with six high stools and to the left of it the bakery display cases and coffee bar. It gave me a chance to chat with Dakota in between her running around taking care of customers.

About five minutes after I'd been sitting there, she came out of the kitchen through the swinging doors.

I sent her what had to look like a manic grin.

"Uh-oh, why do you look like someone pissed in your favorite pair of boots? Wait, no." She held up a finger. "You stabbed someone and you're here to take me up on the promise that I would always help you bury the bodies?"

"I just about had to take you up on it."

A frown cut across her brow. "Did you not get the job? I thought it was basically a done deal?"

"Oh, no, I got it." At least for the time being since it seemed I was on some sort of probationary period, which was ridiculous. I was a hired trainer, not an employee who was supposed to jump at his beck and call.

"Then why are you making that pouty face?" Dakota asked. She started rambling around behind the counter, taking out the ingredients for her famous strawberry iced tea.

She knew it was my favorite.

"Is it a win when you get a job to work for the world's biggest asshole?" I was going to have to get him a customized mug. Was it too early to whip out my Christmas list?

She winced, a perfectly waxed brown brow arching as she poured the pitcher over muddled strawberries. "How bad was he?"

"Well, I'm still alive and not buried in a shallow grave somewhere, so we can at least be grateful for that."

Which was kind of surprising because at one point, I was sure the guy wanted to murder me. Wrap his hands around my throat and choke me out. Or maybe just bend me over his knee.

Who knew.

"Well, that sucks," she drawled as she set the glass in front of me. "I was only teasing this morning. I can't believe Ryder's cousin could be that bad."

"Seriously," I agreed, taking a sip of the strawberry deliciousness. "But the dude was literally the biggest jerk I've ever met. The only saving grace is the horse is gorgeous and the little girl is adorbs. As long as I only have to deal with the two of them, I'll be just fine."

My gut told me there weren't enough stars in the heavens to wish on to make that dream come true. And the really sad part was I couldn't shake this feeling down in my bones at the thought of seeing him again.

"I was wondering what he would be like. You have to be loaded to buy a place like Hutchins Ranch," she mused as she leaned down into the display case to my left.

She plated a bunch of her yummy pastries, an apple croissant and a blueberry tart and something covered in powdered sugar.

I hummed with a nod. "Rich prick to a T. He pretty much fired me on the spot because I couldn't possibly be good enough to be around his pompous ass, then when I went to take off, he told me to stay, and then he turned around and threatened me that I had one more chance."

"What do you mean by one more chance?" Leave it to Dakota to catch it, her pouty, clear-glossed lips ticking up at the edge.

Clearly, she'd come to the quick sum that I'd gotten myself into a mess the way I liked to do.

I cringed, lifting a single shoulder to my ear. "Well, I might have accidentally backed into his Range Rover when I was coming out of the grocery store this morning."

Somewhere along the way, I'd realized it was likely my fault, but it wasn't as if I'd done it on purpose. I'd been blinded by the sun.

Amusement traipsed through her features. "Tell me you didn't."

"But of course, I did. It wasn't a big deal. Just a little bump, but he definitely held it against me when I showed at his place and he realized it was me."

Unease twisted through me at the memory of the way he'd kept accusing me of being reckless. It felt like he wanted to wrap that little girl in bubble wrap, and not in the normal concerned parental way. It was like he was truly terrified something bad was about to happen to her.

"Only you could make such a glowing first impression, Paisley Dae." A tease wound its way through Dakota's tone, the corners of her brown eyes crinkling with affection.

"Well, believe me, his was just as glowing. The second he got out of his car, he started firing off accusations."

Well, after he asked if I was injured, but I'm pretty sure he was just covering his ass to make sure I wasn't going to file a suit or something.

A giggle rolled up Dakota's throat, and she shook her head. "I can only imagine your face when you realized it was the same guy."

"I was shocked, that's for sure. He didn't come close to being what I expected. I figured he was Ryder's quiet, older, reclusive cousin or something."

Dakota giggled. "It's kind of funny that we used to tease Ryder and Ezra that they were making up their rich cousins who lived in Seattle when they were kids, though, isn't it? Maybe that's why we never met him—because they were always embarrassed of him. It's a little sketch that Ryder never mentioned he moved here to either of us until this job opportunity came up, though, don't you think?"

"Um, yeah, super sketch. I think it's safe to say the guy's not exactly a people person. Don't count on him coming in here spending his billions at your fine establishment." I quirked her a grin.

"And here I thought I was about to hit a windfall," she said with a chuckle as she grabbed the two plates piled high with pastries. "Give me a second to deliver these. I'm getting the stink eye from across the room, over here slacking."

"Do your thing."

She waltzed her voluptuous body out from behind the counter and to a booth under the bay of windows at the front. Her laughter rode through the café at something one of them said. Clearly, she hadn't pissed them off too badly.

I couldn't help but watch her from over my shoulder.

Dakota Cooper was the best kind of friend anyone could have. Not in that cheesy way, but in a real, genuine, life-changing way. Someone who was fun and kind and listened. She always had my back, but she didn't hesitate to put her foot down and shake some sense into me when I was going off the rails, either.

We'd grown up two streets over from each other.

Friends forever.

We'd climbed trees together. Played Barbies together. Dreamed together.

As we'd gotten older, we'd giggled and goofed around during class, passing notes, then we'd stay up all night during our slumber parties we'd shared every weekend. We'd imagined all the amazing places we were going to go, and the amazing things we were going to do.

Then we'd grown and matured and began to chase after those dreams. We'd both had some of those dreams crushed, had experienced setbacks and disappointments and tragedies.

But we'd gone through them together.

I had missed her like mad while I'd been living in Arizona.

A soft smile pulled at my mouth, thankful that she'd found so much joy in this place and in her son, Kayden, even though I got a sense that she was holding a pain that hadn't been there before I'd left.

Pain I was hoping she would trust me with now that I was back.

And maybe it wasn't that she didn't trust me—it was something about *herself* that she wasn't trusting or acknowledging.

But at least now I was here, ready for when she needed me.

She checked on a few customers before she turned around and sashayed back my way, her lush curves accentuated by her cute summer dress.

She eased around the counter, eyeing me when she asked, "So, you've got to give me more details on this cousin. How old is this guy?"

Images flashed. His penetrating eyes and the severe cut of his face. The strength that burned through his lean body that had been so potent I'd felt seared by it.

I took a long gulp of my tea. "Um…thirty-five, thirty-seven maybe? Typical suit."

Except he wasn't typical at all, and I had to force myself not to go and chew on my lip as I thought of the ink that scrolled out from beneath his sleeves. The darkness that had radiated from him, this thing that warned of danger and a trap.

"I'm picturing a computer geek. Am I right?"

"Ah, no. He's more *Give me all your money, or I will kill you.*" I gave it a go at imitating that growly voice.

Dakota cracked up. "Girl, you should run. After all that, you agreed to go back?"

"What else was I going to do? I can't let Ryder down, and I could really use the extra cash right now."

"I told you that you could work here."

I sent her my most emphatic groan. "That sounds like a terrible idea."

"Are you trying to hurt my feelings?" She returned it with a pout.

"Um, no, I just don't want my bestie to be my boss." My grin was wide.

Okay, truth was, she was way too organized, and I was basically the opposite of that. We'd drive each other nuts.

Plus, this was my opportunity to finally get back to working with horses.

I'd forgotten how right it felt. It was like the second I'd run my fingers through Mazzy's mane, a place I'd kept locked inside me had unfurled.

A stunted seed that had bloomed.

Dreams rekindled.

"Besides, he offered to pay me double whatever I charged. I'd be a fool to pass that up."

I said it so simply, like there wasn't an undercurrent of something else that had forced me to stay.

She hummed. "That seems…generous."

I snorted. "Generous? More like a bribe to put up with his surly, gorgeous ass."

At least I'd only have to be out there three days a week for two hours at a time.

"Gorgeous, huh?" Her brow popped in interest.

Oops. I had not meant to let that slide.

"Don't worry, what he looks like only adds to the repulsion. He's a grade-A snob, and I will not be crushing on that."

Snob was going easy on him. Because there was more to that arrogance, something cut under the surface that made him almost... scary. Like he might be capable of dangerous things. And the way he interacted with the little girl? It was odd. Like he was terrified of her and would stand in front of a bullet for her at the same time.

I didn't get it.

Couldn't put my finger on him.

And I hated that there was something *reckless* inside me that drew me toward it. Something that made me want to look closer.

My phone buzzed where I had it on the counter.

I cringed when I saw who it was from.

Jeremy: Would you just call me? I told you I was sorry.

Disgust covered me in a shroud of regret. Like an apology was going to cover it? Like it would ever make up for what he'd made me miss? What he'd stolen from me?

Never.

"Who is that?" Dakota must have seen my scowl.

"Ugh, Jeremy. That jerk actually thinks I'm going to go running back to him. It appears I'm a magnet for assholes."

"He is the literal worst. Why haven't you blocked him yet?"

"Good question." I tapped through a few buttons and made it so before I waved the screen at her. "There. Buh-bye, slimebag."

Dakota giggled. "One down, one to go."

I laughed. "We'll see how this one goes. Now feed me food before I get hangry."

Dakota laughed, a tease on her voice, "On it, I wouldn't want my bestie to starve or anything after such an eventful day."

"The eventfulest," I mumbled around a massive bite of the raspberry tart she set in front of me.

"With you, it always is."

∞

I slid my key into the lock and pushed open the door, calling, "Hey, Grandpa, it's me," as I stepped into the old house.

"In here," he shouted back, and a soft smile tugged at the edge of my mouth as I dropped my bag to the floor and tossed my keys on top of it, careful not to jostle the piping hot pot pies that were fresh out of the oven.

I moved through the main living room that was filled with a million memories. It was still decorated the way it'd been since probably the seventies, an orange couch and two oversized chairs to *match* the orange and brown striped carpet.

Knickknacks cluttered every surface, exactly where my grandmother had left them, and the walls were covered in a mishmash of cheap wood frames of every size, each proudly displaying the faces of the family she had loved so much.

It was hideous.

But that sure didn't mean I wasn't pummeled by a wash of affection as I moved through the space. It only hit me all the more fiercely when I ducked through the rounded archway and into the kitchen.

My grandfather was on the other side of it in the small den where he sat in his recliner, his feet up, watching a TV that was as dated as the kitchen appliances.

I set the dish on the brown Formica countertop and moved to him, leaning down so I could smack a big kiss against his prickly cheek. "There's my favorite guy in the whole world."

He was one of the good ones, and God knew there weren't a lot of those.

"How are you tonight?"

His green eyes had grayed around the irises, though they still twinkled as he gave me a lopsided grin. "A whole lot better now that you're home. What did you bring me?"

"Pot pie."

He made a show of inhaling the delicious aroma of chicken and spices and the sweetness of the puff pastry top.

"That's what I thought it was. It smells almost as good as your grandma's."

Light laughter rolled from me, though the sound was clouded with the pain of missing my grandma so much. I hadn't made it back that night when I'd gotten the call that she'd had a stroke.

I'd tried. God, I'd tried. But she was already gone by the time my flight had landed the next morning.

Regret gripped me by the throat, bitter remorse filling me to overflowing.

All because of a dirtbag who in the end hadn't given a shit about me. And of course, once I was gone, he kept trying to get me to go back to him.

That was not going to happen.

"I'll be sure to let Dakota know," I forced around the lump that throbbed heavily in my throat.

"Oh, I'm sure she already does. That one knows what she's doing."

"That's right. Both in the kitchen and in the office."

"She's as smart as a whip, just like my girl." The hinges of his recliner creaked as he pushed down the footrest, and he used the arms to push himself to standing. He winced a bit as he did, and I gave him my arm and helped him hobble over to the round table sitting in the nook.

He settled into his spot, and I uncovered the pot pies and set one in front of him and one in my spot before I went into the kitchen and grabbed forks and napkins.

"There you go," I told him as I set the fork beside his pot pie and pecked a kiss to the top of his head, his white hair sticking up in the back.

"You don't have to take care of me, you know." Still, he was taking his fork and digging it into the pie, his hand shaking so bad I didn't know how he was able to hold onto it.

"Maybe I'm here so you can take care of me." I sent him a soft smile.

He smiled back, and my chest panged with the love I had for him. Appreciation thick.

He and my grandma had raised me from a little girl, since the day my mama had dumped me on their porch when I was three and hadn't turned back. Maybe I was angry at the woman, scarred in ways that wouldn't heal, but I also held a huge amount of gratitude that she'd done it.

Because of it, she'd given me the gift of her parents who were the best people in the world.

"What did you get up to today?" Grandpa asked as I plopped into the chair next to him.

I pulled a piece off the edge of my pastry and popped the flaky goodness into my mouth. "Got a job."

"Doin' what?"

"Training a little girl how to care for and ride a horse."

He tried to hide his smile by ducking his head. "Training, huh?"

Excitement shivered through my veins. I couldn't help it. "Yup."

Grandpa grinned. "Well, if that isn't the best news I've heard in a long time."

"I think so, too, Grandpa."

Even if it meant working for the biggest asshole I'd ever met.

Chapter Six

Caleb

I STEPPED INTO THE BUILDING TO THE SOUND OF A WHIRRING machine and the grinding of metal, so loud it screamed through my ears.

Ryder was bent over some sort of worktable, wearing protective glasses and gloves on his hands, so intent on what he was doing and lost to the roar of the machine there was no chance he could hear that I'd entered through the side door.

Reckless.

In my world, you didn't turn your back like that. You were vigilant. Always fucking watching your back.

I prayed to God I hadn't dragged that world here to Time River. Coming here the way I had, to a place I didn't belong. A place that would never be home. But Ryder had convinced me it was the safest place for us to hide.

The sheet metal he'd been shearing in two cut apart, and the machine wound down, the sound fading off until it was just the quiet of me standing there behind Ryder while the man inspected his work.

He jumped about two feet in the air when he turned around and saw me standing there.

"The fuck, man? Are you trying to give me a goddamn heart attack? I'm too young for that shit." He laughed that low, casual laugh.

"Maybe you should pay attention to your surroundings."

"Maybe you should stop sneaking up on the unsuspecting." He quirked a dark brow.

That had basically been my job, and the asshole knew it.

"You're lucky I wasn't here to cut you." Couldn't stop the grin from pulling to the edge of my mouth.

Laughing again, he stretched out his tatted arms. "Try it. You know I'd take you down."

Ryder was younger than me by five years, his hair black and his eyes close to the same. He was tall and sinewy—all corded muscle. The dude was not to be toyed with, not that I wouldn't give him crap about it, anyway.

"You know I'd kick your scrawny ass." I grinned and pulled out a chair at the square table to the side of me.

At the same time, the side door opened, letting in a bright wedge of light, before it clattered shut again. Ezra strolled in wearing his Sheriff uniform.

"Thought I saw you parked out front as I was driving by—probably could bet on it since you're the only asshole who would drive a Range Rover in this town." Ezra smirked, his blue eyes glinting.

"Seriously. That shit is embarrassing," Ryder said as he swaggered over, wiping his hands with a towel.

I canted them both a scowl. "It's the safest for Evelyn."

In an instant, they sobered.

"How is she?" Ryder asked as he pulled out a chair and flopped down beside me.

I fidgeted in the uncomfortable metal seat. "Quiet. Doesn't say much."

Except for when she was talking about the fucking horse.

Ezra pulled out a chair and sat, too. He had dark blond hair like me, though he was thicker, built like a fucking bulldozer.

All three of our mothers had been sisters. Blonde, willowy, and blue-eyed.

We had to assume Ryder had gotten his dark features from his father, even though none of us knew who he was and, since his mom had passed when he was sixteen, it was doubtful he ever would.

Ezra scrubbed a meaty palm over his face, blowing out a sigh. "Trauma is gonna do that. You just have to be there for her. She'll open up when she's ready."

He knew from experience.

My guts fisted in worry.

"Have no fuckin' clue what I'm doing," I admitted, rubbing my thumb and forefinger into my eyes.

Ryder leaned forward and patted my knee. "You're doing everything you can. That's why you're here."

I barely forced out a nod.

"And it's cool that Paisley is there." He shrugged as he sat back. "She showed this morning, right?"

Irritation blazed beneath the surface of my skin. "Yeah."

Only I hadn't talked to her. I had stayed in my office where I belonged.

Last thing I needed was to get caught in her chaos again and say something I would regret.

"I don't love Evelyn around the horse."

Ezra chuckled. "There are going to be plenty of things you don't like, my friend. Pick your battles."

He had three kids, four-year-old twin boys and a six-year-old daughter. His wife had been killed a year ago during a robbery gone bad here at a bank when she was cashing her paycheck.

Fucking sucked.

Hated it for him.

Hated that he knew what it felt like to have your heart cut out of your chest.

A feeling I knew all too well.

"Not if it's dangerous," I told him.

Ezra's chuckle turned more ominous. "Everything's dangerous, man. Key is to do it as safe as you can."

"That's what I'm trying to do."

"You'll figure this out, Caleb," Ryder said. "Know it feels impossible right now. But you made the right choice, coming here."

My head shook, not sure I could agree.

"What, you're too good to hang out with your hick cousins?" Ryder tossed out the jab.

"Two of you are nothing but shit on my shoe." I grinned.

Ezra threw a punch at my shoulder that kind of fucking hurt. "Screw you, city boy."

"Are you going to arrest me?" I taunted.

He quirked a brow. "Don't give me a reason to."

If he only knew.

I blew out a sigh. "All right, I need to get back and check on Evelyn."

She was with the nanny I was really questioning hiring. She looked good on paper, but every time she scowled at her, I wanted to toss her ass to the curb.

"Just wanted to stop by since I was in town," I added as I pushed to standing.

Ryder stood as I did. "Don't forget Friday night is this asshole's birthday." He jutted a chin at Ezra. "We're celebrating. I'll send you the details."

"Not sure I'm up for that."

"Don't even try to get out of it. It's time to get your ass out of your hidey hole. This is your home now, and you need to get used to it."

Chapter Seven

Caleb

IN MY OFFICE ON THE THIRD FLOOR OF THE HOUSE, I NUDGED the drape to the side where I stood at the window.

Bright rays of light lit the ranch in a blaze of warmth and poured into the room. It did nothing to warm the chill that possessed my soul.

My jaw flexed as I looked down at Evelyn leading her horse by the reins. Paisley had ahold of the bridle, walking right behind her, ensuring the horse wouldn't trample the child. Still, my entire being vibrated in disquiet.

I'd promised to keep her safe.

To give her the best life that I could.

And I felt like I'd placed her directly in the path of a tornado.

That riot of a woman laughed hard, at what, I had no idea, but the force of it bent her in half.

Somehow, Evelyn giggled, too.

Everything clutched.

My heart and my stomach and my mind, fisting in this ridiculous interest incited by her presence, the woman a train wreck I couldn't look away from.

Just because she loved to drive me to insanity, today she'd decided to put on a tight pink tank and even tighter jeans, flared at the bottom to accommodate her boots, and a bright pink cowgirl hat with a ribbon of sequins that made her glitter in the sun like a beacon. A shock of white hair rolled down her back, locks playing like tendrils of temptation around her bare shoulders every time she moved.

The sight of her made me want to fume and did stupid things to my dick.

Talking to her would surely send me over the edge.

But Evelyn's lesson was nearly over, and today was Friday, so I moved to my desk, snagged the envelope that held a check for what seemed an exorbitant amount, and bounded down the two sets of stairs to the bottom floor. Paying Ms. Dae was a task I'd somehow not relegated to my accountant the way I did with the rest of the employees and contractors, but something I'd felt I needed to oversee myself.

She obviously needed someone to keep an eye on her.

Or maybe I was just the twisted fuck who wanted an excuse to get in her space.

I stepped outside and strode down the path that followed the edge of the lawn and led to the stables.

By the time I made it to the barn, Paisley was leading Mazzy through the double doors and into her large stall on the left and two down from the front. Evelyn trotted along beside her, shifting her attention up to the woman.

"Do you think it might be okay if I got to brush her?" she asked in her little drawl, her t's slipping into f's.

"I think that's a great idea," Paisley said in that throaty, sultry voice.

So yeah, I was eavesdropping, unable to show myself, that protectiveness I felt for Evelyn rising up and forcing me to listen to their interaction.

Paisley led the horse into its stall.

The entire time, Evelyn never left her side, attached to her hip.

I paused just inside the threshold and off to the side, remaining in the distance and out of sight as I listened.

"You hold the brush like this and run it over her in this direction.

Nice and slow. Soothing. Just like you're petting her, but you're doing it with a brush."

Their voices went silent for a moment, then Paisley was murmuring, "There you go. Just like that. You're doing a great job."

Evelyn giggled, so quiet and unsure, but still with a joy I prayed one day she would fully possess. "I am doing it, Ms. Dae. I think she likes it."

"You are doing it. You're amazing with her…aww…look, Mazzy loves you. She's giving you kisses."

Evelyn giggled again, though this time loud and giddily, and I could only picture the horse pushing its giant snout to her cheek.

Was that even safe?

I burned with the need to intervene, only I stalled out when Evelyn's little voice barely touched my ears. "I love her, too."

I forced myself to stay rooted.

Finally, they stepped out, and Paisley latched the gate behind them. My eyes narrowed as I watched the way she ran her fingers through Evelyn's hair. "I'll see you on Monday, okay?"

"I think that's okay because it's not even very long? Two days I don't get to see you?"

She held up two fingers, her little face squished in question, a face that sent a shock of pain lancinating through me so savagely I had to bite back the agony that wanted to rip free of my chest.

"That's right. Only two days." A soft smile edged Paisley's mouth, and she gestured toward the door. "Run on back to Ms. Sandberg. She will be waiting for you."

"Do I have to?"

Paisley laughed. "I think you do, but believe me, I feel your pain."

Annoyance spun. I wasn't sure if it was because she was disparaging my employee or because I had a hunch that she was right.

Evelyn scrunched up her nose, clearly not understanding what she was implying. "Okay. I will see you in two days. Don't even be late because I'm going to miss you and I'll be waiting the longest, okay?"

An amused laugh fell from Paisley, and she stuck out her hand to shake Evelyn's. "It's a deal."

Evelyn giggled again, swaying in this sweetness that emanated from her spirit, then she turned and ran out, her brown hair flying behind her. She didn't notice me as she went.

I stepped out to speak with Paisley, only I froze, watching when instead of heading out of the stables, she turned left and walked toward one of the hands who was halfway down the aisle of stalls.

That cocky prick Nate.

I only knew his name because I personally reviewed each employee to give them clearance.

She sidled right up to him, facing away, talking while he grinned and chuckled and tipped his fucking hat like a douche at something she said.

Irritation crawled up my throat. What the hell did she think she was doing?

She patted his shoulder before she spun on her boot and came strutting in my direction. She only slowed for half a beat when she saw me standing there, surprise flashing across her face before she reeled it in and pasted on an infuriatingly big smile. "Mr. Greyson, to what do I owe this pleasure?"

There was no missing the snark laced in her tone.

"It's Friday. I had come to compensate you before I found you flirting with one of my ranch hands."

Why I couldn't keep the spite out, I had no fucking clue. But there was something about her that made me cagey.

Surprise twisted through her expression before she let go of a low, disbelieving laugh. "Who I flirt with is none of your business."

She wound around me, fully dismissing me.

Like a fool, I followed. Clearly, I was losing my goddamn mind. I was right on her heel, chasing her out the double doors, hissing, "It is if you're distracting my employees while they are on the clock."

Condescension rolled from her chuckle, and I came up short when she suddenly spun around and jammed her finger into my chest. "You are something else, do you know that? I mean, I knew you were an asshole and all, but you are a straight up narcissist. Or maybe a psychopath. I haven't decided yet. But what I do know is You. Are. Insane."

She punctuated each one with a jab.

Anger burst in my blood, and I grabbed her finger. Blood sloshed through my veins, chaos bashing through my brain, unable to believe this woman would have the audacity to touch me this way. I angled in close, this unfound fury grating between my teeth. "And you are careless. Thoughtless. Doing whatever you please."

Fury flashed through her moss-colored eyes. "I was asking Nate what supplements they are giving Mazzy to ensure she is getting the right nutrition she needs to grow, not flirting with him or taking up his time or being *thoughtless.*"

She yanked her finger out of my hold. "Not that I have to explain myself to you."

Fuck.

My teeth ground so hard I thought my jaw was going to crack.

I should apologize for overreacting.

But nah, what did I do? I was angling in closer and letting the unjustifiable anger slide out.

"You do when you work for me."

She choked on a sarcastic laugh, disbelief twisting her brow. "That's good then because I don't work here any longer."

Was she implying she quit? Before I could refute her claim, she plucked the envelope from my other hand. "I take it this is for me?"

She didn't wait for me to respond before she waved it in my face like a consolation prize. "Great. Perfect. Then I'll just be on my way because I'm sure as hell not sticking around here."

Spinning on her heel, she stomped toward that monstrosity that was parked off to the far side of the barn, disgust and disappointment burning from her golden skin.

I chased after her.

"We had an agreement, Ms. Dae."

She ripped open the door to her truck, glaring back at me when she spat, "Yeah, I had one more chance. I remember. It seems I just used it. Tell Evelyn I'm sorry. Actually, you know what? You tell her *you're* sorry because this is on you."

She hopped into her truck and slammed the door in my face. She bounced in her seat as she turned the ignition, having to pump the gas to coax the pile to life.

It roared when she did, and I stumbled back when she threw it in reverse and whipped out before she shifted into drive and gunned it down the dirt lane.

A reckless riot kicking up rocks and debris as she left.

Chapter Eight

Caleb

FEAR SLOSHED THROUGH HIS VEINS, THE SOLES OF HIS SHOES slapping on the pitted pavement of the dingy alley. Rain poured from the night-stricken sky, a deluge that covered him in desperation.

"Kimberly!" He screamed it.

Begged her name.

Searched through the disorienting storm that pummeled from above.

Washing him through to reveal the monster hiding underneath.

"Kimberly!"

He dropped to his knees in the blood-soaked puddle, took her face, begged again, "Kimberly, no."

He got no answer.

No reprieve.

No forgiveness for what he'd done.

The only response the vacant eyes that stared back.

I swallowed a bitter gulp of bourbon where I sat in the high-backed chair in my room, staring out the window at the ranch below while thoughts consumed me.

It was cloaked in darkness, still and calm, though I somehow felt the demons lurking in the shadows and playing in the fields.

There was no outrunning who I was or the damage I had done.

Still, I'd attempted it. For Evelyn.

Coming here.

A fresh start.

A new beginning.

But how could you become someone you'd never been? How could you erase the vileness from your consciousness and the deeds you had done?

Impossible when I hungered for revenge. When the thirst for blood soaked me through. The oath that I would track down whoever was responsible, find him, and snuff out his life the way he'd done the others.

Blowing out a sigh, I pushed to standing, set my tumbler aside, and moved out of my room and into the sleeping house. Stillness howled, and I eased down the darkened hall, the barest light illuminating my path from the running lights that glowed from the base of the floor. The wood creaked beneath my feet as I passed by Ms. Sandberg's room. A television quietly droned through the crack she'd left in her door.

One I'd insisted upon.

She was to be available twenty-four seven. There to see to any of Evelyn's needs.

I wanted to be, but I didn't know how, so I spent most of my time held in a void of separation, hiding out in my office or room, the walls thick and my heart harder.

But tonight, I couldn't sit still in it.

Evelyn would have been put to bed two hours ago, and I crept to the door next to Ms. Sandberg's.

It rested halfway open, and a wedge of muted light spilled into the hallway. I kept her room lit in a milky glow in hopes that it would keep the nightmares at bay, that she wouldn't be swallowed by the shadows of depravity that had stolen the safety from her life.

I pushed her door open wider, hovering at the doorway, her tiny frame tucked beneath the covers and her brown hair spread across her pillow.

Peaceful.

Torment gripped me by the throat. A slither of vipers sent to slay.

I was fucking this up. I'd already known that I would. But I was doing it in the most extraordinary way. Completely and irrevocably, scarring the child deeper than she'd already been.

Kimberly would kick my ass if she knew, but she didn't have that chance anymore, did she? She didn't get to raise her daughter—because of me.

And here I stood, fucking inept and incapable.

Trepidation burned through my nerves, this push against the pull that sank like claws into my spirit, my fear against the devotion I held for this little girl. I eased forward, keeping my footsteps light to ensure I didn't wake her. My hand shook when I leaned down so I could carefully set it on her cheek. "I'm sorry, Evelyn."

Sorry that I was ill-equipped.

Sorry that my soul had ceased to exist.

Sorry that she'd lost everything that mattered, and her world had been shattered.

Sorry there was no way to reclaim it or fix it, and I sure as fuck couldn't fill it.

Rage and determination billowed through my bloodstream, and I brushed my thumb along the apple of her cheek, my insides quaking at the contact, at her sweet face that reminded me of every mistake I had made.

"I will at least make this one thing right. Protect you and keep you safe. I promise you, Evelyn."

And I wouldn't stop until I had avenged what had been stolen from her.

For a few moments, I remained there, watching her, knowing there was no hope sleep would come for me.

Finally, I forced myself to stand, and I eased out of her room, pulling the door back to its half-closed position. I headed for my room that was on the opposite wing of the second floor.

The buzz from my phone in my pocket echoed through the heavy quiet of the house. I dug it out, and a scowl took to my brow when I saw it was a text from Ryder.

Ryder: Where the fuck are you?

"Shit," I grumbled as I took note of the time.

Ten-fifteen. I was supposed to be at some bar at ten to celebrate Ezra's birthday.

I didn't know if I'd spaced it or ignored it. Last thing I wanted to do was spend my evening at some grungy bar.

Unease burned through my consciousness.

Or maybe it was my actual conscience that throbbed.

Truth be told, I didn't want to tell him about Paisley quitting today, either. Didn't want to admit I'd been a complete asshole and had run off the one woman who had managed to make Evelyn smile because I couldn't seem to rein the chaos she incited in me.

There was something about her that made me want what I couldn't have, but wanted to control anyway.

Nothing but a selfish prick trampling every good thing beneath my feet.

Me: I never told you I was coming. It's been a long day.

Ryder: No excuses, man. It's Ezra's birthday. Get your ass down here. No one's gonna bite.

Guilt constricted my chest. Before I could respond, another text came through.

Ryder: Know this isn't your thing, but you came here to make a home for you and Evelyn. To start new. You can begin by being a part of this community. Meet some people. Hell, you might even enjoy yourself.

Un-fucking-likely.

Still, I found myself tapping out a response because my younger cousin had always had a way of getting what he wanted.

Me: Fine. I'll be there soon.

Chapter Nine

Paisley

ANTSY ENERGY SHIVERED DOWN MY SPINE AS I STEPPED through the doors of Mack's to the loud thrum of a country band.

After the day I'd had, I was ready to blow off some steam.

I needed a place to dump this fiery frustration, the hurt that sat like a stone in the middle of my chest.

I still couldn't believe one person could be so awful.

And God, he was *awful*.

So presumptive and arrogant and just plain, freaking mean. Tossing his rules all over the place, which were BS in themselves, but also doing it while he had absolutely no idea what he was talking about.

All while doing it with a spite that had struck like arrows.

I might have been the one who'd quit, but he was the one responsible for killing the little spark of something that had lit inside me. A kindle that had flamed. And the jerk had stomped it out in his two-thousand-dollar shoes.

I refused to subject myself to that kind of assholery.

I didn't deserve the misery or mistreatment.

No one did.

I'd already put up with enough, thank you very much.

So, I'd walked, shaking so hard I could barely hold onto the steering wheel when I'd flown from his ranch as fast as I could. No way was I going to let that bastard see me cry.

The second I'd hit the main road? That's when I'd let it go. I let the pent-up anger and disappointment bleed from my eyes, like I could purge it out and make it not matter.

It'd left me in big wracking sobs.

Maybe I'd felt better when I'd finished, realizing working at Hutchins Ranch wasn't my only opportunity.

I could still make this work.

Reclaim what I'd lost.

But when the dust had settled around my heart and the resolution had set in, I'd hated what'd remained. The disturbed awareness that I wasn't the only one who'd been wronged this afternoon.

Evelyn had, too. The one who I'd promised I'd see in just two days. This shy, sweet child who so clearly needed someone to help her spread her wings. To help her see she could believe in herself.

Maybe I was the ridiculous one for getting attached to her so quickly.

I couldn't help it.

Each time I saw her, every cell in my body went soft, and the more time I'd spent with her, the more I was sure she needed someone. Someone to see her. Someone to spend time with her. Someone to encourage her.

Love her.

She obviously wasn't getting affection from that piece of garbage Greyson, that was for sure. I wasn't even sure he was capable of it.

Didn't he see he had the most incredible child? That he'd been given a gift?

Except I'd seen the way he watched over her, too. So intensely protective, as if he were trying to hang onto something he thought he'd already lost.

But I had no control over any of it, did I?

Gulping down the mess of emotions, I pushed up on my toes

and searched through the packed crowd, ready to find my friends so I could dance this bitterness out instead of flying back to that ranch and telling the prick exactly what I thought of him.

Mack's was one big, rambling room. A thick haze saturated the space, the lights strobing from the soaring, open rafters spraying murky streams through the dingy air.

The entire middle of the room was taken up by a giant dance floor that was already overflowing with couples two-stepping.

There was a bar up front next to me, and another on the right wall. On the left was a row of pool tables and darts, and at the far back was the elevated stage where a band currently played a quick, invigorating country beat.

I could already feel my insides quickening with the pulse, ready to let go.

Through the dimness, I scanned the high, round tables that were situated around the dance floor.

Excitement throbbed when I found my friends at a table about halfway down on the right.

I began to wind through the crush, saying hello to familiar faces as I went. Mack's drew a crowd from all around, so while there were a ton of people I knew, there were just as many I didn't.

Like she felt me approaching, Dakota swiveled around on her stool when I was three feet away. "There you are!"

Her face lit in welcome, her brown eyes dancing. Clearly, my bestie was already having a blast.

She had on one of her signature dresses, this one short but flowy and red with dainty pink flowers, her brown hair up in a high, stylish ponytail.

Beth and Chloe were also at the table—two of our friends who worked at the café, as well.

Apparently, I was the only one who couldn't be suckered into working for her.

"Since when aren't you the first to show when there's a good time to be had?" Dakota teased. "Bad day?"

Blowing out a sigh, I plopped my butt onto the empty stool. "Oh, you could say that."

"I thought you told me just last week there are no bad days?" Beth shouted above the mayhem to be heard, lifting her beer glass into the air before she took a sip. She wore her black hair short, her dark skin glowing beneath the lights.

Even when things felt grim, I tried to look to the bright side. It seemed Mr. Greyson had stomped out that flame, too.

"I was proven wrong," I said, my voice droll.

"She's been having all kinds of bad days lately." A wry smile played along the edges of Dakota's mouth. "It seems someone brings out the worst in her. What did that asshat do this time?"

"He did it good. I quit."

Chloe gasped, her purple hair that was cut in a long, angled bob swishing around her shoulders. "From training that little girl? I thought you loved it?"

"I did love it." I just didn't like getting degraded by her father.

"Oh, no, are you serious?" Dakota set her hand over mine. She was the one who understood how much I truly loved it.

What it meant.

I fought the welling of sadness and the surge of anger. It was no use because it still climbed up to knot in my throat. "I basically told him where to shove it. I thought I could handle his rudeness since he'd been making himself scarce the last couple times I'd been there, but nope. The second he opened his mouth, the offenses just came flying out. I'm not going to put up with it."

Beth lifted her glass to clink with mine. Too bad I had yet to get a drink. "To ditching assholes."

"I second that." Dakota gave an exaggerated jerk of her chin, and they bumped their glasses together.

"And I third it." Chloe added her glass to the mix, though her attention was on me. "Life's hard enough without subjecting ourselves to someone who can't treat us with respect. It's his loss."

My stomach tightened. My gut told me it was Evelyn's loss, too.

That child lit up when she was around that horse, her whole

demeanor coming alive. And she'd started to talk a bit to me, too. Very little, but still, way more than the first day I'd worked with her.

"I'm going to grab a drink. Anyone need a refill?" I offered.

Dakota lifted her near-empty glass that swam with a bright pink concoction at the bottom. "Another cosmo for me. I haven't had a night out in months. Prepare yourselves. I'm going lushy tonight."

"I'm going to have to call it at just this one." Beth waved her glass.

"Tell me you aren't already thinking of leaving us. Not when I just got here." I gave her an exaggerated pout.

"I have to be up early in the morning. I'm opening the café so this one can party her cute little butt off tonight." She gestured at Dakota. "Once in a while we need to let our girl out to play."

"Yay!" I tossed Dakota's way before I swiveled to look back at Beth and drew out, "And boooo."

She laughed her husky laugh behind another sip of her beer. "You can't have it both ways."

"I want it all the ways."

"Now there's the abundance mentality I'm looking for," Chloe shouted over the din.

"Mmmhmm…that's your girl right here." I pointed at myself with both thumbs. "And this girl is off to the bar. Be right back."

Dakota leaned back on the stool, swiveling around to shout as I disappeared into the crowd, "Hurry unless you find yourself a hottie to distract yourself with, then I approve."

I already felt ten times better by the time I shouldered my way up to the bar. This was exactly what I needed. A night out to remember that even when things got hard and didn't go the way I wanted them to, I was surrounded by a fantastic group of people.

People who loved me.

Supported me.

Believed in me the way I believed in them.

"Paisley Dae. What can I get for you tonight?" Lilac wiped her hands on a dishtowel. She looked more biker than country, black hair and dark liner, her shoulders and arms covered in colorful ink. Her leather corset was tight and pushed her boobs up to spill over the top.

She was crazy hot and all kinds of amazing.

"Hey, Lilac. I'm going to need a cosmo for Dakota and a mule for me, but that's going to need to be a double."

Chuckling low, she moved into action. "One of those nights, huh?"

"Yes, ma'am, it is definitely one of those nights. You shall be seeing me frequently." I dug into my bag so I could pull out my card when I felt someone nudge my opposite shoulder, the drawl of a country voice rumbling out, "Well look it there. It must be my lucky day."

I tossed my attention that way, and a surprised smile split my mouth when I saw Nate there with his forearms leaned on top of the bar. His grin was sly and confident, wearing the same cowboy hat he always wore, his dimples popping out all over his handsome face.

I guess I *had* found a hottie to distract me.

"Nate, hey, how are you?"

"Better now. I was worried I might not see you again."

Discomfited laughter rolled up my throat. "You witnessed that today, huh?"

His grin widened to a smirk. "I imagine the whole ranch did. Hell, probably the town was able to hear that shoutin' match."

I cringed, but it wasn't like I had anything to be embarrassed about.

"Sorry he treated you like that. I should've—"

I set my hand on his forearm. "Don't apologize. It had nothing to do with you and all to do with him. He apparently has an issue with my mere existence."

"Seems to me he has an issue with everyone's existence."

"Maybe, but that's no concern of mine now."

"For what it's worth, I'll miss seeing you around." His smile kicked, turning flirty. "Guess you'll have to make it up to me with a dance later on tonight."

"Oh, I'll be dancing. You can count on it."

"Good. I'll see you later then." He tipped his hat and winked, which made me want to giggle, but he was super sweet and kind of adorable.

Honestly, I could use a little fun with a guy like him, but I wasn't sure I even had that in me yet. The scars Jeremy had left on me were still raw.

Really freaking raw.

But they'd heal. I knew they would.

Lilac set the drinks in front of me, and I handed her my card.

"Keep it open?" she asked.

"Definitely."

I scooped up both drinks, carefully balancing Dakota's that was filled close to the brim, hoping I wouldn't slosh half of it out before I even made it back.

Martini glasses were the devil.

I somehow weaved back through the thriving crowd with only having lost a few droplets over the side.

"There you are, my darling," I drawled as I set the drink in front of my bestie.

A moan of pleasure rolled from her. "You don't even know how good it feels to have someone serve me for once."

"I'll serve you anytime, Doodle-Boo." I sat back on my stool and started sucking at the little black straw in my drink.

The ginger beer was strong and spicy, just the way I liked it.

"I'm pretty sure what Dakota's missing is service of the male variety." Beth waggled her brows. "How many years has it been?"

Well, take Kayden and add nine months, I was guessing.

"Don't even start." Dakota jabbed her index finger at her from across the table.

Laughing, Beth waved her hand in the air. "Look at all this deliciousness, and you refuse to even sample."

"I have too many other things going on in my life that need attending to. The last thing I should do is go around sampling *trouble*. No, thank you."

"Yet you're encouraging me to get distracted." I gave her a wry smirk when I said it.

She scowled, like she was just then realizing her contradiction.

"Sounds to me like a little trouble is exactly what you need," Beth said. "Nothing wrong with taking a little yum for yourself every once in a while."

Dakota didn't answer since she suddenly got enraptured by something behind me.

Eyes drawn.

Her spirit shifting.

I swore every molecule in her body stood at attention.

I swiveled to look that way, my eyes narrowing to sift through the crowd, peering into the edge of the room where there were a few low tables tucked in the corner, barely visible through the pitchy dusk.

No surprise what she'd gotten tongue-tied over.

Ryder.

She tried to play it off.

But I knew. I just didn't know why she wouldn't tell me her feelings. I was guessing it was because she wouldn't admit them to herself.

He was there, lounged back, as cool and casual as they came, talking up some girl who I didn't recognize.

She might try to hide it, but I knew she hated to witness this same scene with Ryder Nash over and over again. Knew it wrecked her to see him with someone else. Which a revolving door of *someone else's* was the way Ryder did things.

I forced some lightness into my voice when I turned back around. "Oh, nice, it looks like Ryder is here. We should ask him to join us."

It would be the polite thing to do.

Honestly, I loved the man to pieces.

He was one of my best friends.

Like a brother I'd never had.

I guessed it wasn't his fault he had a jackass for a cousin, although I was still a little miffed that he'd suggested I work for him in the first place. He had to know it was a terrible idea.

"Oh, yeah, we definitely should," Dakota said, pasting a smile on her face that at least wasn't too far from genuine. It wasn't like she didn't see the guy almost every day.

I shifted to peer again into the shadows, musing, "Do you think Cody's with him?"

It was rare that Ryder and Dakota's older brother weren't out on the prowl together, but Ryder was the only one I could make out at the table.

Then I froze when someone halfway between us moved to the side, revealing the man sitting next to Ryder.

A cold chill slipped down my spine.

Caleb Greyson.

I'd only learned his first name since it was scrawled across the stupid check I'd snatched out of his hand, even though I didn't think I had the stomach to cash it.

He was angled back in the chair like he owned the place, a leg stretched out in front of him and the other bent, wearing another one of those ridiculous button-downs and tailored slacks. He nursed from a tumbler, what, I couldn't make out in the distance, but I was sure with all his pretenses it was bound to be expensive.

His blond hair weaved with darker browns was styled back, faded close at the sides, his stony face set in the same glower that he always wore.

So out of place but powerful enough not a soul would dare question his presence.

All dark allure and intimidating prowess.

I didn't realize my fingers were digging into the edge of the table and I had no oxygen left in my lungs until Dakota wrapped her hand around my wrist. "What is it? You look like you're about to go banshee right now."

She angled around me, trying to get into my line of sight to find what had me shaking like I'd stuffed my finger into an electric socket.

Confusion curled her brow before I could feel her quickly catching up. "Is that him?" she hissed.

Chloe leaned across the table and Beth whirled around, everyone gaping while I sat there with my tongue stuck to the roof of my mouth.

"What? Who?" they asked.

"Holy shit. It's him, isn't it?" Dakota's voice was held in a whisper, like the man could hear her from all the way across the room and over the raucous noise level. "You said he was gorgeous, but he's…"

I finally managed to tear my attention away, jerking forward as I finished her thought, "An asshole. And I'm not about to let him ruin this night."

"Hell, no, you're not," Chloe said.

Beth lifted her glass, repeating her toast from earlier as she winked at me. "To ditching assholes."

Thank God that time I had a drink, one I clinked with my three friends, then guzzled down.

Chapter Ten

Caleb

"YOU LOOK LIKE A FUCKING RICH PRICK SITTING OVER there."

Ryder kicked the edge of my chair with his boot. I sent him a glare, and he cracked one of his self-satisfied smirks that always made the guy look like he was up to no good.

"I told you I had no interest in coming here."

It was loud and dirty and dark, and it set every nerve in my body on edge.

People were crushed together, their laughter and shouts crashing over the blare of the music.

Chaotic and uncontrolled.

Most believed it fun and games, but I knew full well there were plenty of twisted fucks on the hunt. The depraved. The ones consumed with the thrill of spilling blood. With the love of hearing someone scream.

Hatred burned hot, and my eyes narrowed as I searched through the toiling mass, ready to strike first.

"Loosen up, man." He sat forward, grabbed me by the shoulder, and shook me like he was trying to knock me out of my affliction.

"I know what you're thinking, but you left Seattle behind to start a new life, and you're not going to have any sort of real life if you spend it thinking he might be in the same room with you. You're going to lose your goddamn mind."

It wouldn't be my entire life. Because I would find him. Sniff him out. End him.

"And you haven't come out once since you moved here. It's Ezra's fuckin' birthday, man," he emphasized. "Why don't you ditch the attitude and help him celebrate? He lost someone who was important to him, too."

Ezra came cutting back through the crowd just as Ryder said it, carrying a pitcher of beer. He wore jeans and a white tee that stretched across his muscled chest. The guy might be a cop, but he ran with an underscore of savagery, something that hadn't been there before his wife had been killed.

"Happy Birthday, man." Ryder lifted the scotch he was nursing, angling the neck of it in Ezra's direction as Ezra poured himself a beer from the pitcher.

Air huffed from his nose like he didn't know how to fucking *be* happy.

Not the true kind.

How could he?

"Thanks, man. I'm going to try to make it the best I can."

"Know you will. What do the kids think of the new house?" Ryder asked.

Ezra had moved his kids close to his mother so she could help him while he needed to be at work.

Doing his best to start over, too.

"Oliver and Owen seem to think every inch of it is a playground, and Olivia has decided that she really likes to boss them. Thinks it's her place to keep them out of trouble, and when they don't listen, she comes running to tell me."

Affection rode out with his words, a slight grin edging the side of his mouth.

"She's a sassy little thing," Ryder said.

"Just like her momma." Ezra's expression fell then, though he tried to shuck it off.

I shifted in discomfort.

He cleared his throat and turned to me. "And how about you? That house enough for you out on that ranch?"

A low chuckle came out with the shake of my head. "Not quite. Might have to expand."

"Ah, compensating for something else, I see," Ezra razzed.

Ryder smacked his hand on the table and pointed at me. "You know that's it. Poor Caleb over here, everything so big and shiny to cover up his minuscule dick."

Both of them gloated with shit-eating grins.

I held back a laugh as I took another sip of my drink, lifting the glass to say, "Fuck you both."

Two of them had given me shit for my whole life. Right from the beginning when they figured out the kind of lifestyle I'd lived. What I'd been brought up in. That it was different from them.

Little did they know I'd gladly trade it all in. Take it all back. Give it up if it could rid the depravity from my life.

But it was seeded deep.

Who I was.

Bred and fucking born.

And I knew, deep down, even though I was attempting to change, it was who I was. I needed to remember it before I made someone else pay for the sins that I had earned.

"So, tell me, Caleb," Ryder said, scratching a tatted finger on his temple, something sly riding into his expression. "Is my Paisley-Cakes still making you itch?"

A flurry of unease whipped and stirred, incited in a beat, my guts tangled with the mess I'd created today. My chest still burned where it had met her outrage. I didn't know whether to feel guilty or furious.

I roughed a hand through my hair, taking a swig of my bourbon, letting the burn glide down my throat and land in a puddle in my stomach.

Somehow I got lucky and didn't have to answer since Ryder was a cocky, flirty asshole. Some chick sauntered up and, in an instant, he'd forgotten all about pressing me about Paisley.

The woman was tall and black-haired. Hot as sin and looking for a good time. One Ryder was all too happy to give her, sending her one of his cocky smirks that was sure to get her naked. He had no problem chatting her up, propositions made, while I sat there stewing in the storm that was Paisley Dae.

Or maybe I just felt it.

The chaos that whirled through the building. A bedlam of frenetic energy and the unrest of ill deeds.

I looked up, drawn, searching through the bodies that were crushed in the cavernous room.

It took all of a second for my gaze to tangle with hers. Paisley Dae stared back with a hatred so hot it seared me through.

Like with just a thought, I'd conjured her.

Instant-fuckin'-karma.

My molars ground as a wave of guilt throbbed against the confines of my ribs.

Evelyn was going to be devastated when she found out she wouldn't be returning, not that she would ever know the details. But the reason for her departure wouldn't change the aftermath, wouldn't negate the fact that little girl had been different this week.

Less withdrawn.

Happier.

Not close to the way she'd once been.

And here was this woman, shooting daggers at me like I'd stolen some of her happiness, too.

We froze under the weight of that blazing connection for a second that felt like an age, before she snapped away, turning her back to me in a clear *fuck you*.

Her dismissal made me cagey, too.

I didn't even realize the girl Ryder had been talking to had walked away until he swiveled around in his chair to find where I was staring. Then he cracked a giant grin when he shifted back. "Speak of the devil."

And a little devil she was.

One that looked like a country angel, a cascade of white rolling down her back, sporting another pink fucking tank, this one trimmed in lace and hugging her tits.

"We should go say hi." Draining his scotch, Ryder stood. "Cody's baby sister, Dakota, is over there, plus a couple others who work at the café. These are people you're going to know."

"Not a good idea."

"And why's that?"

"We're celebrating Ezra." Easy excuse that was not going to fly.

Ezra heaved out a low laugh. "Don't worry about protecting me, bro. I see these people most days, and Dakota and her crew are cool as shit. Always a good time, and it's my birthday."

He gave me a wink as he pushed to his feet.

Fuck.

Could this get any worse?

Fucking small towns and the fiery girls who lived in them.

"Let's go." Ryder took the lead, all dark swagger, tatted head to toe, smooth and sinuous as he cut a path through the crowd.

Ezra grabbed his pitcher and followed behind.

Against all sound judgement, I did the same.

I should know better. Should recognize this girl made me insane. That she got under my skin. An irritation I couldn't scratch.

It didn't help that my dick wanted to do a little *scratching* of its own.

"Well, look who's here," Ryder called when he got close enough, spreading out his arms like he was welcoming their table into his home.

"Ryder, Ezra!" A bunch of hellos went up around the table, though Paisley refused to look up from where she was staring at her drink sitting on the table in front of her like it was a wishing well.

Ryder went directly to the woman who was sitting farthest away and facing us and slung an arm around her shoulder. He jostled her a little, making her cheek smoosh into his side.

"I have someone I want you all to meet." He gestured with his chin in my direction. "Everyone, this is mine and Ezra's *much older cousin,*

Caleb Greyson. He just moved into town. Caleb, this is Dakota, Cody's little sister, and this is Beth and Chloe."

He indicated each as he moved around the table. "And of course, you already know my Paisley-Cakes."

Irritation burned through Paisley, her shoulders rigid, though she still didn't offer me a glance.

Her friend Dakota did.

She looked like she wanted to dive over the table and claw at my face.

She wasn't the only one.

Anger radiated from the table, lifting and curling like coils of cigarette smoke.

I fought the urge to bolt.

This was uncomfortable as fuck and completely unnecessary. I never should have agreed to come here.

Dakota peeled herself from Ryder, and she cocked her head to the side, her brown eyes narrowing as she looked at me loitering to the side of their table. "So you're Caleb Greyson."

I stuffed my hands into my pockets. "I am."

Paisley finally shifted to look at me. Eyes the color of the fields glared back, a toil of grassy greens and burnt earth, flecked with glinty emeralds that always made her gaze look like it sparked.

She suddenly hopped off her stool, wearing another pair of those cut-off shorts, frayed threads hanging around her thick, toned thighs.

My teeth ground.

"Oops. Looks like I need another drink. Anyone else?" she said, dramatically waving a copper mug in the air while completely shunning my presence.

"That's my cue." Dakota slipped off her stool, and she hooked her elbow with Paisley's in a show of solidarity.

"Us, too." Beth and Chloe joined them.

"I'll wrangle up another table so we can all sit together for when you get back. It is Ezra's birthday. We need to celebrate our favorite Sheriff. It's party time, baby." Ryder grinned, the smug bastard, and he did it looking directly at me.

They disappeared into the fray heading in the direction of the bar.

The second they were out of sight, Ryder's expression tightened. "What the fuck did you do?"

⌒⋆⌒

This was brutal.

Like he'd promised, Ryder had found another table and dragged it up to the first. I'd settled on the farthest side in an attempt to fade into the shadows, doing my best to ignore Paisley who had moved as far away from me as she could get.

Ignoring me, too, acting like I didn't exist, though she was tossing back drinks like they could douse the fire that had burned between us earlier today.

Their friend Beth had left, needing to work early, and Ezra had also bailed. Even though the kids were spending the night at his mom's, I knew he wanted to check on them.

And somehow…somehow I was still sitting there, a masochist chained to the stool.

Hours had passed, and Paisley still hadn't offered me so much as a word. Not that she owed me anything. She'd made it perfectly clear what she thought of me. Part of me wanted to blame her. Take it out on her. But when it came down to it, I was just a dick.

I felt irrationally angry when she was in my space, irritated energy rushing over my flesh in shockwaves and hitting me with urges that I could barely contain.

I wanted to reach out and take her by the shoulders and shake her.

Maybe kiss her wild into submission.

Fuck it out of her.

Because she provoked something inside me that I couldn't afford to feel.

She laughed loud, her voice becoming slurred, no care as she kept tossing back drinks.

A song began to play, one Paisley and her friends apparently loved with the way they squealed and clapped when the obnoxious twang of it vibrated over the wood floors and grated through the dense, dark air.

Paisley catapulted off the stool and ran with Dakota and Chloe onto the dance floor. That drape of white hair swished around her like the toiling of the sea. The three sidled up to each other in a line along with half the bar.

Oh, I'd heard of this nonsense before, and I couldn't help the way my face twisted into something that had to resemble a snarl as I sat back nursing a bourbon and watching the ridiculous display.

The way her hips moved with the beat as she strutted around, her feet quick to glide through the intricate steps, adding her own flare as she kicked her boots, spinning, sliding, and stomping, moving the opposite direction, the girl a white flame in the middle of this mess.

Her smile was freed and chaotic, the lights strobing over the soft angles of her face in a manic fashion. My guts fisted, and I tried to cool whatever it was that kept rising from the depths, a windstorm that couldn't be contained.

I didn't care about this woman. She wasn't my responsibility.

From beside me, Ryder laughed a disbelieving sound. "Look at you over there about to lose your shit."

My eyes narrowed as I ripped my attention from the woman and set it on him. "I have no idea what you're talking about."

"Right, my friend. You look super cool and collected over there." Sarcasm dripped from his tone.

"I am always cool and collected." Except in the moments when I flew off the handle at this country sprite.

Irrational.

The song ended and the line broke apart as another song began to play, the lights dimming farther as the strobes slowed.

People began to couple up.

Some asshole waltzed up to her in all his swagger, and that *irrational* screamed.

Verging on psychotic.

Exactly as she'd accused me of.

It made me want to squeeze his neck. Drop him to his knees. I didn't exactly have a reputation for playing nice with others.

Only that sensation nearly exploded when the man turned to the side, and I got a good look at his face.

Nate.

That arrogant fucker from the ranch.

He said something and Paisley giggled, and he was slipping an arm around her waist, taking her other hand as he drew her close then began to lead her in some dance the two of them both seemed to know.

My tongue stroked across my lips in hopes of erasing the bitter taste.

Ryder laughed hard that time and clapped me on the knee. "Oh, I see how it is."

"You don't see anything."

"Don't I? It looks to me like you want to dip your pompous dick into my Pais, after you treated her like shit and caused her to quit since you can't seem to keep the asshole at bay, even when you knew she is someone important to me."

Air heaved from my nose, and I did my best to keep my attention on him instead of letting it get sucked back to Paisley.

It didn't work.

Because she laughed loud as she was getting twirled round and round, and I couldn't stop myself from watching.

Guilt grabbed me by the throat, grating like stones as Evelyn's face flitted through my mind. I worked my jaw through the admission. "I didn't mean for that to happen."

Temporary insanity. Although I supposed it wouldn't be temporary when it came to Paisley Dae.

"Then fix it."

"Fix it?"

My gaze snapped back to see her as she stumbled to the side, and she laughed even harder like falling on her ass would be the highlight of her day. It was clear her blood was soaked in alcohol. The woman more untamed than normal.

"Apologize and ask her to dance." Ryder waved with his tatted arm toward her like it was a magic wand.

My brows shot for the sky. "Dance with her?"

He was the one who was insane.

"You know, that thing you do where you move your feet back and forth? Dance. But I'm guessing it's the apologizing part that is going to be the most difficult for you."

A heavy sigh blew between my lips.

This was absurd.

Ridiculous.

Still, I pushed to my feet and left my tumbler on the table, and I moved through the web of bodies that spun and swayed. My teeth ground as hard as my footsteps as I moved over to where Paisley was currently hanging onto Nate's shoulders, flinging herself all over, out of beat and in perfect time.

She was all easy laughter and goofy moves until she found me standing there like a maniac on a short fuse, raging beside her all over again because I couldn't seem to fucking move.

"You," she seethed, untangling her hands from Nate. The fucker looked at me like he wanted to punch me for the interruption. I hoped he did. That I could beat this aggression out on him.

Paisley took two steps toward me, erasing the distance, and started jabbing me in the same spot as she had earlier.

I felt scourged at the connection point.

"You," she snarled, and her eyes squeezed closed for a blink as if she were attempting to control herself or maybe she was just processing all the insults she wanted to toss my way. "How dare you come here and ruin my night. I don't like you."

Few people did.

I should turn and walk. Get the hell out of here because I never should have come in the first place. But there I was, tossing out the stupidity that Ryder had planted in my head. "Would you like to dance with me?"

For a beat, her eyes rounded in surprise before a crash of laughter clanged from her, harsh and grating, full of offense and disbelief. "You want me, to dance, with you?"

"Ryder thought it would be a good idea."

In hindsight, it was not the best thing to say. Fury flared through her angel features, the little devil making a resurgence, and I swore to God her mossy eyes glowed red.

"Ryder thought it would be a good idea? Well, you can tell Ryder that every one of his ideas are horrible and terrible, beginning with the stupid one where he thought it would be a good idea for me to work for you."

She turned on her heel and stormed off the dance floor. It lost its impact as she kept veering left and right.

Chloe and Dakota were already back at the table, and their eyes went wide as they watched Paisley clomp her way back to them, while Ryder sat smirking like the cocky motherfucker he was. By some miracle, she made it back without falling on her face.

"Uh-oh, someone is mad." Chloe said it like praise.

Paisley grabbed a random drink from the table and drained it.

Right. My bourbon.

Gasping through the burn of it, she held the tumbler high before she used the back of the same hand to swipe the liquid that dribbled down her chin. Then she pointed at Ryder. "Your ideas suck, Ryder. Suckity, suck it, suck."

My cock perked up, momentarily confused by what she was talking about.

"I'm out." She dropped the tumbler to the table like it was a mic. It clattered against the wood, then tipped, and I caught it right before it rolled off the side.

"Outta here, tooooo," Dakota sang, nearly slipping off her stool and hitting the floor. Ryder popped up and caught her by the elbow to steady her. Still, she swayed. "I'm so lushy lush. Gotta sleep. Now."

"Yup, let's go. I'll close out tabs then get you all home," Ryder said, instantly shifting into caregiver mode.

Ten minutes later, he was ushering the trio through the double doors and into the balmy warmth of the droning summer night. There was nothing for me to do but follow them, stuck there, held in a twisted sense of responsibility.

Or maybe led by the guilt that felt like a leash around my neck.

Chloe hopped into an Uber that was waiting for her, shouting out the window, "Goodnight, lovie poos!"

"Be safe!" Dakota returned, then promptly stumbled to the side, almost pitching over.

Ryder slid an arm around her waist. "Careful," he murmured, letting her lean against him as he began to lead her toward his car that was parked in the middle of the dirt lot. A lot barely lit, the gravel loose and uneven, the cars and trucks left in haphazard rows.

Paisley was on Dakota's opposite side, and she also slid her arm around Dakota's waist to offer support, though she was lumbering around so badly herself that she nearly sent them toppling to the ground.

They both cracked up, their cackles riding through the waves of darkness that shrouded the lot.

Ryder managed to get them to his car, and he clicked the locks and opened the passenger door.

"You're the bestest of the best, Ryder," Paisley mumbled and tried to reach around and pet his head. Apparently, his sins were already forgiven, the ire she'd thrown at him five minutes before vanished in all her brilliant, blinding light.

She still held plenty for me, though. She kept shooting silver bullets at me from over her shoulder like I was the big bad wolf.

"It's a pleasure to be of service," he teased, laying it on thick.

Dakota promptly bent over and vomited.

My nose curled. I had no clue what *pleasure* he was speaking of.

"Oh, no, Doodle-Boo. You got the pukies." Paisley rubbed her back.

A mortified moan vibrated from Dakota, and she tried to wrangle herself from Ryder's hold.

"Not gonna let you go now, sweetheart. I've got you," Ryder murmured.

"Just leave me here. I'm fine."

Ryder scooped her into his arms.

Gasping, she let out another humiliated cry.

"I've got you," he promised as he settled her onto the front seat. "Besides, your brother would have my ass if I left you out here alone."

"I'll give Paisley a ride so you can get Dakota home."

What I was thinking, I didn't know. I only knew I couldn't leave it like this.

She whirled around, a white, fiery flame, and crossed her arms over her chest. It made her tits overflow from her tank. "No way, buddy. I'm not going anywhere with you. Nuh-uh. I'd rather walk."

"You're not walking anywhere." It came out a growl.

Aghast, her mouth dropped open. "You aren't the boss of me. I quit, remember?"

"No fucking chance would I let you walk home at night alone, so don't even suggest it."

Ryder situated Dakota, the grin he was holding back sly. "Are you sure it isn't too much trouble?"

Oh, I was sure it was plenty of trouble.

Still, I looked at Paisley when I said, "Yeah, it seems I have an apology to make."

Chapter Eleven

Caleb

"THIS IS REALLY GREAT. NOT ONLY DID YOU RUIN MY life, but now you're set on ruining the rest of my night, too. And I couldn't wait for tonight. And then, here you are, right there, ruining everything," Paisley stammered through a scowl. It only served to make her look adorable, her arms still crossed tight over her chest as she clomped in those boots alongside me in the direction of my SUV.

Tiny darts of hatred fired from her flesh, every step that thundered below her accentuating just what she thought of me.

My brow quirked in disbelief. "Ruin your life? Are you sure you're not being a tad dramatic?"

Even in the dusty, pale light that filtered from the streetlamps in the parking lot, those eyes sparked. Emeralds that popped in a field of green. Her mouth dropped open, her heart-shaped face slack with the astonishment at the offenses I couldn't help but keep throwing.

"Oh, don't underestimate yourself, Caleb Greyson. You are the ruiner of lives. Congratulations."

There was something about the way she said it that pierced me to the core. Guilt striking way down deep in that place that promised every word she said was true, reminding me of what my actions had cost.

In it, I was barely able to swallow around the knot of regret that thickened to stone in my throat.

"I didn't mean to ruin your night or your life." I kept my voice as even as I could.

She scoffed. "Oh sure, you say that now when you want to touch my boobs."

My attention whipped her way, stunned she'd allowed that to tumble out of her mouth, her inhibitions steamrolled by the amount of alcohol she had running through her bloodstream.

Not that the girl possessed many of those in the first place.

"Excuse me?"

Another sound of dubiety ripped from her pretty lips.

"Come on. Don't act like you haven't been ogling my girls all night. I know they're great and all, I mean, not half as great as Dakota's because hello hot mama, but I'm pretty happy with them and I think you are, too, Mr. Greyson." The whole ramble fell from her in an accusation, her lips pursing to punctuate her point.

"I can assure you I do not want to touch your breasts." Not going there, and certainly not when she was blundering drunk. And under the circumstances, fessing that I hadn't even noticed Dakota's since I had, in fact, been ogling hers all night seemed highly inappropriate.

A snort of laughter shot from her nose. "Oh, you're even all stuffy and starchy with that stick up your ass when you're talking about boobs. *I wouldn't dream of touching your **very beneath me** breasts,*" she drawled.

She was adorable.

Naïve.

No idea what I would do to that tight body. How I'd fuck her every way. Ruin her for anyone else.

And I could feel every word out of her mouth eroding my control.

"I bet you're a huge disappointment in the sack." She'd shifted around so she could taunt me face-to-face, shaking her head in pity. It set her off-balance, and she tipped to the left. She attempted to right herself, but the sole of her boot slipped on a soft patch of dirt, and it sent her toppling backward, her arms flying as she tried to catch herself.

I didn't think.

I reacted.

She was two inches from the ground when my arms snagged her around the waist. I jerked her upright. It left her pinned against me. We were bent over a fraction, me holding her up while she had no weight on her feet.

So fucking close I could taste her breath. In an instant, I was consumed by her chaos.

Open fields and fucking cotton candy.

I wanted to press my nose to her neck and inhale.

So I did, the words rumbling like a threat at her pulse point. "Are you dying to find out? I would wreck you, Little Riot. You'd do well to watch yourself."

Those eyes widened in shock, and her breaths shallowed out, heaving from her lungs in some disordered pant of desire.

I could scent it radiating from her, saw it streak through her like a flare.

Blood sloshed through my veins in a thunder of want.

How this woman had this effect on me, I didn't know.

I only knew it clouded all reasonable thought in my mind.

I wanted to peel down her shirt to expose the rosy buds of her tits currently peaked like diamonds and rubbing against my chest.

Take each pebbled nipple between my teeth.

Nibble and lick.

Before she had a chance to respond, I righted her, holding her by the waist until I was sure she was steady on her feet.

"Let's get you home." I set my hand on the small of her back as I guided her the rest of the way to my SUV that was sitting at the far side of the lot. Heat blazed at the contact, the woman a shaking mess from the warning I'd whispered in her ear.

Though she'd rebounded by the time we rounded a giant pickup truck and the tail end of my Rover came into view, a snort flying from her nose. "To think a tiny scratch could cause so much hatred. So pretty and shiny and perfect, and little ol' me had to go and ding it up. The shame." She drew it out, derision dripping from her tongue.

A frown pulled tight. She thought I'd been upset by the fucking scratch on my car? Like I gave a shit?

"I can assure you that my frustration had nothing to do with my car, Ms. Dae." I led her around to the passenger door, opened it, and helped her to sit.

"Could have fooled me."

"The car is inconsequential."

Her eyes narrowed, the green coming in and out of focus.

I quirked a brow at her. "But I still would prefer if you didn't throw up in my car."

She giggled then hiccupped, and I flinched as she tossed her booted foot onto the dash and canted me a grin. "That would be priceless."

Her leg was toned and bare, and I itched with the impulse to run my palm up its length. Dip my fingers under the frayed edge of her cut-offs.

Would she let me?

Before I tested the theory, I slammed her door shut, walked around the front, and slipped into the driver's seat.

Her aura punched me in the gut, thicker this time in the enclosed space.

A riot of warmth and candy and the sun.

My jaw clutched as I started the engine and carefully drove out of the lot. "Where do you live?"

"Wouldn't you like to know?" She dragged her fingertip down the side of my arm.

Fire flashed.

She was literally trying to torment me.

Little devil with the angel face.

I deserved it. I did. That didn't mean I would let her get away with it.

"You're playing with fire, Ms. Dae. Now give me your address so I can get you home safely like I promised Ryder I would do."

She went for the doorhandle. "Maybe I will just walk."

"Don't you dare, not if you don't want me to physically chase you down and tie you to that seat," I grated.

My stomach fisted at the thought of her roaming alone, my hands curled tight around the steering wheel, that irrational anger making a rebound, a thousand degrees as it burned beneath my flesh.

Kimberly had been alone.

Afraid.

I braced myself against the grief that slashed through my spirit.

"Why do you always look so mad?" Paisley's voice took me by surprise, soft and quiet and gentle as it penetrated the dense air. I glanced that way, finding the side of her face pressed to the seat as she gazed over at me like I was a riddle to make out.

"I'm not mad," I grunted.

I was fucking irate.

Filled with animosity and a shame so distinct most days I couldn't see straight.

"I think you're a liar, Mr. Greyson. I think you're sad and mad." Care whispered from her simple, profound words, winding me in undeserved comfort, wrapping around my soul that had already been bled dry.

I returned my attention to the road. "It doesn't matter what you think, Ms. Dae."

Hurt blasted from her being at my statement, so heavy I felt it ricochet around the cab. She turned all the way around in her seat and faced the passenger side window.

I scrubbed a palm over my face. Fuck. I was an asshole. A total prick. Completely without the capacity not to destroy everything I came into contact with.

But she couldn't go to those places scarred inside me. I was a danger to anyone who got close.

"Two 'o' two Canter Lane," she mumbled, refusing to look my direction.

At the light, I tapped her address into the screen, and I made a right, winding back through the center of the small town.

Silence held fast to the cab, oppressive and dark, my regret so thick it clotted the flow of air.

Paisley had gone quiet, and I got the striking sense that when she did, that was her true breaking point. It was the moment she'd cut you off. When she'd decided you weren't worth her time or effort because you were only going to bring her misery and pain, and she was far too strong to put up with that.

I headed north up Manchester. At this time of night, Time River was desolate, the window fronts darkened and exuding a peace that seeped from the sleeping souls from within. The town glowed with that quaint country vibe that should be comforting but only served to set me on edge.

Coaxing me into letting down my guard.

It only intensified my vigilance.

Restaurants and shops hugged each side of the road, a mix of older two-story brick buildings with colorful awnings marking their storefronts, interspersed with quaint cottages, their patios overflowing with colorful shrubs and flowering plants. There were a few upscale restaurants, and at the corner of Manchester and Rhoads was a three-story hotel that had been standing for more than a century. It had been renovated, but still oozed character and country charm.

It felt a million miles from what I knew.

No city sounds. No shriek of ambulances. No call of the depraved hunting in the night.

I glanced to where she was twisted away from me, her pale skin painted in a red glow from a neon light cast from a dive bar we passed, the woman rippling with disappointment and disgust.

I wanted to reach out and fist my hand in her hair. Force her to look at me. Confess that I didn't know how to be a good guy, but that I still felt terrible for making her feel like shit.

She didn't deserve it.

The navigation gave instruction for me to take the next right, and I slowed as I made the turn onto Canter. Two perfect rows of humble houses lined each side, towered over by soaring, lush trees. Windows darkened and their inhabitants lost to sleep.

Her house was three down on the right. I came to a stop in front of a pale green, single-story house, a tiny lawn in front of it with a sidewalk cutting up the middle. A light hung next to the door, casting a yellowed glow over the small stoop. There was a single stall garage to the left, and Paisley's truck was parked in the driveway behind it.

At least she'd left that monstrosity at home for the night.

Paisley suddenly jumped out, a hurricane that stormed up the sidewalk.

Without giving it thought, I jumped out and rushed to catch her.

Hating that I'd fucking made her feel insignificant. Like she didn't matter.

I caught her by the wrist, spinning her around.

"What do you want?" she rasped, pain laced in her shaking voice.

I yanked her closer to me, my confession shards. "I didn't mean that."

She shook her head, refusing my words, yanking her arm from my grip. "You can go back to your car, Mr. Greyson. I don't need you."

"I would prefer to make sure you get inside safely."

She scoffed, then stumbled to the side. The alcohol had dampened her senses farther, and I was pretty sure she was getting to that point where she wasn't going to remain standing much longer. "Like you give a crap about anyone but yourself," she slurred.

"I'm not leaving you until I am certain you are safely inside," I reiterated, trying to tame the ferocity that burned on my tongue. To keep it together when she unhinged something within.

Something I'd promised myself I wouldn't have. I'd made an oath. Gave myself to one purpose.

And this woman had me wanting to say fuck it all.

She turned and started back up the sidewalk, tossing words over her shoulder, "I'm a big girl, Mr. Greyson. I don't need you to take care of me. And I think we've already established we don't like each other, so why don't we end this right here?"

She made it to the stoop, and she dropped her bag to the mat and promptly knelt to rummage around to find her keys. Her back to the world, zero caution.

I moved around her and leaned down when she was mumbling and cursing that she couldn't find them.

"Let me do it."

She scowled but let me dig into her bag. It was one giant pit. I dove my hand into it, searching, finally finding them buried at the bottom. I blew out a sigh as I pushed to standing, only having to try three different keys before I finally found the right one and worked it into the lock. I sent her a glare as I twisted the latch. "Do you have any clue of the monsters lurking in the shadows of this world, Ms. Dae? The demons out there waiting to hurt the innocent and unaware? You need to be careful."

"Yeah, from assholes like you."

She wasn't wrong.

I edged the door open to the lapping darkness inside, and she shoved passed me, though she tried to quiet her footsteps as she entered.

I followed behind.

I wasn't about to leave her without checking to ensure it was safe.

In the shadows, I could barely make out what appeared to be a living room, dull-colored couches, every surface littered by trinkets.

Paisley stumbled forward and slung her bag back onto her shoulder. Only she swung it into a lamp, and I rushed forward, catching it right before it smashed to the floor.

I breathed out a sigh, resituating it on the table.

Paisley giggled, pressing two fingers to her lips as she whispered, "Oops."

I blew out a sigh. "We need to get you to bed." I kept my voice equally as quiet.

"I bet you want to get me into bed, Mr. Greyson." She hiccupped.

I took her by the elbow. "Lead me to your room."

"Yes, sir," she slurred, and I did my best to hold onto my patience, not to sweep her off her feet and carry her to her bed and demand she stay there until she'd fully sobered.

She dragged her feet as she shuffled down a hall that was so dark I had to put my hand to the wall to make sure she wasn't leading us directly into one, and she shifted to push her finger to her lips again as we stopped at the first door on the right. "Shh."

There was another door at the end, and I had to assume we were being quiet for a roommate.

Opening the door, I reached inside and flipped on the light. I took a step in ahead of her so I could check that her room was clear.

Clear wasn't exactly how I'd describe it.

It was a disaster.

Piles of clothes covered the floor, crap strewn everywhere, books piled so high on a desk it could not be used.

There was a king-sized bed pushed sideways under a window, the covers a mess, and a mountain of throw pillows tossed on the mattress.

"What are you doing? I didn't even invite you in," she accused, slamming her shoulder into the doorjamb as she came inside.

I turned to glare back at her, trying not to lose my breath at the sight of her right then.

All rumpled and untamed.

White hair a mess and that fiery annoyance on her gorgeous face.

"I am not a vampire, Ms. Dae."

Her brow furled. "Was that an actual joke? Like a *haha* joke or just a warning? Because I am sure you are some kind of monster, I just haven't figured out which one yet. I'm thinking shifter. A werewolf. But not the hot kind that wants to mark you and mate you for your whole life and can't live without you, but the kind that eats you. You're a straight-up horror story, Mr. Greyson."

She was back to rambling as she fumbled into her room.

It was stupid I found some comfort in her no longer shutting me out.

"I will not eat you," I tossed out in a huff. This woman was ridiculous.

"Oh, that's right, you won't be eating me since you're terrible in the sack." A giggle slipped from between her full lips before she stumbled toward me and faceplanted onto the bed with her legs hanging off the edge.

For a moment, I stood stunned.

Just fucking gaping at the delicious disorder spread out on her bed.

The woman was taunting me.

Teasing me.

Getting under my skin in a way I couldn't allow her.

My teeth gnashed as I was punched in the face with the vision of peeling those shorts from her body, spreading those legs wide, and eating her from behind.

But fantasizing about this riot of a woman was not why I'd come here, no matter how hard she seemed to be goading me into going there.

I stared down at her beautiful backside while I raked a hand over my head like it would clear it enough for me to figure out what to say. Figure out how to find the words that could possibly make up for the ones I'd shot at her earlier as if she were deserving of a firing squad.

I hesitated, warred, then feared if I didn't hurry up and get this out, she might fully pass out.

"Apologies don't come easy for me, but I am sorry, Ms. Dae." I forced it out through the anger I could never seem to evade. "Please, give your training for Evelyn a second chance. I'll triple your pay."

At this rate, she was going to be making more than my CFO.

Disbelief left her on a scoff that was muffled by the blankets her face was buried in. "You think I can be bought?"

"It's a job, so yes."

Flipping over, she propped herself up on her elbows, her expression disgusted as she stared me down. "You are unbelievable. Absolutely unbelievable, do you know that?"

I warred.

Warred with the frustration and hate. The truth that I should keep her at bay but wanted to discover her, anyway.

I couldn't have her.

But Evelyn needed her.

I had to remember that.

Scraping a palm over my face to break up the disorder, I forced myself to give her a little of it. "I have no clue what the fuck I'm doing, okay? The only thing I know is Evelyn needs you."

She shifted the rest of the way to sitting, taking a pillow with her.

She hugged it to her chest and tucked her knees under her arms. The green of her eyes entranced like the lull of a rolling field.

Sorrow filled her expression. "Do you even care about her?"

There was no venom in it. No spite. Just this haggard care that seemed to rip her apart.

"You don't know anything about me, Ms. Dae." My first instinct was always to lash out. To destroy a little more.

"That's right, I don't. That's why I'm asking you. I don't know the circumstances of your lives or where her mother is, but the one thing I know is that little girl…" She trailed off, sadness taking over her voice. She looked down for a beat before she returned her gaze to me. "She needs that horse, Mr. Greyson."

I gulped around the animosity. The feeling that came over me that made me want to go on a rampage. Hunt and seek and destroy. "She needs everything, Ms. Dae. Everything I can't give her. And that's why I'm asking you to provide this part for her because I'm not sure there's anyone else who can do it."

"What she needs is to be loved." Her hands fisted on the pillow.

I stumbled back, her words impaling me like blades.

"Are you capable of that?" she pushed, refusing to back down, peering into me as if she could see every sin I'd committed branded on my insides.

Kimberly's face flashed through my mind. Her joy and her hope and the love she had for the little girl who would never know the fierce, full, unrelenting love of her mother.

Grief slammed me on all sides, stoking the rage and confusion and loss.

Hands curling into fists, I battled to get my shit together. To rein the emotions and come up with an acceptable response when there really wasn't one to be found.

Because she didn't understand. Didn't get it.

I rubbed my fingers over my lips as the deluge of emotions rained down.

Regret.

Fear.

The barest of hope that only burned at the edges of this reality. A reality painted in desolation.

"I don't know if I am."

I didn't know if I was capable of loving anyone again.

Loving someone today?

After what I'd caused?

Agony clawed at my throat, pacing like a caged animal searching for a way out.

"So, you hire someone like Ms. Sandberg to watch her?" Paisley's face twisted in revulsion. "Could you have picked anyone colder?"

I exhaled. I'd picked Ms. Sandberg because she'd seemed the most organized. Practical and trustworthy. It'd quickly become clear she might not be the best candidate.

"As I said, I have no idea what I'm doing."

The truth of it barreled into me. I had no idea what I was doing. Had no business raising a child.

Pain cinched down on my heart, unwilling to fathom a different outcome.

I couldn't turn her away.

Couldn't do that to Kimberly.

A soft rush of air left Paisley's nose, and she slowly nodded as if she were processing the sincerity in my words.

"I'll do it," she finally whispered.

Relief punched from my lungs on a rush of heated air. "Thank you."

Choking out a laugh, she hugged the pillow tighter. "I'm not doing it for you. I'm doing it for Evelyn. But if you so much as look at me wrong, Mr. Greyson, I'm going to have Evelyn's horse do the honors of junk punchin' you."

"That seems excessive and cruel." The hint of a smile threatened at the edge of my mouth.

"Cruel? What's cruel is having to deal with your grumpy ass. Now get out of my house. Must sleep. So tired."

That she slurred, like the second the serious conversation had ended, her intoxication had taken her over.

She flopped onto her back and promptly rolled to her side, holding onto that pillow as if it would keep her from drifting away while she slept. It took all of three seconds for her breaths to even out, the woman still wearing the clothes she'd had on at the bar, her booted feet hanging over the edge.

A riot of white curls were strewn across the side of her face, long locks spread out over the pink spread and kissing the soft curve of her cheek.

God, she was a disaster.

A perfect disorder.

One that terrified me. Affected me in a way that made me feel out of control, slipping, without a grip on my next move or thought.

Clearing my throat, I ripped myself away from her and went in search of a painkiller because she was certainly going to need it. There was a door on the opposite side of the hall, and I took the chance that it would be a bathroom.

It was, and I went inside and dug into the medicine cabinet where I found a bottle of ibuprofen. I shook out two then went into the kitchen to get her a glass of water, flipping a switch that cast a dingy light into the room.

I found a glass in a cabinet and moved to the sink.

I froze with my hand on the faucet handle when I felt the presence fall over me from behind.

The hairs lifted at the nape of my neck, and I shifted to look over my shoulder.

An old man stood just inside the threshold of the kitchen. He supported himself on a cane, and his hair that was as white as Paisley's stuck up in every direction. Distrust was carved in the weathered lines of his face. "Who the hell are you?"

Nerves rattled through me, but I straightened myself and cleared the disorder from my throat. "I'm your daughter's friend."

"Granddaughter."

Right. Of course. The man had to be at least in his eighties.

"Yes, your granddaughter. I'm Ryder Nash's cousin, Caleb Greyson. I gave Paisley a ride home. I was just getting her some ibuprofen and water to drink."

I assumed since Ryder had lived in Time River his entire life, this man would likely know him. That it would give him some sort of solace that I wasn't an intruder.

The problem was, I couldn't be trusted.

I was as dangerous as any other monster roaming the streets.

In a different way, but the results were the same.

"That girl loves to go out and find herself trouble." He was still eyeing me skeptically.

"I was hoping to keep her out of it."

He chuckled a low, disbelieving sound as he blatantly took me in. "You look like plenty of it to me."

It was hedged in a warning.

I swallowed around the discomfort lodged in my throat. "I am."

Air puffed from his nose. "She's a good girl."

"I recognize that."

"Good, then you understand she doesn't need any more pain in her life."

Without saying anything else, he turned and shuffled back down the hall while I stood there gaping at the spot where he'd stood, feeling like I'd been bitch-slapped by an old man.

I didn't want to bring her pain, but I had, hadn't I?

Blowing out a sigh, I finished filling the glass and moved back into Paisley's room. I set both the glass and ibuprofen on her nightstand, pushing a magazine out of the way so I could find a bare spot.

Then I turned to stare down at where she had passed out, still wearing her boots with her legs flopped over the side of her bed.

I contemplated, finding I was unable to walk out and leave her like that. I began to work a boot from her foot, then the other. I didn't know if it was exasperation or amusement that pulled through me once I got them off.

Mismatched socks, one bright green and the other red and pink striped.

This absurd, ridiculous girl.

Wild and untamed and everything that shouldn't send my heart sailing in my chest.

I set her boots next to her bed, adjusted her so she was laying the right direction on the mattress, then pulled the pink plush comforter up to her chin.

A moan of pleasure left her as she snuggled under the covers, the angles of her face so goddamned pretty beneath the glow of her light.

Refusing to be the perv staring at her while she slept, I silently moved to the door. I only paused for the barest moment when she mumbled, "Maybe you're not a total jerk. A jerk for sure…maybe not all the way, though. Fallen angels aren't all bad, are they? Can't be," she rambled.

Fallen angel?

No. She had it wrong. There was no angel inside me. Just the darkness I incited.

Chapter Twelve

Caleb

Six Years Ago

CALEB ANGLED INTO HIS FATHER'S OFFICE. CITY LIGHTS spread out below them, the harbor a blackened sheet dotted with lights that shined from the ships and ferries, the islands in the distance twinkling as their inhabitants settled into the night.

It was just past nine, and Caleb's father remained behind the massive industrial desk that sat on the far side of his sprawling penthouse office.

An *upstanding* businessman through-and-through.

Appearances and all.

Respected.

Renowned.

The richest man in the Northwest.

But Caleb knew what was underneath the powerful suit who watched over the city as if he ruled it. He knew how it'd been built. And Caleb was responsible for maintaining it. Continuing its growth by any measure required.

Caleb stood opposite him, his worn, leather jacket keeping out the cold of the Seattle winter, roughing a hand over his head, waiting for his father to give him instruction.

He'd been summoned like the demon he was, called up from the pits where he roamed.

His father leaned forward on his desk, his blond hair short and perfectly styled, and strands of gray had begun to show at his temples. It only served to make him appear more dignified.

He pushed a stack of papers Caleb's direction, irritation pulling through his features. "Frank Aston refused the contract. Your sister has informed me he doesn't want to sell."

Unease billowed through Caleb. He hated that his father had allowed his sister to be a part of this life at all, even though she remained unaware of the way their practices were really handled. It didn't give him any peace, not when their father basically used her kindness as a front.

"I wish you wouldn't have her involved in any of this."

"She is just as much a part of this family as you, no?"

Caleb planted his hands on his desk. "But she isn't like either of us, is she?"

Chuckling, his father waved an errant hand. "Leave her be to do the work she thinks is important. What she doesn't know won't hurt her. And make sure when you leave here, you convince Frank Aston that he does want to sell…whatever measures it takes."

"He's already been offered more?"

"Money is not the issue. He says that building has been in his family for generations. It appears he is loyal to *blood*." His words were underscored. Emphasized.

Caleb easily received the message. "I'll handle it."

"I know you will. And once you take this position when I'm gone, you will be more powerful for it. I only want what's best for my family, too."

Caleb took the contract and tucked it into his jacket, dipping his head in parting before he walked toward the door. When he heard his father's voice, he paused, fighting the irritation that cracked through his nerves. "And take Donovan with you."

Donovan was a prick. Couldn't be trusted. Yet, his father did, cutting him a percentage of each dirty deal they hustled.

"Fine," he grated low, knowing it was no use arguing with him.

He tapped out a message to Donovan as he walked out into the hall.

Caleb: We're on.

Donovan: Address?

Caleb sent it to him, then entered the elevator, dizziness buzzing through his head as it sped forty floors down to the basement parking.

His chest tight.

The sickness of who he was twisting his stomach in knots.

The elevator doors swept open, and he strode to his bike. He started it then flew from the lot.

The back door crashed open, banging against the wall of the sleeping house. He moved through it like he'd been invited in, a storm of darkness that had descended.

Frank Aston tore open the bedroom door, breaths heaving as he gripped a bat to his chest.

Caleb reached out and jerked it out of his hold, then he took him by the back of the neck and forced him down the hall toward the kitchen.

The man stumbled as they went, crying out through fear and fury. "What the hell do you think you're doing? Get out of my house or I'll call the cops."

"Try it." Caleb shoved him down onto a chair at a small table beneath the window.

Donovan turned on the light.

It glared, spotlights on the monsters who'd come to collect.

"I was told you're being unreasonable," Caleb hissed at his ear.

"I have the right not to sell," the man wheezed.

"Of course, you do. We just want to make sure this deal is in your best interest. That this deal lands in your favor," Caleb said. It was filled with a warning.

Venom.

Evil.

Caleb tossed the unsigned contract onto the table in front of him. A picture of his daughter was on top—an 8 x 10 black and white of a beautiful girl that his father had included in the file.

Disgust burned through his being, his conscience in coils of revulsion.

"How could you be so cruel?" Frank begged. "You bastard."

"No," Caleb murmured close to his ear. "I'm just making this deal worth your while. Just sign the contract and you never have to deal with us again."

With a trembling hand, Frank began to sign the dotted lines, sweat pouring from his temples as he quivered in fear and disbelief.

Gathering the papers, Caleb stuffed them back into the front of his jacket then moved for the door that still sat wide open, the cold of winter pouring in.

Donovan didn't follow. He bashed the man in the face with his fist. Blood gushed from the man's nose, and Frank Aston cried out as he lifted his arms to protect himself, "Please, don't. I signed it. Just leave me and my family alone."

Caleb fought the repulsion that scattered through his nerves.

Donovan was a bastard. Out for blood when the man sitting at the table was guilty of nothing but wanting to preserve his heritage. Bile burned on Caleb's tongue, while Donovan cracked a menacing grin. "Just a little something to remember us by in case you get any bad ideas."

He was laughing as they walked out.

Chapter Thirteen

Caleb

"WHAT DO YOU MEAN, HORSES GOT OUT?" I spat into my cell as I paced the floor of my office. The sun had just burst over the horizon, and glittering darts of light speared through the window to pierce the night while the darkness inside me throbbed with the early morning call.

Mert had been hired to run the ranch, to handle all issues that arose. The last thing I needed was to be bothered with its care.

I had enough to worry about in Seattle. I had a billion-dollar business to run remotely. Greyson Industries was the real-estate development company my grandfather had started as little more than a small residential broker when he'd moved to Seattle in his fifties.

My father had built it into the powerful development company it was today, of course, with the help of me and Donovan working on the backend, ensuring deals landed in our favor—by whatever means necessary.

When my father had died, I'd inherited his seat.

For years, it was the only thing that had mattered. Now I really didn't give a shit. Wouldn't care if it all burned to the ground.

As long as I ferreted out whoever hated me as much as I'd come to hate myself, I'd die a satisfied man.

I had to believe it was related to Donovan Paltrow in some way. Believed his older brother had to be involved, a man who was just as much of a scumbag as his brother. I just hadn't found the proof.

But I also couldn't be so narrow-minded to think we hadn't earned enough enemies through the years that it might not have been some-one else. How many contracts had I forced? How much intimidation had I used?

So, I was hunting, sifting through every document and connec-tion because it wasn't like the detectives on the case or my private in-vestigator had found anything. Our misdeeds were buried too deep.

Because of it, I'd known I couldn't remain in Seattle. Not with Evelyn. Not when it felt like every breath and step she took in that city was done with peril and risk.

"Fence was clipped out in pasture three," Mert said. "Fifteen horses got loose and were wandering out in the middle of the main road. Could have gotten hit."

A whirr of unease trickled through my senses. "What do you mean, cut?" I demanded.

"Wire cutters, I suppose. Cut right down the middle."

Apprehension blustered, the low howl of alarm that gathered at the edges of the earth.

I tamped it, trying to control the anxiety that swam through the murky cesspool that had become my soul.

I needed not to make assumptions. Paranoia wasn't going to help me in any way.

"Where is pasture three?"

"It runs about five acres along the main road on Junction 12."

"So, someone wasn't necessarily on my property, and it could have been anyone passing by?"

"Likely was." I could almost see his shrug, as if this was of little consequence. As if I hadn't been stirred into disorder. "It's not the first time one of those fences have been clipped," he added.

Air puffed from my nose.

It was likely nothing. Unrelated.

Some assholes out looking to cause heartache that somehow in their minds was the equivalent of a good time. Still, I wouldn't be complacent.

"Search the area and let me know if there are any tracks or anything left behind. Then see to it the fence is fixed."

"Yes, sir."

I ended the call, exhaling the strain as I pushed the end of my phone to my forehead. I struggled to regain sense, to find solid ground, a baseline when that would be impossible since my life had been purged into this bitter oblivion.

I moved from my office and downstairs, my footsteps quieting as I hit the second floor. I eased down the hall and poked my head through Evelyn's open door.

Her room was empty.

Apprehension bloomed, though I bit it back and kept moving farther downstairs, walking passed the enormous, vacant rooms that echoed emptiness, a cavernous space lacking life.

There was a glimmer of it at the end of the hall where it opened to the kitchen, and the unease that vibrated in me both flared and was soothed at the sight of the little girl sitting at the island eating a bowl of cereal.

Her spirit subdued but looking for a way to break out.

She peered over at me when she felt me at the entry, and a timid smile pulled to her innocent face, one that nearly cracked me in half all over again.

"It's been two days, right?"

"Yeah, Evelyn, it's been two days."

I ignored the energy that stirred in the depths, that wild, chaos of a woman who would soon descend.

She was here to teach Evelyn how to care for and ride her horse. That was it.

I couldn't have her. The problem was, she was becoming everything I wanted to possess.

Chapter Fourteen

Paisley

MONDAY MORNING, I WAS BARRELING DOWN THE DIRT road at five to ten, leaving a plume of dust behind me. Maybe grumbled as we climbed the hill, chugging and lurching, though I was the one chugging for air as we crested the hill and Hutchins Ranch came into view in the valley below.

Miles of green pastures with the gorgeous scenery hugging the land. The river that ran through and the dense woods at the back.

Absolutely breathtaking.

Still, sweat slicked my skin, and my nerves were racing in overdrive.

I hoped to God this wasn't a mistake. Giving in the way I had. Caleb Greyson had already proven he was irrational and bossy and rude, which was so not my thing, and I was not about to be a pushover.

Every time that worry had slithered into my thoughts over the weekend, I'd reminded myself I wasn't doing it for him.

I was doing it for Evelyn.

The tiny white lie jabbed at my conscience, and my chest panged. Bottom line, this really was about Evelyn, but there was also a speck inside me that knew there was something about the way Caleb had stood there pleading with me to return that had softened my dislike of him. Something in his icy eyes that spoke of pain and grief and sorrow.

Exposed in a bare moment of vulnerability.

I knew it was the deep, deep kind that wasn't superficial or easily repaired. I imagined it was the kind that could turn an okay guy into a raging asshole.

Not that it gave him a pass.

It just earned him another chance.

Maybe coasted down the hill, and I wound down the dirt road until I came to a stop in front of the giant barn. Anticipation spiked, a hope that glowed, and a smile tugged at my face as I took in the scene.

Horses of every color, size, and breed were in the corrals and pens, and one was out in the bullpen being run round and round.

It struck me right then.

Something profound.

Coming back here?

Part of it was for me, too.

I needed it.

Wanted it.

An old dream that flared when I cranked open my door and stepped into the warmth of the summer sun burning across the expanse of blue, as a whinny touched my ears and the love of the horses filled my heart.

This...this was what I was meant to do.

That feeling of purpose expounded more when a little voice hit me from behind. "Ms. Dae, Ms. Dae! It was two days and you got here just like you said."

I spun around to Evelyn running across the stretch of lawn, brown hair flying behind her, this enormous smile on her face that spread through me on a whisper of warmth.

I did my best not to take note of Caleb Greyson sauntering along behind her.

All cool but definitely not casual.

Not when he wore another of those button-downs with the sleeves rolled up and those intricate designs rolling across his arms. Dark fury perfectly put together. A dichotomy who stalked along in a pair of tailored black pants, his hair pushed back the way he wore it. The chiseled angles and harsh lines of his face glinted beneath the rays of light, making him appear delicious and dangerous.

Fallen angel, indeed.

A tinge of embarrassment pulled at me when I thought of the way I'd goaded him Friday night.

Implying he wanted me, then straight up saying he would be terrible in bed if he made good on it.

But I couldn't help it when the alcohol had my tongue slack and the man looked too freaking good for *good behavior*.

So there wasn't one single thing about this guy to make me think he would come close to being terrible in bed, not the way the ground trembled beneath my feet the closer he came.

Attraction flared. The kind I shouldn't feel because it was the kind that promised I'd get my broken heart completely tattered. Smashed to smithereens.

Maybe he'd forgotten about it by then or maybe he hadn't noticed in the first place.

Except those ice-blue eyes flashed as they took me in where I stood at the side of my truck.

Sparks of darkness as they moved over me, heat flaring as his gaze caressed over the neckline of my tank and dipped to the swell of my *breasts*.

Oh, he was remembering, alright.

I forced myself to shuck those thoughts. I should absolutely not be thinking about him like that. I didn't even like him. Like, at all.

Okay, that was kind of a lie, too.

Because I liked the way he was looking at me right then.

I liked the way he seemed to be guarding Evelyn as he followed her out.

I liked the way he'd left me buzzy with need when he'd taken care of me Friday night before he'd left, pulling my boots from my feet and tucking me in like maybe he was more than just an *okay guy*.

I liked the way that same buzzing need was humming loud in my veins right then.

But that kind of thinking would only get me into trouble, and I sure didn't need that kind of trouble in my life. I'd had plenty of heartbreak to last me for the next decade or two.

I tore my attention from the way he was looking at me like he really did want to eat me and turned it on the little girl.

Excitement blazed from her, and she ran directly to me, never slowing before she threw her arms around my legs and held on tight.

My heart squeezed like it was in her fist. I bent down so I could hug her back. "Evelyn! I missed you like crazy. How was your weekend?"

"Longest two days of my whole life," she said in her sweet little slur, the hint of a stutter on her t's. "But I counted to keep the best track, and it's finally got here and now I get to see you and maybe I get to ride Mazzy today."

She kept clinging to me while the rattle of words fell from her.

Affection burst in my spirit. A flood of warmth that slipped beneath the surface of my skin.

I shouldn't let it.

I had a whole problem with caring too deep and right off the bat.

Dakota accused me of making instalove a real thing.

But I wasn't going to keep it from this child. She needed it more than I needed to protect my heart that felt like it was ping-ponging against my ribs.

I unwound her arms so I could fully kneel in front of her, and I tipped up her chin. "I was counting the days, too. I couldn't wait to see you."

Shyness danced across her timid features.

Brown eyes soft and trusting and panging in the center of me like I'd been purposed to be there.

Right then.

I thought maybe the heartbreak I'd put up with had been required to be standing in this very spot today.

I should guard myself, but I wasn't the type of person to quiet my emotions.

What was the point of love if you didn't know how to give it?

If you didn't know how to show it or receive it or accept it?

What was the point of keeping it bottled up where it would fester and rot and turn into something distorted and wrong?

Most of all, how could I hold it back when this child clearly needed it so badly?

"You mean you missed me?" She smiled at me like I was her best friend in the world. Or maybe her only one.

My heart squeezed. So tight I thought it was going to implode.

"That's right, I missed you so much."

A shy giggle slipped from her, and I straightened and took her hand. She sidled right up to me, swaying at my side.

My knees only knocked a little bit when I met the heated stare that burned into my cheek.

Caleb Greyson stood there with his hands stuffed in his pockets, grinding his teeth the way he seemed to like to do, as if he were in pain just witnessing the two of us.

Grief lined the harsh hold of his jaw.

God, what was with this guy?

There was something off. Something unsettling about the way he interacted with his daughter. Something that set me on edge but also made me want to dig deeper. Understand what put that haunted look on his face.

"It's good to see you, Ms. Dae." He rumbled it out in that low, seductive voice that hit my flesh like the needy scrape of his palms.

The sound of it did not make me shiver. Nope, not one bit.

"Only time will tell if I can say the same." I curtsied with the razzing.

Mr. Greyson glowered.

Ha. He was so easy to work up.

"I suppose it will."

"And look at me, right on time." I lifted my watch and wiggled it around.

"I noticed."

"Of course, you did."

A grin played at the edge of my lips, and crap, I needed to stop standing there chatting him up like I was there to see him rather than to work with the child.

"What do you say we go spend some time with Mazzy?" I suggested to her, knowing I needed to whip myself into shape and focus on what was important.

"I've been ready for two whole days," she said with her lisp, pushing back the errant strands of brown hair with her free hand that kept falling in her precious face.

Laughter bound my throat. "We better get after it then."

I gave Caleb Greyson a parting glance as I let Evelyn lead me into the barn where Mazzy waited.

Nate was down the aisle a few stalls, and I grinned at him when surprise froze him to the spot. Amused disbelief played through his expression, like he couldn't believe I'd returned, and he was only imagining how it'd come to be.

I only winced a little that he'd had a front-row seat to Caleb Greyson so rudely interrupting our dance, and he'd probably noticed we'd left the bar together, too.

Not that I'd *left* the bar with the guy.

Not the way anyone else would take it, at least.

I'd have to fill him in later. Definitely not while I was on the clock since that would likely cause Mr. Greyson an aneurism, you know, since talking with people was *bad*.

I inclined my head.

Later.

Which maybe I shouldn't give him that because I got the sense he might be expecting something that I really wasn't all that interested in.

I twisted to look over my shoulder when I felt the dark presence hovering at the big doors that sat wide open at the front of the barn.

Caleb.

I felt him like gravity pulling at my back.

A dark vacuum that would suck me into his oblivion.

It should be impossible, but the severe edges of his face sharpened, the man a freaking razor ready to slice.

I gave him a look that told him to watch it because I was still not playing games, no matter how gorgeous he was or that he'd left me a fluttery mess when he'd walked out on Friday night.

I unlatched the gate for Mazzy's stall. My chest squeezed at the sight of her.

The horse was gorgeous, her white coat soft and shiny and dappled in black spots, her black mane long like a shock of ebony hair. Dark eyes kind and soulful. She gave a good huff of her own excitement when she saw Evelyn.

But what really struck me was Evelyn…Evelyn who immediately glowed.

Lit up like the sun breaking at the horizon, casting the brightest rays that cut through the darkness and shined into the hidden places inside this child that seemed so hard to reach.

I eased in front of her, ensuring that Mazzy was calm before I extended my hand. "Come on in. Why don't we get her bridle on and maybe her saddle, too, so you can take your first ride?"

Not that she would really be riding since I'd be walking around guiding the horse at her side. But to Evelyn, I knew this was what she'd been waiting for.

"You really even mean it?" Hope split through her being.

"I think you're ready, Evie-Love. What do you say?"

Chapter Fifteen

Caleb

I WASN'T GOING TO LIE. THE HORSE MADE ME FUCKING NERVOUS. Really fucking nervous. I had my hands shoved in my pockets to keep from marching over and making a bunch of dickhole demands. From getting all overbearing and tyrannical, which was the way I had been taught to run my company, but I was coming to the quick realization that wasn't the way to raise a child.

Not that I'd put my finger on it by any stretch or had been suddenly enlightened.

But by the sharp look Paisley had given me when I'd followed them into the barn, I knew I was about to cross over a line that would be considered rude.

The viciousness gliding through my senses when I found that fucker Nate eyeing Paisley up and down like she was something to eat didn't help things. Not when I had the twisted sense that I wanted to stalk up to her, pull her against me, and stake my claim.

This possessiveness over a woman who wasn't mine welling from the places I needed to keep contained.

So I was really fucking proud of myself that instead of submitting to the urges, I instead rushed up to Paisley when she was both trying to balance Evelyn's small saddle with one hand and hold onto Mazzy's lead rope with the other.

"Let me help you with that." I took the saddle, earning a speculative glance from the woman I hadn't been able to get off my mind for the entire weekend.

Nights spent tossing in my sheets, dreaming of her riding me where she straddled me on my bed, that wild mane of white hair around her, tits bouncing, pink nipples peeking through the locks.

I locked the thoughts down and followed her out to the corral outside the barn. Evelyn had taken her hand, and she trotted along beside her, grinning up at her every second like she was staring at the sun and couldn't look away.

"Put that right there on the fence." She gestured with her chin to the top rail of the corral. I placed the saddle on top of it, watching as Paisley led Mazzy into the corral.

"Okay, let's brush her down before we get her saddle on."

"Got it right here." Evelyn held a pink brush up like a prize.

"You're on it, aren't you?"

"I gotta be if I'm going to take the bestest care of my Mazzy."

Affection spun through Paisley's expression, and she glanced at me for a split second, a beat of understanding as I looked at the little girl, too.

My guts tied in something I didn't know how to process.

Unsure of what it was or what it meant.

Evelyn began brushing the horse the way Paisley had shown her, so careful and full of awe, like every time she stroked the brush down the horse's side, a piece of her mended.

I prayed it would be the case.

Paisley had a larger brush, and she had her arm looped under Mazzy's neck and was brushing down her back. She quirked a grin at me. "You want to give it a go, bossman?"

"Uh?" I hesitated. I had no idea why.

"Scared?"

"That thing might bite off my finger."

She laughed.

Laughed a throaty sound that slicked through me like a warm, wicked dream.

Temptation.

"I can assure you this horse will not bite off your finger...unless you've been bad."

Innuendo spun through her words, a tease that she tried to hide in that heart-shaped face that made her look so innocent.

I was pretty sure innocent she was not.

I eased up to her, pushed my mouth to her ear, murmured, "You have no idea, Ms. Dae."

I didn't know if it was a warning to push her away or draw her closer.

But a shiver traveled her spine. I wanted to trace it with my finger.

Evelyn was still brushing away, oblivious to the exchange.

Paisley cleared her throat. "Okay, I think we're ready to get her saddled. First the blanket."

Evelyn ran over and grabbed it, hoisting it up and groaning as if she were competing in a weightlifting championship, and waddled over to give it to Paisley. She situated it on Mazzy's back, giving Evelyn instructions, while I got the saddle.

"Very helpful, Mr. Greyson." Paisley quirked a light brow, half a tease, half in question.

"It's the least I can do since you're here," I rumbled soft.

Her expression turned the same. "I'm glad that I am."

"Me, too." Gratitude was something I didn't feel often. I trusted few. Cared about fewer. But I felt it right then.

For a moment, the woman just...stared at me...unsure before she turned her head away and showed Evelyn how to properly latch the buckles and secure them.

"All ready." Paisley patted the saddle.

Evelyn danced on her feet, the most excitement I'd ever seen from the child radiating from her spirit. She clapped her hands. "I can't even wait for a second."

Paisley went to pick her up, but I stepped in between them. "Here, let me help you."

I scooped Evelyn up from under the arms, my throat thick as I met her gaze, those brown eyes the same as Kimberly's and full of a joy that had been missing. I tried to ignore it as I settled her onto the saddle. "Be careful, Evelyn, and listen to everything Ms. Dae tells you."

"I'm a great listener," she lisped.

I looked at Paisley, mouthed, "Be careful with her."

"I promise," she whispered.

Then she turned to Evelyn, breaking the connection that kept trying to pull taut between us.

"Hold onto the reins like I showed you…firmly but don't yank or pull unless you're guiding her."

I followed them out then leaned against the railing as I watched Paisley begin to lead them around.

Trusting her.

Something that never came easy.

Giggles floated on the warm breeze, Evelyn squealing as she sang, "Oh, she's moving. She's really moving, Ms. Dae."

"That's right because you're riding her. There you go. Just hold onto the reins," Paisley encouraged.

"I'm doing it." Evelyn's little voice touched my ears, curled into my senses, her joy so potent.

I felt it trying to pierce the dead spots.

The blackened hole that throbbed in the place where my sins reigned.

A place that men like me would never be free of.

"That's right, you are. You're doing a fantastic job. Pretty soon you'll be running through the fields."

I cringed at the visual of the horse galloping over the grass-covered pastures and disappearing into the woods with Evelyn barely hanging on.

"You really think I can be that super fast?" Evelyn asked.

"Well, maybe not this year, but once you and Mazzy both grow a little bigger, you'll be riding her all over the place." A sliver of amusement cut into Paisley's tone.

"I can wait until then, and then we'll get big together, and she's going to be my best friend."

"She'll definitely be. You just love her, and she'll love you right back."

"That's really very good because I love her all the way to the moon. With all my favorites. Will you still ride with me?"

Hesitation brimmed in Paisley for a bare beat before she answered with a slight, "I hope so."

I remained rooted while their conversation floated around me, growing distant the farther away they got. I had a million things to do before I left for Seattle tomorrow, but somehow, I couldn't pry myself from the spot.

They hadn't gone far before they turned and headed back my direction.

In the distance, I watched as Paisley laughed. She tossed her head back, white curls bouncing around her bare shoulders, the woman glowing golden in the backlight of the sun.

"Did you see me?" Evelyn shouted as they made it back to the corral.

My tangled guts fisted. "I saw you. You did a great job, Evelyn."

Shyness blazed on her cheeks, though she looked at me in a way she never had before.

With trust and faith.

Turbulence bounced through my insides, the air rough and my uncertainty thick.

I wanted to be better. Right for her. Give her every good thing possible. But how would I be worthy of that?

"She is a natural." Paisley patted Evelyn's knee, sending me a glance before she returned her attention to the child still sitting on the horse. "Aren't you?"

"Only if you say so because you are the professional."

Paisley laughed. "I'm not sure anyone has ever called me that before, Evelyn. I'll take it."

"I'll give it to you if you want." Evelyn hiked an innocent shoulder, missing the jab I was pretty sure was directed at me.

Amusement tugged at the edge of my mouth. God, there was something about Paisley Dae that lit the darkened places, a fucking light that speared through the shadows. Through the torment and grief.

A ray of hope in the impossibility.

"Okay, we'd better get Mazzy back into her stall so she can get some water. We'll go even farther on Wednesday."

"I won't even see you tomorrow?" It was the closest thing to a whine I'd ever heard come from Evelyn.

Paisley chuckled. "No, not tomorrow."

"Can you stay for lunch then because two days is really very far, and I don't want you to leave. Can she?" Evelyn turned her question to me.

"I don't think—"

"I think that's a good idea." I cut off Paisley's refusal, the words coming off my tongue without permission.

Reckless.

Insane the way this girl made me because I knew better than going after something I couldn't have.

A distraction like her was not something I could afford right then.

Not ever.

Because I refused to drag someone else into the sordid corruption of my world. But somehow, I didn't know how to let her go right then, either.

Not when it was clear Evelyn needed her.

Needed this light in her life, the woman filling in the places that had gone dim.

Chapter Sixteen

Paisley

WHAT THE HECK DID I THINK I WAS DOING, AGREEING to this? But I didn't know how to disappoint the little girl who acted like I was her first friend ever coming over to play. Not a chance.

So I agreed, getting Mazzy settled back into her stall then taking Evelyn's hand and starting up the dirt path that led to the ranch house in the distance.

Okay, mansion. We should really just call a spade a spade.

On another front, I was ignoring that advice entirely since I would never, ever admit that agreeing to stay had anything to do with the way Caleb Greyson had made me feel this morning.

Nothing to do with the way he'd interacted with Evelyn after what he'd admitted Friday night. Like he was trying even though he was scared.

There were so many questions spinning through my mind it wasn't even funny.

Like why was he scared? Why didn't he think he could love this adorable little girl when it was already so obvious that he did? Why had they come here? Why hadn't Ryder spoken about them before?

Not to mention, Caleb and Evelyn's interactions were so...odd.

As if they were just getting to know each other, and I had to wonder if her spending time with him was brand-new.

Was her living here with him only a summer thing? Had he just gotten visitation for the first time? Where was her mother? Were they still together? And why the hell did the thought of that make my stomach sink to the bottom of a stinky pit?

I didn't know anything, but I was burning to. I wanted to ask. Dig deep. Discover who he was. Because there was something about him that compelled me to look closer.

Beyond that gorgeous, hardened exterior that did something stupid to my brain.

I was attracted to him.

At least I could admit that.

Why, I still wasn't so sure. He hadn't exactly proven that he was a good guy. Hell, he was likely a *bad guy*.

I could sense the danger that lurked beneath that suit. Could feel the sins oozing from his consciousness. Could see the demons in his eyes.

But somehow, I knew there was something deeper beneath it. Something that made him desperate to do what was right for this child—so desperate that he'd insisted on taking me home and caring for me.

Intensity radiated from him and covered me in a shroud of his severity as we walked to the house.

The closer we got to it, the more details I could make out. It was this rambling three-story estate. A little stuffy and prim for my taste.

And he called my *Maybe* a monstrosity.

I was seriously not impressed by things, and I wasn't the type to feel out of place, even when the *place* I was heading wasn't exactly in my typical domain. Somehow, I was still feeling all buzzy and anxious as Evelyn dragged me up the seven steps that led to the columned front porch, the wood stained dark to match the stones that made up the walls.

"This is where I live now, Ms. Dae." Evelyn peeked back at me as she led me toward the enormous double doors. "It's really big, and I got my own room, but it's on the second floor, and I'll show you after lunch, but it's already twelve o'clock, so we need to hurry and eat."

Right.

Gotta keep to that schedule.

I fought the desire to look back and scowl at Mr. Greyson. It was freaking summer, and she was five.

"We'd better get a move on, then."

I finally gave into the need to peer back at him as Evelyn was pushing open the door.

Oxygen whooshed from my lungs, the man stealing the air.

I was a fool for giving it to him.

So gloriously rough and sharp, the man a knife that could shear me through.

"Right this way," Evelyn said, bouncing on her toes as she tugged at my hand, pulling me out of the trance.

We entered through the massive double doors, and we landed in a foyer that was as large as my grandparents' living room.

The ceiling rode up the full three stories, and a huge staircase sat on the far side, the wooden railings thick and carved in a delicate design of leaves. The staircase widened the higher it got before it gave way to the second-floor landing.

Above the door was a wall of windows that allowed sunlight to pour into the space.

Still, it felt dark and gloomy, like the rays couldn't fully make their way inside. Maybe it was the dark wood fixtures and the heavy, lavish accents against the textured walls that made it feel confined and constricted, any warmth swallowed by the oppressive formality.

Or maybe it was just the wraiths that seemed to hover in the corners that kept out the light.

The ornate furniture and decorations were so perfectly planned there was no chance an interior decorator hadn't been there.

Everything pristine and unused. Not one thing out of order.

I had to resist the urge to reach out and muss a few things up. Maybe dig into the tank I wore and wiggle out of my bra so I could toss it to the floor. Have Evelyn hop onto the settee and jump on it a few times so it could be broken in.

"This way." Evelyn gave another tug as she turned to the right and led me down a long corridor. We passed a huge living space with a two-story fireplace and mantle situated with oversized brown leather couches, then a den and a formal dining room before we rounded a corner and were in the kitchen.

"This is where we eat because we don't even eat at the fancy table." Sweetness oozed from her as she pulled me the rest of the way into the largest kitchen I'd ever seen.

Equally as fancy schmancy, but different than the rest. It held the first hint of comfort since I'd walked into the house.

The ceiling was not quite as high as the living room, but still, it soared. The cabinets were so tall you'd need a ladder to get to the top shelves, each the color of sage to match the rolling fields.

Fields you could see through the bank of glass that faced out to the North with a gorgeous view of the river and the woods beyond.

A table sat beneath the windows, and I almost groaned at the thought of sitting there and having my morning coffee, waking up to something so breathtaking each morning to set the mood for the day.

I let myself take it all in, the appliances that were brands that I'd never heard of before, the counters a natural creamy stone cracked with white and green veins. In the center of the room was the most enormous island I'd ever seen. Eight stools lined one side, and a freaking chandelier hung from the ceiling above it.

"Wow. Dakota would kill for this kitchen."

A frown curved Evelyn's sweet brow. "That's really not nice."

Chuckling under my breath, I hurried to run a hand through her hair. "I didn't mean literally, Evelyn…I was being facetious."

"What is facetious?" Her tongue lisped all over the word.

"It means you're not being literal."

Her frown deepened.

"It means like…that you don't actually mean something, but you use that word to emphasize what you really mean."

Okay, fine, I was no English teacher because confusion only twisted tighter through her features. "Killing is really bad."

She was back to my original blunder.

Crap.

"It is." Somehow, I had to force it out around the dense energy that had filled the atmosphere, like I'd all of a sudden gotten trapped in a flashflood of grief. Something so horrifying twisting the little girl's face.

And Caleb. I could feel the way he'd gone completely rigid. Stone cold. The way he'd been when I'd first met him.

Evelyn shrugged it off. "Do you want a sammwich? I'm really very good at making them, but I'm not allowed to because Ms. Sandberg has to do it, but I think it's okay if you help me, right?"

She turned to Caleb for the answer.

I cringed, hating the idea of that woman being responsible for her meals, too. It was bad enough she was watching over her the times of the day when I wasn't around.

"That's fine," he answered, though somehow his tone had gone deeper, and he was looking at me like somewhere between the time I'd stepped into his house and standing right there I'd committed a mortal sin.

"I would be more than happy to help." I started to follow Evelyn as she raced off to the refrigerator that was paneled the same as the cabinets, but my movement was incapacitated by the hot hand that took me by the elbow.

Mr. Greyson spun me toward him, and he dipped down, his nose two inches from mine. I tried to fully ignore the rash of shivers that raced across my flesh.

I did.

I tried my best.

I swore it.

But there was no stopping the way the cold lit like flames when his face was right there, the way that attraction flared.

Molten.

Threatening to erupt.

All while he was looking at me like he wanted to choke me out.

"You need to watch what you say around her, Ms. Dae. I've already warned you that your carelessness will not be tolerated."

"I didn't mean—" My head spun, jumping around and trying to figure out what had him so worked up, not that it seemed to be all that hard to poke at his bully.

"It doesn't matter what you meant." His jaw clenched, and still, he held onto me, refusing to let go.

My brow furled in disappointment and ire flamed in my chest. I'd taken another chance on him and, here he was, throwing all his assholery around like it was free.

Well, it was going to cost him.

"Dumb me to think you might not be a total jerk. I should have known you would prove me wrong," I hissed as I tugged my elbow from his grip.

He roughed the hand that had been containing me through his hair. Frustration tightened his jaw, a violent war visibly going down in his heart and mind. He exhaled, the hostility not knowing whether to drain or expand as he angled in, so close but not touching me. "I need you to be thoughtful."

"You think I'm not being thoughtful by staying here for lunch to spend time with Evelyn?" My words were hard and low, hoping to keep them from the child when my anger wanted to fly all over the place. "Or did you get one look at my house and decide I'd only agreed because I can't afford to feed myself?"

He scuffed both those big hands over his face before he dropped them to glare at me. "That's not what I meant."

"What you meant doesn't matter, Mr. Greyson." See how he liked it when someone started firing dirty arrows at him.

He flinched.

I had to stop myself from gloating or maybe from stomping on his foot.

Except I didn't have the time.

Glass suddenly shattered behind us, the sound piercing and echoing on the travertine floors.

I whipped around at the same time Evelyn screeched, her little hands coming up to cover her ears as if the noise had terrified her. Without hesitation, I rushed that way and scooped her into my arms since she was standing in a pool of glass and mayonnaise.

Tears started to track down her face, and I bounced her like she was a baby, running my hand down the back of her head and making all these shooshing sounds.

"It's okay. It's okay. It wasn't your fault. It was just an accident," I promised.

"Are you injured?" Caleb was right there, at our side, his tone deadly. The same as it'd been when I'd backed into his car, though this time, I heard it differently.

Recognized the current.

Terror.

Worry.

Dread.

It knitted it up into harsh syllables and grating vowels.

His fear as stark as the child's.

Evelyn furiously shook her head that was buried in my shoulder. "I broke it."

"That's okay," I told her again, looking at her dad from over her head, trying to figure out what the hell was going on since Caleb looked like he was going to blow a gasket.

Seriously, it was just a mayonnaise jar, not the end of the world, but there was something about the man that gave off the mood that at any second it might be.

That everything was in a constant state of crumbling.

Precarious and unsteady.

"Here...let's just check and make sure, okay?" I didn't know if I was telling him or her, but I had to physically pry Evelyn's arms from around my neck as I set her onto the island. I took one of her arms, scanned it with my eyes, before I ran my hand down the length of it, making sure there were no cuts or scrapes.

"All clear here," I murmured softly, worried if I spoke too loud, it was only going to worsen the situation.

I did the same to the other, then I picked up each of her booted feet and checked them out, but since she was wearing them and jeans, she was completely fine.

Hoping to lighten the tension, I jostled her little pink boots emblazoned with rhinestones, making her flutter kick, my voice twisting into playfulness. "Not a cut to be found…all thanks to these awesome boots you have. Where did you even get these? I need a pair of them for myself."

"You do?" she asked through her tears, her little fists rubbing at her eyes.

"Absolutely. Don't you think I'd look great in them?"

Evelyn barely peeked up at me through the locks of brown hair that had fallen in her face, pieces matted to her wet cheeks. Caution clouded her sweet demeanor, though she sniffled and seemed to let go of some of her fear.

"Because you like horses, too?" she asked.

I brushed her hair back so I could look into her earthy brown eyes. "That's right, I love horses, just like you."

Warily, I glanced to the side at Caleb who was still right there, towering over us. A dark storm. The muscles in his arms flexed as he clenched and unclenched his fists, the designs writhing above.

"She's fine," I promised him.

His throat throbbed heavily when he swallowed, as if he were having a hard time accepting it or wrapping his head around it or maybe just unable to believe it was true.

My spirit thrashed, torn between these two, held in the middle, as if I'd gotten locked in a twisted web of pain and heartache that I didn't understand. Whatever had caused it, I knew it was stark and gutting.

It was the staggering kind that cut out chasms in people's souls.

"Are you—" Whatever Caleb was about to say was cut off by the sharp snap of disappointment that rushed through the air, a click of Ms. Sandberg's tongue as she stood at the edge of the kitchen looking at the mayonnaise and glass on the floor like it was toxic waste.

"What in the world happened in here? I told Evelyn to come to my room immediately once her lesson was finished so I could prepare her lunch. This is unacceptable, Evelyn. Look at the mess you made."

"I'm really sorry. I didn't mean to." Evelyn said it so quietly, and the tears started tracking down her cheeks again.

Maybe it was PTSD, the memory of that same voice echoing in my ear. *You are an impossible child, Paisley Dae. Spoiled brat. I don't know how your grandma even tolerates you.*

I'd had some really amazing teachers in my time, but she wasn't one of them.

"It was an accident," I shot out, unable to tamp that spite in the words. I wondered now what my grandma would have thought if she'd known the things this woman used to say to me. I bet she would have stormed right down to that school and told Ms. Sandberg where to shove it.

One thing was for sure, I wasn't going to allow the vile woman to trample all over Evelyn's soft spirit.

Ms. Sandberg gasped. Sheer offense. As if anyone could possibly dare to disagree with her.

Then she curled up her nose like I was a horse patty she'd just stepped on in the pasture. "I see you haven't changed one bit."

Oh, did she really just go there?

"That's right, only I'm bigger now, and I'll be more than happy to put you in your place."

"Your place is out in the barn, not in this house."

Um, wow. How I wasn't across the kitchen, clocking her, was beyond me. My willpower was stellar.

"I was invited inside, thank you very much."

"Clearly, our employer hasn't yet come to realize the type of person you are."

She lifted her chin at that, elevated and pompous and acting like she was all kinds of something.

All while it was my turn to get gaspy and aggrieved, and the insult was flying out without heed. "And you are nothing but a shriveled-up cunt."

So much for that willpower thing.

At least I'd had the forethought to cover Evelyn's ears before I said it. I was supposed to be watching what I said around her, after all.

I might as well have stabbed the woman in the chest with the way her hand flew to her throat, and she looked to be a second from succumbing to a coronary, choking and gurgling on her spit.

"How dare you—"

"That is enough." A blade of venom cut through the air. Disgust that sheared through the animosity that went back at least twenty years.

Caleb exhaled a hot breath, anger raging through the worry he'd been trapped in a moment before.

Heat blistered from his skin, rising up from his being, crashing over me.

Crap.

Even I could admit I'd gone too far that time.

Evelyn could very well be proficient in lip reading for all I knew.

Except he set that deathly glare on my oldest nemesis, barely held malice vibrating from his flesh. "You are excused, Ms. Sandberg."

She fell into a state of utter perplexity. Apparently, she'd never been *excused* before in her life. "I beg your pardon?"

"I said you're excused. Permanently. Your employment is no longer required. Expect a final check to be delivered to your residence tomorrow with four weeks' severance, although you don't deserve a penny of it."

Holy crap. Did he just can her?

"Well, I never." She clutched her throat.

"I bet you never have." Oops, that ripped right out of me, too.

She glared at me like I was a succubus who'd cast some sort of wicked spell over poor Mr. Greyson who clearly couldn't think for himself.

She stood there like she was waiting for him to come to his senses.

"Get out of my house," he growled.

She gasped, blinking, before she turned and stormed out.

For a moment, none of us moved, frozen in her disbelieved outrage as she banged upstairs.

I finally managed to tear my attention from the spot she had vacated, and I turned it on Caleb whose face burned hot.

The heat of him overwhelming.

A fire in the pit of my stomach.

He'd gone all…papa bear. I liked the look on him.

Oh boy.

That had so just turned me on.

I rushed to fill the silence. "I like old people. I really do. I mean, my grandpa is basically my favorite person in the world. I have mad respect. Just not for that one. And don't you think we maybe should have had her clean up this mess first before you let her go?"

I realized I still had my hands covering Evelyn's ears.

Probably a good thing.

"This isn't funny, Ms. Dae."

I gulped. "I know. I'm sorry I instigated that. She and I have a history."

His teeth ground. "I've been wanting to fire her since she started here. Thank you for giving me a reason to."

"Isn't Evelyn reason enough?" My hands were still covering her ears, the child not even trying to remove them, so sweet and patient.

My and Caleb's voices had gone hushed, as if we were sharing our deepest secrets.

With the way my heart was pounding, I was sure that we were.

"She is the reason." The words were shards. I felt them like barbs hooking in my soul.

"What are you going to do now?"

He blew out a heavy sigh, scrubbed a palm over his face, and looked at the far wall. "Don't know. Find someone new. In the meantime, I'm going to have to ask Ryder or Ezra if she can stay at one of their places tomorrow. I have to go to Seattle."

"You have to go?"

"My offices are located there. There's business I have to attend to."

Darkness flash-fired, a thunderbolt in the ice of his eyes.

I tried not to shudder at what it meant.

"So, you're not a rancher?" I drew out like it wasn't obvious.

He did that scowly thing that I hated to love. "Do I look like a rancher to you, Ms. Dae?"

"Not even a little bit." I hesitated for a beat before I asked, "Then what are you doing here on a multimillion-dollar ranch?"

Rigidness lined his jaw, and his response ground through his teeth. "It's safer than the city."

My brow lifted. "Couldn't you have done it a little more...small scale?"

He glanced at Evelyn. Pain twisted his features in dread. "No."

Evelyn pulled gently at my wrists, and as I dropped my hands, I felt my heart stretching in a new direction. Pulling toward two people who seemed at complete odds, as if they didn't match, as if their worlds had gravitated in different spaces but had come colliding together.

"Am I allowed to listen now?" she whispered like she was in on the secret.

"I think you are, as long as Ms. Dae doesn't have any other choice things to say?" Caleb answered before I could, and he cocked his head.

Amusement played through his menacing features.

God, that looked good on him, too.

I forced some lightness into my tone. "For the time being, I think I'm good, but I can't make any promises for the future."

"I wouldn't dare expect it from you."

The slam of the front door echoed down the hall.

"Good riddance," I said.

"Really good riddance." Evelyn was smiling too wide.

Caleb blew out a breath. "You two are nothing but trouble, do you know that?"

His voice lost its edge, the business-cut suit nonexistent.

"I'm full of it, just ask my grandpa."

"He already told me." A smirk threatened at the edge of his sexy mouth.

My eyes went wide. Crap. They'd met, Friday night, when I'd come in blundering drunk.

For a moment, we stayed there, just watching each other before he stepped away, blowing out a sigh. "I'll get this mess cleaned up, if you could keep her up there while I do."

"Of course."

He went to the pantry and pulled out a broom and dustpan. He began to sweep the glass fragments, taking the oily mayonnaise with them. I was pretty sure the task was below his pay grade.

"How long are you going to be gone on your business trip?" I found myself asking.

He eyed me from where he was bent over scooping all that greasy goo into a dustpan. "Two days."

"I'll stay with Evelyn, if you'd like." It was probably a bad idea, but right then, it didn't feel like it.

Not when this man had just stood up for this little girl.

Proven his care.

His ferocity.

His protectiveness.

In it, it'd felt like he'd been sticking up for me, too.

Plus, I didn't relish the idea of Ryder watching her. I mean, he was amazing, but he'd probably have her down at his machine shop, and I wasn't sure that was the safest place. He was also a bit of a wildcard, a bit careless, living his life without a ton of responsibilities. He would likely be fine with her, but he wasn't used to taking care of anyone other than himself.

And Ezra had his hands full.

Or maybe I was just being selfish.

Finding excuses to tell myself to make the offer okay.

Because I wanted to be there.

For Evelyn.

For this little girl who was coming to mean too much.

"Yes!" Evelyn clapped, far too eager by the proposition. "I really, really like this idea. It's a good idea, Ms. Dae. I think maybe the best."

I wondered if I should have covered her ears again before I'd asked, but I couldn't help but glow that she wanted to spend her time with me.

His brow furrowed in a thousand lines, each carved of worry and question, reservations and relief and so many thoughts I doubted he'd let anyone ever see.

"Are you sure?" he finally settled on.

"I wouldn't have offered if I wasn't."

He blinked, eyes an ice-storm that raged, uncountable secrets and a million regrets. His gaze moved between Evelyn and me. "Yes, I would really appreciate it if you stayed, Ms. Dae. I'll be sure you're well compensated." His tone became business-like.

"I wasn't offering so you could pay me."

"Then why?"

I looked to Evelyn, tipped up her chin, and whispered, "Because Evie here is my friend."

He grunted. "I'm still paying you."

"Just pay me whatever that Ms. Sandberg hag was making, and we're good."

He shook his head and went back to cleaning the mess, and Evelyn was swiping the wetness from her cheeks.

She looked up at me through her soggy face and mess of brown hair.

And she beamed.

Beamed so bright.

And I realized I'd give about anything to see that look on her face.

~⚬~

"Okay, I'll see you tomorrow." I ruffled my fingers through Evelyn's hair where she was at the table beneath the windows in the kitchen, sitting up high on her knees as she finished her sandwich.

"Only one day...it's so fast." She held up her pointer finger while shoving her sandwich into her mouth with the other.

My chest squeezed. "That's right."

I cast a glance at Caleb who remained at her side, his demeanor different, bigger somehow. Darker and lighter. As if a layer had been peeled back and I was seeing a different man underneath.

This one was scarier, somehow, because I felt my pulse quicken in my veins as he looked at me with those eyes. Polar caps that burned blue flames. Licked and wisped and blazed.

Clearing my throat, I forced a smile. "I'll see you tomorrow at eight."

I turned and made a beeline out of the kitchen, suddenly feeling like I needed to escape whatever was growing in that room.

Something that built from the depths and became powerful.

Because I didn't need to go falling for this man, grabbing onto a crush that caught like a wildfire, incinerating the promises I had made to myself.

I might be strong, but my heart was fragile. It'd been broken, and I felt those fragments trembling, shifting like they were trying to take new shape.

A shape that would be as dangerous as the man who'd been looking at me like I was exactly what had gone missing. Or maybe like something that had never been there in the first place.

I'd almost made it to the front door when I felt the presence cover me from behind.

Intensity gushing out on a wave. That buzzy sensation vibrating in my veins.

I froze with my hand on the door latch, keeping my back to him because I wasn't sure I could look at him right then.

He approached, the soles of his shoes heavy on the floor, his presence so powerful I lost my breath.

"Thank you." The words were issued close, so close to the shell of my ear that chills lifted in their wake.

Flames that licked a path down my spine and settled in the pit of my stomach.

"I'm more than glad to."

He shifted closer.

Electricity crackled.

A storm of volatility.

I finally sucked it up and turned to face him.

Blood sloshed and sped at the sight.

So intimidating, all harsh angles and sharp, sculpted beauty.

His throat bobbed when he swallowed. "Are you sure you're up for this?"

"I wouldn't have offered if I wasn't. Are you having second thoughts?"

He lifted his hand, and my breaths turned shallow as he caught a lock of my hair and twisted it around his finger.

His head angled, so close that I breathed his aura.

Power and wealth and deep-seated secrets.

It felt as if he were devouring me on all sides without even really touching me.

Consuming.

Overwhelming.

"I question everything, Ms. Dae, but I'm having a hard time questioning you."

His confession speared me, staked me to the wood. The truth that he didn't trust anyone, and he was giving it to me.

"Your daughter is incredible. I would do anything for her."

Pain blanched his face, his eyes squeezing shut as if my saying it punctured his wounds anew.

When he opened his eyes, he fisted a whole handful of my hair, gripping on like he didn't want to let go.

Chest hitching and his breaths coming hard.

The same as mine.

His forehead dropped to mine, and he just remained there breathing me in, like he craved whatever I was emitting before he edged back and set his palm on my face, his words ragged when he let them go. "Thank you for coming back."

"Thank you for proving that I should."

He held my stare for a moment before he nodded, then he peeled himself away, forcing two feet of space between us.

"I'll see you in the morning, Ms. Dae."

Turning, he strode back down the hall. At the end, he shifted to look at me, and a smirk pulled to his face. "And don't be late."

I didn't know whether to laugh or give into the disorder that blustered through my being.

Caleb Greyson was a storm. And I was the fool who was getting swept away.

Chapter Seventeen

Paisley

"I THOUGHT WE HATED HIM?" DAKOTA POPPED A FRY INTO her mouth, one she'd stolen right off my plate, the sneaky little thief.

She was on the other side of the counter at the café, grinning at me where she had her elbow leaned on top.

I swatted at her hand. "Hey, those are mine."

"And I made them."

"And I'm paying for them."

Her brows quirked all over the place, her voice playful and wry. "Are you? Because the last I checked, you've been running up a tab since the second you got into town."

A twinge of guilt poked me in the chest. "I get paid on Friday. First stop I'm making is coming in here and paying it off."

Dakota waved a hand. "Stop. I'm only teasing you. You know you don't have to do that. Love is on the house."

"But your fries shouldn't be." I sent her a smirk.

"Food is my love language, don't you know?" She snatched another fry, her brown eyes glinting.

I laughed around the bite I took off my enormous, juicy

cheeseburger. "Oh my delish. Your love language has just become mine. You are a wizard in that kitchen."

"Why else would half of Time River currently be in my restaurant?" She gestured to the packed house behind me.

"Um, because you're awesome-possum in every way. My bestie is slaying. You worked your butt off for it and look what you've built. I'm so proud of you, Doodle-Boo." My voice softened at that, sincerity taking over. She had poured herself into making this place work.

"I'm pretty proud of myself." Awe filled her voice before she stole another fry then winked.

I laughed. "You punk."

"That's why you love me. Now back to the one we hate. Let's get this straight…" she said as she pointed a finger at me. "Friday night, you were set on never seeing him again, let alone acknowledging him, and then you climbed right into his SUV and let him take you home, and now you're spending two nights at his house to watch his little girl? Do I have this right?"

In contemplation, my head shook back and forth as I took another yummy bite, humming around the food as I chewed. "Well, he apologized."

"He apologized?" Disbelief took a free ride to the sky on her perfectly waxed brows. "He doesn't much look like the apologizing type. Besides, talk is cheap. You and I have both learned this from experience."

"The apologizing type he is not," I agreed, still having a hard time putting my finger on why I'd taken him at his word since his words were all kinds of rash and rude. I was glad I had.

He'd been…different today. Really different.

I quirked a brow at her, taking us back to the way things had actually gone down on Friday night. "And let's be real. It's not like I asked the guy for a ride home. Ryder basically dumped my ass in the parking lot so he could whisk you away."

I made sure to paint the words with innuendo.

Redness touched her cheeks, though she scoffed. "Hardly. He just wanted to get me home as fast as he could since I'd already puked on his shoes."

"Tell me you didn't get the shoes," I moaned.

Her face turned a dazzling shade of mortification. "You wouldn't think I'd get lucky enough not to have, did you? Got his pant leg, too. I'm sure his car is going to smell like puke for months. Go me, making myself unforgettable." She pumped a sarcastic fist in the air.

"Oh, that bad boy doesn't mind a bit."

Dakota ground out a sound of disagreement. "Ryder is just a friend, you know that. Family really. Cody would lose his ever-lovin' mind if I even thought about dating his best friend. And you're the one who needs to be real, anyway, Paisley-Cakes. We both know there's no chance Ryder wants me. The only reason he's always hanging around is he considers me his little sister and thinks it's his job to look after me."

Her teeth clamped down on her bottom lip, and I saw her mind spinning, her insecurities rearing their stupid head.

"Not want you? That's crazy talk. You're grade-A amazing."

She huffed as she glanced down at her lush curves like they were a curse. "Hardly."

"Don't do that," I told her.

"What, be realistic? I prefer to be honest with myself, Pais."

But it was all the ignorant, vapid lies that had convinced her of that untruth. Anger pulled against my ribs, wanting to break out and beat down anyone who'd ever put my bestie down for not being a fucking size 6.

"So how about some honesty on your part," she continued. "What's actually going on in that pretty little head of yours? Because the Paisley I know would tell that guy to go fuck himself."

I didn't even realize she'd stolen another fry until she made a circle around my face with it.

"Hey," I whined. I was going to starve at this rate.

She snatched my plate and dragged it across the counter. "None for you until you fess it up."

"There's nothing to fess up. I really like the little girl, and she needed someone to babysit her for a couple days, plus I could def use the money. Simple as that."

Oh, simple it was not.

I could still feel his breath on my cheek, his fingers in my hair, the need that had whirled around me like a stupid drug I hadn't known I should resist. The way I felt compelled to lean into him. Dip my fingers beneath the stony surface.

With the way my pussy had clenched when he'd had me backed against the door.

Clearly, I was in need of a good lay. Maybe I should go after Nate. He seemed like he wouldn't mind getting his cowboy on with me. Too bad missing was the lusty flare one Mr. Greyson lit in me.

"You know, he looked like he wanted to rip that Nate guy's jugular out just for having the audacity to dance with you on Friday night."

She said it as if she'd known exactly what I'd been thinking.

I reached over to snatch the plate back from her. "Well, are you surprised? He seems to jump on every opportunity to be an asshole."

"Or maybe he just wants to jump on you."

"Haha. Hardly."

Too bad an errant flame licked up my insides.

"We know what was *hard*." Playful suggestion widened her eyes.

I swatted at her. "Don't you dare put that visual in my head. Not when I'm trying to eat dinner. I might gag."

"I bet you'd gag."

"I hate you," I pouted.

"I prefer honesty, remember?" The tease danced through her features, her full lips quirking as she tried to hold back her laughter.

I poked my tongue out at her, but then she was totally ignoring me because her mother walked through the door, her sweet boy hooked on his grandma's hip. Kayden's little arm flew out, his pointer finger going right toward his mom. "Momma!"

Joy burst in Dakota, her devotion and loyalty so thick I could taste it, the magnitude of it radiating toward him as if she could touch him from where she stood. "Hey, you."

"I see you," he spluttered through his tiny voice.

Kayden was all dark hair and big brown eyes like his momma's, a roly-poly, dimple-faced, angel boy who giggled and laughed and shined his joy into this world. He was also kind of a stinker. Getting into things left and right. He kept Dakota and her mom, Pat, on their toes, that was for sure.

"I see you, too," she sang as she moved that way. She took him from Pat, hoisting him up high then bringing him down to smother his face in kisses. He giggled and kicked and tried to kiss her back.

"How was he today?" Dakota asked her mom.

Pat watched Kayden during the days, which was a huge relief to Dakota, knowing he was safe and cared for, plus she brought him in often so she could get quick snuggles.

"A handful," Pat said, though it was pure affection as she ran a loving hand down the little boy's back.

"I a good boy," Kayden proclaimed, dipping his head in two deep nods, like just saying it and smiling that way could erase every bit of trouble he'd gotten himself into during the day.

Laughing, Dakota hugged him tighter. "You are, aren't you? Are you hungry?"

"Pancakes?" he asked, clapping his hands.

"I think that can be arranged."

"Playing favorites again, I see," I said, giving her crap since they stopped serving breakfast at eleven thirty.

She sent me a smirk. "Do you need me to have them whip you up some pancakes, too?"

I popped the last fry into my mouth then grinned. "Nah. I'll just take another order of these fries."

Chapter Eighteen

Caleb

DARKNESS FELL IN A HAZY SHEET WHERE I WAITED IN THE side alley of the six-story building. The first floor was a coffee shop and an electronics store, and the upper levels were apartments.

I leaned against the dingy bricks, my hands stuffed in my pockets. The sounds of the city shouted, ambulances screaming and voices carrying. Engines whirred as cars sped up the inclined streets.

The air was cool, the city held in those few coveted weeks that offered Seattle fair weather in the summer.

I might as well have been in the fall of drizzly, dreary rain. The storm that surrounded, my heart a mad thunder where it beat at my ribs. Viciousness crawled as I waited.

My head jerked to the left when a heavy metal door rattled open, spilling light into the alley before it slammed shut behind the man. He turned to walk toward where his car was parked, his back to me, the murky light spreading out in front of him as his footsteps clacked on the pitted pavement.

I moved.

Quietly.

Stealthily.

Different than the way I used to handle things all those years ago.

My position at the company might have changed, but underneath, the same man remained. Even if I tried to repent, it was still there, this wickedness that turned my blood to oil. Venom that beat in my veins.

I had the knife pressed to his throat before he even knew I was there.

He flailed, a gurgled sound spilling from his mouth before he stilled, fear radiating from him as I leaned in close to his ear. "It's so good to see you again, Tarek."

Donovan's brother was a piece of shit. I didn't mind shaking him down, and I'd do a whole lot more if I found he was responsible.

"Greyson," he wheezed. "What the fuck? Haven't you already stolen enough from me?"

I grabbed him by the back of the neck and hauled him over to the trunk of his car. I shoved him forward until he had his hands braced on it, and I reached into the inside of my suit jacket.

I tossed the first picture down and forced him to look at it.

"Oh God." Tarek moaned, trying to turn his face away like he was sickened by the gore tossed to the glossy shine of his trunk.

"Look at him," I demanded.

Raffi stared back with lifeless eyes, his throat slit, blood spilled around him where he'd been left at a worksite where an old building had been dozed to make room for a new luxury apartment building. My Director of Project Management.

"Look at him, Tarek. Look at him. Did you do this?"

I tossed down the next.

Miles. Our corporate attorney.

In the same position, outside in the alley that ran the side of his house where he'd been climbing into his car to come into the office that morning.

Lifeless. Cold. His throat cut open.

Tarek Paltrow wretched.

"Did you do this?" And why now? All these years later?

"What? You think I'm responsible for this? Are you fucking insane?"

I might not have thought Tarek was a monster like Donovan, but he was slime. And I knew he hated me for what I'd done to his brother. Hatred made you irrational. Made you thirst for revenge. Wickedness your master. Donovan's fate had never been confirmed, but Tarek knew. Of course, he did, since I'd threatened the same result would befall him if he ever came near Kimberly.

Now, I was sure that he had.

Bile rose up my throat as I threw down the last, agony sharper than the knife I held at the fucker's throat.

Kimberly.

Her brown eyes wide. Unseeing. Gone.

Her body found behind the Greyson Industries building.

Hatred filled me full, sickness boiling from the abyss that festered inside, my voice haggard when I demanded low, "Did you do this?"

"No," he whimpered. "I heard about it, on the news." He gulped and trembled. "But it wasn't me. Swear to God."

Of course, he'd heard. Everyone in this city knew. There had been an immediate connection between the killings and Greyson Industries. They were tied. Related. The investigators had no idea who. But I knew well enough it was done as retaliation. That someone out there hated us enough to hurt people who had not earned the retribution.

Innocent.

I might deserve it, but they did not.

My gut told me it was this fucker.

"I will find out. I promise, I will find out." I hissed the threat at his ear. "If you did? There is no place I won't find you."

I shoved him forward farther, and I gathered the pictures and stuffed them back into the inside of my suit jacket. Without looking back, I headed in the opposite direction down the alley.

Loathing ran on a circuit. Every molecule in my body throbbed with abhorrence. I just didn't know who it was directed at.

By the time I made it back to my building, I could hardly breathe, revulsion marching over my flesh, like I was on my hands and knees in the sewers, crawling with the rodents.

Covered in disease.

I rode the elevator to my penthouse apartment, and I went directly to the shower in the en suite. I turned it to hot and peeled my clothes from my body like it could peel away the atrocity.

Make me someone else.

I stood beneath the scalding water as if it could make me clean.

Wash it away.

The vileness that filled my soul.

Because I'd been responsible for it. Responsible for it all.

My skin was bright red as I toweled off. I pulled on a fresh pair of underwear and roamed into the massive, vacant room.

Below, the city was at my feet. The harbor bobbing with ships and boats that twinkled in the blackened night.

I'd once felt the king of it.

Higher than them all.

But I'd been brought to my knees. Forced to see what my sins had caused.

I sank down onto the side of the bed, dragging my fingers through the wet strands of my hair before I reached for my phone and thumbed into my texts.

I went back to the last one that Paisley had sent earlier today.

It was a picture of her and Evelyn, their two bright, smiling faces plastered on the screen.

It was followed with a thumbs up and a *Having a blast!*

My stomach twisted in hope and dread.

I had one purpose left.

Ensuring that Evelyn was safe.

I had nothing more to give than that.

Knowing me was peril and risk.

My soul emptied by the mistakes I had made.

Loveless.

Lifeless.

Still, I ran the pad of my thumb over their faces.

Wishing I was different.

Chapter Nineteen

Paisley

I GALLOPED UPSTAIRS WITH A PEAPOD ON MY BACK, HER GIGGLES wild and unending. Her little arms clung to my neck, and mine were wrapped around her back, keeping her safe and supported as I clomped up the stairs, snorting and whinnying and bouncing her all over the place.

"You are the most fastest horse I've ever seen," she managed through her giggles that kept coming. Each one made me grin wider.

I bucked her a bit when we got to the second-floor landing. "That's because I'm a Thoroughbred. If you're the bettin' kind, I can't be beat."

More giggles rolled. "Don't be crazy. I'm only five, and I'm not even allowed to bet, and I only got five dollars. And my mommy said betting is really bad so I'm never even gonna do that."

I nearly screeched to a halt, my knees going weak as my heart hitched.

It was the first time she'd mentioned her mom, and it rolled out of her so easily, like second nature, but what I felt more was the way her arms tightened around me once she realized what she'd said.

In an instant, she'd gone quiet and still.

The last thing I wanted was for her to fall into somberness, but I didn't want to ignore the importance of it, either. So, I bucked her again, keeping my voice light when I told her, "Your mommy is totally right. Betting isn't the smartest thing you can do with your money. It's best to save it up so you can buy what you want. What are you saving those five dollars for?"

"Another horse." With the way she said it, she might as well have tacked an *obviously* onto it.

My chest expanded. Of course, she was. I galloped down the hall, my feet clomping on the wood, a raucous disorder filling up the vacancy that echoed through the space.

Evelyn lightened again, and I made a sharp right, making her laugh as I darted through her door and galloped into her room. Spinning around, I bucked up so I could dump her in the center of her bed, careful to lean almost all the way back to keep her safe.

Laughter ricocheted as she bounced on the mattress. It hit the walls and my heart, and it only grew when I spun around. She was on her back, those long locks of brown spread around her in a total mess.

It was pure cuteness overload as she grinned up at me as she struggled to get her hair out of her face so she could see me, her smile growing by ten times when she finally did.

"I like it the best when you're here, Ms. Dae."

Everything slowed as a wave of affection overpowered me. A tsunami that knocked me from my feet. I climbed down onto my knees at the side of her bed, suddenly so thankful that I'd gotten to have this time with her.

"I really like it, too," I told her. "So much."

It was our second night, and Dakota might tell me I'd completely lost it, but I thought staying here had been one of the best experiences of my life.

I looked down at the little girl who had made it that way.

She was wearing a pink nightgown with three unicorns printed on the front. Last night, we'd painted our fingernails and toes a rainbow of colors.

I took her little hand, running the pad of my thumb over the back.

I couldn't help but think she was the most adorable thing I'd ever seen.

She curled her fingers around mine, lifting them between us. "We match."

"That's right, we do."

"And we like horses so much and the same."

"Mmhmm, we both love them so much." I could almost remember being her age and forming my obsession around them. How I couldn't wait to get to my uncle's small ranch on the weekend, begging my grandma and grandpa to go early so I could spend the day in the barn.

"Does that mean I'm in your favorites, too?" she asked, her voice turning timid, though it was underscored with hope.

Everything soared. Was it possible to fall for a child? Like completely, irrevocably lose your heart? Apparently, since I was sure mine now belonged in her little hand.

So very reckless, like Caleb Greyson had accused me of, since I would be leaving tomorrow afternoon, my time here limited. And it wasn't like the lessons were going to go on forever.

But I knew I wanted them to.

"You are definitely in my favorites, Evie-Love," I admitted.

"That's good because I don't got a mommy anymore, and I never even had a dad."

She might have stabbed me in the heart with the way it seized.

Stopped beating.

I moved so I could run my finger along the length of her jaw, careful how I chose my words. "I'm very sorry for that, but I think it's very good that you're in my favorites, too."

"It makes me really sad because I miss my mommy lots." She whispered that like a secret, her tiny voice riddled with things no child should have to feel.

Her torment tore me in two, and I raised up on my knees so I could get closer to her, so I could slip my arm around her back and lift her to me.

I hugged her fiercely.

So tight.

She clung to me, different this time, her fingertips scratching at my back as if they were looking for a place to sink into. A place where she belonged.

"It's okay to miss your mommy," I whispered against her head.

Pain sheared and slayed, and I hugged her tighter, never wanting to let her go.

"My uncle said she's gone forever."

I froze for a beat, lost to a crash of confusion, before everything came rushing in on a flood.

The pain on Caleb's face every time I called Evelyn his daughter. The way she'd never called him dad. How her mother had never been mentioned.

Oh God, how had I been so oblivious not to add it up?

Caleb was her uncle.

It made so much sense. His overprotectiveness and his inability to connect.

Too much sense, and I hated the reality of it for this little girl so violently that I would do anything to erase it. But there was no erasing it. There was only holding her and loving her through it.

My spirit shook, a trembling, a sickness that had become my own.

Because I saw it in her eyes. The grief kept there, brimming below the surface and seeking a way out. She just hadn't felt confident enough before to release it.

A thousand questions burned on my tongue, but they weren't mine to ask.

She was five.

That was an invasion of privacy.

Manipulation.

So I gave her what I could.

"It's an awful thing to lose someone we love, Evelyn, but you should know you don't ever have to feel bad for missing her. You don't have to feel bad for still loving her or for being sad that she isn't right here with you. But what's also really important is that you find joy and do all the things that make you happy because that is what she would want you to do. I bet she's looking down right now, so happy that Mazzy makes *you* so happy."

I might be overstepping, pushing past a line I shouldn't cross, but I believed it. Believed a bond that great couldn't be broken.

"You think she got happy for me?"

God, that didn't mean this wasn't painful.

Excruciating.

I squeezed her tight then eased back to brush my fingers through her hair. "I do."

A soft exhilaration filled her expression, something that looked like rejoicing, and I wondered if she'd felt completely alone and isolated since she'd lost her. How long ago that'd been, I couldn't say, but I had to guess it was recent.

A fresh, raw wound cut into this little girl.

"I like that," she murmured.

My heart panged, and my smile was soft. "Me, too, and I like you."

"A lot?" Hope filled her words.

"A whole, whole lot."

God, I was getting myself in deep. So deep that I wouldn't be able to get out. Setting myself up to get my heart ripped to shreds because I was falling for a little girl who wasn't mine to love.

"Okay, time for bed."

"Do I have to?"

"It's already thirty minutes past your bedtime. But shh…" I pressed my finger to my lips. "Don't tell anyone."

Predominantly the stickler who'd given me five pages of printed-out instructions about her care, her schedule down to a T.

I was going to have to talk to him about that.

But it made Evelyn giggle, so I was happy for that. She snuggled down under her covers, and I pulled them up to her chin. Leaning over her, I pecked a kiss to her nose. "Goodnight, Evie-Love."

"Night-night, my favorite day."

Everything squeezed, and I held onto the sensation that felt like my heart weighed ten thousand pounds heavier, so full that it throbbed against my ribs.

Cherished it because I'd never felt anything like it before.

"Sleep tight. I'll be in the room right next door if you need anything."

"Okay."

Turning onto her side, she closed her eyes, and within a minute, she was already breathing deep.

I brushed my fingers through her hair once more, then I reluctantly stood and crept out, pulling her door halfway shut, lingering at the threshold while I listened to her breathing.

Knowing my heart no longer belonged to me.

Chapter Twenty

Paisley

I JOLTED IN THE SILENCE WHERE I STOOD OUTSIDE EVELYN'S door when my phone buzzed in my pocket.

I shouldn't have been caught off guard since Caleb had texted me pretty much every two hours since the moment he'd left.

But everything about it felt different now.

The man so much more than I'd expected. And seeing his name light on the screen?

Butterflies scattered.

What was I even supposed to say to him now? Did I ask him about it? Pretend like I didn't know there was something horribly wrong in this house? Ask him what had happened to who I was guessing was his sister? I could only surmise he was related to Evelyn's mother since Evelyn didn't seem to know anything about her father, but really, what did I know?

Nothing more than there was a grieving little girl sleeping in her room.

And I wanted to understand.

Fully.

I was invested. Wanting to be here for the child in a way I'd never wanted anything before. And I wanted to be there for him, too.

I tiptoed back to my room next to Evelyn's, the room lit in a faint glow from the lamp on the nightstand.

I hopped onto the unmade bed and propped myself against the headboard and thumbed into his message.

Caleb: Update.

A grin tugged at the edge of my mouth. So stuffy and precise. Still, my spirit thrashed in the middle of it, sure there was so much more to him.

My fingers hovered over the screen, unsure of what to say. I decided to keep it superficial.

Me: It was a really good day.

Me: You?

Caleb: How my day went is of no consequence.

Irritation flash-fired, but I schooled it, remembering what I'd learned tonight.

Me: Because it's none of my business or because you don't want to talk about it?

So maybe I was pushing him a little. Maybe this concern had seeded itself deep and had already sprouted, growing into something I shouldn't let it.

But it was already there. Tendrils curling through my consciousness and drawing me toward a man I shouldn't want.

It took forever for him to respond.

Caleb: Because Evelyn is what is important.

There it was. I was sure of it. Where his commitment lay, from where every choice he made originated.

Me: I think you're important, too, Caleb, but somehow, you don't believe it. You can talk to me, if you want.

Caleb: I'm not looking for a friend, Ms. Dae.

I saw it for what it was. He was trying to build a wall between us. Erect a barricade around his hurt.

Me: What is it you're looking for?

It felt like an eternity passed before he finally answered.

Caleb: I'm not a good man, Ms. Dae. You'd do well not to ask me what it is that I want.

There was something about his response that snapped through me like static electricity. Lifting the fine hairs on my nape and running down my arms. Sex painted his tone a greedy red, coded in the warning that I couldn't seem to heed.

Me: I'm asking anyway.

Caleb: And what if I wanted something I shouldn't have?

Me: I say we go after what we want.

Caleb: You're asking for things you can't handle, Ms. Dae.

Me: Oh dear, Mr. Greyson, have you even met me? I'm sure I can handle you.

I was only subtly aware of the fact I was digging myself a hole. Weaving the innuendo into the words, letting the attraction flame and flare and rise with each text that came through.

I was asking for trouble, flirting with him this way.

Dakota might not like to go after it, but apparently, I did.

Because my heart was fluttering at the exchange, my stomach lighting up in a way it hadn't in so long.

I liked his demon.

This fallen angel who looked so damned good. I wanted to crack through the polished stone and discover what was hidden inside.

Caleb: Reckless girl.

Was that really what he thought of me?

Me: It's only reckless if you regret it in the end.

Caleb: You'll regret it. I can assure you that.

Me: And what if I don't? What if I want to know exactly what you're thinking right now?

I was pushing him. Or maybe it was just this need, *this interest* that was pushing me. Desperate to find out if he felt the same spark between us every time he came into the room.

Caleb: Is that what you really want? To know exactly what I'm thinking right now?

It didn't matter if it was a text. It was coated in a warning.

Me: I do.

Caleb: So you wouldn't mind if I told you I'm thinking I want to fuck you? That I want to trace my tongue over every inch of your body? You wouldn't care if I told you I know your cunt is the sweetest thing, and I've been dreaming of tasting it? Propping you on my desk and eating you for lunch?

A roar of lust bounded through my veins, pounding in my ears and thundering through my body.

Holy crap was I ever playing with fire. But I couldn't stop. My fingers flew across the screen, incited by this need that boiled and blistered.

Me: Ahh...so you would eat me. I bet you want to see my boobs, too.

I let the tease weave into it, trying to maintain the lie that this didn't matter. That his confession hadn't scored me with desire. That I wasn't sitting on this bed writhing, burning with lust.

I nearly hit the ceiling when my phone suddenly rang with a video call, Caleb's number lighting on the screen. My hands were trembling like crazy when I answered it, and in a moment, I was staring at the harsh, striking angles of his face.

The man was hewn in severity, a barely controlled fire that threatened to spiral into tragedy.

And he told me that I was chaos.

"Are you trying to drive me to madness, Ms. Dae?" His jaw was clenched, the words a low threat.

I lifted my chin. "Would you meet me there, Mr. Greyson?"

The man growled. It sent a rash of shivers skating across my skin. I had no idea why I wanted this guy so much, but the thought of having him had embedded itself deep.

This curiosity. The attraction. The strange connection I didn't quite get.

"Is Evelyn asleep?" The man always made a question sound like a demand.

"Yes."

"Shut your door and lock it," he ground out, his breaths shallow and hard.

I wasn't just looking for trouble. I'd found it. Jumped right in because I was hopping off the side of the bed and padding barefoot across the room like I was on a secret mission, my heart jackhammering in my chest while I snapped the door the rest of the way shut.

The click of the lock turning rang through the room.

Sealing my fate.

And I was getting all gaspy and short of breath as I edged back toward the bed, wondering what I'd gotten myself into. How it'd gone from some *harmless* texts to this man staring me down through the screen. In the dim light of whatever extravagant room he was in, those icy eyes burned blue fire, and I was slowing beneath the severity of them, waiting for his next instruction.

Nothing but a silly sheep waiting to be slain.

But death by whatever wicked pleasure he was about to bring seemed like an okay plan right about then.

"Is this a line you want to cross?"

"If it's with you, I do." Vulnerability seeped into my tone, though I lifted my chin in challenge, sure I wanted to test these waters. Explore the way he made me feel.

"Let me see you," he rumbled, and my tongue stroked over my dried lips, palpitations pounding my heaving chest.

"What do you mean?" I asked.

His chuckle could only be construed as menacing. "Don't get shy on me now, Ms. Dae. You know exactly what you were asking for. Hang up right now if you don't want it."

Standing at the side of the bed, I lifted my phone up high, my head tipped back, angling the camera to give him a good show of my cleavage that more than peeked out of the top of my tank. "Is this what you wanted to see?"

"Take off your underwear."

Um, what?

Well, okay, I guessed I'd totally heard him because I was already complying, a fool who raced toward destruction because clearly this man held the power to annihilate me.

I kept the phone held high, peeking at him every couple seconds, while my free hand skimmed down my front until I found the hem of the sleep shorts. I slipped my fingers under them, catching my panties as I went. I wiggled out of them, pushing them down until they slipped the rest of the way to the ground.

I stepped out of both.

A hard breath panted from his mouth. "Good girl. On the bed."

Cool air hit my heated center, and chills were racing far and wide, clashing with the fire that was going to burn me up. I climbed back onto the bed, a riot going off in the middle of me.

"You're turn," I told him, trying to sound like I was the one in control.

Hardly.

Because he rumbled, "Already done."

He pulled his phone away so I could see more than his face. "I was already thinking about you."

His image was dulled by the muted light, but the subdued shadows outlining him still ripped the breath from my lungs.

He lay on a bed, surrounded by silky linens, his light skin in stark contrast against the black sheets.

His chest was bare, packed with that lean, corded muscle that made him look like a viper, coiled and ready to strike. His body written in a severity that howled of danger. Just like I knew he was, something wicked beneath that suit that he tried to keep contained. His rippling flesh was covered in tattoos, and I tried to take them all in, to categorize this paradox of a man and peer into the mystery he kept so powerfully hidden away.

My attention caught on a broken clock that rested over his heart. The hands were forever frozen at 11:42. Fractured, shattered fragments scattered off to one side as if they'd been taken by the wind, and an eye peered out from the middle of it.

Everything about it felt ominous and dark.

As dark as the need that blazed in his eyes.

Then the air was yanked from my lungs when he drifted lower, over the hard planes of his abdomen, the cuts and grooves flexing and bowing with his movements.

Because he had his cock in his hand, jerking himself in harsh, rigid strokes. The man was massive, thick and long, his crown engorged and fat. He curled his palm over the tip before he ran back down.

Arousal dripped out to soak my thighs, and a shudder ran through me in a freight train of need.

"Shit," I whimpered.

"Do you still think you can handle me, Ms. Dae?" His voice rang with the challenge.

Nope. No. I definitely did not, but I really wanted to give it a go. I wanted to know what it would feel like to have him over me, filling me, taking me violently the way he was stroking himself.

"Look at you," he murmured. "So fucking gorgeous. That face could ruin a man."

I didn't even realize he was paying attention to my face. Not when I couldn't look away from the sight of him, but I had to when he moved his phone so I could only see the intensity burning on his.

Eyes aflame.

My stomach twisted and blood thundered through my veins.

"Have you been thinking about me, Ms. Dae? Fantasizing about me?"

I pressed my knees together while I gave him an erratic nod. "Yes."

"Your turn," he said, his voice dark, pitching with each stroke of his hand. "Show me what you've been dreaming about."

I only hesitated for half a second before I decided if we were doing this thing once and only tonight, I was going to give the man the full show. I leaned over and dragged my bag out from under the bed, and I rummaged around for my vibrator.

The truth was, my fingers weren't going to do.

Not when he sparked this deep, guttural ache. I wanted to be stretched wide and filled to the brim.

"Shit," it was his turn to hiss when he saw my toy.

"I'm not the type of girl who doesn't like to come prepared, Mr. Greyson."

So maybe I'd been worried the house was going to smell too much like him, that I was going to be inundated with his presence, that the growing attraction toward him was going to burgeon and sprout and become all-consuming.

I'd thought I might need relief, but what I'd never, ever expected was this.

This need that throbbed and glowed and begged to be filled.

Lying back on the bed, I rested my head on a pillow and lifted the phone high. My breasts strained against the confines of my tank, and I tipped the phone to capture where the hem had ridden up enough to expose my belly button.

Quivers rocked my thighs where I had my feet planted on the bed.

"Let me see your pretty cunt," he demanded, his voice a rasp, and he had his phone held up high, too, the man giving me full vantage to the miracle that was his dick.

There was a piece of me that wanted to be shy right then, so exposed, letting go, trusting him to hold this private moment.

But I realized I did—somehow, I trusted him with this.

I sighed out when I gave it to him, angling the phone so he could see.

"Look at you. Your pussy is perfect. Gorgeous. Is it aching for me?" he groaned. "You're dripping, aren't you?"

"Yes."

"Turn it on and let me see you fuck yourself, Ms. Dae. The whole time, you'd better be wishing it was me."

"So bossy," I told him, my voice too gaspy to allow it to come out light.

He growled. "Have you met me?"

"Unfortunately." I couldn't help but taunt him, tease him the way he was teasing me, the man ruining me with each second that passed.

As if I wouldn't be wishing it was him, but the last thing I wanted to do was admit how desperately that I did.

I was sure he could tell the truth, anyway, the way I moaned when the tip of the vibrator hit my slick entrance. It slid right in since I was soaked and ready.

I moaned, "Caleb," like he was the one penetrating me.

It was much smaller than him, and I'd always considered it more than sufficient in the past, but as I began to pump it in and out, the little nub hitting my clit each time, it didn't come close to being enough.

"You have to be the most perfect thing I've ever seen. Perfect chaos." His words had grown harsher, deeper and desperate as we both drove ourselves toward climax.

That buzzy energy hummed through my body. He fisted and stroked himself, faster and harder, the man beautiful in that powerful, arrogant way.

Hedged in darkness.

His demons playing in the shadows that surrounded him.

But me?

I got to see him undone.

Coming apart.

His teeth ground and his jaw clenched and every glorious muscle in his body bowed when he split.

An orgasm rocked him, and he was grating, "Come with me, reckless girl. Finish what you started."

At the sight of him jerking and spilling on his stomach, I did. I followed him into his blissful ecstasy.

Pleasure ripped through me.

A firestorm.

An inferno that devoured everything in its path.

A cry nearly busted out, and I shifted to bury my face in the pillow to keep it contained.

Ripples of this rapture rushed through, wave after wave.

I laid there gasping with aftershocks rocking through my body while Caleb Greyson fought to steady his ragged breaths.

Finally, the haze of lust cleared.

Something shifted in the stone of his gorgeous face.

It almost looked like tenderness.

"You surprise me at every turn, Ms. Dae."

I swallowed around the rocks in my throat. "In a good way?"

In that same moment, the tenderness was gone. "I have no room for distractions in my life right now."

Inhaling, I tried to find some fortitude for my heart that already felt like it might get shattered. "It seemed like you were looking for one. What, you don't have a girlfriend there in Seattle to keep you warm, and you needed to call me?" I did my best to act like this didn't matter. Keep it light. The fakest smile on my face when it felt like my chest might cave.

If he did, I was absolutely going to stab him when he got home. And I was realizing I knew absolutely nothing about him. So little. And I was the fool who wanted to hold any pieces he would give me.

"I don't have girlfriends. I fuck, and it ends at that."

Another warning.

Right.

Of course.

"Well, I'm glad I could keep you entertained for a few minutes." There was no keeping the spite out of my voice. But what had I expected? A confession of love?

I had to be a fool.

He blew out a strained sigh, and he sat up, only his profile visible as he scrubbed a palm over his face. "I didn't mean it like that."

It was then I noticed how haggard he looked.

Frayed.

As if he'd aged five years since he'd gone.

"Then what did you mean?" I whispered it.

"It means I won't let you get twisted up in the mess I have made."

The questions burned again.

I wanted to ask him about Evelyn's mother. About what had happened to her. About his life. About who he was once he walked out this door because every single thing about him was written in mystery.

"Life is always messy."

His laughter was hollow. "No, Ms. Dae, not like this. I already told you I'm not a good man."

Emotion gathered at those rocks in my throat, and I was struggling to speak. "Yet you would do anything for the little girl in the next room."

Somehow, I knew it was the truth. Their interactions might be strained, he might be fearful, but I saw what blazed from his being when he was in her space.

"She's the only thing that matters," he murmured. Darkness clouded his features. Grimness dulling his frame.

"She's wonderful."

"Thank you for taking care of her while I'm away."

"It's been my pleasure."

More than a pleasure.

It'd been life changing. But I didn't think I should admit that.

He exhaled again, and for a second he looked at me like he wished things were different. "You should get some sleep. I'll see you tomorrow."

"Have a safe trip home."

He ended the call, and I flopped back onto the pillows, groaning as I covered my face with my hands.

What the hell had I done?

Chapter Twenty-One

Paisley

EVELYN'S SWEET LAUGHTER RANG THROUGH THE AFTERNOON air, her joy profound as she held onto the reins while I guided Mazzy by the lead rope.

"I really love her so much, Ms. Dae. Like a lot and a lot."

Mazzy gave a snort like she agreed, bobbing her long neck.

"She definitely loves you a lot," I told her.

Mazzy whinnied.

"Did you hear that? She's saying you are pure awesomeness."

Evelyn giggled. "I do got the awesomeness."

A peace unlike anything I'd felt before had settled over me, at war with the disorder deep inside over what I'd instigated last night.

Evelyn and I had been out with Mazzy for over two hours, and we'd wandered over the grass-covered plains before we'd found ourselves following a path beneath the towering trees that ran the edge of the river.

The air was clear and clean, close to crisp if it weren't for the warmth of the summer sun that blazed from the endless span of blue sky.

I thought today that sky might go on forever.

No end.

The possibilities eternal.

But I still couldn't help but worry that after last night I might be coming up on a quick dead end. Heading in a direction that would lead nowhere good.

I mean, what were the chances he would fire me when he got home? Say it'd become a conflict of interest?

It really was. On both our parts.

But like I'd told Caleb, it was only reckless if you regretted it.

It might have been stupid, but I'd do it all over again.

Bare myself for the sake of getting a moment of his vulnerability.

The memory of his gorgeous cock wasn't going to hurt all that bad, either, except for the fact I was sure I'd never find anything comparable.

Men like him ruined you like that.

My only regret would be if it harmed what I had with Evelyn.

My heart squeezed in rejection.

Now that? That would be a travesty. But I guessed it was a risk I'd taken, asking to know him more, even though now I was a little terrified of what it might mean.

Either way, I knew as Evelyn and I strolled along the edge of the river, the sound of it rushing over the rocks and the whisper of the wind calling through the trees, that I'd come to the place where I belonged.

Coming to Hutchins Ranch had reminded me of what I really wanted.

Rekindled those dreams.

Time River was my home. Where I wanted to be. Where I was going to build a brand-new life with all the old pieces that I'd loved and left behind.

As Evelyn and I roamed, I hoped she would always be a part of that, in whatever capacity that might be.

As her teacher and mentor.

As her friend.

I glanced up at the delicate features of her face. Her smile was accentuated by the rays of sunlight that speared through the leaves in the trees.

It lit her like the little angel that she was.

My chest tightened, and my spirit hummed.

Devotion expanded, and I had the sudden urge to reach out and touch her cheek.

Promise I would always be there for her.

That I would stand at her side.

That she wasn't alone.

I knew what that feeling was.

Love.

I loved her, and I worried merely being her teacher might not be enough.

"Did you even think I'd be this good at riding my favorite horse, Ms. Dae?" Evelyn asked.

"Of course, I knew you would be. You screamed natural the second I saw you."

"Just like you?"

Soft laughter rippled out. "Just like me."

"You got to ride on your favorite horse when you were five, too?"

"I did. I didn't have one at my house, but my uncle did, and I thought his house was the best place in the world because I got to see his horses."

"How many did he have? As many as me at my house?"

"Oh no, not even close. He had three."

I doubted there was anyone in Time River who'd ever had as many horses as Caleb Greyson did.

Evelyn gasped like it was an atrocity. "And you didn't even have one?"

"Nope, even though I thought of them as my own."

"Well, we can ask my uncle if you can have one. Which one do you like the very best? I think he's got a lot and he won't even mind."

My heart throbbed at her sweet innocence. "That's really nice of you, Evie-Love, but that's okay. I'm going to save up just like you and buy my own horses."

Or really, the hope would be other people would bring theirs to me.

"You're saving just like me? We really are the same, and we must be in all our favorites."

"I guess we do have a whole lot in common, don't we?"

"We match, remember?" She lifted her little hand with her rainbow nails as proof.

Affection pulsed. "That we do. So, what do you say we try something new?"

"I like that idea."

"We're going to have Mazzy go into a trot. Just an easy one, and you need to make sure you're holding snuggly onto the reins, but also don't tense up. You don't want her to feel like you're nervous. Remember, she's listening to you and taking all her cues from you, so you stay calm and in control, and she's going to, too."

"I already learned all that the other day when you told me," she rambled out, "because I am a very good learner and a good rider."

God, this kid made me happy. "That you are. Okay, just nudge her real gentle with the heel of your boots."

"Will I hurt her?" Horror filled her voice.

"Nope. You just keep it gentle, like a love pat."

She only hesitated for a second, looking down at her boots like she was checking to make sure they weren't weapons, before she sucked in a big breath and barely knocked her heels against Mazzy's flank.

Mazzy began to trot, super slow, while I jogged along beside them.

"There you go, just like that," I encouraged.

I stayed right beside them in case there was an issue, even though I was pretty sure Mazzy would protect the child with her life. The horse was completely in tune with her, the two connected in that special way that would last a lifetime.

"You're doing great."

Evelyn squealed, giggles riding on the summer air. "I can't even believe it, Ms. Dae. We're running so fast, I bet I could even win a race."

We were barely more than walking, but I wasn't going to correct her.

My phone buzzed in my pocket. It would be Caleb checking in after his flight had landed.

This morning, I'd woken up to the first text of the day. He'd reverted to the typical dry tone of his texts.

Update.

Update.

Update.

Didn't he know I'd let him know if anything had changed?

He hadn't mentioned last night.

I supposed I should be thankful for that.

Water under the bridge.

Because I really didn't want things to become uncomfortable between us.

Complicated.

Too bad I felt like I'd been completely *complicated* by him. Spun up in a way I wasn't sure I'd ever before been.

"Time to head back." I shifted course to head in the direction of the barn.

My stomach sank at the thought of leaving soon. He was probably climbing into his Range Rover at this very moment and starting the hour drive it would take him to get the rest of the way home.

Nerves scattered, pinpricks against my heated flesh.

I was both excited to see him and dreading it at the same time.

I needed to boot the reaction. I couldn't go around feeling like this.

He'd already made it clear he didn't have time to strike up something with me, and I didn't even want that, did I?

"Is it time to go back already?" Evelyn slurred in her adorableness, squinting as we hit the trail and came out from beneath the shade of the trees and into the glare of the day.

"It is. Your uncle is going to be home soon, and it's going to be time for me to leave, but don't worry, I'll be back soon."

"I think I like it the most when you're here, Ms. Dae. It makes it feel good right here." Evelyn rubbed the center of her chest.

My heart nearly exploded out of mine.

"Mine feels really good when we're together, too," I whispered around the clot of tenderness. Tenderness so fierce it made me feel like I might suffocate.

"That's because you're my favorite day."

I slowed the trot, and I shifted so I could touch her chin, so I could meet her eyes when I said, "You are my favorite day, too."

She beamed, a bursting flame that struck me to the core.

When we made it back to Mazzy's stall, I helped her down and showed her how to remove the saddle, even though it was far too heavy for her to do it herself.

She moved toward Mazzy the way I taught her, slowly, without making any quick or jarring motions. She pressed her little face to Mazzy's muzzle, her little arms going up to wrap around the horse's neck.

Air puffed from Mazzy's nose.

"I got the best horse in the whole world."

"That's because she has the best owner."

My phone buzzed again.

Caleb was likely to lose his shit since I hadn't returned his texts immediately.

"All right, we'd better get back in." I stretched my hand toward her, pulling her out of the stall and closing the gate. I tugged at it to make sure it was locked.

I started to dig into my pocket for my phone since I could then safely check my messages, only to gasp when I saw movement in the periphery to my right.

I let go of a small laugh when I realized it was Nate. He was leaned against the wooden slats of the stall next to Mazzy's.

He grinned, all his dimples popping out as he kicked a casual boot back on the wood. "You are a jumpy thing."

"Not usually. Just extra cautious right now."

I tipped my head toward the little girl at my side, and his attention slipped to her, his smile shifting from sly to warm. "That's more than understandable. You have an important job to do."

Then the flirtiness reclaimed its spot when he returned his gaze to mine. "Boss is heading back. You about off? Thought maybe we could hang out tonight. Get a bite at Time River Market & Café? I've heard it's good."

"It's delicious. My best friend owns it." I could never help but shout praises for Dakota.

His grin kicked at the edges. "Your best friend, huh? Are you sure you're not just saying that then?"

"Heck no. It's truly the best. But I think I'm going to have to pass tonight."

Okay.

I was going to have to pass forever.

It wasn't like I owed Caleb Greyson anything, but I couldn't imagine going out with Nate after what'd happened last night.

I blamed it on those sculpted cheeks and that stony jaw and those full, red lips. Those icy blues that cut through me with the force of a knife.

A freezing cold that had managed to light a fire.

I really would do best to put out that fire, but the truth was, I liked his grumpiness and surliness and outright severity. That energy that felt like a coming storm. Like it might break me apart at any moment and without warning.

I'd liked the way he'd looked at me last night. Like maybe I could burn him alive, too.

I couldn't have it, but that didn't mean I was going to string poor Nate along when my feelings had slanted in the direction of my boss, either.

Ugh. Why did this all of a sudden feel so messy?

There was only a flicker of disappointment in Nate before he pushed off the stall. "Rain check, then."

"Sure."

Damn it, Paisley. Don't do that.

I resolved to tell him we could be friends but nothing beyond that when we didn't have an audience. It really wasn't a discussion Evelyn needed to be privy to.

Caleb was right.

I needed to watch what I said around her.

"See ya around." He tipped the brim of his hat before he dipped his chin and said, "Miss Evelyn."

Then he turned and strutted his really nice ass in his fitted jeans down the aisle.

I blew out a sigh, then glanced down at Evelyn who stood there with her hand swinging in mine, grinning up at me, totally oblivious to the exchange.

"All right, let's get you a bath before your uncle gets home."

Calling him her uncle sounded so foreign on my tongue. A mind-fuck. All my assumptions twisted, chewed up, and spit out.

"He probably isn't going to appreciate that you're covered in horse kisses and mud."

In my humble opinion, that was exactly the way she should be.

"I like the horse kisses," she said.

"That's because they're the best," I told her as we left the barn and started down the dirt trail that led back to the house.

Evelyn skipped along at my side, holding onto my hand. "I had so much fun for all the days you have been here. How many days until you come back?"

She squinted up at me through the rays of light that cut through the leaves, using her free hand to rake back the matted locks of hair from her face to give me a better view of that adorable grin.

"I should be back tomorrow, so only one." As long as things hadn't gotten weird.

Evelyn suddenly released my hand. "Watch me, Ms. Dae, I bet I can run just as fast as Mazzy!"

"You think so, huh?"

"Yup!"

She took off in a clumpity sprint, her little pink boots kicking up a plume of dust. Strands of brown hair whipped like a horse's mane behind her.

"You are so fast!" I shouted, laughing at her joy because she was laughing, too.

"As fast as Mazzy?"

"Faster!"

She turned to look at me from over her shoulder, her smile so wide and free.

Then the sole of her boot skidded on a loose rock.

My heart clutched. I started to shout at her to watch where she was going, only it was too late, and the toe of her boot caught on a larger rock, tripping her. She toppled forward, her little arms flailing.

There was no stopping the fall.

She hit the ground with a hard thud.

"Oh my God, Evelyn." The words wheezed from my lips, and fear crashed through my senses.

I ran for her. I was at her side in the flash of a second, right as a shattered wail ripped from her lungs.

That fear screamed, and I was on my knees so I could gently peel her from the gravel and roll her over, one arm beneath her back to keep her supported.

My gaze was frantic as I searched for wounds. "Evelyn, oh my gosh, are you okay? Are you hurt?"

Tears streamed fast down her cheeks, leaving streaks of mud in their wake. I cringed when I saw she was holding her left arm protectively against her chest.

"I think I got broken," she whimpered.

Oh God, that was not good. Not good at all. Dread seeped into my bloodstream, slogging like sludge through my veins.

At the commotion, a bunch of ranch hands came running up from the barn.

I shooed them back. "She's fine, you're all going to scare her if you get up on her like that."

Mostly, I didn't want anyone to touch her. Didn't want any more harm to befall her.

I wanted to wrap her up and keep her safe and protect her.

I'd certainly done a bang-up job of that, hadn't I?

"Can I see it?" I murmured, trying to keep the worry out of my voice.

She nodded warily.

Gingerly, I lifted it. Her wrist was already swollen, and a big scrape ran about three inches up her forearm. A bunch of tiny pebbles of gravel were embedded in the wound.

Crap, crap, crap.

"Does it hurt if I move it?" I really couldn't even do that for fear that I would cause her additional pain.

More tears streaked down her face. "It hurts really bad, Ms. Dae."

I held back the slew of curses that wanted to whip from my tongue.

"You're alright, Evie-Love. We're just going to take you into town and get it checked out. How does that sound?"

Nate was the only one of the hands who hadn't taken off when I'd told them to go, and I could feel him hovering about twenty feet back. I turned to him. "Get me some ice and a towel?"

"Sure thing." Without hesitation, he ran back for the kitchen in the barn.

I pushed to my feet, careful as I lifted Evelyn, and I carried her shaking form the rest of the way around the trail to where I'd parked my truck in front of the house.

Nate was already running up to us by the time I was loading Evelyn inside. I secured her in the booster Caleb had only left for *emergencies*.

This qualified, right? I sure as heck hoped so. At least my gut told me this was what I needed to do, even though I was pretty sure he was going to kill me, anyway.

I set the ice on her wrist. "Hold it right there."

She nodded, her face pinched and a mess, dust covering her head to toe.

I shut her door, then turned to Nate.

"Would you mind staying with her for a second? I need to grab my keys and some documents Mr. Greyson left."

"Of course, Paisley. Anything you need," Nate assured me.

"Thank you." I turned and ran inside, boots clomping as I bounded upstairs to retrieve the folder Caleb had left with a document saying I could seek medical care for Evelyn. The second I had it, I darted back downstairs and grabbed my keys and wallet where I'd left them on the entry table.

I'd done it just to muck up the order a bit.

Racing back out, I tapped out a message to Caleb in response to the five I'd had in the last ten minutes since I hadn't immediately responded earlier.

> **Me: Change of plans. Evelyn is okay, but she had a little accident. I'm taking her to the urgent care in town to get her checked out. Meet me there.**

"Thanks, Nate," I said as I whipped open my door and hopped inside.

Then I set a reassuring hand on Evelyn's forearm, the words thick when I forced them out. "Listen to me, Evelyn. I want you to know you're amazing and wonderful. Kind and smart and beautiful in every way, and you're going to be okay."

She would be.

I knew she would.

But I also worried it might be the last time we'd be together this way.

Because I had a hunch that Caleb Greyson was never going to forgive me.

Chapter Twenty-Two

Caleb

Six Years Ago

RAIN DRIZZLED FROM THE GRAY-STREWN SKY. COLD OOZED through his jacket and seeped to the bone where Caleb stood at the edge of the grave, surrounded by a drove of people dressed in black.

The gleaming gray casket streamed with droplets of water that dripped down into the open ground.

A giant spray of red roses lay on top as if it could disguise the stench of the man who lie inside. Conceal the truth of who he had been.

Kimberly squeezed Caleb's hand tighter, as if she were seeking strength. Or maybe she was trying to offer it to him.

He wanted to receive it. Take this moment to end one chapter and start another.

Begin again.

His father's voice echoed in his ear.

"It's time for you to step into the spot you were always destined for. I worked my entire life to give it to you, the same as your grandfather did for me. Promise me, you will protect it. Everything we have built."

"I promise," he'd whispered where he'd sat at his bedside.

He'd promised. Made an oath.

One he knew he had to keep.

⌒⌇⌒

Caleb sat at the same desk where his father used to reign, staring at the news report on his phone.

A local small-business owner had been killed in an apparent botched robbery.

Caleb's chest twisted and twined as he stared at the name.

Frank Aston.

Hot hatred curled through his being.

Botched robbery.

What fucking bullshit.

That was right when Kimberly burst into his office and tossed the stack of papers onto his desk.

"What is this?" she demanded.

Caleb rocked back in his chair, gritting his teeth as guilt clotted off the flow of oxygen.

Their father never should have brought her into this. Given her the position.

She'd been oblivious.

Innocent.

The way she should have stayed.

And now this had spiraled so much deeper. A line crossed that couldn't be uncrossed.

He forced the casualness that he always wore, though it was underlined in coldness, never able to just speak the fucking truth. "It's a contract."

Kimberly's brown eyes were wide with horrified disbelief. "I know it's a contract, Caleb, but I want to know why you have it. I worked with that family for months to come to a deal, and they did not want to sell." Her words came in short, hysterical gasps. "Mr. Aston's great grandfather built that home, and his grandfather was born there. Mr. Aston had zero interest in selling. None whatsoever. And now he's dead?"

She tripped over the last, the words abraded as they fell from her mouth.

"I had nothing to do with that."

"You had nothing to do with it? There's a contract and now the man is dead? I don't believe you, Caleb."

Tears blurred her eyes, and she began to shake, her hands fisting in the fabric of her sweater as desperation took her over. "Tell me what you did."

"Kimberly." His teeth grated, and revulsion at this life hardened his voice. "You never should have been involved in it in the first place. Dad never should have brought you into this company."

She suddenly threw herself against his desk, her fingers clawing at the wood as she angled across at him. "Tell me you didn't do it."

He gulped. "I can't."

Because in the end, he was responsible. This was his company now. And it was time he fully stood for what that meant.

Change it.

But he doubted there was anything he could ever do to erase the way Kimberly was looking at him right then.

His teeth ground harder as tears fell faster down her cheeks.

His heart thundered, and his stomach twisted.

She was the one person in his world he couldn't stand to look at him like that. The one person he cherished. The one person he'd ever allowed himself to love.

She shoved off the desk, nodding as if the reality of what Greyson Industries was had just sank into her consciousness.

She turned and walked out, quietly clicking the door behind her.

Still, it rang with finality.

Because it was the last time she ever spoke to him.

Chapter Twenty-Three

Caleb

AGITATION CRAWLED ACROSS MY FLESH AS I SPED ALONG the barren two-lane road in the direction of Time River.

Seattle had left me on edge. Edgier than normal.

That bitter taste still boiled, both for myself and Tarek Paltrow, the sickness of that life that I would never shake. Each time, it only grew worse, this life I had come to not want to live.

There was something about the way he'd reacted to the images that had left me shaken, a gut sense that he was seeing that horror for the first time.

And that left me starting from the beginning again.

Digging back through every person we had wronged because it wasn't like the detective had found any clues or leads. Most of the time, I thought he believed I deserved it.

Karma.

But none of those people had deserved what I had earned.

Allen had already been through everyone, all the way back to when my father had first taken over the company. Most had moved on, accustomed to the money that had been forced into their hands.

Rebuilt.

Others had moved away and started new lives.

Some had passed.

We'd pressed the three who'd seemed most likely. Other business owners who'd been hurt the most. Their livelihoods taken.

The whole time, I'd scanned, searched, looked over my shoulder as if I could dig him out of his hiding spot.

Sense his depravity.

Taste the wickedness.

The hunger to destroy him, hurt him, cause him the type of pain he'd inflicted, had intensified with each step that I'd taken around the city.

A year had passed since Kimberly's body had been found. She'd been the last. Now, I waited for him to strike again. I knew he was out there lurking. Waiting for the moment to come for me.

I would find him first.

Cut him off.

End him for what he had done.

Ensure that Evelyn would forever be safe, the last to hold the Greyson name.

I glanced at the screen on the dash. Irritation clawed at me that Paisley still hadn't returned my texts.

The whole time I'd been away, my stomach had felt hollow, filled with worry at being away from Evelyn for so long. I itched with the need to see her for myself. To know she was safe and whole and fine.

Last night hadn't helped this anxious energy in the least.

Fuck.

What had I been thinking, giving into the lust that Paisley Dae incited?

I didn't know which of us had pushed for it first, but it'd been me who couldn't do anything to stop myself from making the video call.

Desperate to know if it was real.

If in that moment, she was consumed with thoughts of me the way I was of her.

I scrubbed a palm over my face like I could rid myself of the image of that riot of a girl spread out on the bed, white hair all around her, pumping herself with that vibrator while she lie there drooling over my cock.

How could I be in her space now without thinking of reaching out and taking her?

Touching her.

Bending her over my desk and fucking her from behind.

I'd wanted to ever since I'd found her perched on the corral fence that first day with her ass in the air.

Gritting my teeth, I glanced at the screen, willing a text to come through as I barreled down the two-lane road in the direction of Time River.

I pushed the button on my steering wheel to record another message.

Me: Update, please.

How difficult was a simple response? A quick, *all is well*. Hell, I'd even take one of those obnoxious thumbs up emojis.

I passed by a sign that marked Time River was twenty miles away. The sight of it allowed me to draw a small measure of oxygen into my aching lungs.

I was almost there.

Finally, a text dinged through from Paisley, and that ball of aggression released, allowing solace to slide into its place.

I tapped the button to listen.

Paisley: Change of plans. Evelyn is okay, but she had a little accident. I'm taking her to the urgent care in town to get her checked out. Meet me there.

Fear clogged my pores. A dagger driven straight through.

I'd made one oath.

One fucking oath.

To protect the little girl.

And this was what Paisley had given me? That she was *okay*? No other details? The only thing I knew was it was bad enough that she needed to be taken to the urgent care.

I pressed down on the accelerator, the speedometer rising to a hundred. The countryside sped by in a blur, and my heart beat erratic and out of time.

Flying as quickly as the SUV.

I punched at the button to dial Paisley's number. It went to voicemail.

"This is Paisley. If you're getting this message, you don't know what year it is."

"Is she fucking kidding me?" I spat, wanting to demand that she pick up but also knowing I'd printed her out an instruction manual five miles long on Evelyn's care. It had included an explicit statement that under no circumstances was she to use her phone if she was ever driving Evelyn anywhere.

Panic sieged me. That feeling of being out of control. The feeling the things that mattered were slipping through my fingers.

I forced the Rover as fast as I could as I blazed across the desolate road.

My shallowed breaths came quicker when the boundaries of Time River finally came into view. The town was quaint and quiet and peaceful, the pace slowed and easy.

Tree-lined streets and cozy businesses with a backdrop of mountains that could coax you into believing you'd cut yourself a small slice of heaven.

Only a fool believed in that.

The rural road intersected at Manchester. My tires screeched as I came up fast on the stop sign. Anxiety ripped through me as I waited for one car to pass before I gunned it as I made a left.

I raced through the small town, skidding around corners as I took the three turns it took me to get to the urgent care.

It was a plain, one-story brown-brick building with double doors at the front.

I whipped into the lot and flew into the parking spot directly next to the monstrosity that was Paisley's truck.

The sight of it sent a wave of protectiveness curling through me, too.

I couldn't believe I'd allowed Evelyn to ride in that thing.

Jumping out, I peered through the passenger window to check the cab.

It was empty except for Evelyn's booster seat.

Something manic lit in my nerves.

I ran up the sidewalk, ripped open the door, and moved directly to the elevated counter at the reception desk. Grabbing onto the edge, I leaned toward the woman sitting behind a computer.

"Where is Evelyn Greyson?" The demand fired from my tongue.

Without looking up from the computer screen, she held up a finger since she had a phone tucked between her ear and shoulder and was inputting something on her computer.

Irritation blazed.

Fuck.

I knew she was doing her job, but I didn't have time for this bullshit.

The door to the left opened, and a man led out his hobbling teenage son. I didn't hesitate, I moved that way, grabbing the handle of the door like I was being courteous and holding it open for them.

Only the second they made it out, I slipped through and into a long hall lined with closed doors.

I banged on the first. "Evelyn?"

The next. "Evelyn? Paisley? Where are you?"

"Sir, I'm going to have to ask you to return to the waiting room." I looked over my shoulder at a petite woman wearing blue scrubs.

She stumbled back two steps.

Apparently, my expression was as dangerous as I felt. "I'm looking for Evelyn Greyson."

A gush of air heaved from my lungs when one of the far doors popped open, and Paisley poked out her head.

"What in God's name are you doing? We're right here. A little patience never hurt anyone."

Patience?

I stormed that way. A volcano that would soon erupt.

"Where is she?" The demand sheared through the air.

"She's right in here and totally fine." Paisley held up her hands like she could calm me down.

"If she was totally fine, she wouldn't be here, would she?"

I pushed inside the room before she had a chance to respond.

Tension boiling, eyes darting around in desperation.

I stumbled to a stop when I found Evelyn sitting on an exam table, sucking on a red lollipop.

Awake and alive and whole.

No blood in sight.

Relief heaved from my lungs, and I drew in a shaky breath.

That tension flared when I saw her left wrist wrapped in an Ace bandage.

"You were injured."

Regret constricted.

I was supposed to protect her.

I'd made one promise at Kimberly's grave.

And that was I would keep her daughter safe.

The child sent me the smallest smile. "Just a little bit, but I'm not even broken. It barely even hurts a little so you don't have to worry."

Relief nearly dropped me to my knees.

God. I was going to lose it.

Because I didn't know how to do this.

How to handle this.

How to be in charge of someone else's life without destroying it.

"I told you she was okay." Paisley's throaty voice hit me from behind. The brush of her fingertips down my back scored me like an electric prod.

I whipped around.

That veil of hair framed her face like white flames.

Or maybe I could only see fire.

I had the horrible urge to wrap her in my arms. Hang onto her. Seek comfort and give it.

Because she might have acted like everything was fine, but I could see the tension lining those mossy eyes.

I towered over her, ragged juts of air raking from my lungs as I tried to control the madness.

Paisley's face was tipped up toward me as I stared down at her chaotic beauty.

Reckless Angel.

Her mayhem burned through my blood.

"She's hurt." It came out deadly. A curse. Half pain and half a demand. Paisley blinked, and I was having a hard time not leaning toward her and pressing my nose into the fall of her hair.

To keep myself from inhaling everything she was.

"It was an accident, but she's okay." Her voice shook, too, caught in a turmoil she was trying to play off.

"That fucking horse…" I hoped my voice was low enough that Evelyn couldn't hear, but I wasn't sure that was true.

I had known from the beginning the horse was a terrible idea. It was dangerous. But I hadn't known how to tell the child no.

Paisley's brow pinched in uncertainty. "The horse?"

"I knew she would get hurt on it. That it wasn't safe." The words were an accusation I threw at myself.

Her brow curled in understanding. In sympathy. In a softness I didn't know how to accept. "The horse didn't hurt her. She tripped and fell while we were walking on the trail back to the house. She sprained her wrist. That's it."

Her tone changed, threading through me like a plea, like she was trying to get to the place where this animosity glowed.

"That's it?" It scraped through my teeth.

"I didn't mean it like that. I meant that she is going to be fine. And don't you dare tell me it doesn't matter what I *meant* because you and I both know it does. I'm sorry it happened, and I wish I could have stopped it, but I won't stop her from experiencing the joy of being a child, either. I know you're going to hate me over it. I accept that. But you should know I was every bit as worried as you on the way over here."

Hate her?

I wanted to.

I wanted to fucking hate her as fiercely as I hated the whole fucking world because she made me feel too goddamn much.

Before I could say anything, a light tapping sounded at the door, and I turned to find a woman peek inside. She was likely in her mid-thirties, dark hair held in a sleek ponytail.

She smiled when she saw me. "Oh, good, you are here."

"I'm not sure how you could've missed him with the entrance he made," Paisley mumbled under her breath.

I sent her a glare, then forced some of the strain out on a long sigh, roughing my hands over my head in an effort to tame the mess boiling inside. It took me until then to realize I was drenched in sweat.

"I'm Dr. Moore. Evelyn is great, other than a small sprain of her left wrist and a superficial scratch that we cleaned out. I assumed that was all, but we went ahead and got an x-ray at Paisley's urging. Everything was clear, so Evelyn can continue to wear the wrap until the swelling goes down, but she shouldn't have any limitations. Any questions before we get her discharged?"

"Will she need any medication?" I asked, voice trembling because I couldn't seem to get that shit contained.

"She shouldn't, but if she seems to be in discomfort when she's trying to sleep tonight, you can give her some children's acetaminophen."

"Thank you."

"It's been my pleasure."

"Bye, Mandy." Paisley poked her head around the side of me and waved.

"It was good to see you, Paisley. So glad you're back in town. Let's try to catch up soon."

"I'd love that."

Then Dr. Moore turned to Evelyn and gave her a high-five. "Thanks for being awesome."

Evelyn giggled around the sucker. "Ms. Dae told me I'm pure awesomeness, so I guess I gotta be if I got this." She took it out for a second and waved it like a gold medal.

Dr. Moore laughed. "Sounds right to me."

She moved to the door, opened it, then paused to peer back. "You can check out at the front desk, and feel free to call the office if there are any issues, but I wouldn't anticipate any."

Then she slipped out.

By then, the rage had dissipated a fraction. Enough that I trusted myself to approach the child. Like a fool, I touched her face, unable to keep the coarseness from the words. "Are you sure you're okay?"

"I told you I'm not even broken because Ms. Dae got me here

so fast, and they looked at me and took care of me. Don't you think that's really good?"

It was the most she'd ever said to me at once.

Everything panged.

My heart and my conscience and the promise I'd made.

"That's really good. Let's get you home."

Reaching out, I carefully picked her up and into my arms, a pained breath leaving me as I drew her to my chest.

I'd picked her up before.

Out of necessity.

Times when she'd fallen asleep in the car and needed to be moved. Or set her on a chair so I could tie her shoe. When I'd lifted her onto Mazzy for the first time.

But I'd never held her like this.

Had never let her *reach* me.

But right then, I didn't know how to keep those boundaries high. How to shut it down or shut it out. How to keep from hugging her tight as the relief finally barreled through me.

A flashflood.

My throat locked, and my heart slammed against my ribs.

She patted me on the back with her little hand.

"I'm really very okay," she promised in her tiny voice, so close to my ear.

I fought the ball of something sticky that caught at the base of my throat.

Feeling unraveled.

Frayed.

Warily, I turned to look back at Paisley who lingered by the wall, this expression on her face that slayed me through.

Too real.

Too genuine.

Too good.

Every-fucking-thing I was not.

Chapter Twenty-Four

Paisley

WARILY, I FOLLOWED THEM OUT THE URGENT CARE doors and into the warmth of the waning summer day. Evelyn was still in Caleb's arms, and I wondered if maybe he would never let go.

I hoped that were the case.

Hoped he finally saw how amazing she was, this little gift just waiting to be adored.

I saw everything so differently now that I'd learned she was his niece. His reservations and his fear and the rigidness in the way he'd interacted with her.

He handled her like glass he was afraid would break.

My chest squeezed.

How well had he known her before?

She almost seemed a stranger to him.

Foreign.

His deepest fear and his greatest burden.

I ached to ask what had happened to Evelyn's mother, hoping he'd confide in me, but I was unsure if that was ever going to be a possibility after what happened today.

The terror he'd worn as he stormed in, the man a rampage and looking for somewhere to place the blame.

And that blame might land on me.

I'd accept it if it did.

Take it if it made him feel better. If it'd driven him to this moment where he held her like she was a treasure and not an obligation.

That was a sacrifice I would gladly make.

My footsteps were cautious as I traipsed through the rush of emotion he left behind them as he carried her down the sidewalk to where he'd parked.

Without saying anything, I went to Maybe so I could grab Evelyn's booster, my movements even slower when I returned and edged around to the driver's side where he'd opened the passenger door.

"Here, let me get this situated for you," I told him.

My heart crashed in my chest like a battering ram. Hurting for a man who probably deserved to be hurt, but I couldn't help but want to hold some of his pain because I had become sure there was something deeper than the malice and animosity.

I knew it.

Saw it.

Felt it simmering around him like a dark gloom trying to break free.

The man was in mourning.

Grieving.

Lost.

Reluctantly, he stepped aside. I set the booster on the seat, my gaze soft as I eased out of the doorway so he could strap her in. He took the longest time and care in ensuring she was securely buckled, murmuring once more, "You're okay."

No doubt, he was reassuring himself.

Then he seemed to war, unsure if he wanted to turn around and look at me or not.

My knees knocked when he finally did.

Ice-blue eyes stared back, his gorgeous face written in sharp angles, acute and exquisite.

Fierce enough to annihilate.

Beautiful enough to decimate.

I did my best not to think about him bared last night.

Exposed and beautiful.

The most gorgeous thing I'd ever seen.

In unease, I gestured at my truck. "I'm going to swing by your place to get my things, and then I'll be on my way."

He hesitated, like he wanted to say something, before he gave a short nod, his plush lips sealed as if he were refraining from saying what was on his mind.

I wished he would just lay it out.

To my heart, I knew it was an accident, but I also knew how scared I'd been when she'd fallen.

Looking back, I probably should have given him a few more details, but I'd thought by stating it the way I had, I might save him some pain.

But he didn't say anything.

He just climbed into his SUV and drove away.

$$\sim\!\!\ast\!\!\sim$$

I stuffed the dirty clothes I'd left on the bedroom floor into the duffle bag and tossed my toiletries bag on top, totally ignoring the way my stomach tilted when I glimpsed my toy stuffed at the bottom.

That baby was always going to remind me of Caleb Greyson.

I was pretty sure it was going to have to be retired.

Zipping up the bag, I blew out a breath as I glanced around the room.

Heaviness sat on my chest.

A ten-thousand-pound boulder I couldn't budge.

I'd gone straight to the guest room to gather my things, giving them space, the time he had seemed to need with Evelyn. It felt like he'd turned a corner, even though that corner was still bound and riddled with fear.

Evening was approaching, the sky still light, though the intensity had dulled, as if a grayed filter had been placed over the heavens, giving it that moody vibe.

Or maybe it was just a filter of melancholy that had been painted over me.

It was really my fault that I'd let myself get so attached. That it felt wrong that I was about to leave. That I wanted to stay when I needed to remember my staying here had just been a job.

Hopefully, if he wasn't too freaked out, I would still be welcome to return for Evelyn's training tomorrow.

I tossed the straps of my duffle over my shoulder and headed out of the room. A stilled quiet held fast to the house, not that I'd have been able to hear someone talking or moving around on the other side of it, the place so big and vacant it echoed the loneliness.

I just hoped that maybe now something new would fill it. That Caleb had come to a turning point. The stupid part of me wanted to stick around to witness it, while the logical girl who wasn't going to let herself get trampled again knew I really should run.

Turn my back on these emotions that had begun to run rampant.

Caleb Greyson was dangerous to me. I knew it, felt it in my soul.

I took the stairs at a clip, my boots booming on the wood like thunderclaps.

A racket in the perfect stillness.

I almost grinned that I was the one causing it.

I hit the landing with a thud, pinned a bright smile on my face, and went in search of Evelyn so I could tell her goodbye.

At the thought of it, a knot formed so tight in my belly that I thought I might throw up.

Crap, I'd gotten in too deep. I really should cut the cord. It would be better. End whatever this was before it got out of control.

Except that cord started to strangle when I finally heard the low murmuring of voices coming down the hall from the direction of the kitchen, one low and deep, smoothly rough, the way Caleb Greyson was. The other was timid and shy but brighter than I thought it had ever been.

Wearing the casualness I kept trying to don, I peeked through the archway. "Got my things. I'm going to head out."

"Oh man, you have to already? But I'll see you tomorrow!" Evelyn peeped from where she sat on one of the stools on her knees and leaned on the island, not paying that much mind to her injured arm.

At the sight of her, tears pricked at the backs of my eyes.

I was definitely in danger, and I knew it was time I put up some boundaries. I'd never wanted to hold back affection from the child when I knew she needed it so desperately, but that affection had become something I shouldn't let it.

It was the kind that was absolutely going to crush me.

Panic welled, a rising tide, dragging me so deep I thought I was going to drown. And if I got any deeper, I was not going to make it.

Sweat slicked my neck, and it hit me so fast and hard that it nearly knocked me from my feet. Where my stupid heart had gone. I'd put it right there on the chopping block because this child wasn't mine, and she never could be.

"I'm not sure, Evie-Love."

Caleb had been jabbing at the microwave buttons like he'd never used it before, and his attention whipped toward me when I said it. Something passed through his stony features. Regret, maybe? Anger? Hard to tell when he remained all glowery and rigid.

A frown marred Evelyn's sweet brow.

"But you get here on Mondays and Wednesdays and Fridays. Friday is tomorrow." She held up a finger as proof. I came to stand at her stool, spun her toward me, and knelt so we were face-to-face.

"I think maybe you're ready for a teacher who knows more things than me, that way you can learn to ride superfast." I couldn't help but run my fingers through her hair that was still matted and littered with dirt.

She definitely needed a bath. I had the thought to tell Caleb, but that was not my place.

"That's okay. I already go superfast." She grinned, her tiny, gapped teeth on display.

My heart fisted in my chest. This was harrowing. But it only got so much worse when a swell of blazing energy slashed through the air.

I snapped up to find Caleb looking at me like I'd committed another one of those mortal sins.

Except this time, I felt like I had. Guilt constricted, cutting off the flow of oxygen that breathed life, cutting off something that had come to feel intrinsic.

That right there was where I'd gotten myself into trouble.

But I'd gone hunting for it, hadn't I?

Begged for it.

I ripped myself from that steely stare and turned it on the child.

"I love teaching you, Evelyn, but I'm not sure it's a good idea for me to come here anymore."

"Why not?" Sadness twisted through her little face, her disappointment so thick I choked on it.

I didn't think I could answer that, so I leaned down and pressed a kiss to her forehead and murmured, "I'm sorry, Evie-Love, but I think it's for the best."

"But you're my favorite day." Heartache saturated her innocence, this sweet, sweet girl I wanted to keep.

Grief welled in my chest, and I could barely force out the haggard words as I touched her cheek. "You're my favorite day, too."

And that was why I had to go.

Because I realized I wanted them all.

I lingered there for too long before I forced myself to straighten. I looked at Caleb.

Another feigned smile contorted my face, though I was pretty sure the tear that escaped and slipped down my cheek gave me away.

His jaw clenched.

"I'm sorry about what happened today," I told him.

Then I dipped out without allowing anyone to say anything else.

I beelined for the front door.

I'd almost made it out when that dark presence enclosed on me from behind.

An ice-storm that froze everything in its path.

Me included.

I couldn't move where I faced away, my hand on the knob, my escape right there, but I couldn't peel myself from the spot.

"Where do you think you're going?" His voice was low, sharper than a blade.

Inhaling a shaky breath, I forced myself to speak. "You asked me to stay with Evelyn for two days. I finished the job, and now I'm going home."

I went to open the door, but a hand crashed down on the wood above my head, slamming it shut.

Those vacant walls rattled.

My heart pounded at a ravaged beat.

The air grew dense. Dark and volatile.

"And let me get this straight…you don't plan to come back."

There was no question behind it. Just anger as his hot breath breezed over the back of my ear, sending a wash of chills sailing across my skin.

"It's time, don't you think? I let her get hurt."

"You said it was an accident."

My ravaging heart hitched, and somehow, I found the lie. "This afternoon was just too stressful."

"Coward," he grumbled that time.

Heat radiated from his skin, flames licking out to burn me alive.

"Why didn't you tell me you're her uncle?" I knew I shouldn't dig deeper, but the question clawed out, anyway. Needing to know. To understand.

The air whooshed from his lungs.

I slowly turned to face him, needing to see what was written in his expression.

I shouldn't have.

He was right there. All fierce and powerful, barely contained strength bristling in his tall, towering body.

Fury underscored it all. A fury I was a fool to want to understand.

He was right. I was reckless. Totally and completely reckless that I kept coming here. That I'd offered him that piece of myself last night. That I'd fallen for a little girl who wasn't mine to keep. It was why I needed to leave.

Yet there I was, staring up at that blaze of blue while he worked his jaw so hard I thought it might crack.

"How do you know that?" he ground out.

"She told me," I said on a whisper, the words coming out in some sort of plea. "She told me her mother was never coming back. You can't expect her to never speak of it again. She needs support, Mr. Greyson. Someone to talk to. She needs to be able to be herself here in your home. Feel safe and cherished and loved. I've never even heard her call you uncle. Why is that?"

I blinked through the torment that raged in the space between us. Sorrow flared in the middle of it, pouring out from the fury of his storm.

"Fuck, Paisley, I hadn't even met her before Kimberly died." Shame filled his voice, and I barely registered that it was the first time he'd called me by my first name.

Because I stumbled back against the wood, unprepared for that blow.

How?

He must have read it on my face because he scrubbed a big palm over his, trying to control himself. "We had a…" He stumbled over the confession before he forced out, "A falling out. I hadn't talked to her in more than five years. I knew she'd become a mother. Had done my best to keep tabs on her while respecting her wish to keep me out of their lives. After she died, her will stated that she wished Evelyn's custody go to me."

Agony radiated from him, filling the oxygen like lead. "You asked me if I had the ability to love her, and the truth is, I don't know how. The only person I've ever loved is my sister. And she's gone." His voice wheezed with grief. "And she left a child with me. One I have no idea what to do with."

"You might think you don't have the capacity to love her, but you do. You do because I saw it when you came into the clinic. I saw it in your worry. I saw it in the way you held her after. That's love, Caleb, whether you believe it is or not."

It was the first time I'd called him by his first name, too.

This was no longer business. It was personal.

I guessed I'd solidified that last night.

His throat bobbed as he swallowed, those blue eyes gluing my shaking boots to the floor.

His aura wisped through the space.

Power and wealth and deep-seated secrets.

He moved even closer, and I leaned farther against the door.

My fingernails scratched at the wood, as if it could ground me, keep me standing and steady.

He inched forward, nearly touching, and for all the trying I was doing, it was no use. My shaking hand reached up, and I curled my fingers into his shirt.

A fool who wanted to hold him.

The pain.

The secrets.

The shadows that crept through his tormented gaze.

His head shook, his voice hard. "My only job is to keep her safe."

"You're more than that."

Vulnerability bled into his tone. "I'm not equipped for this, Paisley. I have no idea why my sister chose me to care for her daughter...to raise her...after everything I've done."

"I think you're equipped for so much more than you believe. You wouldn't have accepted her into your life if you weren't."

"I owe it to my sister." Agony sheared out with that, and I wanted to ask him a thousand things. What had happened to her, and why did they have a falling out?

I pressed my palm to the thrashing of his chest, wading deeper into the darkened abyss of his sea. Waters dragging me under.

That panic shivered just under the surface. The whole reason I knew I needed to leave.

Because if I didn't go now, it was going to be too late.

I was falling. Falling into a man who wouldn't be there to catch me.

He must have read what was in my expression because he pushed closer, plastering me to the wood, hands clinging to the caps of my shoulders. His mouth at my ear and his spirit weaving into mine.

"Please don't walk out that door." His plea was sandpaper. Rough as it scraped into my consciousness. "I need you to stay."

He ran just the tip of his nose along the length of my jaw.

"What do you mean, stay?" I hated that it came out a stammer.

"I want you to take Ms. Sandberg's place. Stay here. Live here."

That panic screamed.

So, of course, I was trying to cover it with the lightness that didn't stick. "Tell me you never had Ms. Sandberg pressed against the door like this."

Caleb growled, and he angled back, cupping my jaw in one of his hands. "I've never had anyone like this, Paisley. Have never needed anyone the way I need you."

Oh, but that statement was so conflicted.

Convoluted.

Tangled up in too many things that I had no idea what he was asking of me.

I was pretty sure he didn't know, either.

"I'm not a nanny."

I had no qualifications for that.

And being under the same roof as him?

Staying with Evelyn like this?

My spirit soared. Diving low. Falling fast.

Caught up in this mystery of a man who had tapped into something inside me that no one had before.

"I'm not asking you to be her nanny. I'm asking you to continue to look at her the way you do, spend time with her the way you do, and I'll pay you for it. There is no one I trust the way I do you."

And I knew, more than ever before, what a danger he was to me.

Because my stupid fingers tightened in his shirt.

"That's still a nanny, Caleb."

"Call it whatever you want," he grated. "The only thing I know is there isn't anyone better for Evelyn. She needs you in her life. Since she met you, she's been happy for the first time since she came to live with me."

Reservations spun through my mind. "But what about my

grandfather? Spending time with him and helping to take care of him is really important to me. Plus, I have Dakota and my friends…" My tongue stroked out as I hesitated with what to give him. "I have goals. Dreams I want to live."

"Make a schedule. I'll watch over her in the times you cannot."

A discordant laugh skipped up my throat because this was crazy. "I don't even like you."

Icy eyes flamed with the same intensity from last night. "Oh, but I think you do."

Air rushed from my lungs, arousal whispering through my veins. "This is a bad idea."

"I know," he agreed.

"No more outbursts?"

He actually smiled, though it was sly and smirky and did stupid, stupid things to my insides, my pussy clenching as I was struck with a rush of lust.

I was going to get my heart smashed.

"Would you expect anything less of me?"

"Oh, I expect plenty from you, Mr. Greyson." Crap, I was flirting with him again.

Wading deeper and deeper.

Dark waters lapping at my thighs.

"I promise I'll try, Paisley. Promise I'll try with you." Sincerity wove into his tone, even though there was a hardness underlying it.

"I reserve the right to junk punch you if you even look at me wrong." I forced lightness into my tone, unwinding myself from his hold.

If I was going to do this, I had to maintain my distance.

His severe brow lifted. "Junk punch?"

"That's right."

"Those are your terms? You get to junk punch me if I lose my temper? And here I thought you were going to have Evelyn's horse do the honors."

"This seems more personal."

"And you don't want to know what I'll be paying you?"

I shrugged, like all of this was no big deal when I'd just set myself up to get trampled.

But Evelyn—Evelyn was worth it.

"I'm sure it's fine, Mr. Greyson. Throwing around your money and your tantrums seem to be your favorite things to do."

Air huffed from his nose, and he stuffed his hands into his pockets, forcing himself to take a step back.

"Thank you," he said.

"I'm doing it for Evelyn." So many lies because I knew right then I was doing it for him, too. "I need to go pack some things."

"When will you be back?"

"Not sure."

"I'd like a time." It was a grunt.

"Don't even try to get bossy with me, Mr. Greyson."

I went to step out, only a gasp ripped from me when he reached out and grabbed me by the wrist and dragged me back inside.

In a flash, he had me pushed against the wall and he was framing my face in his big hands.

So much for distance.

His breaths filled the air, heavy and harsh, his chest pitching in some kind of demand.

What the hell was he doing?

Better question was, what the hell I thought I was doing?

Because I was frozen where I was pinned beneath him. I couldn't move. The most problematic was I didn't want to.

Everything flashed, hesitation and need and every sort of reservation, right before we crashed.

Shockwaves of heat blistered through my body as his mouth descended and devoured, his hands so fierce where they held me by each side of the jaw.

He controlled the demanding kiss.

Mastered it, the man so fucking bossy, and I was the fool who liked it so much.

His tongue slipped into my mouth.

Tangling.

Stroking.

Mating.

My legs went weak, the air too thin to breathe. So I was breathing him instead, inhaling his secrets like I could hold them, my nails digging in like I could find my way inside.

He kissed me and kissed me like it was the first time he'd ever done it, and he never wanted it to end.

Lightheadedness swept me through, and I thought I might pass out from the rushing desire.

He finally pulled away, though he continued to hold me by both sides of the face. He tugged me close, so close I could taste his words as he gritted them at my lips. "Just to be clear, if you touch my cock, Paisley Dae, you're going to end up on your knees with it in your mouth."

Chapter Twenty-Five

Paisley

I TAPPED AT THE DOOR BEFORE I PUSHED DOWN ON THE LATCH, popping my head into the wisping shadows of my grandfather's house. "Grandpa, it's just me."

"In here," he hollered back.

Heaviness overwhelmed my heart as I stepped into the house. Torn.

Called between two different places that felt equally important. Yet, I was making a decision, wasn't I? Picking one over the other?

I crept forward until I was standing in the archway, emotion cresting as I looked at where my grandfather sat in the same recliner that he'd had for as long as I could remember. So many times, I'd sat at his feet while he told me wild stories, and other times I'd sat perched on the arm, eager for comfort or wisdom.

And there I stood, for the second time in my life, feeling like I might be letting him down.

"What's wrong, sweetheart?" He pushed forward, closing the leg rest, his white hair wild and sticking up all over the place.

I attempted to swallow around the knot in my throat. "I need to talk to you about something."

"Are you hurt?" Anxiety shot into his voice, and I shook my head, easing forward to sit on the hearth that was near his chair. "No, I'm not hurt."

"Then what's put that sad look on your face?" He leaned forward, reaching out and swiping the pad of his thumb over my cheek as he studied me. "Funny, there's also hope in those eyes at the same time."

I choked over a soft laugh. "Because I'm feeling both, Grandpa."

He nodded his head as if he'd already read the convoluted mix of melancholy and the spark of something too bright that was shining out of the middle of it.

Glowing from the center where this new feeling had lit.

"I got offered a job," I continued.

Belief spread through his expression. "Doesn't surprise me one bit. Working with horses?"

Hesitation brimmed, and my tongue stroked out over my bottom lip. "Not exactly. The little girl I've been training? You know how I spent the last couple days babysitting her?"

"Sure."

"It was offered to me as a permanent position."

I left what it really meant hanging in the middle of us. Grandpa pushed right into it.

"And what's the sad part? You aren't sure you want to do it? It's not exactly a full-time training position with horses, but you'd still be out there on that ranch and working with the horses? Am I right about that?"

"Yeah."

"Then what's the problem, unless you don't want to have to spend your time caring for a child?"

My chest expanded. "No, it's not that. I really…" I hesitated, not sure I wanted to say it aloud. Showing my cards would reveal too much. "I really enjoy spending time with her. And the horses…"

"Then what's the problem?" With the way he said it, he already knew. He was just pushing me to lay it out.

"I'm not sure I want to leave you."

Air huffed from his nose, and he took my hand. "I love having you here, Paisley, but me and your grandma didn't raise you to get stuck under this roof. We raised you to live. To chase after your dreams and everything that burns inside you. To find the things that make you happy. And you're not gonna find that here with me. You have to go where you're being called. And if you're bein' called out to that ranch, then you follow it. If you're being called somewhere else, then you go there. And maybe you want to spend some time exploring and figuring out where you really want to go and what you really want to do, and that's just fine, too. Thing is, you have to step out that door to find it."

"But what about you being here alone?"

He huffed, a sly grin cracking in the wrinkles around his mouth. "What, you think this old man is too old to take care of himself?"

"Of course not, Grandpa, but you're no spring chicken anymore, either." I forced some lightness into my voice, praying it didn't twist on the truth that I worried about him.

Hated for him to be alone.

He breathed out a slow sigh, and he enfolded both his hands around mine. "I never imagined I would get to spend the years I did with you, Paisley, and I might not have ever approved of what your mama did, but I will tell you your grandmother and I took it as a blessing. Getting you was like getting a bonus on life, and I promise the only thing we ever wanted was to see your joy."

"I just hate the idea of you being here by yourself, Grandpa. When I went to Arizona…"

The words were too bitter to speak.

His hands squeezed tighter. "You went there for someone else, Paisley. And you did it out of love, but when the kind of love you're offering isn't returned, it becomes sour. A distorted memory that makes it impossible to see your original purpose. Don't you ever feel bad that you left in search of happiness. I'm just sorry you didn't find it there, but you can't let that keep you from still searching."

"Grandpa," I whispered. A tear slid down my cheek.

He wiped it away. "Besides, you're gonna be right here in town. It's not like we're not gonna see each other. That is unless that suit tries to keep you locked away in his tower."

Rough laughter ripped out. "You met Caleb."

"I did." There was something in his features then, something he wanted to say but held back. Instead, he asked, "That is his little girl you've been watching?"

I nodded. I didn't feel right confessing the intricacies. Not when I didn't understand why Caleb had seemed to keep it secret.

"What's she like?"

"Amazing." Awe infiltrated my voice.

Understanding wobbled through his nod. "I think your heart already knows where it wants to go. And I'll be just fine here. I've got my friends, and I reckon I can call Dakota if I start to starve."

He quirked a grin.

A soggy giggle got free. "You know I'd never let you starve."

He sobered. "I know that, sweetheart. You've always been good to us. More than good."

Pushing to standing, I wrapped my arms around him. "I love you so much."

He patted my back. "I love you more than you'll ever know. Now get out of here before I pack your bags for you."

I swiped at my tears, smiling too wide. "Oh, I see how it is. I really was just a burden, and you're ready to kick my butt out of here."

"That's right. Last couple days were the best of my life. Quiet as could be." He winked.

"Except for that television. You have to have it set to at least forty."

He settled back in his chair, grumbling, "I don't know what you're talking about. Can barely hear it."

Grabbing a throw blanket, I spread it over him then kissed his temple, whispering at the spot. "Thank you, Grandpa."

$\backsim$

"Excuse me?"

I was blazing down the two-lane road in the direction of Hutchins Ranch, talking to Dakota through the speaker on my phone. It had been close to ten by the time I finally got my things packed and got on my way.

"I said, I'm going to be nannying for Evelyn. You know, on a full-time basis." I shouted it over Maybe's grumbling engine.

"I heard you just fine. And it seems like what I'm hearing is my bestie has lost her mind and is making bad choices. I thought we hated him?"

I hemmed and hawed, rolling my lips to keep back the dirty secrets I was keeping from her.

"Don't we?" she pressed.

"I only kinda hate him." Damn, that was painful to admit out loud.

"Kinda?"

"Well…" I drew out over the thunder of the engine.

"Uh-oh, I distinctly recall you saying you would definitely not be crushing on him, but I am pretty sure I detect some crushing."

"Um, crushing? Heck, no. No way. Who me?" It rambled out way too fast. "It's just about the money. Okay fine, it's about the little girl. And don't forget the horses."

At least the last part was true because this whole thing had long since ceased to be about the money. Not that I didn't enjoy earning. But it became something else entirely when you'd do it for free.

"And it has nothing to do with a hot as sin single dad who's a total asshole and owns the most gorgeous ranch in the county?"

My spirit pinched, and I found myself whispering over the drone, "You can't tell anyone this, Dakota, but he's her uncle. He took her in after her mother died."

Silence curled through the line before she said on a hush, "Oh my God. That is so sad. That poor little girl."

Evelyn's confession from last night rolled through me. Tugged at my heart and wound in my spirit. Her sadness that I'd wanted to hold. To wipe away. Erase.

"It's really awful. So, like I don't think he's a terrible person. A jerk and kind of intimidating and scary, but not terrible. And he's a really good kisser."

That got out before I could stop it.

"What?" she screeched.

I rubbed at my forehead as I watched out at the deserted road in

194 | A.L. JACKSON

front of me, darkness all around and the center line winking by in a blur.

"He kissed me tonight before I went to tell my grandpa my plans... after we maybe might have had video sex last night," I rushed.

If I was confessing things, I might as well confess it all.

That time she cracked up.

Cracked up so hard her laughter shook the cab of my rattling truck. "You didn't?"

"Oh, but I did." I blew out a heavy sigh. "I'm an idiot, aren't I? Tell me I'm an idiot. And on top of it, I'm getting way too attached. Evelyn fell today and sprained her wrist, and it was about the scariest thing that ever happened to me. You don't even know how freaked out I was."

Soft air puffed from her nose. "Believe me, I know. Every time Kayden falls, I have a mini-heart attack. I don't know how I'm still standing. Being a mother is both the best thing you'll ever experience and the most painful. The worry is constant."

"Well thank God I'm not a mother because I couldn't imagine going through that kind of torment every day. Y'all are masochists." I forced the teasing around the clot constricting my airways, this brand-new feeling I didn't quite understand.

"Just wait. You'll know one day."

"You know that's not in the cards for me." Too much sadness got wrapped around that.

Dakota caught it. Sympathy filled her sigh. "You've always said you didn't want to be a mother, which is just fine if it's because you really don't want to be. But every comment you've ever made makes me believe you're terrified of repeating the same mistakes your mother did. You're worried you've got that selfishness running through your veins. But you aren't her, Paisley. Not even close."

My spirit clutched. "Well, it doesn't much matter, does it?"

"Doesn't it?" she pressed. "You think I can't hear what's in your voice?"

Panic blustered in my senses. "I don't know what you're talking about."

And she was getting way, way ahead of herself.

"You do, and I know you well, Paisley, and I know you're scared right now, and the only time you get scared is when something really means something to you."

Awareness throbbed. Throbbed in that place that knew I'd fallen for a little girl over the last two days. In that place I knew that my heart was hers.

My heart that had already been battered.

Dreams crushed.

And with Evelyn, those dreams had been breathed back to life.

Bigger than they'd been before.

And maybe the scariest part was I thought there was a chance Caleb might steal a part of that fractured heart, too.

"I don't want to get hurt again, Dakota. It seems like every time I turn around, I leave myself in a position to get myself shattered." I let the fullness of it come out.

The memory of Caleb saying the only person he'd ever allowed himself to love was his sister beat through my brain.

I was setting myself up for destruction.

Getting involved with a man who wouldn't keep me.

One who would hold the power to rip away everything I'd come to love.

Now *that* was the scariest part.

"Anytime we love, we leave ourselves in a position to be shattered, Paisley. Every time. You have to decide if taking that chance is worth it or not. So, let's weigh this—just how good was that phone sex?" Her words shifted into razzing.

"Wouldn't you like to know."

"Um, yes, I would very much like to know. I'm forever living vicariously through you."

I groaned. "I'm basically ruined for life."

"It couldn't have been that good."

"Oh, but it was."

I would never get the sight of him out of my mind.

My heart thrummed, nerves scattering at the thought of moving in under his roof. Having no clue what he really wanted. What his intentions were.

I just had to hold onto mine.

The bottom line.

Evelyn.

I needed not to lose sight of that.

"Sounds like you've gotten yourself into trouble."

"Don't I know it."

I felt it in the shift of the earth when the turnoff to Hutchins Ranch came up quick.

I heard a clattering on her end of the line. "I have to go, Ryder is here to fix a leak under the kitchen sink."

"At ten-thirty at night?"

"He just finished up at the shop, and it was the first chance he had to come over."

I laughed a low sound. I doubted much that I was the only one who was in trouble.

"But you call me tomorrow. I want details about what's going on with that bad boy. And I need to make sure he doesn't have you buried on that ranch somewhere."

I giggled. "You have got to stop watching true crime. That paranoia is getting the best of you."

"It seems to me he has secrets."

Unease rattled me to the core.

He did.

I knew he did.

"Just be careful, okay? And go after what makes you happy. It's time, and you deserve it."

"Thank you, Doodle-Boo. I'll try. How about you do the same?"

She sighed. "Someday, Paisley. Someday."

She ended the call, and I made the turn onto the long dirt drive.

Somehow knowing my life was about to change forever.

Chapter Twenty-Six

Caleb

HITTING THE FIRST-FLOOR LANDING, I STARTED TO PACE down the hall toward the kitchen, needing to do something with the nerves ticking my muscles into agitation.

Rattled.

Shaken.

This chaos I'd been asking for. Invited into my life because I couldn't seem to stop myself from going after what I couldn't have.

First convincing her to stay here, then going so far as to kiss her like a lovesick teenager who had his first goddamn crush.

But the truth was, it was the first time someone had made me feel that way. Like I wanted to sink my fingers into her.

Hooks and snares.

Keep her for my own.

Fucking *reckless*.

She hadn't returned for more than five hours, and my guts were tangled with the dread that she might have changed her mind. I should be relieved. Thank every star in the sky that she'd come to her senses since I didn't seem to possess any when it came to her.

But no, I paused to peer out the blackened glass at the stillness of the ranch, itching like a beast. Wanting to dig out my phone, call her, and demand to know where she was.

Find out if she was safe.

If she was okay.

A flicker of something caught my attention in my periphery.

My eyes narrowed as I more perceived the movement than saw it.

I stepped closer to the glass, peering out into the nothingness that echoed back.

But still, it felt like something.

Intuition kicking.

Unease wrapped me in a bow of adrenaline. I moved back for the door and slipped out onto the front porch.

My eyes darted through the wisping shadows that breezed through the night.

Trees whooshed with the summer storm that threatened at the far end of the horizon, and blankets of lightning struck against the sky above.

Stillness whispered through the breeze, the intermittent whinny of a horse woven in the gusts.

Nothing seemed out of place.

Yet something felt…off.

Unsettled.

An omen that hung like venom in the air.

I slowly climbed down the porch steps, gaze narrowed as I took another pass over the areas of the ranch I could see.

Nothing.

Clearly, being in Seattle had set me on edge.

That edge lessened when I heard the rumble echoing somewhere in the distance. Finally, hazy lights came into view at the top of the hill that enclosed the valley, that monstrosity growing louder the closer it got.

I watched as she wound closer, passed by the barns, and eased along the sprawling lawn before she pulled to a stop off to the right side of the house. Silence held fast when she cut the engine, then she stepped out, slowly, peering at me through the crack in her open door.

White hair billowing around her shoulders.

That chaotic recklessness sparked in the darkest places inside me.

The girl a match.

A perfect flame.

"Am I late?" The tease curled from her decadent mouth.

I fought a grin. "I had begun to wonder if you were going to return."

"And here I am."

"And here you are." It came out like possession as I began to ease that way.

She remained rooted to the spot as I rounded the front of her truck to come to her side.

Her teeth raked her bottom lip, her features glowing in the glinting beams of the moon, her aura effervescent.

Blankets of lightning flashed in the distance, and a low rumble rippled through the air.

Standing that close to her, everything enclosed, the heavens drooping so low I thought I could drag my fingertips through the abyss and stir the stars.

Reshape the constellations.

Rearrange their meaning.

God knew, I'd do it if I could.

Take back what I'd done.

But my mistakes were all written there, carved in the firmament.

I needed not to forget.

But somehow, I stood there wanting to kiss her again.

Dip my fingers into her flesh and my body into her soul.

"Let me help you get your things."

Suspicion arched her brow. "Were you standing out here waiting for me?"

"No, I was checking on things."

Not that I wouldn't have come running the second I heard her coming up the drive.

"Ah, and here I thought you were being chivalrous."

I took a step toward her, towering over her gorgeous frame, my hand catching on the edge of her door to keep myself from getting too close. "Is that what you want, Ms. Dae? Chivalry?"

Vulnerability slipped into her expression. "I honestly don't know what I want. Have no clue what I'm doing here."

"Makes two of us, Little Riot," I mumbled beneath my breath, forcing myself to step back.

I moved to the back of her truck, pulled out the bag she'd left with that now appeared to be stuffed twice as full, and handed it to her before I grabbed the two suitcases she also had back there.

We started toward the house. The woman trailed behind me by one step.

Her presence consumed.

So potent I felt like I was breathing her.

Her energy.

Her goodness.

That chaos that wouldn't let me go.

It only increased when we got inside and climbed the staircase.

"Is Evelyn asleep?" she asked so quietly as we hit the second-floor landing.

"For a couple hours now."

"Would it be okay if I went in and talked to her?"

"I think that would be good. She was upset after you left."

I glanced back at her as I set her suitcases in front of her door. Regret filled her expression. "I hate that I left that way."

"She did, too."

Understanding passed between us before she quietly tiptoed into Evelyn's room. I stopped in the doorway as she knelt at her bedside. She barely nudged her awake, her voice held in hushed sincerity as she whispered, "Evelyn. It's Ms. Dae. I'm here."

"Ms. Dae?" It was a confused, sleepy question. "Are you back?"

Paisley brushed her fingers through Evelyn's hair. "Yeah, I'm back."

"Because you missed me?"

"Yes, I missed you."

"Good because I would miss you so much, too." Grogginess filled her voice, and her eyes drooped closed again.

I could feel Paisley gulp. The emotion that leapt as she leaned up higher and kissed the side of Evelyn's head and murmured, "Goodnight, sweet girl. I'll see you in the morning."

It tremored like an oath. Like she was promising she would be there for one of them for the rest of Evelyn's life.

My chest stretched tight with that feeling I kept trying to ignore, and when she stood, I moved out and took Paisley's suitcases the rest of the way into her room.

She stood behind me.

The air sparked.

A shiver of greed.

Antsy and alive.

I turned, and need pummeled me at the sight of her standing there. I wanted to lay her out on that bed she'd been spread out for me on last night and take her the right way.

Make her beg and scream and moan.

Feast on her pussy.

Devour her body.

Instead, I edged toward her, set my palm on her cheek, and murmured, "This is your home now, Paisley. Whatever you need, it's yours. Don't hesitate to ask for it." The words came out low. Too fucking possessive.

Because I wanted her. Wanted her in a way I'd never wanted anyone or anything before. I just didn't know how I could keep her.

Chapter Twenty-Seven

Caleb

THUNDER CRASHED AND RAIN POUNDED AT THE WINDOWS.
It mixed with the roar that ripped from my mouth.

Guttural.

Pained.

A staggering agony that shot me upright in bed.

"*Kimberly. No. No.*"

Visions continued to flash, no matter how hard I squeezed my eyes to try to stop them.

The drizzle of freezing cold rain.

The puddle of blood.

Lifeless eyes.

What I had done.

I ripped at my hair as I fought the cry that wanted to erupt from my throat.

Guilt and grief slaying me through.

I couldn't breathe.

Couldn't see.

Could only feel the wraiths and demons spinning around my room.

Their playground.

The wickedness I had invited in.

As if I'd summoned them, then cast them out on three innocent souls. I'd been bred to be a monster, but I'd been aware. For years, I'd done it like it was my duty. Without question.

With bloodthirst and greed.

A light tapping sounded on my door, and I jerked my head up, glaring at the wood.

"What?" It left me on a growl. The last thing I wanted was for someone to see me like this.

The knob turned, and a wedge of muted light poured in from the hall when the door was pushed partway open.

Paisley stood in the doorway, hanging onto the knob, hair a glowing white halo around her head.

Reckless Angel.

Having no clue what she was stepping toward.

"Are you okay?" she whispered.

"I'm fine." It was rough, piercing the dense, toiling air.

She padded forward like she refused to accept what I'd said.

A beautiful temptation.

She came to stand at the edge of my bed.

Lust fisted my guts, and I clenched my teeth as I looked at her through the shadows. "You should go back to bed."

She set her knee on the bed, then climbed up. "How about I stay right here?"

She slipped under the covers and snuggled into me.

Shock locked my tongue as that energy crashed through the room.

Foreign and so right.

"Paisley," I finally managed to warn.

"I'm afraid of the thunder." She snuggled closer where my heart was ravaging at my chest.

"Liar." Still, my arm instinctively curled around her body, tugging her close, relishing the heat. The connection. This need.

"You can tell me," she whispered.

"No, I can't," I rumbled at the top of her head.

She hummed like she would take it on, anyway.

Thirty seconds later, she was asleep in my arms, and I was wondering what the fuck had just happened.

This girl in my bed.

Her breaths steady.

Her goodness spreading into my room.

Chaos and light and life.

I should send her back to her bed.

Untangle myself and go sleep in another guest room.

Instead, I pulled her closer, whispered, "Reckless Angel, I already warned you I'm not a good man."

⌒⌒

"Hello, do you want eggs?"

I blinked out of the momentary stupor when Paisley waved the spatula in the air to get my attention.

Oh, but she'd had my attention.

It took me until then to realize she'd been asking me a question. I'd been too fixated on the way her lips moved around the words that I hadn't begun to process what she'd said.

Because there she was, all bright, shiny rays standing in my kitchen at the stove.

Wearing the same outfit that was going to drive me to disaster, the soft curve of her butt cheeks peeking out from the sleep shorts, the girl barefoot and that mane of white tossed into a messy heap on top of her head.

I cleared my throat. "I didn't hire you to make me breakfast, Ms. Dae."

The hint of a smirk played at the edge of her mouth as she began to plate scrambled eggs.

"Well, since I'm already in here making them for Evelyn and me, I don't see the harm in you reaping the benefits of having me here."

The smirk went full-fledged.

"I don't typically eat breakfast," I ground out. I had to keep some semblance of professionalism between us if we were going to make this work. Difficult when I wanted to stride forward, drive my fingers into her hair, and kiss her like she was mine.

"I don't think he even eats food. I've never even seen him one time."

It was then my attention finally snapped to Evelyn. She waited at the square table that sat in the nook beneath the windows, leaning her elbows on top of it, her shoulders rocking back and forth in the cutest sway.

My chest squeezed.

"Oh, I think he eats, Evelyn."

My gaze flew right back to Paisley who sent me a sly grin.

My teeth clenched in dwindling restraint. "I'm just here to grab some coffee."

I moved deeper into the kitchen, giving myself some distance when I wound around Paisley. If I got too close, I worried I would be sucked into her atmosphere. Pulled into the gravity that was this woman, and I was never going to find my way out.

Only she grabbed me by the arm as I passed. Fire streaked over my flesh.

"You should sit." Her voice was lowered, and she angled her head toward the table in emphasis.

Sit with Evelyn.

Spend time with Evelyn.

But I had no idea what I was doing. How to do this right. How not to mess up a little girl more than she'd already been.

Reservation billowed through my spirit, the fear that kept trying to creep up and this feeling that terrified me more.

"Are you the hungriest you've been in your whole life?" Evelyn asked, her little face gleaming below the morning light that streamed in through the windows.

My chest tightened as I looked at her. Took in the dimple in her chin that matched my sister's, her hair the same shade of brown.

A constant reminder of what I'd done.

Of what I'd cost.

Trepidation coursed through me as I moved to the small table and took a seat.

206 | A.L. JACKSON

"He is the hungriest, Ms. Dae." Evelyn grinned. "You better give him lots and lots."

"Well, I cooked a dozen eggs, so that should be plenty."

Evelyn's eyes went wide. "A whole million?"

Paisley laughed. That deep, throaty sound that spread through me like a caress. "Not quite but close enough."

"Did you know breakfast is really the most important food of the day?" She'd turned her sweet gaze to me. "We have to have lots of energy if we're going to ride horses. Do you want to ride horses with me and Ms. Dae? We are going to ride the whole day. It would be really fun."

Anxiety screamed. The warning that I was getting too close. That this was too much.

The dread and the worry and the urge to reach over and brush back the lock of hair that had fallen in her face.

But I knew better than to get too close.

Yesterday had proven I was slipping.

Falling in a direction neither of us could afford.

I'd care for her.

Protect her from the fate of those who got too close to me.

But I had to be careful. Keep from tainting the child with who I was.

"I have a lot of work to do today. Maybe another time." The words scuffed off my throat.

Disappointment dimmed her expression. Then she whispered, "That's okay, you got really important work to do."

Is that what she thought? That what I did was important? What would she think when she realized it was what had stolen her mother?

Rocks sank to the pit of my stomach, and I jerked when Paisley's voice hit the air. "Can I bring you your coffee?"

Sympathy contorted her face.

Like she could read every thought that ran through my mind.

"Sure," I forced out.

She grabbed a mug and poured coffee into it, then took one for herself, dousing it with a ton of creamer before she waltzed our way.

I felt her coming like a landslide, all chaotic power and energy.

"There you go," she whispered close to my ear, her fingertips dragging down the length of my arm when she set it in front of me.

"Thank you." How I managed to get it out around the lump in my throat, I had no clue.

"Not a problem." She pranced back to the other side of the island and gathered three plates.

"Need help?" I asked. At least I could try to be a gentleman.

"Nah, I work here, don't I?"

Except she placed all three down at the table and plopped onto a chair as if she were right where she belonged.

Without delay, she took a bite of her eggs.

"So very employee-esque of you," I muttered under my breath before I took a sip of steaming coffee.

"Well, you may not like food, Mr. Greyson, but I'm a fan. Besides, I think someone told me to *make myself at home* last night." Her voice dropped on the last, and those green eyes sparked, dragging over me slowly.

Softly.

My brow arched. "Oh, I like food, Ms. Dae. I just have particular tastes."

"Mmmmm," she hummed. "I look forward to getting to know what those are."

She was asking for it.

Or maybe I was.

This enchanting girl who had me mesmerized.

That connection throbbed between us.

A livewire that flamed.

Luring.

Tempting.

Taunting.

I had to stop myself from reaching under the table and squeezing her knee, from letting it glide up the inside of her thigh so I could watch her squirm and shake and come undone.

"I love these eggs the most." Evelyn's wholesome voice smacked me out of those dangerous thoughts.

"That's good, Evie-Love," Paisley said so easily, though it was still riddled with care. "Because it's about the only thing I know how to make. That and spaghetti. Don't be expecting any gourmet meals around here, and if Mr. Stuffy Pants over here has a problem with that, he's going to have to hire us a chef."

My head whipped her way.

Mr. Stuffy Pants?

A giggle slipped from between those plump, pink lips. "Are you denying it?"

"It's Mr. Dressy Pants," Evelyn corrected around a forkful of eggs. "He's got the fancies on every day because he has important work to do."

"I think he just doesn't know he lives on a ranch and not in the city." Paisley canted her head to the side, taking a sip of her coffee.

Teasing.

Playful.

Lighting up a dark spot inside of me.

"Eat your food, Ms. Dae," I grumbled, fighting a grin.

She angled my direction, feigning a whisper, "I stand corrected. It's Mr. Bossy Pants."

Evelyn giggled like it was the funniest thing in the world.

That time there was no stopping myself, and my hand was under the table, gripping the woman by the top of the thigh.

Heat flash-fired.

A blaze across our flesh.

Paisley inhaled a shallow breath, and I leaned her way, so close to her ear that only she could hear. "I'll show you bossy, Ms. Dae."

She managed to grin around the flush that rushed up her neck. "I sure hope so."

Chapter Twenty-Eight

Paisley

LIVING HERE WAS LIKE LIVING IN A DREAM. THE PEACE OF the ranch. The beauty of the land.

Like walking through quicksand.

Slipping slow before you'd realized you'd begun to get sucked under.

Like floating in shallow, cool waters, drifting before you'd realized you'd gone too far. You were in the deep end, and you'd forgotten how to swim.

But you never realized any of it because the sun was still shining on your face. Rays streaking through the leaves of the lush trees just like it was as Evelyn and I meandered back down along the river, Mazzy slowly plogging along with the little girl on her back while I held onto the lead rope.

We'd gone far today, a few miles to the northeast, exploring this gorgeous place, discovering some of its secrets and history.

I'd been here for two days.

Caleb and I had slipped into a strange sort of comfort—tiptoeing around each other, always aware, unimmune to the attraction that threatened to burn down the house every time we got in the same room.

Last night, I didn't sneak into his room again, even though I'd lain awake desperate to go to him, that gravity that pulled between us so tempting.

The call.

The lure.

I didn't even know why I was trying to resist it.

But I'd managed it somehow, trying to go back to the terse banter he and I had shared at the beginning because being enemies was probably a whole lot safer than what I was feeling right then.

The way the ground shook as Evelyn and I came out from beneath the trees and rounded the front of the house just as his shiny Range Rover pulled into the detached garage off to the left of the house.

Quicksand.

Nothing solid beneath my feet.

He appeared at the tail of his car, so rough beneath the polished stone, gorgeous and hard and powerful.

The garage door dropped closed behind him, and he began to stride our way, carrying his laptop case and a stack of mail, the dark blond locks of his hair stirred by the breeze, the ends kissing the sharp angle of his jaw.

My knees wobbled just a bit, nearly gave when those icy eyes tracked over us, clearly searching to ensure Evelyn was safe as we neared each other, the man who thought he couldn't care so obviously *caring*.

But I still had no idea how to break through that. How to get him to understand what he was coming to mean to Evelyn. I doubted he had a clue. Doubted the calluses covering his heart allowed the truth to bleed through.

I doubted he understood it when she grinned so wide when he came closer, the excitement when her little voice hit the air when she shouted, "Hi, Uncle Caleb!"

She'd taken to calling him that. Like once she'd confessed it to me, said it aloud, it'd become a permanent part of her.

"Hello, Evelyn," he said.

For a beat, those eyes traced over me, his teeth grinding when his attention roved over my pink tank and cut-off shorts. I was prepared for the day when he decided I had to wear a uniform since he clearly didn't appreciate my attire.

But it was hot as balls out here. Who could blame me?

"We went so very far on our ride today, like a thousand miles, and guess what we found?"

That pulled Caleb's attention back to Evelyn, his brow quirking. "What did you find?"

"An old cabin!"

"An old cabin, huh?"

"Yep, and I think it was even haunted."

"Haunted?"

A soft laugh rolled up my throat. "Well, it might not be haunted, but I would bet it definitely has a few stories to tell. It's way up along the river. Pretty dilapidated. I would guess the first homesteaders might have built it and lived up there long before this house was built. It's gorgeous."

"It has spider webs and broken windows. I think it's definitely haunted." Evelyn's eyes widened like she was trying to convince Caleb of the fact.

"You didn't go in it, did you?" The question slanted out like a dart. Sharp and accusing. I knew him well enough now to know it was worry that had it coming out.

"Of course not. We just peeked at it from the outside," I told him.

"You should ride on a horse sometime so you can go see it with us!"

Caleb worked his jaw.

I laughed a low sound, rubbing at Mazzy's neck as I looked at the man who stood there itching like it was his worst nightmare. "Not sure we could get him on a horse to save his life."

I cringed a little when I realized what I'd said. I was trying to be careful with the way I phrased things around Evelyn, to be cautious of her precious heart. At least she seemed not to notice it that time.

And Caleb just grunted. "The only thing I ride is a motorcycle."

My brow arched for the sky. "You ride a motorcycle?"

"Before...yes." He seemed to leave a thousand details out.

The man this mystery.

A dichotomy.

Everything I never expected.

A chuckle pilfered out, just picturing it because against all odds, it fit. My tummy stirred, liking the idea of it too much.

And maybe I liked the way he stood there, just kind of smirking, like he wanted to be with us right then.

Like some of those walls were crumbling. Getting knocked down.

A gust of wind came up without warning, and it picked up a few pieces of mail that Caleb was holding.

Envelopes whipped up by the wind before they fluttered to the ground.

One landed at my feet. I reached down and picked it up to hand it to him.

He went to grab it, then he froze with his fingers gripping one side of it as he looked down at his name written on the front.

Any easiness he'd worn drained off his face.

He went a pale, pasty white, though darkness flashed in his eyes.

He finally took it, his entire demeanor stiffening, something that looked like horror edging into his frame.

"Are you okay?" It left me on a wheeze.

"I'm fine." It cracked through the air. Then he turned and hurried into the house without a parting word.

And I knew he was definitely not fine.

Knew it as I led Mazzy and Evelyn the rest of the way back to the barn. As we settled Mazzy back into her stall, brushed her, and watered her down. As I cleaned up Evelyn, fed her lunch, then tucked her into bed for a nap.

Knew it in the fear and hatred that clouded the air like a noxious storm when I stepped out of her room.

It floated down from the third floor.

Emanated from the man I didn't understand.

And I'd done so good at minding my business. Keeping space.

But this time, I climbed the stairs, wobbling on my unsteady feet.

Quicksand.

I eased across the floor, trying to keep my boots as quiet as possible on the wood.

I could barely breathe by the time I made it to the door that sat halfway open. I pushed into the space, drawn, unable to stop myself.

In his sprawling office, he stood with his back to me, staring at the wall of bookshelves behind his desk.

Blankly.

Frozen.

A stone statue that bled agony. The energy painted in violence.

Dark and menacing.

Chained and held, thrashing through the stillness for a way to be released.

I knew when he felt me hovering at the doorway. His shoulders tensed more than they already had been.

"What are you doing up here?" The question was fragments of glass. Slicing through the dense, dense air.

"I needed to check on you."

"I don't want you to be concerned about me."

"But I am." I took a tentative step forward.

"Where is Evelyn?" Worry tripped from his mouth.

"She's down for her nap."

He seemed to let go of the breath he was holding, like he found some kind of comfort in knowing she was fine for that moment.

The fear he always held that everything was close to falling apart was blatant.

And somehow, I knew whatever it was had everything to do with whatever was in that letter.

"What happened out there?" I whispered it as I slowly approached, footsteps so careful I might as well have been walking through a field of landmines.

He didn't speak, caught in the disorder that whipped around him.

I was standing behind him before I knew it, my hand on his back that shivered with unfound rage.

He jerked at the connection, though I just pressed my palm flatter, like I was pressing myself into the darkness that stirred his spirit and scourged his soul.

"You can tell me, Caleb."

A shudder ripped down his spine.

"You should leave." It was gravel.

"Maybe I shouldn't. Maybe right here is where I'm supposed to be."

"You're asking to go somewhere that is only going to cause you pain."

"But that's what you open yourself up to when you care about someone. Their pain. Sharing it with them."

"I'm the last person you should care about."

"Too late." It wisped out on the connection I couldn't contain.

Energy crackled.

Dark, dark light.

"That was a letter from my sister's murderer."

Shock stumbled me back a foot. I was not expecting that. Not even close. No word had ever been given of what had happened to her.

I'd thought an accident or cancer or something equally as terrible.

Grief speared through me when I realized where Evelyn's fragile mind had gone when I'd said Dakota would kill for the kitchen downstairs. How she'd taken it literally. How the idea of it had to have been scarred into her psyche.

Caleb turned around then. Viciousness carved his face into severity. "When?"

"A year ago."

My uncle said she's gone forever.

Dark misery passed through his features.

"I'm so sorry."

A sneer twisted his mouth. "Don't tell me you're sorry for me, Paisley. Not when it was my fault."

My heart hitched on the magnitude of his pain.

Fracturing.

Shattering.

So devastating I had to reach behind me to hold onto the edge of his desk to keep myself steady.

He acted as if he wasn't capable of love, but there was no missing the truth of it right then.

You didn't hurt this badly without love.

"How could it possibly be your fault?"

Hatred puffed from his nose. I could feel the way it was directed at himself.

"I told you I wasn't a good man. Someone was looking to retaliate against me. Some sin I committed. Some selfish act. I don't know which because the list is so long. Two of my employees were slaughtered, the same as my sister. I hadn't spoken to her in five-fucking-years, and still, some twisted monster used her to get back at me."

He kept coming closer and closer, his aura covering me whole.

Power and wealth and deep-seated secrets.

I wanted to reach out and hold them. Take some of what was pouring out of him and dip my fingers in to experience them.

"I can't believe it's your fault."

It was a whisper.

A promise.

Belief.

Because I'd seen glimpses of what was inside him.

"You keep trying to make up your own reality, Paisley. Make me someone I'm not. But the proof of who I am lay strewn across Seattle. Their bodies left mangled, close to unrecognizable, all a message to me. And now, he sent another."

His attention shifted to the desk behind me. Off to the side was an unfolded letter.

The words imprinted so deep into the paper they might as well have been written with the tip of a knife.

The destroyer hunts, and the casualty watches and sees. He knows what has been stolen from him, and he will not rest until it has been reclaimed. He who suffers will mete the suffering.

Oh God.

My knees went weak, and I was having a hard time remaining upright.

This person was free.

Roaming.

And I suddenly made the connection to the news stories from a year ago. The three gruesome murders connected to the richest man in Washington.

The way Ryder hadn't mentioned him or given any details.

"He knew I was in Seattle. He's watching. Calculating. Planning." It was haggard, his chest heaving with each pant.

"And you brought Evelyn here to protect her."

"I told you I would do whatever it took to ensure it. To make sure she's safe until I find him. Snuff him out. And you can rest assured that I will." He'd moved to murmur those words at my ear.

A threat.

A warning telling me to run.

"You think that makes you a bad person? That you want to end him for what he did?"

God, who wouldn't want revenge?

"It's not just a *want*, Paisley. I won't stop until I see to his end. Until I bury him six feet under. And I will do it slowly. Painfully. The same as he did to them."

My spirit quivered, and I tipped up my chin, the man right there, consuming everything.

Dark and dangerous.

Boiling with wrath.

He suddenly locked his arm around my waist, tugging me against the hard planes of his body. With his free hand, he took me by the jaw. "I will do whatever it takes to ensure he dies at my hands. To ensure that Evelyn is safe. To ensure that anyone associated with me is safe. To ensure that you are safe. I promise you."

This.

This was why he was so cut off. Refusing affection or love or any semblance of hope.

He didn't think he had any.

He thought he would only bring misery to those around him.

I couldn't tell which of our hearts were beating so loud, this manic pounding that ricocheted through the room.

Energy buzzed. Loud in my ears and banging at my heart.

Wrapping me in a fiery sheet that made me feel like I was burning up.

Caleb Greyson an inferno set on devouring everything in his path.

He dipped his mouth down to my ear, his breath a shallow grate when he drew out, "This is your chance to go, Paisley. Run before it's too late."

Blood sloshed through my veins, and my fingers curled in his shirt. "I'm not going anywhere."

Chapter Twenty-Nine

Caleb

NEED POUNDED THROUGH MY BLOODSTREAM, BUT IN THE middle of it was something so much more powerful. Something that fucking terrified me.

But still, I couldn't let go where I had her plastered against me.

Inhaling her like she was mine to breathe.

Open fields and cotton candy.

I could no longer take it.

This need that stalked me. Itching to taste her mouth. To feel the flutter of her fingertips across my skin.

Bile still thickened my throat, the revulsion and loathing so intense I felt it scar my flesh.

That fucking letter sitting open, taunting me with the truth that the monster was out there.

Watching.

Lying in wait.

Right under my fucking nose when I'd been in the city, thinking I had been sniffing out the bastard when he'd been the one watching me.

It made my skin crawl.

Problem was, I wanted to crawl right into Paisley because of it.

I knew better. Knew better than giving in. Knew better than

dragging her into my debased world that would only hurt her in the end.

But her breaths were short and shallow, her tits heaving with each desperate pant, her warmth as strong as the desire she'd lit.

I brushed my thumb over the apple of her cheek. "Reckless Angel."

Mossy eyes sparked, strikes of emerald in the endless night.

It was me who was loaded with the recklessness that was this girl.

Because I had no control left. Not when it came to her.

"You're driving me to insanity, Paisley Dae."

"I think you already have me there, Caleb."

My mouth watered with her confession, and I spun her and bent her over my desk.

That fucking letter was a foot to the right of her.

Taunting me with what it meant.

The insanity flared, the desperation to unleash this hostile energy.

To replace it with something else.

She gasped a shocked sound, like she hadn't known what would happen when she pushed me against this razor-sharp edge.

When I no longer possessed any faculties except for this desire that drove everything else.

I leaned over her, plastering myself to her back, my hands gliding down her bare arms. She trembled below my touch. I threaded my fingers through hers. "This will be a mistake."

"I don't care." Her breath was a wisp of need.

My swollen cock ached at her lush, full ass.

She had on another pair of cut-off shorts, the tightest fucking pink tank wrapping her like a dream.

Lust clouded my sensibilities.

Oxygen raked from my lungs in haggard pants as I buried my nose in the fall of her hair.

Sweet sin and reckless intentions.

I slipped my hand around her waist, and my palm flattened over her quivering belly. I pulled her harder to my dick that raged against the zipper of my pants. My mouth moved to the soft shell of her ear, uncontained words rumbling out. "Tell me you don't want this."

I couldn't tell if it was a demand or a plea.

I twisted the fall of her hair around my hand and pulled it to the side to expose the delicious slope of her neck. Angling down, I pressed my lips to the soft flesh and inhaled, like I could suck all her goodness into my soul. "Tell me."

Desire escaped her on a whimper. "That would be as big of a lie as you saying you don't care about anyone but yourself."

The words whispered from her mouth in a torrent of greed.

My heart fisted at her accusation, and I fought against the feeling that kept trying to rise to the surface.

I wanted to refute what she'd said. Remind her that she didn't know what the fuck she was talking about.

She didn't know me.

Had no idea what I was capable of or what I'd done.

But finding that note had stirred my guts into mayhem, and the girl had stirred my body and mind into lawlessness. It was a dangerous concoction because the only thing my lips were doing were whispering over the flesh of her neck, tongue flicking out to taste the goosebumps that scattered over her nape.

The girl a hook I couldn't seem to evade.

"You're so fucking gorgeous. Did you know that? I know better than taking you, but you make me want to say fuck it all and take you anyway. Screw the consequences."

"And maybe we're both right where we belong." Her words were throaty, curling through me.

Ribbons that possessed.

"You have any clue what you've been doing to me, Paisley Dae? The way you have me so spun up, thinking about the things I want to do to you?" I murmured it as my lips roamed, over her nape and up her neck until I was nibbling at the lobe of her ear.

Paisley whimpered. "I hope it's as good as what I've been imagining you doing to me."

She ground her ass against my cock to emphasize her words.

The shudder that ran through me was so overpowering I didn't know how it hadn't dropped me to my knees.

"What I want to do to you will ruin you."

Or maybe it was only going to ruin me.

Fire stoked.

Flames licking through my insides.

Singeing and scarring. The promise I had made howled in my ear.

I'd allowed myself to love one person in my life and look what that had caused. I wouldn't make the same mistake twice.

"Caleb." Paisley breathed my name.

How that slight sound shouted louder than the rest, I didn't know, but it clouded the commitment and slayed my resolve.

I spun her around so quickly she was gasping again.

I propped her on the edge of my desk.

The girl looked like a prize.

Her chest pitched, those tits spilling out over the top of the pink tank.

I swore the woman wore them day after day just to push me to the cusp of her recklessness.

My gaze traveled south. Over her quivering stomach and down to the tiny cut-off shorts that barely covered a thing, those thick, toned thighs trembling with need.

"Reckless Angel."

So slowly, I eased my gaze back up, tracing each curve with my eyes.

I dragged my attention the rest of the way up, to the contour of her face that was so pretty and soft.

But it was those mossy eyes flashing with greed that did me in.

"I'm not feeling much like an angel right now."

A low chuckle rumbled free.

"Chaos," I told her. "Reckless. An angel sent to tempt me."

"Is that the way I have you feeling, Caleb? Reckless?" It was a fucking tease that slipped from those plump, pink lips.

Daring me to take her.

I gripped her by the back of the neck and jerked her forward.

Bringing us nose to nose. Our lips nearly touching. "What do you make me feel? Everything I'm not supposed to."

"Maybe feeling is exactly what you're supposed to do." Her tone had gone soft, her fingertips even softer where she fluttered them down my jaw.

A caress.

Like I meant something. Like I might be more than the demon who'd caused this grief.

"Fuck, Paisley." I took her in a bruising, desperate kiss.

Our mouths moved in a violent give and take.

Desperate to get closer. Tipping over an edge that we never should have crossed.

But I was there anyway, in the bowels of my selfishness where I took and took.

I pulled her bottom lip between both of mine, sucking the sweet flesh, before I moved to the top and did the same.

Desperate hands fisted in my shirt, and she moaned, her mouth parting in invitation.

My tongue stroked against hers in a gambol of gluttony.

I felt enraptured.

Fixated.

Entranced.

Maybe she was a little devil after all.

Except the sounds she was making were far too sweet for that. Her fingers too gentle when she dragged them up the back of my neck and tangled them in my hair.

I wound myself between her thighs, and Paisley wrapped her legs around my waist. My hands slipped under her so I could get a handful of that full, lush bottom while she set to rubbing her heat all over my dick.

I pulled back from the kiss, my forehead rocking against hers, the words scraping in the frenetic space between us. "Fuck, Paisley. What have you done to me?"

I forced myself to sit on my chair before I lost it, though my hands clamped on the sides of her thighs.

Refusing to let go.

Gaze drinking in the sight of her where she sat propped on my desk.

A fucking treasure.

The kind that was forbidden and would destroy everything if you kept it in your possession.

Waves of white hair framed her striking face, her lips swollen and wet, her chest heaving.

"Did you know I've wanted to touch you like this since that first day?" I leaned in and kissed her throat, riding down until I was nuzzling my nose in the cleft between her tits. "Since I saw you propped on that fence."

I dragged the temptation of that pink tank down.

A riot of need stirred through the air.

She mewled in approval, and her fingers curled into my hair as I kept kissing her cleavage.

"A really dumb part of me wanted you when you were glowering down at me when I backed into your Range Rover." A tiny giggle came out with that while she continued to cling to my hair, her voice throaty and raw and cracking with need.

I chuckled at her flesh. "You made quite the impression."

"What can I say? I'm unforgettable."

Another chuckle rolled free, and I yanked at the hem of her shirt. "Take this off."

She hesitated only for a second, but it was to pull her phone from her pocket. The monitor I kept in Evelyn's room was on the display, her sleeping form illuminated in the faint strains of sunlight that burned through the edges of her window.

My chest stretched tight.

I fucking loved that her first concern was for the little girl napping downstairs.

She set it to the side then peeled the fabric over her head.

Air ripped from me on a grunt, my cock straining so hard I thought I could go off just looking at her.

Her large breasts bare and on display.

Pert and round, but heavy enough they sagged a bit, her nipples tight and pebbled and as pink as her lips.

I stroked my tongue over one, pulling her nub into my mouth, sucking and licking while I twisted the other with my fingers.

"Caleb." She whimpered my name.

Energy bounced around the room. Banged against the walls.

Alive and bright and burning through me like an electric shock.

Prodding me to life.

"What do you need, reckless girl? Do you want me to make you feel good? Is that why you came up here? Because you've been dying to have this, too?" I rumbled at her breast, unable to stop the inane words from flooding out.

A fucking fool.

It didn't matter because I was eating up her tits like they were dessert, lapping each taut nub, before I was kissing back over the thunder pounding in her chest. I licked up her throat before I took her mouth again.

"I came up here because I care about you," she mumbled against my lips. "Because I couldn't stand the look that took over your face."

Her words should have stopped me in my tracks.

But I was kissing her deeper, my tongue stroking against hers like in it I could find reprieve.

One hand wound in the fall of her lush hair and the other explored each curve of her body. Riding down her side.

Her waist.

Her hip.

Gliding down until I gripped her by the knee.

I spread her, then angled back so I could run my fingertips along the sweet juncture between her thighs.

She gasped, and she held onto my shoulders as she reared back, looking down at where I touched her over the material of her shorts.

"Are you wet for me, Paisley?" It was a growl of desperation, my cock so fucking hard it took all the restraint I possessed not to rip myself out of my pants and sink my dick into her cunt.

She moaned. "So wet. I hate how much I want you. How much I've wanted you since the first time I saw you. And after that night…"

Vulnerability slipped into her tone, and I was assaulted with the vision of her fucking herself with that toy.

I wanted to tell her to go get it. Do all manners of dirty deeds with it to her gorgeous body.

"Good because I hate how much I want you, too." I popped the button of her shorts and dragged down the zipper, then I hooked my fingers in the waistband. "I've been dying to taste you since I got to watch you shoving that toy into your pussy while you dreamed of it being me."

Need shocked through her low groan, and her hands shot out to cling to my shoulders as I tugged both her boots from her feet, dropped them to the floor, then began to wind the shorts and underwear down her legs.

My appreciation left me on a hiss. "Look at you."

She was completely unclothed, and I took her by both knees and propped her feet on the edge of my desk, spreading her so wide her slit parted.

Glistening.

Every sweet spot on this girl hewn in pink.

I drove a single finger deep into her body.

She arched from the desk. "Caleb. Yes."

I fucked my digit in and out, measured and deep, slowly coiling her into a messy bow of want.

Her hands shot behind her to keep herself upright as I took her by the outside of each thigh and dove in.

Tongue diving between her swollen lips.

I devoured her pussy the way I'd been aching to, thrusting my tongue into her walls, lapping and licking.

She was nearly screaming by the time I moved to focus on her clit. Her flesh was engorged, as needy and throbbing as her walls when I sank two fingers deep inside her.

"Oh, Caleb, yes. Please," she whimpered.

I swirled my tongue around her sweet nub and fucked her with my fingers in slow, deep thrusts.

She was back to ripping at my hair, the girl panting, winding up so fast I knew it would only take a minute for her to explode.

"I want your dick," she begged.

Fuck.

This girl.

Chaos.

Too much.

Everything I couldn't have.

"We aren't going there, Paisley."

Like it fucking mattered. Like I hadn't already broken the vow I had made. But denying myself the pleasure of fully taking her felt like a semblance of control.

A taste without fully giving in.

"Why? I want to. I want to feel you," she begged.

"I will take care of you, angel." I shifted my fingers, curling them, rubbing her faster as I licked and sucked her into oblivion.

I could feel the bliss beginning to gather. The way her fingers ripped and tore and her breaths became ragged. Every cell in her body glowed, expanding, racing toward the beauty I wanted to be the one to give her.

One second later, her walls spasmed around my fingers, and she flew. Her entire being bowed with ecstasy, rocked and trembled and rolled.

Wave after wave.

A cry ripped up her throat, and I leaned up so I could swallow it, kissing her as she rode out the orgasm by writhing on my hand.

I held her there while she quivered and shook. She twitched and jerked for the longest time, and I knew it'd take but a touch to have her completely wound up again.

I slowed the manic kiss, waning the intensity until our lips were barely touching. Her pants wheezed through the connection, filling my lungs, like she had become my air.

An angel who'd come to calm the storm.

But how could I let her go there?

How could I be so selfish to drag her into the mess that I had made?

I already knew what my selfishness had cost.

The ultimate price.

I would never put her in that position.

Never.

She edged back, still panting, those eyes delving so deep into mine. Sifting around in the mayhem. Slipping through the cracks of who I'd become and who I wanted to be.

Her spirit rushing out.

Entwining.

Enchanting.

Soothing the sting and this ache.

Reckless Angel.

She pushed me back farther into the chair. A groan got free when she climbed down onto her knees. My guts flexed in greed, the girl so stunning as she knelt fully bare at my feet.

All that hair and those eyes and that beautiful heart she needed to protect.

My thumb traced over the contour of her cheek. Soft against the chaos battering my ribs.

"Paisley."

"I want to taste you, too." She tugged at my belt. "I want to touch you. I want to know you. I can't stop thinking about you. About this body, but I'm thinking about the inside places, too. About this man who carries so much pain. One who's cast himself aside like waste. A man who needs someone to stand at his side and show him what he really means."

My hand fisted in her hair as she unzipped me. "Fuck, Paisley. You can't go there."

"You're wrong, Caleb. I'm already right here. Right here." Then she angled up and hooked her fingers in the waistband of my pants. "You just have to decide if you want to meet me there or not."

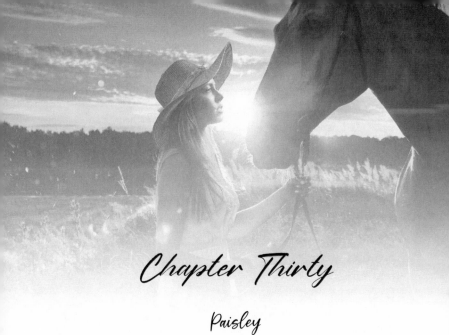

Chapter Thirty

Paisley

DESIRE CRACKLED, AND I HELD ONTO THE WAISTBAND OF his pants like they were a lifeline. Something to keep me grounded while I rested on my knees in front of this man.

An offering.

Myself.

My body.

My belief.

I knew he didn't believe he deserved it. I'd seen the self-hatred scored in his eyes when he'd revealed the horrors he'd left behind in Seattle.

The loathing.

The disgust that radiated out and twisted with the hunger for vengeance that shook from him so violently I'd felt it penetrate down to my soul.

I knew I was in the crosshairs of it.

That I'd placed myself in the position to get trampled.

But Dakota had been right. I had to evaluate the risk, and my gut told me he was worth it. On top of it, I was going after what my heart wanted, just like my grandpa had said.

I didn't want fear to stand in my way, even though it'd taken on new layers with the confessions Caleb had made.

His ghosts grimmer than I ever could have imagined.

But I'd hold them, too. Chase them away.

Aftershocks from the orgasm he'd given me still trembled through my veins, but it was the sight of him staring down at me with those icy eyes burning with lust and reservation that ricocheted through my chest.

Knocked me senseless and made me want to chase after whatever he had to offer.

Desire bristled and blew.

Energy thrashed. No longer just a hum, but a loud thrumming that echoed in my ears and reverberated in my heart.

I needed to touch him. Bring him the same kind of pleasure he'd brought me.

"You make me crazy," he growled. "How the fuck am I supposed to resist you?"

"You don't, Mr. Greyson. You take it because I'm offering it." I tipped my chin his direction, ripe with a challenge.

Ringing with the plea.

He swiped the pad of his thumb over my lips, sending sparks shooting down my spine.

I eased up higher so I could drag his pants down, and Caleb lifted to allow it.

His cock sprang free of his underwear.

A flash of need slammed me, one so intense I nearly bowled over.

Desire lashed. An inferno that lit in a flashfire of greed.

I wrapped my hand around his hard cock, as stony as the rigid expression that lined his face.

The video hadn't come close to doing him justice. The man so thick I had no idea how I was going to get him in my mouth, so long I trembled with the idea of taking him into my body. Knowing he would consume me in a way I'd never been consumed before.

Fill me.

Score me.

Ruin me.

My tongue stroked over my parched lips.

"Fuck me." He grunted it, words scraping like need dragging over my flesh. "I like it hard, Ms. Dae. Don't get shy on me now. Show me what a good girl you are on your knees for me."

The command was gravel, and my heart hammered at my ribs in a wild, uncontrolled beat.

"Bossy." It barely made it above a whisper.

"I warned you I'd show you just how bossy I could be."

My survival instincts were clearly lacking.

I was begging for a breaking.

This man was going to do me in.

But I'd already known I was a goner the second he'd kissed me in a way I'd never been kissed before. Had known it when I'd sneaked into his bed.

When for a moment, he'd let me hold the torment he kept hidden away. Emotion thickened my throat. This felt so much bigger than anything I'd experienced before. So much bigger than I should have let it.

Alight.

Glimmering.

Drawing me to unavoidable places.

As if he sensed my heart going there, he reached out and cupped my cheek, thumb brushing over the hollow beneath my eye. "Reckless Angel. Told you to stay away from me."

"The problem is, I don't think you meant it."

He slipped his thumb into my mouth, and he pushed down on my tongue before he withdrew it and coated my lips with my saliva. The next thing I knew was he was fisting himself and nudging the fat head of his penis to my mouth instead.

"You're right. Now let me see those pretty lips wrapped around my cock."

Desire throbbed, building up brand new, this man so hot it sent a shudder ripping down my spine.

My thighs squeezed together, and I couldn't stop the way a thrill went sailing through my system, playing this dangerous game.

Except I was stupid enough that I had the sense that I was playing for keeps. There was something about Caleb Greyson that felt like home.

"Now suck me. Undo me the way you've been dying to do."

"Yes, sir," I murmured. I'd wanted it to come out a tease, a taunt, but it was far too shaky for that.

Possession flashed through his features. "Oh, Little Riot, you're in trouble now."

He pushed to his feet, towering over me, so ridiculously fierce where he stood at his full, imposing height.

He didn't hesitate. He pushed his giant cock into my mouth, so deep I almost gagged, my mouth stretched so wide drool dribbled out at the sides.

"That's right," he grumbled.

With one hand, I gripped him by a thigh to keep myself steady, and the other I wrapped around the base of his cock. Searching for some semblance of control, for a way not to fully lose myself even though I knew that ship had long since sailed.

I was a goner.

I began to suck him like he'd told me to.

Taking him in as deep as I could, riding back up to swirl my tongue around his head, licking him up and down and doing my best to drive this man to the ends of ecstasy where he'd driven me.

"Fuck…you feel so good. So nice. Perfect, baby, that mouth, what you're doing to me." The words fell from his lips like praise.

Close to incoherent.

It didn't matter. Each one pierced through me like arrows.

Stakes that would claim.

"I knew this smart mouth would be perfect. I knew it."

I took him deeper.

Faster.

More and more as he began to rock his hips in time.

I met him jut for jut, my hand wrapped around him to stroke what I couldn't take.

And that buzzy energy glowed brighter. Blinding light with flashes of darkness.

Wound with his intensity.

Severity whirled around him like a force field.

I wanted to break through it.

Reach inside to the places where he was hidden away.

Find him.

A frenzy struck in the air.

The kind of need I'd never known.

And I thought that maybe Caleb felt it too when he fisted a hand in my hair and began to lead me, taking what he wanted, what I wanted to give.

"Paisley." He breathed my name like it was the first time he'd ever said it.

Like he sang it.

Like he meant it.

I unlocked my jaw so I could let the man pound into my mouth, the fat head of him hitting the back of my throat with each desperate thrust.

He was so much.

So big.

So powerful.

All-consuming.

Overwhelming.

I was struck with a flood of everything I had no idea I needed until I'd met this man.

Heat seared me through.

Scarring me in some way, or maybe burning through to the scarred places.

My nails curled into his thigh, praying I might be scarring him, too.

"Shit. Fuck. Yes." A slew of curses tumbled from him, and his snaps became frantic.

Every packed, beautiful muscle in his body coiled.

Ready to blow.

The hand in my hair tugged, pricking my scalp in pleasured pain. "Harder, Paisley. Need it."

I grabbed him by the ass and let him fully take control.

He pushed in as deep as he could go, and I felt when the tightly wound pieces of him ripped apart.

When the orgasm blistered through him.

The man a fire when he roared in pleasure.

He jerked and spasmed, and I swallowed the cum he poured into my mouth.

Sparks of pleasure at undoing him lit in the middle of me.

We slowed, his cock jerking and twitching as the tension drained from his body.

A second later, his hand was back to running the length of my jaw as he struggled to find his breath.

"Paisley," he murmured. For the first time, those icy eyes were completely soft. But beneath the melted snowcap was torment. "You're fucking perfect, Paisley Dae. Perfect. Wish I could be the same for you."

"I don't need perfect, Caleb. I just need the man who is fighting for the safety and joy of that little girl downstairs."

Something like hope bloomed through the bleakness before he shuttered it, clearing his throat as he tucked himself back into his pants, leaving the waistband open as he reached out a hand to help me stand.

He leaned over and helped me back into my shorts.

Tender.

Gentle.

So freaking sweet.

Apparently, orgasms were his love language.

He pulled my shirt back over my head, let his fingertips play along my belly as he dragged it down, his voice thick when he whispered, "I forgot what it was like to want something other than revenge until I met you." Blue eyes flashed in the brightness of his room, a shockwave of guilt and regret. "I shouldn't, but I do."

"There's more to you than you think there is, Caleb Greyson. There's so much brimming beneath the barriers you've built. I can feel it." I brought my palm up to cover the life beat that thundered in his chest.

Severity pulsed through his blood.

Devotion and loyalty.

Goodness he didn't know he possessed.

"I don't know what you did in your past, Caleb, but I do know the man who is standing in front of me right now. You get to choose which one he's going to be."

He blinked, torn between the wrath that whispered in his soul and this pull that neither of us could resist.

I hesitated for a beat, teeth raking my bottom lip, glancing away before I looked at him and asked, "Do you think she's in danger?"

Aggression cracked through the room.

A thunderbolt.

Then he was clinging to me again, his arm looped around my waist as if it could stop him from coming apart. "I don't know, Paisley. I thought coming here was the right choice. Hiding her away. But sometimes I swear I can taste the wickedness in the air."

"It's because you worry about her."

His head shook and he pulled me closer, mumbling the words into my neck. "I'll do whatever it takes to keep her safe."

"I know."

"You should leave this place." His arms only tightened.

I cleared the lump from my throat. "I already told you, I'm not going anywhere."

Chapter Thirty-One

Paisley

THE BED JOSTLED, AND I BLINKED MY EYES OPEN TO FIND A little peapod bouncing on the mattress at my side, her beaming grin shooting affection straight into my bloodstream.

"Are you going to wake up today? You've been sleeping for a thousand hours, and I've got the hungries because I need all the energy so we can go on our ride by the river. Mazzy will be waiting because I already told her that's what we get to do. Can we pack a special lunch?" Her little voice slurred with the thrill.

Pushing up onto my elbow, I glanced around. The room was still a bit dim, though morning light pressed in at the drapes, claiming a new day.

I reached out and brushed back a wild lock of Evelyn's hair, giving her a soft smile. "Someone is excited. It's not even six yet."

"I've been awake for two whole hours, and I had to wait the whole time. Are you ready?"

Most mornings I was up with the breaking of dawn. But Caleb had come into my room last night right as I was drifting to sleep. He'd climbed onto my bed, peeled my sleep shorts down my legs, then devoured me with his mouth all over again. Then I'd stroked him with my hands until he'd come all over my fingers.

I'd wanted to ask him to stay. For us to explore this. But I was afraid neither of us knew what it meant.

"Well, we'd better get a move on, hadn't we?" I touched Evelyn's dimpled chin.

"We better. The early bird gets the worm, you know."

Soft laughter rolled from me. "And you're an early bird?"

"I'm an Evie-Bird." She flapped her arms.

"I thought it was Evie-Love?" I teased.

"Because you love me?" Hope glowed around the child like the rays of light streaming in from the window.

My heart expanded. Pushed at my ribs. Threatened to burst.

My fingers kept brushing through her hair, the air both heavy and light. "That's right, Evelyn. Because I love you. So much."

And that glowing that surrounded her like a halo turned luminescent.

"I love you because you're my very most favorite day," she said, her smile showing off the gaps in her teeth.

My spirit thrashed, and I cupped her cheek. "And you are mine. So, what do you say you and I go make this day amazing?"

Hopping on her knees, she grinned. "I like this idea very much."

I tapped her nose.

"You go get dressed, and I'm going to, too, then I'll meet you downstairs so we can get breakfast and pack our lunches."

"Deal." She shoved out her hand.

I was caught in her sweetness. Her adorableness. Everything I hadn't known I'd been missing.

I shook her hand. "It's a deal, Evie-Love."

She scrambled off the bed and hightailed it out of my room in the direction of hers, and I tossed off my covers, stretching.

A residual pleasure danced through my body.

Tiny tingles of rapture.

A grin tweaked at the edge of my mouth as my thoughts spiraled back to yesterday. That rigid, stony man going pliable in my hands.

I went into the en suite bathroom and washed my face and brushed my teeth, then I changed into some jeans and a tee and grabbed my hat, heading downstairs and into the kitchen.

Caleb was at the table, lit up like a dark god where he sat beneath the window tapping at something on his laptop.

My fallen angel so gorgeous there beneath the light that kissed the sharp edges of his face.

He looked up when he felt me hovering at the periphery of the room. A scowl was etched into his brow. I couldn't hold back the laugh that crawled up my throat.

So damned grumpy.

"You're looking awful cranky over there. And here I thought I blew your mind twice yesterday." I let it go as a tease.

Caleb all but growled. "I'm not cranky."

"No?"

"No," he gritted. "I'm trying to get in touch with the investigator in Seattle. He didn't return my calls yesterday when I tried to let him know about the letter I received."

All the teasing drained from my being. I hated that I hadn't picked up on where his distress was coming from.

I was also thankful that he'd offered the information.

Trusted me to hold it.

"Does it usually take him awhile to get in touch with you?"

Air puffed from his nose as he tapped at his keyboard while he spoke, "He's completely incompetent. But it doesn't matter. Finding him is my job."

He looked up at me.

Intensity fired from the fiery depths of those icy eyes.

Right.

He wanted to be the one.

Fear curled down my spine. Sickness landed like a stone in the pit of my stomach at the thought of him being hurt. Of him finding the same fate as his sister.

Of it happening to Evelyn.

Horror rolled up my throat without permission, and my hand

went to the island for support. I couldn't imagine it, and I knew I'd do the same to protect her as Caleb was contemplating.

"I hate that you're afraid. Are you sure you don't want to leave?" Regret passed through his features.

"It's not me I'm afraid for, Caleb." It came out choked. Hard and furious and filled with the type of devotion I'd never felt before.

Tearing myself from his gaze, I moved deeper into the kitchen, heading directly for the coffee pot that he'd already brewed. I hiked up on my toes so I could grab a mug, then I froze when I felt the presence enclose from behind.

Severe.

Sharp.

Overpowering.

I gasped when he plastered his hot body against my back, his cock hard at my ass.

He leaned over me, his mouth coming to my ear. "For the record, you more than blew my mind yesterday, Paisley Dae. You demolished it."

Pleasure sparked in my belly, then I froze when the tiny giggle flooded the air. Our attention whipped to the left.

Evelyn stood at the far side of the kitchen, wearing her adorable boots with her jeans bunched up where she tried to tuck them inside. She was grinning like mad and trying to shove back her messy hair that kept falling in her face so she could see us better.

"Are you guys going to have a baby?"

I tried not to choke on the surprise that gushed up my throat. Half laugh and half horror.

Caleb peeled himself away, and his spine went ramrod straight. Unease had him resituating the cuffs of his button-down shirt.

"Of course not, Evelyn. I was just helping Paisley reach a mug from the cabinet."

Evelyn frowned like she was disappointed. "Okay, I guess."

I blew out a strained breath, peeking over at Caleb, not sure what to make of him or any of this. It was the first time he'd ever called me

Paisley in front of Evelyn, and there was something about it that made that vulnerable spot in my chest warm and expand.

Caleb went back to where he'd been working at the table like nothing had transpired, his attention fully focused on his laptop.

But I noticed the shift.

He hadn't escaped to the third floor like he usually did.

He was downstairs.

With us.

I turned my attention on Evelyn. "What would you like for breakfast?"

"Eggs, please."

"On it," I told her.

We set to work. I whipped up eggs and toast, and she buttered the slices, the two of us a total team.

We ate quickly before Evelyn pulled a stool up to my side so she could help me make turkey sandwiches for lunch that we packed into a small cooler.

She kept grinning over at me while we worked, her sweet spirit light, her joy easy. It made everything easy for me, too.

I tossed the strap of the cooler over my shoulder and reached for her hand. "All right, let's do this."

Caleb closed his laptop and stood, his eyes dragging over us where we held hands. Something flashed through his gaze before he cleared his throat. "I need to head into town. Please be careful while I'm away. Call me if you need anything."

"We will be," I promised.

I wanted to cross the room and kiss his face.

Somehow, I managed to leave him there gathering his things, and I led Evelyn out.

Chapter Thirty-Two

Caleb

I TOSSED THE LETTER TO THE TOP OF EZRA'S DESK BEFORE I SAT down across from him. He scrubbed a beefy palm over his face as he sat forward in his office chair, eyeing it like it might be a bomb. That was exactly what it felt like.

A bomb going off in the middle of my world, but it wasn't like I had expected peace. I just wanted to be the one delivering the violence.

"Shit. First communication like this?" Ezra asked, glancing between me and the evidence I'd placed in a plastic bag, hoping someone might be able to get some prints off it. But considering the monster never left a trace of anything behind, I didn't hold out hope that this would amount to anything.

But if it did…

I gave him a clipped nod. "That's right. It came overnight to the post office box I have here in Time River. It had been forwarded from where it was sent to my address in Seattle."

"And you didn't hear from the investigator there?"

"Not yet, but I'm not surprised. Would prefer to leave him out of it, if I'm being honest."

Ezra looked over at me, my cousin seeing through the polished exterior to what lie underneath. He was no fool. He knew the corruption by which I'd lived. The blood I'd spilled in my father's name. The vile things I had done to pad my own pockets.

It wasn't like Ezra hadn't been involved in his own depravity before he'd made a change for something better.

Still, he shifted in unease, cursing under his breath. "Shit, man. This is shady as fuck. Doesn't sit well. This has serial killer vibes. Not a hired hand coming at you for some wealthy businessman you did wrong. Looks deeper to me."

Dread thickened my throat. "I don't care who it is, I want him to bleed."

Ezra pushed out a heavy sigh. "Only you would sit across from me while I'm wearing this uniform and admit that."

"Admit what?" Ryder pushed through the door, strolling in with that salacious expression on his face. Dude always looked like he was up to no good.

Ezra sighed again. "Asshole is trying to put himself in a situation he can't come back from." He shifted to look at me, his voice dropping low. "He's either going to get to you first, or you're going to land yourself behind bars. This is too fucking high profile, Caleb. I don't care how much money you have to cover it."

Ryder smacked my shoulder as he plopped down in the chair beside me. "And your ass is way too tempting for you to go to prison, my friend."

I sent him a scowl. "Do I need to be concerned you've been looking at my ass?"

He laughed, tapping a tattooed thumb against his thigh like it was a drum. "Hey, just looking out for my favorite cousin because we know it's not that ugly cocksucker over there."

He pushed his shoe up on the edge of Ezra's desk, giving it a teasing shove.

Ezra sent the collector baseball he had sitting on his desk whizzing toward Ryder.

Ryder's arms shot up to deflect the blow. "What the hell, Ezra? You trying to take me out? So testy. The both of you."

He was all grins like this wasn't a life-or-death situation.

"Focus, man. This is serious," Ezra said, words low. "Caleb got a letter. Whoever this creep is was watching close enough to know he went to Seattle. It's like he's begging Caleb to come after him. Drawing him out. Toying with him."

Ryder sobered, worry threading through his demeanor. "And there still aren't any clues? No idea who this deviant is?"

"Not one."

I dropped forward, elbows on my thighs and my head slumped between my shoulders as I pushed my face into my palms.

"We're going to find him, Caleb." Ezra's voice broke through the torture, and I forced myself to look at him. "Promise you that. You stepped up for me when I needed it, do you think I'm not going to do the same? I'll go to Seattle myself to track this fucker down if that's what it takes."

Severity coated Ezra's pledge.

"You know I'm there," Ryder added. "Whatever you need."

"I wouldn't put either of you in the path of this."

It was already bad enough I'd come here. But they were the only family I had left. The only family Evelyn had left. Not that I'd allowed her out to get to know them. Keeping her locked away within the confines of the ranch, terrified someone might follow us here.

"Keep telling you that we're your family, man." None of the razzing was left in Ryder's voice, just a quiet ferocity. "What the hell do you think we're here for?"

My head shook. "I would never want to bring danger to your doors."

"Sounds to me like we're going to have to go find it." Ryder looked at Ezra, the promise of violence rippling beneath his tatted arms.

I knew they'd step in the line of fire for me, but I would never allow it.

My teeth ground. "I will find him. These are my sins."

Ezra blew out a strained breath. "Let the detective there do his job, Caleb, and I'm going to see if I can't dig around myself from here. Uncover something that's been missed. But you need to move on. Let

Evelyn live. You're stagnant, refusing to let yourself breathe, and it's time you did."

Not until he was dead.

"Don't do something stupid you can't take back." Grimness filled his warning.

"Speaking of, Dakota's little boy, Kayden, is having his second birthday party this Saturday," Ryder cut in. "Ezra's kids are going to be there." He jutted his chin at Ezra. "It's time Evelyn met her cousins, don't you think?"

The need to protect her surged. Gushed up from the dark places. My hands curled into fists. "I don't know if that's a good idea."

"Come on, man, these are people you need to get to know. Our friends," Ryder emphasized. "People we consider family. And it's time you became a part of that. It's the whole reason you came to Time River."

I'd come to Time River to keep Evelyn safe.

"And you know Paisley is going to be there." Ryder wagged his brows.

I grunted. "What does that have to do with anything?"

Everything.

The thought hit me before I could stop it.

Ryder cracked up. "Oh, you think I haven't heard you have that girl holed up at your mansion? You think I don't know what you've gotten up to? I knew you wanted to dip your dirty dick in my Paisley-Cakes."

I kind of wanted to throw my fist through his smug face. *All brotherly-like.*

"Evelyn needed a nanny." The lie tasted sour where it whipped off my tongue, even though it was true.

Evelyn needed a nanny.

She needed Paisley.

Fucking problem was I was beginning to need her, too.

"Sure, asshole. You keep telling yourself that."

Ezra chuckled. "At least someone like Paisley can whip this surly fucker into shape."

"You're calling me surly?" I looked pointedly at Ezra. He was the grumpiest motherfucker I knew.

Not that I blamed him after what he'd been through.

"What are you talking about? I'm a ray of goddamn sunshine." He grunted it, fighting a grin.

At least not all his joy had been stolen. At least there was a piece of him that held onto a faith I'd long ago ceased to believe existed.

"Seriously, Caleb, you need to be there," Ryder urged. "These people are important to me. Important to Ezra."

"And you remember what happened the last time I let you convince me into going out." It wasn't even a question.

"Yeah, you got your girl back. You're welcome." The cocky bastard reached over and patted my cheek.

I grunted.

Chuckling, he stood. "Come on. Thought we were going for lunch. I need a beer."

My phone pinged, and I dug it out as I pushed to my feet, heart lurching just seeing her name.

> **Paisley: Hey, my best friend is having a party for her son on Saturday. I'd really like to take Evelyn, and I'd really like you to come, too. Pretty please? I'll even put a cherry on top if you want me to.**

Reckless Angel, bursting into my world and jumbling everything. Reason and sight. My jaw clenched before I typed out the response.

> **Me: I think that could be arranged. Cherry required.**

Ryder smirked where he looked at the message from over my shoulder. "That's what I thought."

Chapter Thirty-Three

Caleb

"THAT'S DAKOTA'S RESTAURANT—TIME RIVER MARKET & Café. She lives right behind it in this cute house, but it's way too small for the party, so that's why it's going to be at her mom's house. Have you eaten there yet? It's seriously delicious. She took that baby from a total diner dive and made it something extra special. The kind of special only Dakota can do. It's closed today, obviously, since everyone is going to be at Kayden's party."

Paisley chattered on from the front passenger seat, filling me and Evelyn in on every detail of this small town and the people who made it up, while my insides coiled into intricate knots of agitation.

Unsure of why I'd agreed to this.

How I'd thought it would be a good idea.

"Do you think we can get to go there and eat sometime really soon?" Evelyn asked from the backseat. "You know how much I love the delicious foods, and we don't have a lot of that at our house except for eggs."

Our house.

It struck me.

A stake to my consciousness.

One that got shoved in deeper when Paisley shot me a coy grin before she shifted to look back at Evelyn. Feigning offense, she touched her chest with her fingertips. "Are you accusing me of being a bad cook?"

"No way, I didn't even mean it that you're *bad*. I only mean that you're not good." It was completely serious and sincere.

A chuckle rolled up my throat.

Paisley gasped. "I'm not good?"

"You should really stick with horses," Evelyn told her as if she were giving her financial advice.

"Well, that's a good thing since cooking isn't part of my job description. I was just doing it out of the kindness of my heart."

"That's because that's one of your *good* parts," Evelyn slurred in her little voice. "I really like your heart."

Affection pulsed through the cab, pouring so distinctly out of Paisley I felt it slam into me.

Bounding and reverberating.

Saturating the space.

Taking over the air.

Paisley blinked rapidly, her eyes moist, and fuck, I didn't know how to process it. What this meant. How this woman had come in and changed everything.

"I like your heart, too, Evie-Love," she whispered, her voice soggy.

She shifted back around. "Oh, crap, make the next right."

The *next right* was about two feet away, and I had to ram on my brakes to make the turn.

Paisley giggled. "Oops."

I sent her a glare.

Little Riot, driving me wild.

I made the turn off Manchester and onto another tree-lined street.

The quaint neighborhood was similar to where Paisley's grandfather lived, though here, the houses were larger, fronted by elevated wood porches and perfectly manicured lawns.

The trees were enormous, clamoring for the sky, their soaring branches shading the yards and giving respite from the warmth of the summer day.

"Are we going to be at the party right now?" Excitement erupted from Evelyn, and she bounced in her car seat, trying to get a better look.

My chest tightened as I glanced at the woman who sat smiling next to me. Knowing this was right. That this was what Evelyn needed. To become a part of something that she'd lost.

A family.

I mean, fuck, I didn't even know what she'd been taken away from. If she'd had friends. If Kimberly had carved out a community for them.

Paisley smiled back.

That fall of white hair was curled in soft, fat waves. She wore a dress for the first time since I'd met her, white with pink flowers, thin spaghetti straps showing off her bare shoulders and the expanse of her chest. The neckline dipped down just enough to hint at the swell of her tits, so fucking sexy it made my mouth water.

But it was what was under it that made me truly thankful.

Thankful she was here.

Making this impact on Evelyn's life.

I'd made mistakes every step of the way, but Paisley Dae was not one of them.

"Yep, we're almost there, Evie. It's that house right there." She pointed to the left at a single-story house. A ton of cars were parked in the driveway and overflowed onto each side of the road.

I found a spot on the opposite side from the house and killed the engine. Paisley immediately popped open the door.

A fresh round of nerves prickled through my system.

I scrubbed a palm over my face as I looked at the house painted white and trimmed in blue. Balloons were tied to the wood railing of the porch, and there was a giant sign on the lawn in the shape of a two.

Was I really doing this?

"Second thoughts?" At her voice, I looked back to my right where Paisley had climbed out. She had her head poked back inside, wearing one of those flirty grins that claimed she knew me better than I wanted her to.

"There were always second thoughts," I grumbled.

She laughed and waved her hand. "Come on, Mr. Grumpy Pants, it's going to be a blast."

"A blast, huh?" I asked.

"Um, have you ever even been to a two-year-old's birthday party before?"

"No." Who exactly did she think I was?

"Time of your life, I tell you." A giggle that was nothing more than a razz rolled up her throat.

"I'm sure." I let the sarcasm bleed into the response, though I clicked open the door and stepped out. I opened the rear driver's side door and unbuckled Evelyn while Paisley grabbed the stack of presents bound together by a big blue ribbon from the backseat.

Evelyn slipped off her booster and stood at the side of the door, and I hoisted her up from under the arms to help her down.

Only when I set her on the ground, she didn't step back or withdraw the way she always had in the past.

She took my hand.

I gulped around the knot in my throat when I looked down at her, as she turned her little face up to me, beaming this smile that pierced me in the chest.

"Don't worry, I don't know anybody, either, and we can stick together and take care of each other if we get nervous, but I think it's going to be really a lot of fun because I haven't never been to a two-year-old's birthday, just like you, but I think it's going to be really good."

My heart fisted.

A feeling swept through me that I wasn't supposed to possess.

"I know you're going to have a wonderful time, Evelyn." My voice croaked when I forced it out.

That storm was suddenly at our sides, chaos that spun and the light that shone.

An angel who'd appeared at the edge of our dejected world.

"Are you two ready or what? I was never about the whole fashionably late thing. Why miss out on a second of the fun?"

"I'm ready!" Evelyn swung our hands between us.

Paisley started across the street, and we followed behind her. I probably should have gotten in front so I didn't have to watch her ripe, lush ass swaying back and forth in that dress or the defined cut of her calves accentuated by her wedge heels.

Hindsight and all.

Because lust twisted in my guts, hungry for another taste.

Paisley moved up the sidewalk and onto the porch. Without knocking, she pulled open the screen door and walked in. She kept moving through the living room that was cluttered and a bit of a mess, the furniture worn and well-lived in.

Voices echoed, loud and uncontained, laughter and shouts that were coming from the backyard.

Paisley breezed into the kitchen at the back of the house.

"Paisley, hey!" A young woman I'd never seen before was grabbing a tray of vegetables and dip from the countertop that was completely covered in food. Bowls, trays, and half used packages covered every surface.

"Hi, Kayla! How are you?" Paisley asked.

"Great. It's so good to see you."

Paisley dipped in and pecked a kiss to her cheek. "I know, it's been way too long. What can I do to help?"

"We're just setting the food up outside. Gift table is out on the back porch. You can set those presents down, and then grab any of these dishes. I swear, Dakota overdid it this time."

Instead of taking the presents outside, Paisley turned around and shoved them into my free arm. "Hold this."

"Uh…sure." I shifted on my feet, so out of my element I had no fucking clue where to stand.

It only got worse when Paisley waved a casual hand my way. "Kayla, this is Caleb Greyson, and this is our sweet Evelyn."

Another arrow staked me through.

Ours.

Except neither of them could ever truly be mine. I needed to fucking remember it.

I gave the most pleasant smile I could find but probably looked half deranged when Paisley gestured at the woman. "Caleb and Evelyn, this is Kayla, Dakota's baby sister."

"Nice to meet you both. Come on out back."

No other choice but to follow since Evelyn went skipping that way, still holding onto my hand and dragging me along. "It's so nice to meet you, Ms. Kayla. Is the party this way?"

"You are definitely heading in the right direction," Kayla told her.

Warily, I glanced back to where Paisley had taken two large bowls from the counter and was balancing them in her arms.

Evelyn hopped out onto the deck a step ahead of me.

Streamers and balloons hung from every surface.

A fresh bolt of excitement blazed through the child. She clapped her hands before she clasped them in front of her like she was issuing up a prayer, her shoulders rising to her ears. "Oh my goodness, it's a real party, Uncle! Look it!" She squealed when she saw a piñata hanging from a tree. "I'm going to get so much candy!"

My gaze traveled, and I spotted Ryder and Ezra sitting in Adirondack chairs beneath a tree to the right of the yard. Another man I didn't recognize was with them.

Ryder sent me a smirk from behind the beer bottle he was sipping from, the strength of it growing when Paisley stepped up to my side.

Anxiety itched through me as I stood there with Evelyn and the ridiculous stack of presents.

I could only imagine what it looked like with the three of us there together.

Paisley moved to set the bowls down on a long buffet table before she strutted back my way.

Need gutted me at the vision.

God.

How was it possible one woman could affect me this way?

"Here, let me get that." Casually, she took the presents, set them on the table, then immediately returned.

Evelyn bounced at my side. "Look at all my new friends," she whispered as she gazed out at the mass of children screeching and running and playing on the lawn.

My spirit clutched.

Ezra pushed to standing and meandered our way. Ryder followed behind. We climbed down the porch steps to meet them.

"Nice to see you, brother." Ezra leaned in and gave a clap to my back. Ryder did the same before he picked up Paisley and swung her around like a ragdoll. "There's my favorite Paisley-Cakes. What are you doing hanging out with this guy?"

The ribbing was all there, though Ryder was slanting me a knowing eye.

"If you wouldn't mind putting her down," I grated.

I didn't care if I sounded like I was making a claim.

Maybe I was.

"Down boy." He winked while he was still hugging her.

"Yeah, stop manhandling me, you brute. I'm wearing a dress. Can't you see I'm a lady?" Paisley's laughter was all throaty and low, the tease dripping from her tongue.

Ryder chuckled as he set her onto her feet. "Ah, I see how it is."

Did he? Because I sure as shit couldn't make sense of it.

Ezra leaned down in front of Evelyn. "Hi, Evelyn. Do you remember me?"

Ezra and Ryder had been there to help us move in. Evelyn had been shell-shocked then. Close to mute. Barely eating. Barely sleeping, and when she had, she'd wake up wailing for her mom.

My chest tightened, thanking God that she had come out of it.

That this angel had shown up at our door, as reckless as she was.

"I remember a little bit," she said, shyness in her voice.

"Well, remember when I told you I have three kids? That they're your cousins?"

"Yes."

"Would you like to meet them?"

"I would like that very much, yes please. Is that okay?" She looked up at me.

"Of course, Evelyn," I said.

A smile split her face, and we followed Ezra toward the group of kids playing on the lawn.

"Olivia, Oliver, Owen, come on over here please."

The three of them came running, meeting us halfway, and Ezra knelt in front of them.

Each was as blond as their dad.

"Evelyn, this is Olivia, and these are my twins, Oliver and Owen."

Oliver and Owen shouted, "Hi," before they got distracted and started chasing after a balloon that'd gotten free.

Olivia remained, a year older than Evelyn. Soft spoken, shy, holding that same kind of sadness I'd witnessed often in Evelyn. "Do you want to play with me?"

I wondered what their relationship would be like when they discovered how similar they were.

What they'd lost.

"I really like that idea."

Evelyn let go of my hand, and she skipped off with Olivia.

Paisley touched my arm, her smile soft, tender with joy as she looked at me. "I'm going to go help Dakota with the games and hang out with Evelyn and the kids. Why don't you grab a beer?"

Unable to say anything, I dipped my chin.

My throat too thick.

Ryder handed me one. "Got you covered."

"Thanks." The three of us wandered over to where they'd been sitting. Ryder gestured to the guy I hadn't recognized. "Caleb, this is Cody, my oldest friend, Dakota's older brother. Cody, this is my cousin Caleb I told you about."

"Ah, the infamous Caleb Greyson." He leaned forward and shook my hand, no hostility in his voice. He took up most of the chair, his long legs stretched out far in front of him, the guy built and giving off the vibe that he likely spent most of his days working out in the sun. "Used to be jealous as fuck of you, every time these assholes came back after spending their summers in Washington, bragging about the shit you all pulled. Good to meet you."

I chuckled low as I took the chair next to Ryder. "Best days of my life."

I meant it.

It was in the days before I'd let the greed set in.

Before I'd become the type of man I'd never thought I could be. But he'd been there, waiting to slip in and take over.

Laughter rang through the summer air, and I looked out onto the rambling lawn.

Paisley sat on the grass with her legs crisscrossed, and Evelyn was on her lap, her back to Paisley's chest. Paisley had her arms wrapped around her, holding her close and rocking her back and forth while they sang some children's song that I'd never heard.

Paisley leaned forward, hugged her tight, before she shifted to peck a kiss against Evelyn's cheek.

Everything throbbed.

Light and heavy.

Perfect and wrong.

It made me feel like I was coming out of my skin.

Ryder squeezed my shoulder. "Maybe it's time you took those days back."

Chapter Thirty-Four

Paisley

TWILIGHT EASED OVER THE BACKYARD, THE HEAT OF THE day giving way to a cool breeze that played through the pinks and purples strewn across the sky. Dakota had some country music playing softly through the outdoor speakers, the sound of it threading a peace through the atmosphere.

Overhead, the trees swayed, and the kids had gathered under a massive oak where the piñata hung from a rambling branch that covered about half the yard. Giggles rode on the air as each of them took their turns jumping up to grab a string hanging from the bottom of the piñata that was in the shape of a 2, hoping to be the one who broke it apart.

I stood off to the side, watching since the guys had taken over this activity.

Cody, Ryder, and Ezra, plus two other dads, Grant and Joel, lined the kids up and gave them instruction.

But what made it impossible to look away was Caleb had joined them. He was out there wearing dress pants, radiating that fierce intensity that made my knees weak. But sometime throughout the afternoon something had changed.

The harsh, rigid planes of him had slackened.

Loosened.

His gaze soft as he watched the children play, his attention constantly going to Evelyn who'd had a blast. Fit right in. Became a part of this patchwork family. Right where she belonged.

I looked to my left when someone jostled their shoulder into mine.

Dakota stood there, brown hair tied in a high ponytail, something sly infiltrating her expression. She took a sip of her margarita as she reached out and touched the edge of my mouth. "Here, let me help you wipe some of this drool off that you have running down your chin."

I swatted at her hand. "Don't you even start with me."

"Oh, I'm about to start with you. Because from where I'm standing, it looks to me like you're doing a whole lot more than just crushing on that man."

I blew out a sigh, though the smile taking to my mouth was soft, riddled with the confession of what I was actually feeling. Knowing it was true but sure it was probably going to cost me my heart. "I have no idea what I'm doing, honestly."

"He's different than I thought," she mused, angling her head as we watched as Caleb hoisted Owen up so he could reach a string. The little boy howled and laughed, kicking his feet as he pulled one free before Caleb set him back on his feet and the child ran back to the end of the line.

Evelyn was next. She tried to jump up and reach one herself, but she couldn't, so Caleb lifted her, too. Though this time it was different. Riddled with something deep and profound and beautiful.

The way his features both hardened and curved into this gentleness I'd never seen in him before.

My spirit pitched, thrashing and moaning in a bid of want.

"So different," I whispered. "So much more than I'd imagined."

"When you were only imagining he was wicked hot, and you thought it wouldn't hurt to take him for a little ride?" Her voice went wry.

The scuff of a laugh rolled up my throat. "I never thought that."

"Um, you wanted to climb that bad boy from the moment you

saw him. It was written all over your face, don't even try to deny it," she teased.

I hummed. "Well, I guess he turned out to be a whole lot more than just someone to hate, that's for sure."

"I'm thinking you don't hate him at all."

Emotion climbed high when he glanced at me, the way those icy eyes sought me out, like he just needed the confirmation that I was still there.

A tether that kept him in place.

Heat keened through the connection.

A livewire.

Electricity.

It was suddenly feeling very difficult to breathe.

"Oh, Paisley. You're in love with that man." Dakota whispered it low, like a secret I might have a chance of keeping, when in all likelihood there was a neon sign hanging over my head proclaiming it.

Gushing up from the well where I'd tried to keep it checked.

Shining out like a beacon that sought to call him home.

I guessed I'd never been so good at curbing what I felt.

"I just want to be there for him," I said instead of admitting it aloud. "So much is going on in his life. He needs someone there who believes in him."

"Just make sure he believes in you, too, okay? Though from where I'm standing, it looks like you might just be the meaning of it."

"No, I don't think that's in store for us." It was a breath, terrified of believing it myself. Because I knew I had myself in the most precarious position.

Falling hard and fast for a man who'd already fallen himself, but in an entirely different way.

Only when he'd gone over a cliff, he'd hit rock bottom, had gotten battered and broken, and he didn't know how to climb out of it.

How to come back from the things he'd done.

I didn't know details, but I had a hunch they weren't pretty.

Ryder lifted Kayden high so the sweet little guy could tug free a string. He wasn't strong enough to do it himself, so Ryder gave him an edge up. The piñata busted open. Candy and inexpensive toys scattered on the lawn.

"You did it! The birthday boy did it!" Ryder shouted.

Kayden giggled like mad while Ryder soared him through the air before setting him onto his feet just as a bramble of children dove in, screeching and stuffing as much candy as they could into their bags.

I let go of a soft laugh. "You're trying to start a war out there."

"I probably should have thought that through, but I couldn't resist when I was ordering everything. Can't believe my little man is already two."

"You're doing a good job, Mama."

"I hope so."

"I know so."

"Ms. Dae! Ms. Dae! Look what I got. I got a whole bag and so much candy!" Evelyn held her bag over her head as she ran my way, her face filled with this smile that sheared me through.

So perfect and free.

My chest ached and another piece of me shattered.

"Hmm…looks like someone else is doing a good job, too." That Dakota muttered before she roamed away just as Evelyn got to me.

I knelt in front of her. "Let me see what you've got."

She opened it so I could peek inside. "See! I got a whole bag. Which do you like best? I'm going to share all of it with you."

"What, are you really going to share your spoils with me?"

Her nose curled. "Spoils?" she drew out in a question.

Affection left me on a soft chuckle, then the breath was getting sucked from my lungs when I felt the presence enclose.

Encircle and surround.

My heart stumbled into a scattered beat.

I looked up.

Caleb was three feet away, those hands in his pockets.

Intimidating.

All harsh angles and sharp, sculpted beauty.

But I felt his spirit that had gotten locked inside. Fighting for a way out, so constrained and hardened and packed down I wondered when it was going to blow.

I found myself pushing up to my feet. Tremors rocked the ground as he came forward, and my stomach tilted at the way a smirk took to the edge of his delicious mouth. "You know, I never got that dance."

I nearly tumbled back onto my ass.

Wait.

What?

Was he asking me to dance?

Right here?

My attention darted around the backyard. Most of the kids had moved to the jungle gym, and the adults were chatting casually as the day waned away. Darkness crawled across the grayed blue of the sky, stars blinking to life just as the timed twinkle lights had lit in the trees.

Music continued to play, the tune a soft love song.

A discomfited giggle slipped up my throat. "Are you serious? People will be watching us."

And it wasn't like I was shy or anything. But this was Caleb Greyson we were talking about.

"Let them watch."

He stepped forward and looped an arm around my waist, tucking me against him.

Fire flashed.

"Have you lost your mind?"

His hand slipped to my cheek as he began to lead me in a slow sway. "I told you that cherry was going to be required."

"And this is the cherry on top?" I choked around the clot of laughter. The clot of emotion. I couldn't even discern all that I was feeling right then.

"I think getting to touch you will always be the cherry on top."

I thought it was the first time I knew what it felt like to swoon. The way lightheadedness gusted through my brain. The way my heart whooshed.

A shy giggle snapped me out of it, and I looked down to Evelyn standing there swaying in time with the music. "Are you going to have a baby now?"

Before I could answer, Caleb hoisted her up, holding her in one arm while he wrapped the other around me. Evelyn wrapped both her arms around our necks, squeezing us tight. "No, Evelyn, I just wanted to be lucky enough to dance with my girls."

Everything clutched.

Constricted.

Then rushed to overflow.

A dream I floated through.

I held on tight to both of them like I could do it forever.

Like they were mine, and I wouldn't ever have to let go.

Something flashed in my periphery, and awareness slammed me like a fist to my face.

I jerked to look at the person standing at the bottom of the porch steps.

Curling and uncurling his fists.

Jeremy.

Jeremy with his brown hair and dimpled cheeks. All boyish good looks. Artificially charming until the real dickhead was revealed underneath.

He came off the last step and began to storm across the lawn like he had the freaking right.

Caleb must have felt the way I went rigid because he shifted to look over his shoulder at the man who was coming my way like I was the one who'd done him wrong.

Selfish asshole, ruining this moment.

"What the hell do you think you're doing, Paisley?" Jeremy hissed when he came within earshot.

Was he for real right then?

Anger surged, bubbling up from the depths.

Reluctantly, I let go of Evelyn and Caleb, taking a step his way, quieting my voice to shield this nonsense from the kids. "What am I doing? I think the question is what you're doing here. The last time I checked, you weren't on the guest list."

Awareness rippled through the guests. A ton of people had already left, so it was mostly close friends and family.

But that didn't mean this intrusion was acceptable.

"You need to leave right now. You're making a scene," I demanded.

"Not until I talk to you."

Ryder, Cody, and Ezra had come forward, and Dakota was suddenly there, whispering, "Hey, Evelyn, why don't you come with me, sweetheart? I was just going to start a movie inside since the party is winding down."

She untangled Evelyn from Caleb's hold, and she sent me a worried glance.

"Go on and take the kids inside," I told her. The last thing I wanted was for them to witness this.

She nodded, though she looked at Jeremey, disgust riding off her tongue. "I can't believe you have the nerve to show your face on my son's birthday."

She walked away, carrying Evelyn, and she and her mother Pat rounded up the kids and herded them inside.

All while the hostility flared.

Aggression vibrated from Caleb.

And not just a little bit.

He looked deadly right then.

All the things he'd warned me about rising to the surface.

Savagery honed in every muscle of his body. A stone that rippled and shook.

"Who is this prick?" Caleb growled. The polished suit that I knew had gone poof. Something dark taking its place.

I turned to him, touching his forearm. "He's no one important. It's fine. Just give me a second to get him out of here."

Caleb's jaw clenched, restraint barely enough to hold back whatever was boiling inside.

Ryder and Ezra edged up behind him.

I eased toward Jeremy who stood five feet away, words quiet but cutting through the dense, malevolent air. "I can't believe you would come here."

"I've been trying to get in touch with you, and you fucking blocked me, so what else was I supposed to do but come here?" It came out sounding petulant. Like I owed him something.

I scoffed. "And you're too stupid to get the message that I don't have a single thing to say to you. I don't know what you think, Jeremy, but you can turn around and haul your ass back to Arizona because I don't want anything to do with you."

"Said I was sorry, Paisley. That it won't happen again. I love you. I want you to come back to Scottsdale with me. Where you belong."

Remnants of hurt bubbled in my consciousness, but I realized it wasn't because he'd left me with a broken heart. It was just that he'd left me bitter. Had stolen the time I could have had with my family. With my friends. Took me from the place I loved like the selfish bastard that he was. I'd let go of my dream to give him his.

And he clearly didn't know one goddamn thing about me if he thought that was where I belonged.

"I don't care about your apologies, Jeremy. I don't accept them because they don't matter. I've long since stopped losing sleep over you. So why don't you take a hint and leave because you're not welcome here. It's bad enough you showed up to mess up Kayden's party like this. Have a little respect."

Except he clearly had zero respect since he sneered, grabbed me by the wrist, and jerked me toward him. "This is about him? Because you're fucking this rich asshole? I never took you for a gold-digging slut."

Oh, I wanted to claw his eyes out for that.

But I didn't get the chance.

Caleb was set on doing the honors for me.

He had him by the collar of his shirt.

A fist smashed into Jeremy's nose. Hard enough it knocked Jeremy from his feet.

Jeremy hit the ground, but he hopped back up, swiping away the blood that gushed from his nose. "What the fuck? You're dead, motherfucker."

He took an arrogant step toward Caleb.

And Caleb descended.

Dark intensity sweeping in.

A fallen angel who'd come to collect.

I didn't even know how he'd gotten him there, but he had Jeremy pinned to the table to the left, the man nothing but a blur of fury.

Caleb was over him, pounding into his face. Jeremy struggled, kicking his feet as he tried to break free, though it didn't take long for him to go limp.

Caleb continued his assault, and I finally got myself together enough to rush to him. I grabbed onto the back of his shoulders to try to pry him back. "Caleb. That's enough. Stop. Please stop."

He continued to pour his wrath on the man who wasn't worth our hate.

"Please. Stop," I begged him.

Ezra was suddenly there, dragging Caleb off him. "Enough, man."

Caleb stumbled back, his entire body quivering with violence. I fully wrapped myself around him from behind. Holding him.

"It's okay. It's okay," I whispered.

Jeremy moaned from the table, and he managed to sit upright.

But oh, God, was he a sight.

Blood covered his face, his eyebrow and lip both split open, his breaths strained.

Air huffed from his nose as he raked the back of his hand over the blood running from his pompous mouth. "You really are just a selfish bitch, Paisley Dae."

I tightened my hold on Caleb because there was no question he wanted a second round.

"You get anywhere near Paisley again, and I'm hauling you in," Ezra warned. They'd once been friends, but obviously that ship had sailed.

"Ezra's going soft on you. I see your face around here again? You won't be walking out next time," Ryder added.

Jeremy slipped off the table and staggered toward the side gate, though he paused to glare back over his shoulder. "I'm not finished with you, Paisley."

"I can assure you that you are." Caleb's warning was as sharp as a razor blade.

Jeremey lifted a finger just before he disappeared around the side of the house.

"Fucker is begging for it," Ezra rumbled.

"Yup," Ryder agreed.

While Caleb stood there trembling in my arms.

Fury shook him to the bone.

"Come with me," I whispered, and I took him by the hand and led him in through the back of the house, slipping down the hall until we were closed in the small bathroom.

He leaned against the countertop while I dug a washcloth from the cabinet and ran it under warm water.

Energy buzzed.

Intense.

Potent.

Taking his right hand, I dabbed the cloth to the open cuts across his knuckles.

"You don't need to take care of me," he grumbled. Shame tumbled out with the words.

I peeked up at him.

Icy eyes blazed at a million degrees.

"That's what you were doing out there, Caleb. Taking care of me. Standing up for me. How about you let me take care of you, too?"

I doubted he'd ever had anyone do it.

"Only thing I want to do. Take care of you. Take care of Evelyn."

"I know, but that's how this thing works. We take care of each other."

"This thing?"

"Yeah." Whatever it was. This thing that swirled through the enclosed space, this thing that kept knitting us closer.

"I keep warning you I'm not a good man."

I choked out on my disbelief. "You think I minded what you did back there?"

He stroked the pad of his thumb over the hollow beneath my eye. Ferocity lined his features. "I scared you."

"I wasn't scared. I just didn't want your cousin to have to arrest you." I tried to make it come out a joke, but it was too thick.

Saturated with everything he'd come to mean.

He blew out a sigh. "We should get Evelyn home."

"Yeah."

I tossed the cloth into the hamper.

We eased back down the hall and into the living room. The volume on the television was quiet, the lights dimmed, the kids starting to doze from their full, fun day.

The second she saw me, Dakota got off the couch and met me at the end of the hall. "Are you okay?"

"Yeah. Not sure Jeremy is, though."

I glanced back at Caleb who lingered a few feet behind me before I returned my attention to Dakota.

Her brows lifted. "So I heard."

"I'm sorry he came here and messed up Kayden's birthday."

"Don't you dare apologize. That was on him. Some guys don't know when to give it up, though I'm pretty sure he received the message loud and clear this evening."

"I would sure hope so," I said.

She gave me a tight hug then looked around me, eyeing Caleb. "I'm really glad you brought Evelyn. It was great to get to know her."

"Thanks for having us." His voice was still strained. Hard and coated with the residual violence.

"You're welcome any time."

He edged around us and moved into the living room where Evelyn was on a blanket on the floor next to Olivia. "Come on, sweetheart," he murmured as he lifted her into his arms.

She was already close to sleep. Sleepy when she wrapped her little arms around his neck. "Are you still mad?" she slurred.

He hugged her tight and muttered, "No, I'm not mad. Never at you."

He carried her out the door, and I followed, glancing back one more time at Dakota who gave me a knowing wave. "Be careful out there. Thank you for all your help this afternoon."

"Of course. What is it you say? Love is on the house?"

A soft smile pulled at her mouth. "Love is always on the house."

Then I followed Caleb out, across the front porch, and down the walkway.

I came up to their side, and from where she had her head rested on Caleb's shoulder, she gave me a sleepy smile.

"Are you tired, Evie-Love?"

"So tired, but sometimes tired is worth it."

"Now if that isn't some sage wisdom, I don't know what is. We have a smart one here," I whispered.

We.

Because that's what it felt like. I opened the rear driver's side door so Caleb could buckle Evelyn into her booster seat, and I shut it once she was secured.

For a moment, Caleb and I stood in the withering darkness that seeped over the earth. Shame radiating from his spirit, toiling with the rage he couldn't seem to let go.

"It's okay, Caleb," I promised him again.

Throat bobbing with his hard swallow, he gave me a tight nod, and I dipped my chin at him before I rounded the back of the SUV to the other side.

A gasp tore from the middle of me.

Horrified disbelief.

Caleb raced up behind me, instantly on guard. "What is it?"

He recoiled when he saw what had been painted in giant white letters on the passenger side door.

The word glaring in the moonlight.

SLUT.

My stomach fisted in disgust.

In hate.

Caleb spun around, searching the shadows, busted hands curling back into fists.

I knew exactly what he had on his mind.

"I will fucking destroy him, Paisley."

I grabbed him again, hugged him to me, and whispered at his back, "No. Stay right here. With me."

Chapter Thirty-Five

Caleb

I CARRIED EVELYN'S SLEEPING FORM UPSTAIRS THROUGH THE rippling silence of the house.

A house that whispered omens and morbid prophecies.

I tried to slough it off and not allow my mind to go there, but it was impossible.

The feeling like I'd once again been unable to stop someone I cared about from being hurt.

The uncontrolled spiral that threatened to suck me under.

Chaos that blustered through, banging at the walls and curling through my spirit.

I knew my volatility had a whole lot to do with receiving that letter after months of nothing.

When it felt as if I was no longer the hunter, but the hunted. The demon I'd chased enclosing with the promise to strike.

The two of them together made me feel like I would lose my mind.

I hugged Evelyn tighter as I hit the second-floor landing and moved left down the hall in the direction of her room. Paisley's presence covered us from behind.

I entered Evelyn's room, dragged down her covers, then settled her onto the bed. A contented moan slipped from her lips, and I thanked fuck she was completely unaware of the offenses that had occurred tonight.

I wanted to kill that bastard.

End him for having the audacity to hurt this woman who was the brightest, most brilliant thing. But that was the thing about having that kind of light in your life. When you lost it, you realized you'd do anything to hold it again.

He'd made the mistake of trying to get it back.

I'd wanted to hunt him down and show him how much I meant it.

Make him pay for it.

But it was the plea coming from Paisley's mouth that had staked me to the spot.

"No. Stay right here. With me." Her words had rang with more than that moment.

They'd rang with permanency.

Forever whispering from her lips.

So I'd turned and dragged my hand through the paint to smear the word into ambiguity instead of hunting the fucker down.

A promise of my own.

I watched then as Paisley went to Evelyn's dresser and took a nightgown from the top drawer, inhaled the peace of her aura as she returned and the two of us worked quickly and silently to remove the sundress Evelyn had worn.

Together we got her ready for bed.

Evelyn blinked her eyes open as I lifted her so Paisley could slip the nightgown over her head.

Pools of brown stared back.

An emotion I'd never seen in them before shone.

"There we go." I pulled her covers over her as she lay back on her pillow.

My chest tightened, and I found myself kneeling at her bedside, my fingers stroking through her hair.

Her tiny mouth twisted in comfort, her words that sweet slur when she said, "Today was really my favorite day in my whole life. Just like Ms. Dae is my favorite day, and you're my favorite day, too."

Her statement speared me to the spot.

I felt…

Staggered.

Shattered.

Unprepared for the rush of affection that surged, rushing through my veins and infiltrating all the places I didn't want it to go.

I leaned over her so I could press my lips to her temple.

"You're my favorite day, too," I whispered, terrified by its truth.

Standing, I turned to find Paisley in the middle of Evelyn's room with her hand pressed to her throat.

For a moment, we just stared at each other, held in this uncertainty.

Then she turned and slowly walked out into the hall.

I followed.

Drawn.

I pulled Evelyn's door partway closed, and I found Paisley facing me in the dim light of the hall.

Energy crackled.

Sparks of desperation.

Every-fucking-thing I could no longer ignore.

"Caleb." My name barely hit the air.

At the sound of it, I broke.

I crossed the space. No restraint left.

My hand dove into her hair at the side of her head, and I curled the other around her waist and tugged her against me.

We collided in a torrent of greed.

Mouths and tongues and spirits that no longer knew how to exist without the other.

We spun, gripping at each other, desperate to erase every inch of space.

Her back banged into the wall, and she arched into me as I kissed her.

Kissed her with a madness that burned me to the soul.

This girl who'd scored herself into the places I wasn't supposed to let her go.

But she was there, sinking her fingers into my shoulders and raking them down my chest. "I need you," she mumbled at my lips.

"I've never needed anything the way I need you," I admitted.

I forced myself to plant my hands on the wall over her head, pulling away a fraction, my breaths shallow as I stared down at the beauty that stared back. "I would lose it all for you, Paisley."

Her head shook. "This isn't about losing anything, Caleb. This is accepting a gift. This is about finding what was meant to be."

My chest tightened at her promise.

"No one will fucking touch you. No one but me."

The words were shards.

An oath.

I swept her off her feet and carried her into her room, kissing her as we went.

I laid her sideways in the middle of her bed.

She was covered in that sundress that had driven me out of my mind the entire day. White hair cascading around her delicate face, those lips parted and damp and her eyes doing those wicked sweet things that I'd always known would ruin me in the end.

"Do you hear me? No one will touch you but me."

"I hear you," she whispered.

"Do you have Evelyn's monitor?"

Nodding, she fumbled to pull her phone out of her dress pocket, and she set it on her nightstand. I moved back to the door where I clicked it shut and locked it.

The alarms were set around the perimeter of the house, no way for anyone to get in.

I strode back to her, my hand going to the side of her face and slipping into the soft locks of her hair. I tipped her head back.

"I need you, Paisley. I need to feel you. I need to know that you're whole and safe."

My voice was rough, harsh and pained and vibrating with the wrath. The wrath of the day and the wrath of what I knew was to come.

Because I could feel it trembling all around us.

Lawlessness.

Her fingers curled into my shirt. "You have me, Caleb. You have me."

Chapter Thirty-Six

Paisley

I GAZED UP AT CALEB WHILE HE STARED DOWN AT ME WITH A severity that I'd never seen in him before.

Icy eyes burned blue flames. So hot they seared me through.

I curled my fingers tighter into his shirt and tugged him closer, reiterating the promise. "You have me."

He did.

Wholly and completely, even though I doubted he understood the extent of it. What he'd come to mean.

His mouth crushed against mine. Demanding as he fisted a hand in my hair. Our lips pushed and pulled in a war to get closer.

His tongue delved inside, stroking in greed and necessity as he hovered over me in all that violent savagery.

Like he couldn't have this any other way, either.

Like he needed me as badly as I needed him.

My fingers tore through the buttons of his shirt. Frantic, I got them undone, and I shoved the fabric over his shoulders. He left me for a second to twist it free of his arms.

I gasped a little at the sight of his bare chest.

Awestruck at his masculine beauty.

I'd only seen it through the haze of the video that night. I wasn't prepared for the full impact of him.

Lust radiated from his ink-covered flesh, the designs rippling with the packed muscle that vibrated in power.

I couldn't do anything but kiss over the broken clock held frozen in time over the thunder that raged in his chest.

Wanting to hold whatever it meant.

A shiver went sailing through him. Hand tightening in my hair, he tugged my head back, forcing me to look at him. "Are you sure you want this?"

"I want you, Caleb. I want you more than I've ever wanted anything."

There was my heart, trying to climb out of my chest and into his hands. But it was already there. Beating fast and alive and fully for the first time.

And I wasn't afraid.

"Reckless Angel. I don't deserve you. I'm nothing but a thief sneaking into your room to steal the treasure that you are."

"Everyone deserves to be loved, Caleb."

His head shook, pain emblazoned in his eyes, unable to accept it.

But just because he didn't believe it didn't make it true, and I knew the only thing I could do was show him.

Show him what he meant.

"It's not stealing when it's offered to you."

In a flash, his mouth was back on mine. He dragged down the zipper of my dress, and his palms smoothed over the caps of my shoulders, pushing the fabric down.

I eased back so he could tug it over my hips and down my legs.

Cool air hit my bare flesh.

I was only wearing underwear, and my chest heaved, matching time with his.

For a moment, the two of us were held in this gravity.

Spirits spinning around the other.

Desperate to mesh.

He tugged each of my heels off, dropped them to the floor with a thunk, then reached out and peeled my underwear down my legs.

He stepped back and toed out of his shoes, unfastened his pants and shoved them off.

A fire lit, so bright, so hot, I thought I might pass out.

He climbed over me.

So powerful.

So intent.

His cock heavy and hard where it bounced between us, pressing at my belly that trembled in want.

Shockwaves of desire pounded through the air.

A roar of that recklessness he kept accusing me of.

I took him by both sides of the neck, emphatic words pitching from my mouth. "All of it, Caleb. I'm offering all of it to you."

"I should refuse it, but I don't know how," he rasped at my mouth before he dove in for another kiss.

All the things he didn't know how to say or even believe were true gushed out with it, pouring into me.

"I need you," I mumbled through the kiss, my fingers raking down the hardened planes of his back.

"I want to possess you, Paisley. Fuck you. Mark you. Ruin you," he warned as he let his mouth travel along the length of my jaw.

"I'm already ruined for you, Caleb. Take my body, too."

Need rumbled in his throat, and he kissed a path down the column of my neck, his mouth opening as a rough pant escaped.

Fighting to keep the control I could feel fraying inside him.

"Don't be gentle with me."

"I don't ever want to hurt you," he murmured.

I dragged my fingernails up his back. "You won't."

I prayed I was right. That I could find him in the middle of his storm, meet him there, and that one day, we would walk out of it together. He edged back off the bed. He stared down at me, a conflict of emotions flashing through his being.

Lust and want and fear and regret.

Those eyes caressed over me.

The man looked at me like I might be a priceless painting hanging on his wall.

A treasure.

Something to be adored.

But it was the sight of him bare and hungry for me that sent chills crashing across my flesh.

A naked, fallen angel where he stood at the edge of the bed.

Darkness dripped from his aura, and all that intimidation glowed beneath his skin. He thought I was the angel. But didn't he know he was the savior Evelyn had needed? One I had needed, too? Because after Jeremy, I wasn't sure I'd ever fully give myself to a man again. That I'd ever really let myself go.

Let myself fall or trust or love.

"Look at you, spread out for me. Most gorgeous woman I've ever seen, Paisley Dae. Dripping sex and sweetness and spinning my world into chaos."

It came out coarse, scraping the air with the lust that addled the atmosphere.

My hips jerked off the bed, begging for him.

He reached out and dragged his fingertips between my trembling thighs.

His jaw clenched in that way that I now recognized was barely-hinged restraint.

"You're soaked, sweet girl. Soaked for me. What I'm going to do to you."

"Caleb, please. I need you," I whimpered.

He slowly nudged two big fingers into my center.

A moan got free, and my legs parted farther as I arched from the bed. Tiny pinpricks of pleasure lit up behind my eyes. "Yes. Please, Caleb."

"Do you have a condom? Since you're the girl who doesn't like to come unprepared?"

His head cocked at that, the teasing threat slipping from his wicked tongue.

A throaty laugh got loose. Why did I love that he remembered the taunt of that first night?

"Bottom drawer under my book."

He opened that drawer of the nightstand and rummaged around inside. What sounded like a growl rumbled in his chest. "Little Riot. What I'm going to do to you."

He'd definitely found my toy stuffed in there, too.

Slamming the door shut, he straightened to his full, imposing height.

The man a glorious shadow that moved back to the edge of the bed.

I burned as I watched him ripping open the condom, burned beneath the weight of his stare as he rolled it over himself.

Urgency was carved into every harsh angle of his unforgettable face.

That unfathomable energy.

Electric sparks.

Shockwaves that blistered through the air.

I wanted him. In every way.

He climbed onto the bed and wound himself between my shaking thighs. He came all the way up until his hands were planted on either side of my head, and he leaned down, mouth a hairsbreadth away.

"I'm taking you, Paisley Dae, and I won't fucking let anyone else have you. Do you understand?"

I tipped my chin up to him. "Don't you know I already belong to you?"

Possession flashed through his gaze, and he clutched me by the back of the neck and edged away enough so he could guide himself to my center.

For one second, he stared at me, his promise so stark in the fiery ice of his eyes.

Then he had me in one single stroke.

So deep and overwhelming.

My mouth dropped open on a cry, and my hips jerked off the bed, nails raking over the bowing muscles of his back.

"Fuck," he rasped.

The pleasure of him filling me was close to pain.

Perfectly devastating.

"I told you I would ruin you, Little Riot. How perfect you are around my cock."

His palm slipped all the way down my side until he had me by the inside of the knee, and he was pushing me wide.

He pulled out then drove back in.

If it was possible, deeper that time.

Stealing my breath.

My sanity.

My mind.

I gasped around the feel of him. "Caleb."

He pulled me closer. Chest to chest. Our breaths mingled and our spirits danced.

He took me in deep, powerful strokes. "You are perfect, Paisley. Nothing has ever come close to the feel of you."

I lifted my hips to meet him thrust for thrust.

Our lips brushed and our tongues caressed.

Soft.

Hard.

Everything in between.

Pleasure sparked and grew, glowing at the edges of my sight.

Gathering strength.

Caleb pushed my leg up higher as he began to pound into me.

Faster. Deeper. Owning me.

Possessing me.

Taking me to a place I hadn't known existed until he'd touched me.

Ruining me like he'd promised.

Lights shimmered and danced.

He slipped his hand between us and began to play with my clit.

His fingers stroked.

And that bliss pooled in my belly, bright and blinding as it built. "Caleb."

"I have you, Paisley. Let go."

And that buzzy energy I'd felt from the beginning took new shape. Rose from the depths.

It became a roar.

A roar in my spirit and soul.

A roar that erupted as an orgasm split me apart.

Bliss sped through my body.

Ecstasy carved deep.

Speeding and spreading. Touching every recess. Every cell. Every hidden place.

My nails tore at his back as the pleasure seared me through.

Caleb jerked and spasmed, and he buried a growl in my neck when he came.

He bowed and shook and clung to me as the pleasure rocked his foundation.

I could feel it.

The way everything shifted.

The cracks lining up to match.

He curled an arm around the top of my head, his lips against mine as he panted. "Reckless Angel...what did I do to get to have you right here, with me?"

"Stay with me?" I whispered at his ear as I ran my hand through the dark blond locks of his hair at the back of his head, holding onto him the way he was hanging onto me.

"Where would I go?"

Chapter Thirty-Seven

Caleb

DARKNESS CURLED THROUGH HER ROOM. VAPORS AND shadows. The night deep and so utterly quiet that I could almost reach out and run my fingers through the dense stillness.

Peace and a contentment I'd never known before blustered through it, lulling me into the sanctuary of this woman's arms that were still wrapped around me. Two of us clinging to each other, our hearts beating in sync.

Still, the tranquility was marred by the gloom that covered the house in a foreshadowing.

A coloring of evil that I could feel crawling across my flesh. Unease burned through me as I thought of what she'd come to mean. How I knew I would fight for her just as furiously as I would Evelyn.

Nerves rattled as that emotion fought to break free. The one only she had evoked.

I pressed a kiss to the side of her head. "I'll be right back."

I unwound myself from her and moved into the bathroom. I flicked on the light, ridded myself of the condom, then wet a washcloth under the sink, coming to stand at the doorway and looking at her on the bed.

She'd shifted, pulling down the covers and slipping underneath. She held the comforter to her chest and was gnawing at her bottom lip as she stared back at me.

Hair a wild halo of white around her.

Reckless Angel.

My chest tightened as I edged the rest of the way back to her, and I tugged the covers down, revealing every fucking gorgeous inch of her body.

She wheezed a sigh, and I pressed the warm cloth to her cunt. "Don't know what I'm supposed to do now that I've experienced this perfect pussy, Paisley Dae."

It was true.

She was fucking perfect.

Perfect for me. Everything I would be a selfish bastard to try to keep.

The hint of a smile played at the edge of her mouth. "I think the answer to that is clear, Mr. Greyson." Her voice had gone flirty, drawing my last name out like a tease, and a low moan rolled from her as I cleaned her with the cloth. "You experience it again and again."

A groan vibrated my chest, and I tossed the washcloth to the ground before I eased closer so I was on my knees hovering over her, her mouth an inch away. "You should be worried how often I might take you up on that."

"Do I look worried to you?"

"You should be." The warning came out, and the easiness drained from her, seriousness taking its place.

"Do I hate what you've gone through, Caleb? What Evelyn's gone through? Do I worry for you because there is some sicko out there who wants to hurt you? Of course. But that doesn't mean I'm not willing to stand by your side. Just like you came to mine tonight when my ghosts showed up."

"You need to understand the graveness of what I'm talking about, Paisley. He comes after the people I care about." The true terror of what I felt ground between my teeth, and I couldn't do anything but fist a hand in her hair, tipping her head back, trying to get her to grasp what was at stake.

Her head shook, and she reached out, clamped me around the back of the neck and dragged me closer to her, her lips whispering over mine. "We're in this together."

Rage curdled beneath the surface of my skin at the thought of something happening to her. Of my putting her in danger. It was at odds with the need to keep her close.

"Lay with me," she urged, and she lifted the covers. I looked at the spot she'd carved out for me. An asshole for taking it, but I climbed down at her side, propped myself against the pillow, and pulled her into my arms.

She rested her head against my chest, and she played her fingertips over my pecs. Mossy eyes glinted in the bare light as she looked up at me.

The picture ripped the oxygen from my lungs. The woman the thief of my breath.

Her fingertips tapped a quiet song over the thunder that raged in my heart, over the clock imprinted on my chest. "What is this?"

A knot grew tight in my throat.

Reservations spun through me, telling me to get up and go. I wasn't supposed to be here. I didn't have the right.

Instead, I pressed my lips to the top of her head, inhaling her goodness, like it might assuage some of the pain that would forever hold me prisoner. "It's the moment my heart fully died. The moment it ceased to beat. The minute I discovered my sister's body in the alley of our building."

Horror ripped from her lungs.

I breathed out a shattered sigh, both tormented and relieved at saying it aloud.

Paisley tightened her arms around me as I confessed the harsh words at the crown of her head. "I found her, Paisley. I found her. I couldn't stop it from happening. Couldn't stop her from being hurt. Because of me. Because of the things I did. So, I marked myself with the time when I'd found her so I would remember each time I looked in the mirror what I'd done. What I'd caused. I'd destroyed the one person I've ever allowed myself to love."

Each word became more haggard than the last.

Paisley shifted and pressed her lips to the scar I'd imprinted on my flesh. A scar that was imprinted on my soul. "I'm so sorry you lost her, Caleb. I am so sorry. But I know you are so much more than that moment."

My arm curled around her head as she kept kissing her belief into my skin. Like she could erase what it meant.

"You keep trying to find the things that aren't there."

"But they are, Caleb. You've just lost sight of them. Or maybe you'd never seen them before. Never believed yourself more than who you'd allowed yourself to become. Or maybe he's brand new. But he's here, right now."

God, she was perfect. Too good. Chaos that had come from out of nowhere, a disturbance that was nothing but a balm.

I urged her up to look at me, my thumb stroking over the apple of her cheek.

Her eyes were wide and trusting.

Lips pouty and trembling with her faith.

"Reckless Angel, shining your light into my life. You deserve so much more than the scraps left of me, and I'm the asshole who took you, anyway."

"But you're my favorite asshole." Somehow, she teased it in the middle of the disaster I'd created, and a chuckle rumbled as I pulled her back down to me.

"Do you expect anything less of me?"

"Never." I felt her smile against the skin of my chest. "I've come to like him quite a lot."

"I'm sorry for losing control today," I whispered low, my fingers playing over the soft expanse of her back.

Fury simmered in the depths at that bastard I wanted to end.

Her head shook where she was plastered against me. "He came looking for trouble, Caleb. Jeremy thinks he's God's gift. It's no surprise that after all these months he thought I would still drop to my knees at the sight of him. He likes to take what he wants and doesn't like it when someone tells him no. He never should have come here in the first place, but he crossed a line today, and he suffered the consequences."

"I want to hurt him, Paisley."

She quirked a wry smile my direction. "I think you already took care of that."

"And he was the fool to push it farther with what he painted on my car."

"He's an idiot. A spoiled brat throwing a fit. He's not worth it."

"Did you love him?" The thought of it made me irrationally angry.

She hesitated, lost in thought, before she softly answered, "Yeah, I did. I should have known when he put his dreams in front of mine that he wasn't worthy of that love, but I know that now."

I brushed my fingers through the silken locks of her hair. "What happened?"

Hopeful sadness washed across her face, and she cleared the roughness from her voice. "You know how much I love horses?"

Softness swelled, and I kept brushing my fingers through her hair as she looked at me through the shadows. "Yeah."

She pressed her lips together for a moment, the smallest amount of shyness taking hold. "I always knew they were my passion. Where I belonged. From when I was just a little girl, about Evelyn's age. My uncle had horses, and I was obsessed from the first time my grandparents took me there one Sunday afternoon. I'll never forget it, the way something in me felt complete for the first time."

Air huffed from her nose. "I started riding then, learning everything I could about them. When I was ten, I started doing the rodeo thing. Barrel racing. My grandparents would drive me around to all the towns, supporting me, believing in me."

Wistfulness edged her mouth. "My grandpa always said horses were in my blood. But as I got older, it was training them that really got me. Taking a horse that was scared and unsure, an owner that was scared and unsure, and bringing them together. Teaching them how to trust each other. But it's more than that..."

Her head dropped as if she were embarrassed.

I tipped up her chin, needing to know.

"It's love, you know?" she said with a small shrug punched with emotion. "Being with a horse that way. It's seeing the beauty of creation. The ability for two species to come together, a human and a horse, and share a bond that is so strong. I love being a part of that. When I was twenty, I started saving. Scraping together every penny to buy a little plot of land. Five acres. Five acres where I was going to make my dreams come true. And I did. Time River Equestrian Center. I was so proud of what I'd built there, thankful for the people who started to bring their horses to me."

"What happened to it?"

She let go of a hollow laugh. "I'd finally built it up a bit, but it was the land that had become most valuable. I'd been dating Jeremy for a couple years, and he convinced me to sell it and invest the money into a restaurant he wanted to open in Arizona. He'd made it out like he couldn't live without me, like he needed me with him, and there were plenty of horses there that needed help. He'd promised to help me start over there."

Regret shook her head. "I should have known he wasn't sincere if his dreams were more important than mine. But I'd done it, anyway, and it was the biggest mistake of my life. He took that money and used it up and expected me to be working at his restaurant night and day. Worst part of it was I'd missed being here for when my grandma got sick. She'd had a stroke, and I didn't make it back in time. But while I was here for her funeral, trying to be here for my grandpa, he cheated on me. One of the servers who I'd become friends with had let me know, texted me proof, not that I needed it because by then, I'd already realized just how selfish Jeremy was."

She gave another tiny shrug. "So, I stayed here, where I belong."

Rage pulsed deep, and my fingers dug deeper into her hip to keep myself from flying from this bed and going after him.

As if what he'd pulled today wasn't enough.

"I can't fucking believe a single man could be so stupid."

Giving up a girl like this. Treating her like she wasn't the most important thing in his world.

Fucker should have worshiped the ground she walked on.

The angel that she was.

"It was a lesson learned, Caleb. A hard lesson I won't repeat." Redness pinked her cheeks, and shadows danced over her face as she peered up at me. "Don't worry. All's not lost. I'm going to rebuild it. I knew the second I crested that hill and saw your ranch sitting below in the valley beneath me that dream wasn't over for me. I was going to chase it. And I'm going to get it back."

I traced my fingertips along the curve of her side, riding up over her hip, wanting to sink back inside. "You belong with horses. With people like Evelyn who need them."

Her nod was tight, affection so fierce I felt it drive deep into my spirit. "With people like Evelyn."

She hesitated for a moment, her throat locked, before the confession wheezed from her. "I love her so much."

Grief constricted. "And she loves you, too."

Tears welled in her eyes, and Paisley shifted to straddle me. So fucking gorgeous. Hair all around. Tits large and pert and round. Stomach quivering. Pussy bare. But she was so much more than that.

This chaos that battered at the walls inside me, fracturing and cracking and seeking a way through.

"I need you to know you deserve to be loved, too." Her nails dragged over the clock that sat over my heart.

"Reckless Angel," I murmured because I couldn't respond. Couldn't give her what she wanted, what she needed, even when the foolish side wanted to give it to her anyway.

"Reckless for you."

She pushed up onto her knees, took my dick in her hand. I was instantly hard, and she guided me to her throbbing heat. She whimpered as she sank down, her pussy wrapping me tight.

And Paisley Dae rode me.

Rode me into chaos.

Into carelessness.

Into this abandon I couldn't keep from falling into.

Chapter Thirty-Eight

Caleb

Five Years Ago

"**Y**OU'RE DONE." CALEB STARED DOWN DONOVAN Paltrow who sat on the opposite side of his desk. The man was slung back in the chair, an ankle hooked on his opposite knee, smirking back at Caleb like he had forgotten his place.

Obviously, he had.

Donovan chuckled like Caleb was ridiculous, roughing a hand over the top of his black hair. "I'm not sure what you mean, Mr. Greyson."

He almost sneered it, as if the fucker thought when Caleb's father died, he would be the one sitting in this seat.

"I said you're done. You no longer *work* for Greyson Industries."

As if that could be what it was considered.

Incredulous, Donovan scoffed. "You're *firing* me? And for what reason would that be?"

Disdain wrapped around the disgrace, tendrils that constricted, Caleb's conscience on fire. He knew what he deserved. The penalty. It wasn't as if he were any more innocent than the disgusting man sitting across from him.

But Frank Aston's blood should never have been on his hands.

"Did I give you an order to *handle* Frank Aston?"

Donovan rocked back in the chair with a grin sliding up the edge of his too-thin face. "Got a tip he was headed for the police, so I simply headed him off."

"You didn't have authorization to do that."

"I made the choice I had to make. You should be thanking me for saving your ass."

"Thank you? You killed an innocent man."

Derision puffed from Donovan's nose, a scoff of a laugh riding in behind it. "Who knew you were such a pussy, Greyson?" He sat forward. Aggression riddled the dark amusement that played through his features. "It seems your father picked the wrong man to lead this company. You know you can't do this without me."

"I'm absolutely doing it without you. Now get out of my office."

Donovan shot to his feet. "What, you think you can just toss me aside after everything I have done for your father's company?"

"It's my company now."

And he was making a change.

The atrocities wouldn't be committed any longer.

Caleb was fucking sick of it. What they stood for.

He was richer than God. As if he needed to add another dime to his fortune.

Donovan planted his hands on his desk, snarling, "I think you've forgotten who you're talking to."

"Oh, I'm fully aware." Caleb strode around his desk, malevolence riding out in front of him as he leaned in close to Donovan. "I think it's you who doesn't know who you're dealing with. Now get the fuck out of my office."

Air puffed from Donovan's nose, and he stood his ground for a moment before he turned and moved to the door. Only he paused with his hand on the handle and looked back. "I guess you've left me no choice but to take this matter up with your little sister."

Caleb sat in his car on the opposite side of the street in front of Kimberly's house. Darkness covered him, the rain a steady drizzle that fell from overhead.

He watched out the passenger window at the renovated Victorian hidden in the thick foliage and trees. Lights burned from the windows, and he could feel his sister's warmth spilling out.

He'd been there every night for the last two weeks, waiting for the man who had made the mistake of threatening his sister.

Or maybe he just wanted to catch a glimpse of her since she'd written him from her life.

He didn't blame her. It was better this way. His world was sordid and ugly. He didn't want her a part of it. But maybe someday things would be different. Maybe he could rectify enough of this disgusting mess that he could be good enough to be a part of her life again. That the depravity of it wouldn't bring danger to her door.

Caleb's chest tightened as she came up to the long-paned window and stared out through the drizzle.

Sorrow poured from her spirit and battered into him.

One day, maybe he would be better.

She moved deeper into the house, and he blew out a sigh. He went to push the button to start his car.

Only he froze when he saw the shadow creep through the night at the edge of her house.

He didn't even have to think it through. He stepped from his car and strode through the rain.

"You piece of shit. You don't actually think you're going to get away with this?" Donovan sneered where he was on his knees in the deserted dock by the harbor, spittle flying from his mouth as he thrashed, hands bound behind his back, his feet weighted with industrial blocks.

Caleb's building loomed from behind them, ominous and powerful and sleek.

But he wasn't that man right then.

Caleb put the gun to the back of Donovan's head, and he felt zero remorse when he pulled the trigger and kicked him over the side.

Because he had one purpose.

To protect his sister from the depravity brought on by the Greyson name.

And he would gladly suffer any consequence to end that threat.

Chapter Thirty-Nine

Caleb

I AWOKE WITH HER IN MY ARMS, MUTED RAYS OF MORNING LIGHT streaming in to illuminate her face.

She slept curled up at my side, this precious gift I would never deserve.

Guilt closed off my throat, and I reached out and brushed the pad of my thumb over her cheek.

And I knew, if I had the ability to love today, it would be her.

Chapter Forty

Paisley

I STOOD AT THE ISLAND WITH EVELYN AT MY SIDE. SHE WAS ON a stool, carefully placing our lunch into the small cooler pack we used when we took long rides.

"Can we go the farthest we've ever even been today?" she asked.

I handed her the slices of apples I'd cut so she could place the baggie inside.

"The farthest ever? Are you sure you're not pooped after all the fun you had yesterday?"

God knew I was pooped. Exhausted in the best of ways. Deliciously sore.

But it was my heart that had been stretched and transformed and reconfigured.

"Pooped?" Evelyn drew out in confusion.

A soft chuckle got free. I loved how she took everything so literally. I pressed a kiss to the top of her head then ran my fingers down her hair. "I just thought you might be tired from playing so hard yesterday, is what I meant."

"I'm not even tired a little bit. I slept the whole night because I fell asleep in the car, and you and my uncle took really good care of me."

My chest expanded, a wash of love, then my emotions were flailing when I felt Caleb enter the kitchen.

His presence potent.

Distinct.

A gravity that had drawn us together from the ends of the earth.

Nerves prodded at my consciousness. I had no idea what things were going to be like in the light of day.

I peeked his way, teeth roughing at my bottom lip at the sight.

The man an imposing force that could annihilate me.

Drop me to my knees.

But this morning those icy eyes were soft, lingering long as he moved deeper into the kitchen, his fingertips gliding over the small of my back as he passed.

"Good morning," he murmured.

"It is a fine morning, isn't it?"

"A very fine morning," Evelyn peeped up.

I bit down on my lip like it might contain the rush of everything I'd never thought I'd possess. Because I wanted to hold it forever. Cherish it.

This beautiful gift.

Caleb went to the coffee pot and filled a mug. "What are you two up to today?"

"We are going to take Mazzy on a super really long ride, the farthest we've ever been. We're packing a lunch. See?"

Tenderness filled his features as he turned to look at her. "I see that."

"You wanna come?"

I saw the reservation flash through his eyes. Something close to revulsion. I laughed. "I think we already established riding horses is not his thing, but he's super happy that you and I love it so much, isn't he?"

I looked at him when I said it.

A low chuckle roughed up his throat, a tease rolling through his demeanor. "Super happy."

My heart went giddy.

"All right, I think we're all set, Evie-Love."

"Let's do this!" She turned and jumped off the step stool, giving me a high-five as she went. Her little boots hit the floor with a thud.

"Be careful out there." His features turned to stone when he said it.

"Of course," I promised.

I stood there with Evelyn's hand in mine, wanting to go to him.

Kiss his rigid, beautiful face and tell him I would guard her with my life.

But I think he already knew it with the way the hardness eased free. The way his shoulders dropped and his lips parted on a soft breath.

Yep. I was done for. Nowhere else to fall because I was already at the bottom. Floating in his dark, dark waters. Never a chance to come up for air.

"We'll see you later," I said, forcing myself to move before I stood there a love-struck fool gaping at him all day.

"Bye!" Evelyn sang, trotting along beside me as we moved out the door.

Sunshine rained from the bluest sky, and we started down the path toward the barn.

"I think it's going to be the bestest day in ever, don't you think? Because I got the best horse Mazzy, and she loves me so much, and I got seven new friends and three new cousins."

She held up the five fingers of her free hand.

My spirit pulsed. Too full. Too perfect. And I was sure in that moment the amount of love I had for her might strangle me. "That's right, you have so many friends and so much family who care about you."

"Family and friends are really important."

I clung tighter to her hand. "That's right, they are, Evie-Love."

We went into Mazzy's stall, and I saddled her with Evelyn's help, then led her out to the exterior stall that we always used. I tied her lead rope to the middle rung and packed the saddle bags with our lunch and supplies.

Only when I turned around, Evelyn wasn't there.

My heart climbed to my throat. "Evelyn?"

"I'm right over here," she shouted back.

292 | A.L. JACKSON

The worry eased off when I saw she'd wandered over to a patch of wildflowers, bent over picking a handful of them. Then it regathered when I realized where she'd ended up.

Close to the pen where a brand-new colt was being kept. He'd arrived two days ago.

His coat a glossy brown, as gorgeous as could be but as wild as ever.

"Evelyn," I called, "you need to stay away from that pen over there. That colt isn't broken yet."

She straightened at my voice. "It's okay, I know to stay away from the fences because those horses are so big and fast and I'm not even old enough to ride one yet."

The colt whinnied and kicked, agitated by her presence.

She started to trot my way, grinning as she skipped, her hand held out in front of her with the bouquet of purple wildflowers she had picked. "I'm coming, and I got you a pretty present!"

"They're so pretty," I told her. Still, agitation had me shifting on my feet. "Hurry, sweetheart, we need to get a move on."

Behind her, the colt banged against the gate.

It busted open.

Horror streaked down my spine.

Ice cold.

My stomach spilling onto the ground.

The colt came bolting out, kicking and bucking.

"Evelyn." It was a prayer from my soul.

I sprinted her way, my boots pounding as my heart pounded out of my chest.

I dove for her, pushing her out of the path of the horse a second before it would have run her over.

I toppled to the ground where she'd been standing.

She was safe. She was safe.

That was right before the colt trampled over the top of me.

Chapter Forty-One

Paisley

"WOULD YOU STOP FRETTING OVER ME? I TOLD YOU that I'm fine. I'm not even hurt."

Caleb scowled that look that promised he would, in fact, not stop fretting. Since he'd been doing it the entire day, I shouldn't have been surprised.

He was angled where he sat on the side of my bed, one knee drawn up and his other foot planted on the floor so he could get close to me. Fingertips traced down the edge of my face where I was propped against the headboard supported by what had to be every pillow in the house. "Don't ask me to stop worrying about you, Paisley, not when taking care of you has become my reason. The way taking care of Evelyn has become yours."

My heart fluttered. God, I had not expected this man. This completely unexpected, intense, hard, broken, beautiful man.

Caleb had *insisted* on taking me to the emergency room where I'd spent half the day being examined, getting a battery of tests that he had also *insisted* upon.

The entire time he'd trembled. Shaken in this possession that had wrapped around me like a perilous embrace.

Everything was negative, the way I'd said it was going to be. My side was just a little sore from where the hoof had struck me. I had no cracked ribs and the MRI had cleared me of a concussion.

"Thank you for protecting her today," he murmured.

Reaching up, I covered his hand he had set on my cheek. "I would protect her with my life, Caleb."

Tenderness and fear traipsed through his features, that strong jaw clenching in the bid for control he always fought for. "You did. You risked it all for her."

"Just like you would do."

"Yes, just like I would do. The same as I would do for you." His voice was gruff, filled with all that severity that bounded around me in a fiery warmth that flooded me to the depths.

"Are you trying to wreck me, Caleb Greyson?" I fought for lightness. For a tease. So hard when my chest felt like it was going to explode with the pressure of the love it contained.

"I warned you that I would." His words were all rough and rumbly.

"I never thought the ruining would be quite like this." Mine quivered with the weight of what I felt.

And God, I wanted to tell him. Lay it all out. But I could still see the terror roiling in the frozen sea of those eyes.

"I can't believe that horse got out. When I find out who was so careless…" He trailed off, his hand tremoring at my cheek.

"I know, Caleb. It was reckless. Dangerous. But unfortunately mistakes like that happen."

"Not at the cost of Evelyn. Not at the cost of you."

"I'm right here." I tried to sit up so I could fully face him.

He pressed his big palm over my chest to stop me. "You need to rest."

"And you need to quit fretting over me. I am fine." I gathered his hand and brought it to my lips. "I'm fine. I promise. I'm not hurting a bit. And I really need to stretch since you've forced me to lay around in this bed all day."

"Half the day," he corrected.

Light laughter got free, and I nudged him back. "Yeah, because during the other half, you were forcing me to get poked and prodded."

Reluctantly, he stood, then he stretched out his hand to help me onto my feet.

Truthfully, I wasn't in much pain at all. The spot where I'd been stepped on was a little tender, but when considering how bad it could have been, I felt like I'd come out of it unscathed.

And Evelyn was safe. It was the only thing that mattered.

Caleb watched me carefully. Like I might all of a sudden crumble. Like he might have to pick me up and piece me back together.

I knew that he would.

That he'd hold me and protect me and care for me.

"See." I raised my arms over my head and turned in a small circle. "As good as new."

He growled a deep sound. It rattled against my walls with devotion and need.

I wore an oversized tee, the hem landing at mid-thigh. So maybe I knew him seeing that would send his restraint crumbling a bit.

Because what I didn't want right then was restraint.

I just wanted him.

Caleb smoothed his palms down the outside of my thighs, angling in to bring us chest to chest. He groaned a greedy sound like he couldn't help himself and felt bad for it.

Ridiculous since he was right where I wanted him.

Because beneath the warmth of his hands, chills skated across my flesh. A tumble of my own greed lighting in my center.

I played my fingers along the collar of his shirt, my face tipped up to the harsh cut of his. "See, this body is right as rain."

"This body is more than right, Paisley." Those palms went to exploring, riding up my hips and gliding over my bottom, careful as he took a handful of each cheek. "This body is everything. Everything I want to protect. Everything I want to possess. Everything I need."

"It's yours." It was a breath, and he inhaled as he began to slowly sway us in my room.

Night all around, the sounds of the ranch beyond the window whispering at the glass. The play of the branches where the breeze bustled through the leaves of the trees, the bugs humming their night song, peace wrapping the house in a blanket of comfort.

Evelyn was sleeping in the room next to us.

Safe.

Whole.

And Caleb was holding me close.

And I knew that I didn't want to be anywhere else than right here with this man in that moment.

Right here with this man I'd come to love.

Right here next to the little girl who'd stolen my heart.

Every part of me belonged to them both.

Caleb swayed me in a slow dance, the rhythm our own time, the drone of the stilled night our tempo.

And I gazed up at him while he stared down at me, tenderness thawing the ice of his eyes.

He ran the back of his hand up my jaw before he shifted his hand and weaved his fingers through my hair. Softly. His hand tangled in the locks before he cupped the side of my head. "I need to ask you something, Paisley."

"Anything."

He brushed the pad of his thumb along my temple, and his hand began to shake.

"What is it?" I almost begged it, caught in the swell of his uncertainty.

"If something happens to me, I want you to take Evelyn."

My heart raced, and I curled my fingers in his shirt. "What do you mean?"

Sorrow glanced through his expression before ferocity rushed in to take its place. "I told you before that I would do whatever it took to put that monster in the ground. I don't know what's coming. What the cost is going to be. But I have to return to Seattle soon. Find him. End this. And if something happens to me, I want you to take Evelyn. Raise her. Love her the way you do."

My God. He was asking me to stand for her like a mother. Love her and cherish her and adore her forever. I also understood what he was implying. Where his true fears lie. A fear I couldn't handle. One I couldn't imagine.

"Of course, Caleb. Of course." My fingers curled tighter as the thought of losing him wrapped me in shackles of dread. "But nothing is going to happen to you. I won't let it."

Denial of what I said fueled his words. "I've done terrible things, Paisley. Things that have earned me pain and grief."

"Let me hold those mistakes, too."

He pushed on like he couldn't accept what I'd offered, grating the plea, his biggest fears and highest hopes and most profound purpose placed on a platter for me. Trusting me with it. "Promise me, Paisley, if something happens, you will be there for her. There is no one who will love her the way you do."

Agony crested with the affection. "I promise."

He swallowed hard, his thick throat bobbing around the relief. "I'll call my attorney tomorrow to get the paperwork drawn up."

"Okay."

His nod was slight. "You're a miracle, Paisley. A chaotic, reckless miracle that Evelyn needed."

Didn't he get it? I needed this miracle, too, the same as he needed it.

The three of us tossed together by a tragedy neither of them should have had to endure. But that tragedy had brought us here anyway.

Each of us clinging to the other because we'd found what we'd needed.

What we'd been missing.

He kept swaying me slow as I began to work through the buttons of his shirt, unable to look away from the stony strength of his features as I did. Understanding and wanting him in a way that I'd never thought I would.

Wholly.

Permanently.

Desperately.

He pressed a big hand over both of mine to try to stop me. "What do you think you're doing?"

"What does it look like? Undressing you." I whispered it like seduction. I was going to have to play dirty to get this bad boy to give.

That steely jaw clenched. My stomach lit in a bout of giddiness, knowing how ferociously he wanted me, how ferociously he wanted to protect me at the same time. "Not going to happen."

"Oh, it's going to happen, Mr. Greyson. I'm not injured, so you can go ahead and stop treating me like glass. And after you promised to *ruin* me." I pushed up on my toes and murmured the last at his ear.

His arm tightened around my waist, and he pulled me against him on a groan, his body arching around mine like he might fully consume me.

Draw me in, suck me under, never let me go.

"It's you who's ruining me." Hot hands splayed out over my back. The man all around.

Arousal throbbed.

"Well, I guess we're a good team then, aren't we?" I unraveled myself from his arms and stepped back, peeling the tee over my head as I went.

I tossed it to the floor, standing in front of him bare except for my underwear.

Electricity sparked in the air.

Gluttony and greed lighting in his icy eyes as he took me in.

"Angel with a devil's streak." It was a grumble of praise.

A giggle slipped up my throat, and I swore I had to be half delirious, the way dizziness rushed through my head and sloshed through my body.

So light and heavy and perfect in his eyes.

"Mmhmm," I purred as I peeled myself out of my panties and twisted them from my ankles, leaving myself completely nude. "Take me like you mean it. I expect you to do your best, Mr. Greyson."

Chapter Forty-Two

Caleb

"O N THE BED, Ms. Dae," I ORDERED, FUCKING SHAKING from the need she'd lit.

A frenzy.

A fire so hot I couldn't resist.

A fire that promised we both were going to get burned. But I would stand in the flames with her.

She giggled like the little seductress she was, this woman who could strip me of every reserve, shred me of all restraint. She slipped back onto the bed, lying angled in the middle of it toward me.

Her knees swayed back and forth like she was trying to hypnotize me.

Entrance me.

Giving me glimpses of the sweet spot between her thighs. "Your cunt is perfect, Paisley. Perfect. I could fuck you forever." It came out rough, as desperate as I felt.

"It's yours, Caleb. And you should make good on that, don't you think?"

Need spun me so tight, this woman who took it all like she couldn't live without the disaster I had to offer.

At the side of her bed, I began to slowly undress. "You're sure you aren't hurting?"

"The only ache I have is the one only you can fill." She purred it as I shoved out of my pants, standing before her, my cock hard, every muscle in my body coiled in desire. She was leaned back on her elbows, and I climbed over her, hovering high, taking that sweet mouth that sang with ecstasy. Her tongue that danced with rhapsody.

Holding my weight up by one hand, I took her by the back of the head with the other so I could control the kiss.

Demanding it of her which was unnecessary since she seemed set on relinquishing everything to me.

This treasure in my hands.

I pushed two fingers into her molten pussy. Paisley's mouth parted in the middle of our kiss, desperation taking her over as she curled an arm around my neck and began to rise up to meet my hand. "Caleb, yes. Harder. I need you to mark me. Show me I'm yours."

Fuck, she was such a fiery thing.

Strong and wild and good.

I broke the kiss and pushed off the side of the bed.

A whine climbed from her throat.

A hard chuckle rolled free. "What, you think I'm not going to take care of you?"

"You'd better," she rasped.

"I'll always take care of my girl." It was out before I could stop the claim. What she'd come to mean.

Possession wound me tight, chest stretching in a bid of too many things as I gazed down at her chaos on the center of the bed. Propped on her elbows, her tits pebbled and peaked, all that hair raining down around her like a dream.

Body shuddering in want.

Everything I'd come to need.

"On your hands and knees," I told her.

Without delay, she scrambled onto all fours facing away, her delicious ass in the air. She looked back at me from over her shoulder with this expression that pierced me to the core.

Trust and need and belief.

The woman was already keening in desire, and I'd hardly even touched her.

Lust pounded through my bloodstream. So intense I could hardly see. Could hardly control what was driving through me with the force of a hurricane.

Wild and messy and so fucking reckless I couldn't make sense of the toiling in my chest.

My spirit thrashed.

Alive for the first time since I could remember, if it had ever even beat before at all.

"So damn perfect," I rumbled.

I moved to rummage around in the drawer of her nightstand, and I pulled out her vibrator and her lube and tossed them onto the mattress beside her.

She whimpered. "Caleb."

I climbed up behind her and took her by both hips. "You said you wanted me to ruin you. Is that what you want?"

I took a fingertip and swirled it through the lips of her pussy. "Yes."

"Look at you." It was a moan because shit, this girl was too much, rocking back in an attempt to claim what she wanted.

"Have you even looked in the mirror? You're the hottest man I've ever met, Caleb. But you're more than the man who made my knees weak the moment we met. You're everything."

I reached over and took her toy, flipped it on, before I opened the lube and coated it.

She moaned as I brought the vibrating tip to her entrance. I barely pushed it inside, stretching her as I pushed it in, inch for inch, teasing her the way she'd teased me with it. "You nearly wrecked me the night you pulled this out, Paisley Dae. Shocking me at every turn. Wild, beautiful girl. How many times did you fuck yourself with this, thinking about me?"

A moan left her as I pushed it deeper. Deep enough that the nub rubbed over her clit. "Every night. Every night since I met you. How many times did you touch yourself thinking of me?"

She always threw it right back. I loved it, loved that she took what she wanted, that she wasn't shy, that she demanded what she needed.

"The second you drove off this ranch that first day, I went directly into my room and wrapped my hand around my cock, closed my eyes, and saw your face. I did it every day after until the day you wrapped that sweet mouth around it instead."

"Every day," she whimpered as she drove back onto her toy that I fucked into her pussy. "Every day."

There was a plea behind it.

I coated my fingers in the lube, swirling the tips around the entrance of her ass. I gave a soft nudge at her puckered hole. "Have you been fucked here before?"

She shook her head, that veil of white whipping around her as the air heaved from between her lips.

"Only with my vibrator, by myself."

She looked back. Vulnerability and trust and a desperate need churned in those mossy eyes.

A groan rolled up my throat.

Nothing but a siren.

My weakness.

My demise.

"Good girl," I murmured. I angled down and ran my lips down her spine, kissing her as I fucked her with her vibrator and slowly began to ease my fingers into her ass.

"Please," she whimpered. Her hands fisted in the covers of the bed.

I drove them deeper, in sync with her toy.

She began to rock.

Her body begging to be filled.

"Who do you belong to?"

"You. You, Caleb. And I need you. All of you."

I covered my cock in lube, then I shifted her around onto her back, taking her by both knees and spreading her.

"Do you trust me, Little Riot?"

"Yes." She lifted her chin. "I want you everywhere. Take me."

I lifted her by the hips enough that I could line myself at that sweet hole. "I'm going to make you feel better than you ever felt before."

I left her toy vibrating within her walls while I slowly began to work myself into her tight ass, teeth grinding to dust as I carefully nudged inside.

Paisley whined and pushed up on her shoulders, her hips lifting higher. "Caleb."

"I know, baby, just relax."

She raked her fingernails across my chest as if she were going to slash her way inside.

But she already had, hadn't she?

My vision hazed over, every nerve-ending coming alive as I filled her in a way no one else had ever filled her before.

I'd promised her I was going to give her more pleasure than she'd ever experienced, but I was wrong. It was Paisley who was giving it to me.

I nearly blacked out at the feel of her squeezing my dick. At the vibrations that rolled through her that were created by the toy, at the orgasm that hit her so intensely and from out of nowhere I felt it like a shockwave through my body.

Racing up my spine and spreading out to saturate every cell.

I almost came without even moving.

"Caleb, oh my God, Caleb."

"Are you okay?" I gritted through clenched teeth.

"I didn't expect...you just...I...it's so good." A ramble of incoherent words rolled from her mouth.

"I'm just getting started."

"I don't think..." She started to protest when I withdrew then slowly pushed back into her again. A low moan rolled up her throat, and she tossed her head back, hair all around her, her chest arching as she begged for me to take her deeper.

Her tits pointed toward the ceiling, her belly quivering with need as she yanked at the bedding below her.

Climbing onto my knees, I gripped her by the hips, holding her up so I could spread her wide.

I took her like that, fucking her ass while orgasm after orgasm rolled through her, her hands fisted in the covers like she was going to float away if she let go.

Mine.

The thought came so swift and unbidden as I looked down at her.

Mine.

My perfect match.

The one I was sure had been created for me.

And I wanted to hold onto her forever.

Keep her.

Take back every selfish, horrible deed I'd ever committed.

Be good enough for this perfect, chaos of a girl.

"One more, Reckless Angel," I told her.

Because bliss gathered fast, racing down my spine and tightening my balls. Too bright and too blinding. And I was losing focus, a haze of euphoria clouding my sight. The only thing I could see was the woman who writhed, her tits bouncing with each thrust, her hands reaching out for me, stroking down my face as she whispered, "I love you, Caleb."

The confession danced on her tongue as I let go.

I bucked into her, and a wall of pleasure split.

Breaking apart and spilling over.

An ocean that rose.

A dark abyss.

Starlit heavens.

Everything.

Everything.

I pulled out in time to spill my cum on her stomach, my body jolting as I spasmed with a pleasure greater than I'd ever known.

She shivered and shook.

Trembles rolled through her.

Sparks of life lighting on her gorgeous skin.

But her face. It was filled with the evidence of the words she'd just given to me.

And I wanted to admit it, too.

Say it, but I didn't know how.

Paisley ran her fingertips down my lips, my chin, brushed them down until they were fluttering softly over the clock imprinted on my heart.

The day my bleak world went completely dim.

"You might not believe it, Caleb, but you deserve to be loved, too."

Chapter Forty-Three

Paisley

LOVING HIM WAS LIKE FLOATING ON CLOUDS OF BLISS WHILE
tiptoeing through shards of broken glass littered on the floor. Joy
wrapping you in boughs of comfort while you waited for the moment
you'd be cut.

His touch impassioned.

His need profound.

Oh, but his fear was so great.

I watched him as he stared at the man in the mirror as if it were a
demon staring back.

Riddled in guilt and grief.

And I wished for a way to hold it. To share it with him. The blame
he carried for what had happened to his sister and the two men who'd
worked for him.

But Caleb Greyson wouldn't let me pry it away.

He held onto it like service.

Like debt.

The days passed like that—ten days where I loved him with all that
I had.

Ten days of me praying one day he would love me back.

That he might look in the mirror and see something different.

That he'd see the man who owned me—body, spirit, and mind.

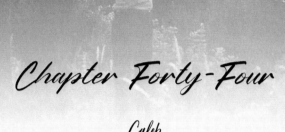

Chapter Forty-Four

Caleb

MOVING TO THE WINDOW IN MY OFFICE, I NUDGED THE heavy drape aside and peered out. Blue sky went on forever, the sun casting an endless warmth on the summer day.

Or maybe that warmth had everything to do with the sight of Evelyn and Paisley. Maybe they had everything to do with the way my chest expanded and the blackened mess that had been my heart pushed at my ribs.

Beneath a towering oak, its arms thick and its branches covered in green, they'd spread a blanket out on the lawn. A picnic basket was open beside them, and Evelyn was on her knees in front of Paisley, her hands animated as she flung and danced them through the air, clearly telling a story she'd conjured from her mind.

She'd been doing that a lot lately.

Playing.

Giggling.

Imagining.

Paisley's head rocked back, and she let her laughter ride toward the sky. I couldn't hear it from there, but I knew it'd be throaty and low. Just the thought of it sent a gnarl of greed to my guts.

A second later, Evelyn dove at her, wrapping her little arms around

Paisley's neck and sending her toppling back onto the blanket. Evelyn wrestled around on top of her, and Paisley began to tickle her, the two becoming a flailing pile of joy where they played beneath the sun of a perfect day.

Emotion crested.

Devotion so thick it obstructed the flow of oxygen.

I would do anything for them.

Absolutely anything to keep them safe.

My phone rang from my pocket, and I dug it out, jerking myself from the view out the window and pacing back into my office.

My chest tightened when I saw it was Mert. He only called when there were major issues he could not handle. The last time he'd called was to tell me Paisley had been in the accident with the horse. Suffice it to say, I did not relish hearing from him.

"Greyson," I answered.

"Mr. Greyson, it's Mert."

"What is it?" I couldn't keep the hardness from my voice.

He hesitated for a moment before he released a shaky breath. "We have an issue out in pasture nine."

"What kind of issue?"

"The kind of issue you're going to want to take a look at, sir. I sent one of the hands, Manny, to pick you up. He'll meet you out front of the house."

"I'm heading down now."

Dread curled through my senses, tightening every cell in a fist.

Always on edge.

I would need to return to Seattle soon. End this threat that waited for us there because I would never rest or find peace until it was done.

It only lurked, waiting around in the fringes of my mind and spirit, reminding me Evelyn would never truly be safe until it was done.

But each day here with the two of them made it harder to do.

This place that had become a fairytale.

A sanctuary in the storm.

But I needed to return to it before I became complacent.

I felt the truth of it as I bounded downstairs and stepped out into the blinding rays of light.

Could feel it on the breeze that wisped through the branches of the trees.

A vileness that crept up from the darkest places.

A shroud that had gathered in the moments of peace that I'd allowed myself.

Blood thugged through my veins, heavy and hot.

As if she felt the extremity of it, Paisley's attention snapped my way where she was hugging Evelyn to her chest.

Questions raced through her features, and I squeezed my hands into fists to keep the chaos at bay.

It didn't work, though, it only followed my every step, growing as I strode down the walkway and hopped into the front seat of the grimy work truck waiting for me at the drive.

Confused concern knit Paisley's brow, as if she could feel the apprehension radiating from me in noxious waves.

I didn't know what it was, but I felt pieces of myself flaying.

Fraying.

Wanting to come apart.

Manny gunned the accelerator, and I forced my attention out the windshield.

I struggled to reel in the disorder.

But I couldn't shake it as we sped down the dirt road.

About halfway up the long drive, he made a sharp left onto what could hardly be considered a path, just two worn tire tracks that led over the rolling fields and alongside the copse of trees before it opened up about three miles to the east at pasture nine.

"Here we are." Manny skidded to a stop, and I jumped out, striding through the gate that sectioned off this area. Four cowboys loitered at the top of a hill, their stances grim as I moved their way.

I couldn't help the spark of annoyance that Nate was one of them.

He wanted Paisley. I knew he did. So what if I was a selfish, possessive bastard for wanting to ram my fist in his face for it.

Tamping the irritation down, I edged to where they were gathered around something on the ground.

Vultures circled overhead.

A stench filled my nostrils the closer I came, and that dread grew in the pit of my stomach with each step that I took.

I shouldered through the group as the irritation rose.

Only I came to a quick, horrified stop, rearing back as nausea spun my guts in disgust and bile rose up the back of my throat.

I gagged at the sight and smell, while revulsion spiraled through my consciousness.

It was a black horse.

A black horse that had to have been laying there for days, its belly bloated where it had been gutted.

But what made me want to drop to my knees was it'd been slashed across the throat.

Visions flashed through my mind.

Kimberly.

Kimberly.

Her eyes vacant.

Her body mangled.

The slash across her throat.

My body tilted to the side, knocked from its axis.

He'd been here.

He'd been here.

Fuck, he'd been here.

I grabbed onto the back of my head with both hands to try to control myself while foreboding whirled through my mind.

Mert scrubbed a gloved hand over his mouth, gray hair sticking up at the back, his hat hooked on his knee. Disgust dug trenches into the lines that were already on his weathered face. "What do you make of that, sir?"

"I think some monster killed this horse," I forced out through the crushing awareness.

A message for me.

A warning.

A reminder of the sins I'd committed.

The things I had done.

Rage screamed through the fear.

"How long has this horse been like this?" I demanded.

Mert shook his head. "Four, maybe five days."

Shit.

He could be anywhere by now.

Violence burst in my blood, this sticky dread dumping into the vat of rage that boiled in the darkest recesses of my soul.

"Shit," one of the other hands spat, fighting his own anger. "Who would do somethin' like this? Horrible. Mean."

Terror pierced through me, as sharp as the knife that had slain this horse.

"You got any enemies?" Mert asked, still crouched beside the animal.

Grieved laughter stuck in my throat. "Yeah."

I forced myself to shove off the shock and focus on what needed to be done. Because I couldn't sit idle. Not when the threat loomed alive.

So close.

Too fucking close.

"Who has access to these fields?" I demanded, shifting into action.

Mert gave a half shrug. "About anyone could sneak on. You have miles and miles of land. Gates are locked, but it doesn't take much to go through one of these fences. Fences are intended to keep the horses and cattle in, not keep people out. Just like we had that cut fence a while back."

I began to pace, roughing an agitated hand over the back of my head that was dropped between my shoulders.

It'd been him.

It'd been him.

It had to have been.

Fuck. Fuck. Fuck.

"I want surveillance cameras added to each field."

The man had the nerve to chuckle, peering over at me like I was insane. "You won't be able to track everything, sir. It's probably nothin', anyway. People do weird, sick shit just for the hell of it. We can all keep out an extra eye."

He had no idea what was at stake.

No clue of the demon that had descended.

My hands curled into fists, so full of fury that I had to stuff them into my pockets. "Just get it done. I need to get back to the house."

"Of course, sir, whatever you want. Might take a few days."

"Let them know the urgency. I'll pay whatever they need to get them out here sooner."

I turned to the men who still loitered around the remains. "Nate, you're on watch here. Make sure no one comes or goes until the Sheriff gets here. The rest of you get back to work."

He dipped the brim of his hat. "Yes, sir. You mind if I sit back by the trees? Might be a bit for the Sheriff to make it out this way."

"That's fine." I turned my attention to Manny. "I need to get back to the house."

He nodded, and we both rushed back to his truck and jumped in. He whipped it around and gunned it as we took to the trail.

"Please hurry."

"Of course."

Dust whipped behind us.

A billowing storm.

Convoluted chaos.

Fear and hate and the violence that fought for release.

The sickness was so thick by the time he pulled back up in front of the house that I thought I would puke. Because on the drive, I'd come to the conclusion of what I had to do.

It was going to be the most painful thing I'd ever done.

But there was no other choice.

I flew out of the cab, not saying anything to him as I slammed the door shut behind me and immediately headed in the direction of Evelyn and Paisley who were still sharing their picnic on the grass.

Mossy eyes flared, strikes of emeralds that flashed as I stormed their way.

Panic thundered beneath my footsteps.

"What happened?" she whispered, the words raw.

"Get up." I could barely force it out around the agony that threatened to drop me to my knees.

A frown marked her brow. "What?"

"Get up."

"What's happening?"

"Come with me."

Each blunt command tore me to shreds.

I turned on my heel and started back in the direction of the house, and Paisley got up and clamored behind me, tugging Evelyn along by the hand. "What's going on, Caleb? Talk to me."

"Inside." I opened the door and thundered upstairs. My heart crashed in my chest as I turned left down the hall.

"Evelyn, please go to your room and shut the door," I instructed, each word barbs as I forced them from my throat.

Confusion and fear rippled through her innocence, and I fucking abhorred that I was the one to cause it.

But I had no choice.

No other choice than this.

I'd been careless in thinking he wouldn't come here. Thinking I would be the one to hunt him down in Seattle. A fool to believe this place a haven that couldn't be touched.

After everything? It was me who was the reckless one.

Evelyn slowly moved toward her room as if it were difficult for her to walk through the sludge of apprehension that dripped from the walls and oozed across the floor. She peeked back for one moment before she slipped into her room and clicked the door shut behind her.

The second she did, I turned and went into Paisley's room. The room where I'd shared the bed with her for the last ten days because we wanted to be as close to Evelyn as possible.

I went directly for the duffle bag I knew she kept stowed under the bed.

"Caleb, what is going on? Please tell me what's happening." Alarm filled her voice.

I dragged out her bag and threw it onto the bed. "You're fired."

She jerked back, slammed so hard with what I said, I might as well have struck her. "What?"

Pain sheared through me. Hot razors across my flesh. I ground my teeth. "I said, you're fired, Ms. Dae. Pack your things and get off my property."

I had to get her out of here. Out of my life and away from the danger that I had dragged to her door.

"You can't just fire me. Not when we've been…" She trailed off, unable to bring herself to say it. She kept blinking through the bewilderment, trying to catch up to the turn of events.

Events that had come from out of nowhere.

But I should have felt them coming all along.

I should have known he would come here.

That it wasn't safe.

That my life wasn't safe, and I refused to cost one more person I cared about their safety.

Their life.

The ultimate price paid for my sins.

And now he was out there, lurking in the shadows, waiting to strike.

"What can I say, I've had my fill." I managed to sneer it. The sound grinding from my throat was genuine enough, supplied by the hatred that boiled me in a vat of venom.

Paisley laughed a hollow sound, and her head slowly shook, that fall of white swishing around her gorgeous face as she watched me with a disappointment so severe it cut me in half. "You're such a coward, Caleb Greyson. A coward and a liar. You think I don't know what's going on here?"

"You don't know anything."

"Oh, I know plenty, and I know you're terrified right now. We're supposed to be in this together. Don't you dare push me away. Whatever has happened, we'll figure it out together."

"I can assure you I'm not pushing you away. I'm simply letting you go. Evelyn and I will be moving out of state tomorrow, and your services are no longer required."

Pain speared through her at the words I spat. I saw them penetrate. Strike her so deeply I wasn't sure she would ever recover from them.

But at least she would be safe.

Disconnected from me.

No attachment.

Tomorrow, I would take Evelyn to safety, away from this place, and find somewhere to leave her where she would be protected. Then I wouldn't stop until I'd put an end to this threat. The attorney already had the paperwork that would give Paisley custody in the works.

In time, they would be reunited.

"Don't you dare do this, Caleb Greyson. I'm right here, and I'm not going anywhere, just like I told you before."

I lifted my chin, my frozen-over soul that she had lit cracking down the middle. "You don't have a choice in the matter, Ms. Dae. Pack your things and get out of my house."

Hell, I'd do it for her.

I turned and began to drag open the drawers, stuffing everything I could into the duffle before I ripped open the closet door in search of a suitcase.

"Stop it, please, just stop this," she cried out, trying to get me by the wrist. "Please, stop."

I wrenched out of her hold and tossed a suitcase to the bed next to her duffle. I flopped open the lid and began stuffing more of her things inside.

"Stop it, Caleb, please." Her voice turned frantic, low and desperate as she kept trying to take hold of my arm. "Stop and look at me. I don't care what is happening or what you think you did. What you think you do or don't deserve. The only thing you need to know is I love you, and I love Evelyn, and I need you to love me back. Love me today. Right now. Please. Please love me back. You can't leave me. Please don't leave me."

I squeezed my eyes closed and forced out the words, "I warned you that you kept trying to see something that wasn't there, and it's not. It's time for you to go."

She held me for a moment, trembles rocking her through, her sobs contained.

Waiting for me to change my mind.

For me to take it back.

When she realized it wasn't going to happen, she let go.

She let go.

And I thought she must have been holding me up from going over a ledge where I'd been teetering. A lifeline that had been severed. And I was falling backward into a black hole.

Flailing.

A scream of the truth locked in my throat, forever forbidden from coming out.

Death waiting to consume me when I hit the bottom.

She slowly backed away.

Energy howled.

The tether ripping between us.

Heartbreak cracked in the room.

Banged and thrashed and battered the walls.

Then she turned on a stifled cry and rushed to the dresser where she snatched the keys to that monstrosity and grabbed her purse.

"Take the Range Rover," I growled, facing away from her as I continued to pack her suitcase, unable to look at her, knowing I would falter if I did.

"Screw you, Caleb Greyson." She didn't take her things. She ran out, her boots pounding on the stairs as she went. Below, the door slammed shut behind her, and the old truck grumbled to life when she started it.

I choked over the gnarl of torment.

Misery curdling my blood into venom.

But I'd known from the beginning.

I had no right to love.

I had one goal.

One fucking goal.

And I'd almost lost sight.

Chapter Forty-Five

Paisley

I forced Maybe to the limit as I barreled down the long dirt drive. Agony blurred my eyes, and I swiped at the tears, but they fell as fast as I could wipe them away.

I choked over the knot of torment in my throat.

He was leaving. With Evelyn.

Oh my God.

I couldn't breathe.

My spirit ached, howling for a way to go back.

I swiped over my runny nose as I tried to see through the haze of misery as I drove up the high hill. When I crested it, the ranch disappeared behind me, and with the way I felt my heart crack down the middle, I knew I'd left half of it there.

That it belonged there.

With Caleb and Evelyn.

And he was forcing me away.

Putting up those walls we'd finally knocked down.

Cutting me with those shards of glass I'd been tiptoeing through, and now I was afraid I was going to bleed out.

His words had hurt, but I knew they were lies. I knew something was wrong. Terribly wrong. That whatever had taken him away in that work truck had destroyed the little belief we'd begun to build.

I sniffled as I approached the end of the drive, the sign claiming Hutchins Ranch taunting me where it was inverted in my rearview mirror. I came to a stop, looking both ways before I turned left and accelerated onto the paved two-lane road.

A disorder blustered through, everything so heavy, weighted, and I couldn't shake the sensation that my spirit was being dragged back in the direction of Caleb and Evelyn.

The engine chugged, like Maybe felt it, too.

That disorder galloped and raced as I came up on a hill and saw the red and blue lights flashing on a white SUV that approached in the distance.

Unease festered and swelled the closer we came until I pulled over to the shoulder and it buzzed by at high speed, Sheriff painted on the side, Ezra Sutton at the wheel.

Fear clamored through my senses.

Oh God, what was happening?

Every part of me begged to go back. To be there for them. To be a part of whatever they were going through.

But how could I stay when he was pushing me away?

When he was leaving and taking Evelyn with him?

When he'd shunned every promise I had made him?

A cry erupted from my throat, and I struggled to focus on driving, on putting distance between me and the only place I wanted to be.

By some miracle I made it into town, and I choked over a sob when I realized I didn't even know where I was going.

I ended up in front of Time River Market & Café. I found a spot in the front, killed the engine, tossed open the door, and slid out onto unsteady feet.

Floating through the misery as I fumbled through the entrance.

Beth was behind the register in the gift shop.

She flew around the counter and toward me as I stumbled in.

"Oh, God, Paisley, are you okay? What happened?" When I

couldn't speak, she wrapped me in her arms and hugged me to her chest. "Dakota is back at her place. Why don't we head over there?"

I could only nod, and she tossed out some instructions to one of the other employees before she curled an arm around my waist and led me back outside.

We wound around the building to the gate that led to the house at the back of the property. It was two stories and attached to the far side of the restaurant, and there was a big fenced in yard where Kayden could play.

Beth unlatched the gate and led me the rest of the way to the stoop. The front door was open, the screen door keeping the bugs out. I could hear her singing a silly song to Kayden inside.

Beth rapped her knuckles at the metal frame. "Dakota! It's Beth and Paisley!"

In a flash, she was there, smiling through the mesh. But the smile melted off her face the second she saw me, and she flicked the lock and held open the screen door.

"Oh my God, Paisley, what's going on?"

I went right into her arms, sagging against her as she hugged me tight.

She just held me there while I sobbed.

While I sobbed and sobbed.

For a little girl who had stolen every part of my heart, and the man who had crushed it in his hands.

"They're leaving tomorrow." I choked it into her chest.

"What do you mean?"

"Caleb and Evelyn are moving away tomorrow." Pain slashed and sheared at saying it aloud. "They're leaving me, Dakota. They're leaving me behind."

It was a heaving tumble of words, soaked in this misery I couldn't escape.

"Shh," she whispered at my head. "It's okay."

"It's not okay," I wept, unable to keep it together. "It's not okay. Not when I love them this much. It hurts. Oh God, it hurts."

Beth rubbed my back, shushed me, too. "It might not be okay right now, but it will be."

"What did he say?" Dakota asked, still holding me up.

"Nothing except that they were moving out of state, and that he doesn't need me anymore. But it's a lie, it's a lie. He needs me. They need me."

Just as much as I needed them.

⌒

I was completely numb by the time I wandered up the walkway to my grandfather's little house. A place he'd invited me into, had promised was my home for as long as I needed it, a place I loved.

The problem was, it no longer felt like where I belonged.

Where I belonged was thirty miles down a deserted road, likely where they were packing their things so Caleb could run again.

Hide.

Leave.

Turn his back because it was easier for him to hate himself, to succumb to the fear, than to give into the love waiting for him to accept it.

Darkness had come an hour before, the night stilled and quiet.

Morbid and wrong.

I turned my key in the lock, then knocked at the door to give my grandpa a heads-up that I was there.

Cracking it open, I called, "Hey, Grandpa, it's just me."

It came out sounding like a croak with the amount I'd been crying, but I didn't have it in me to try to hide it.

Inside, it was almost completely dark, and I tossed my keys and bag to the floor and fumbled my way through the living room and into the back room where I could hear the drone of the news on the television.

The only light in the room emanated from it, illuminating him just enough that I could see the warmth in his expression.

"Well, what a nice surprise."

Except his excitement dulled and that warmth expanded when he saw my face. I could only imagine the mess that I was.

My eyes were swollen, and my lips were chapped, and I was pretty sure there was a wound gaping open in my chest where my heart had been ripped out.

"Oh, Paisley, sweetheart, what happened?"

"I went and got my heart broken, Grandpa."

He shifted in his chair and held out a hand, and I moved the rest of the way over to him and eased down on the arm of his recliner. I snuggled into his chest, and he wrapped his arm around me.

"I imagine it was that boy in the suit. Do I need to get my shotgun after him?"

He was so old school, fighting for my honor since I was a little girl.

"No, Grandpa, I'm pretty sure he punishes himself enough."

Grandpa hummed. "It's hard for a man to love when he's got demons shouting in his ear."

"You saw them?" I whispered, tears streaming free again and soaking into his shirt.

He pressed a gentle kiss to the crown of my head, the way he'd done when I was a little girl. When I'd get my knees scraped or my feelings hurt.

But this hurt was so big, so enormous he couldn't soothe it away, even though I knew he would do everything to try.

"I didn't talk to him for long, but it was clear enough to see he was haunted when he was standing there in my kitchen. There's something always missing in a broken man's eyes."

I sniffed. "I don't know how to battle those demons for him when he won't let me."

I felt him shake his head. "No, you can't because you'll just be fighting a losing battle. Never works unless someone picks up their sword and fights beside you."

More tears streaked, and I tried to contain the sob that busted through anyway. "I love him so much, Grandpa, and I love that little girl, too. More than I ever knew I could love anything or anyone. I feel like I was given a family, and a moment later they were ripped away."

I struggled over the soggy words, the pain in my chest making it impossible to breathe.

He squeezed me tighter. "You love her like your own."

I nodded where my head was tucked under his chin. "I do, and I'm not sure I'll ever heal from that."

"Breaks my heart for you, Paisley. I'm sorry."

I nodded against his shoulder. "Is it okay if I stay here for a little bit until I figure out what I'm going to do?"

"This will always be your home, Paisley. You don't ever have to ask or wait for an invitation."

"Thank you." I hesitated, then whispered, "You always warned me that life hurts sometimes."

"A whole hell of a lot of the time, but that just means we've gotten to experience love."

"Is it worth it?" I choked into the lapping shadows of the den.

I could almost feel my grandmother's spirit hovering in the corners.

He only hesitated for a moment before he said, "I wouldn't change a thing."

⌒⌒

I tossed most of the night on the small twin bed that had been mine since I could remember.

I'd sent Caleb a text at midnight, asking him to trust in me, telling him I knew the risks of loving him, all the dangers that went along with it, and that I didn't care.

I'd still stand by his side.

We could face it together.

But I hadn't gotten a response.

I had to accept it. Stop fighting it. Caleb had made his choice.

That didn't mean I didn't float in the misery of that choice the entire night. Dark waters dragging me under.

Holding me hostage.

The gutting reality that I hadn't only lost one person I loved, but two.

I felt empty.

A cavern cut out from the place inside me where my love for them had grown.

My grieving so intense for a little girl who'd become my very favorite day.

All of them.

Every single one that I'd been lucky enough to have spent with her.

With the first hint of the sun lighting at the curtains on my window, I climbed out of bed. I dressed, unable to stand being in the loneliness of that small room for any longer.

I grabbed my phone, already knowing my plea had remained unanswered, though it still sent a billow of despondency rippling through me when the last message on the thread with Caleb was the one that I'd sent him last night.

Needing to get out of the house before I lost it, I sent an SOS to my bestie.

Me: Tell me coffee is already brewed.

Two seconds later, she responded.

Dakota: We've already been open for an hour.

Me: See, and this is why I refuse to work for you.

I did my best to joke. To remember it wouldn't always feel this bad, except I worried I was only telling myself a lie.

Dakota: Yet you're awake at this ungodly hour. Sounds like you need to get your cute butt down here.

Me: Yeah, couldn't sleep and I don't want to be alone right now. Is it okay if I come hang with you at the café?

Dakota: Of course. You know you're always welcome here.

Me: Be there soon.

I tucked my phone into my back jeans pocket, brushed my teeth, then pulled my hair into a ponytail.

I scribbled a note for my grandpa and left it on the counter, promising I would be back later.

I stepped out of the front door and into the approaching day, the air cool and crisp as it brushed against my skin.

I inhaled it, trying to stave off the shivering that shook me to the soul.

Then I squinted through the misty light at the pickup truck that slowed then came to a stop in front of the house. Its headlights were still on, and I couldn't make out who it was.

I climbed down the two steps from the porch, and I started down the walkway when the passenger window rolled down.

Confusion twisted my brow.

"Nate? What are you doing here?"

That was when I heard crying from the backseat.

Evelyn.

"Ms. Dae! I need you! I need you!"

My heart rate kicked into a sprint, and I ran that way. "What happened?"

The truck only had two doors with the extra small cab in the back, and I ripped open the passenger door and climbed in on my knees so I could get to her, leaning over the seat.

"What happened, Evelyn? Are you okay?" It came out haggard, riddled with confusion and this sense of dread that whirred at the back of my mind.

"I want to go home." Her face was splotchy and red, brown eyes terrified. She was only dressed in her pink nightgown with the unicorns on the front, and her feet were bare. The seatbelt was strapped around her, but she wasn't in her booster.

Ice slicked down my spine.

I whirled back to Nate.

"Where's Caleb?" I demanded. "What's going on?"

He grinned with those dimples that had always made him appear cute. "Don't worry. We're just goin' for a little ride."

I could barely process the flash of metal before I realized it was a gun. That was one second before the butt of it cracked against my skull.

There was no time to react.

No time to scream.

Because in an instant, everything went black.

Chapter Forty-Six

Caleb

I WAS IN MY OFFICE, STUFFING ANYTHING OF IMPORTANCE INTO a case, my laptop and the few paper files I would need, trying to keep my fucking hands from shaking, but the bedlam going down in the middle of me was making it nearly impossible.

Agony stark.

My chest stretched so tight I thought I would implode with the force of it.

This misery that gathered from the darkened depths, inflating with the hatred of what I had to do.

I'd already packed what I needed in my bedroom and bathroom. I'd been up throughout the entire night, anyway, raging like a beast, pacing the floor as I kept checking out the window, waiting for the disgusting fuck to show his face.

Unable to sleep or settle.

Torn by what I had done.

The decision I had made.

But it was required.

There was no other choice.

I had to get Evelyn out of here before it was too late. Before the monster caught up. Before the one thing I was supposed to protect was harmed.

Visions flashed, images that I couldn't stomach of a little girl sustaining the same fate as her mother.

My sister.

I swallowed down the bile that stormed up my throat.

I couldn't fathom it.

Couldn't even consider it.

Wouldn't allow myself to think it because I *wouldn't* allow it to happen.

I'd failed at every other turn, but protecting Evelyn would not be one of them.

I glanced at my phone that I'd set on the desk.

My teeth ground as I warred with the urge to pick it up. Respond to her text. Tell her I was a fucking liar, and I hadn't meant a thing I'd said.

Confess the only thing I wanted to do was protect her. Save her from the fate I brought to those closest to me.

Save her from me.

I picked it up, staring at her plea, her promise that we could do this together, my insides a riot of desperation and need.

I forced myself to shove it into my pocket.

Responding would only make it worse.

I needed to end this.

Sever it before it was too late.

But it already felt too late, didn't it?

Like I'd dragged a hot blade through both of our spirits, rending them apart.

Spilling our hearts out.

Gutting pain was the only thing left.

Daybreak hovered at the edge of the sky, a hue of gray spreading over the heavens that should usher in warmth but sent a cold chill slipping beneath my flesh.

I would have to wake Evelyn soon.

Break her heart all over again.

Zipping up the case, I reminded myself there was no other way. Staying here and putting the child in danger was not an option. I never should have believed it would be safe in the first place.

Never should have given.

Never should have settled into this comfort.

Never should have fallen.

I carried the rest of my things down to the first floor where I'd already set a bunch of bags at the door, then I forced myself to return upstairs, preparing to once again be the one to destroy the child's joy.

The one to bear news I never wanted to give.

Only the last time, there'd been a wall of stone between us, a vacant place where this connection hadn't lived.

Could I be enough to comfort her this time?

My jaw locked as I hit the second-floor landing. I kept my footsteps quieted as I took the path toward her room, and I ignored the piercing agony that struck me as I passed the emptiness that echoed from Paisley's vacant room.

I couldn't contemplate it right then.

Only I felt that same emptiness echo from the bare crack of Evelyn's door. An awareness that hit me as hard as slamming face-first into a brick wall.

A spindle of dread curled down my spine, and I nudged the door farther open.

A dusky haze infiltrated her room, the space still trapped in shadows, though I had no issue recognizing that her bed was empty.

Her covers pushed back, the spot where she had slept divoted and vacant. I had just checked her monitor thirty minutes ago, and she had been there.

"Evelyn?" I pushed inside. I spun in her room while my heart thudded out of time. When there was no response, I rushed into the en suite bathroom. The door was open, and I flicked on the light, searching the barren space.

Nothing.

I ran back into her room and dropped to my knees to search beneath her bed.

Nothing.

Ice shivered through my soul, and I rushed back out into the hall, shouting, "Evelyn? Evelyn, where are you?"

Ominous silence shouted back.

My pulse raced, a vicious banging that pounded through my veins in a thunderclap of desperation.

Fear and torment and agony.

I blew into Paisley's room, searching every inch the way I'd done Evelyn's.

Again, it was empty.

I barreled back out and into the next guest room that had been vacant since we'd come here, my voice frantic and edged with a plea. "Evelyn? I need you to answer me. Right now. I know you might be upset with me over what happened with Paisley yesterday, but I need to know you're safe. Please."

The stillness screamed.

I darted in and out of rooms, the chaos in my chest beating harder with each room that was empty.

The downstairs was just as desolate as above.

The horse.

The horse.

It finally occurred to me where Evelyn would have sought sanctuary, and I rushed out the front door and ran down the path to the barn. I busted through the double doors.

Hope drained out of me when I found Mazzy alone in her stall.

"Evelyn!" I ran the length of the barn, shouting it from the top of my lungs. "Evelyn!"

Mert appeared at the open doorway, squinting through the murky film of morning light that streamed in through the cracks in the walls. "What's going on?"

"I can't find Evelyn."

"You check the house?"

"She's not there." I couldn't keep the bite out of my voice. "I want everyone up, searching every inch of this ranch for her."

"Yes, sir."

Mert turned and walked out, and I dialed 9-1-1. "9-1-1, what's your emergency?"

"My daughter is missing."

And I realized it was the first time I'd said it.

Claimed it.

Understood what it meant.

I gasped as the agony clawed and ripped at my chest, talons that tore through flesh and muscle and bone, flaying me open to where only spirit and soul existed.

I gave the woman all the information I could then I dialed Ezra's number. He answered, his voice garbled with sleep. "Caleb, what's going on?"

"Evelyn…she wasn't in her bed this morning, and she's nowhere to be found. He was here. He took her."

My knees went weak, and I reached out to hold on to a beam to keep from falling to them.

I knew he had her. Knew it down to the bitter emptiness carved in the middle of me.

"Shit," he rumbled, and I could hear rustling on the other end of the line. "I'm on my way."

"Hurry."

Then I called the one number I'd sworn to myself I would never call again. Terror ridged my spine, every molecule that made up my being held in desperation as it rang and rang. Her voicemail came on, the same annoying one that I'd come to love, her sassy, throaty voice playing through me in that recklessness that was this woman. "This is Paisley. If you're getting this message, you don't know what year it is."

Panic sieged my senses, and I begged, "I can't find Evelyn. Please call me back."

I dialed again, pacing back and forth three steps, counting the rings, each sounding off like the tolling of death.

No answer again.

I texted her, pleaded with her through the words to answer.

Ten minutes and ten calls went by without any response.

I dialed Ryder. He answered on the third ring. "What the hell, man? It's not even six in the morning."

"Evelyn is missing, and I can't get ahold of Paisley, either."

"She isn't at your place?"

"I ended things yesterday." The words were barbs. "There was a horse found on the property. Slain. The same as my sister. That monster is here. I know it, Ryder. I should have known I couldn't escape this. I was leaving this morning to find a safe place to take Evelyn."

"Fuck, man. What were you thinking? Why didn't you call me?"

"I need Dakota's number," I told him, rather than answering.

He rattled it off, then said, "I'll head over to her grandfather's place and see if she's there."

"I would appreciate that."

"You're family, Caleb. Of course. I'll let you know what I find out, and you do the same."

"Okay."

The moment the call ended, I dialed Dakota. It went to voicemail, too.

"This is Dakota. I'm probably baking something delicious. Leave me a message."

"Dakota, this is Caleb, I need to know if you've seen Paisley. She's not answering her phone. It's…important. Life or death. Please call me back."

Then I ran back to the house to do another search, a frenzy in each step, my blood cold by the time I'd covered every room and had come up empty again.

I could hear the shouts of the crew outside, Evelyn's name called again and again.

I stumbled back out the front door when two SUVs came blazing down the drive, their lights flashing as they came.

At the same time, my phone rang.

"Dakota," I wheezed when I answered, her name gushing out of me on a petition. A fucking prayer that Paisley was with her.

"Hey, Caleb…Paisley texted me that she was going to come into the café, but that was like an hour ago, and I can't get ahold of her." Worry laced her tone. "What's going on?"

Dread slicked beneath the surface of my skin.

"Evelyn is missing."

"What?" It was a breath of horror.

A horror I felt sink so deep it was the only thing I felt.

Fear. Horror. Desperation.

"I need to go. Please let me know if you hear from Paisley."

My phone rang again. That time, it was Ryder. He didn't give me time to say anything before he was shouting, "Her truck is there, but she's nowhere to be found, and her cell is on the sidewalk. Fuck, Caleb, this doesn't feel right."

The two SUVs skidded to a stop in front of the house.

Mert rushed up behind them, taking off his cap as he approached. "Sir, I thought you should know that it looks like Nate has skipped town."

Chapter Forty-Seven

Paisley

PAIN SHEARED THROUGH MY HEAD, SO INTENSE IT FELT LIKE an icepick had been stabbed into my brain. I moaned as I blinked against it, fighting the torture of opening my eyes.

I didn't have the luxury of giving into the agony trying to suck me back into oblivion.

Because I could hear them…her little cries coming from somewhere across the room.

Evelyn.

My chest squeezed in torment, desperate to climb to my feet, to claw my way to her, to make sure she was okay.

I finally managed to force my eyes open enough that I could take in my surroundings. I lay on my side on a hard, wood plank floor, the kind that was worn and uneven, aged and unkept.

It appeared to be one large room.

Dust coated everything, the rays coming in through the window clouded by the dirt caked on the glass.

But what I noticed most was the fact my wrists were bound together in front of me. That and the man who stalked back and forth in front of the door, raking an agitated hand through his hair with a huge knife clutched in the other.

Fear flash-fired, speeding through every cell of my body.

I couldn't see Evelyn, though by the sound of her, I knew she was likely against the far wall opposite me, out of my sight but not close to being out of my heart.

My heart that ran rampant, so loud it beat in my ears in time with the throbbing in my head.

Adrenaline a thunder, desperation whipping through the disorder that pumped.

I calculated, tried to process, my mind coming up with the horrible sum too fast.

Evelyn was being held hostage in a room with the same man who'd killed her mother. The same man who'd killed those two men to get back at Caleb.

A monster who raged in front of us.

A man I'd thought sweet. One I didn't have the first clue how to handle.

But I had to figure it out quick.

Be smart.

"Nate, what's going on?" I whispered, the words cracking on my dried tongue. I tried to keep it soft, without judgement, like I could keep the deranged from fully coming unhinged.

At the sound of my voice, he whirled around, and for the first time, I saw the delirium spinning through his gaze.

"Oh, good, you're awake. How are you feeling?" His voice was eerily tender, the way it'd been all along, like he was filled with concern for me, though now I recognized the way it was edged in mania. The edges of his words sharp. One misstep, and he would completely snap.

"I am. Why am I tied up?" I tried to play it off like I had no idea who he was or what he'd done.

"Well, I wouldn't want you to go running away from me now, would I?"

"Why would I run from you?" I had to swallow the vomit that rolled up my throat in order to get it out, my words far too sweet as they slipped off my tongue. I prayed they were more than saccharine to his ears. That he took them as genuine.

It made it freaking hard when my little Evie-Love whined from the corner, and I realized she had to be gagged with the way it was slurred and garbled. I wanted to beg him to let her go. Tell him she was just a little girl. Promise him I'd take whatever he had planned for the two of us, that he could hurt me as much as he wanted, just as long as he set her free.

But I knew it was the wrong move. It would only incite a madman. Because I could feel it, the vibration that pulsed beneath his skin, the wickedness that churned through his veins. Wickedness he thought he was entitled to.

His jaw creaked as a rush of rage rippled through his body. "You fucked him, didn't you?"

God, I wanted to cover Evelyn's ears. Protect her from this. But there was nothing I could do but lay there and play along.

I forced a frown to my face. "Who?"

"Mr. Greyson. You're impure, just like her." His voice hissed in an accusation.

Confusion swept through me, twining and twirling through my consciousness. I fought to figure out what to say. How to get through this.

"Mr. Greyson is just my boss, just like he is yours."

He scrubbed a flustered hand over his face. "I see the way you look at him."

"I'm just nice to everyone."

"You left with him that night when you were supposed to leave with me," he argued.

"Only because my friend Dakota was sick. I thought I was riding with our other friend to take her home, but Mr. Greyson insisted on driving me back to apologize for being a jerk. He's a jerk a lot, you know."

I forced the tweak of a smile to the edge of my lips, hating with all of me every word that dropped from my mouth.

"But you moved in with him."

"That's because I'm Evelyn's nanny. I'm just there to take care of her. To keep her safe." I didn't even want to speak her name or bring attention to her, but I didn't have a choice in the matter. Not when I was fighting for our lives.

His attention flashed to her, and something moved across his face that twisted a knife through my guts. "Yes, we have to keep the little one safe. He took her from me, and he's trying to take you from me, too."

What the hell was he talking about?

I was lucky I was able to keep from spitting it aloud.

Panic thrummed, if possible, harder than before.

"I don't know what you mean, Nate. Let's just…talk. You and me." I shifted so I was sitting against the wall, groaning against the pain splitting my brain. I held my arms out in front of me, silently asking him to cut the rope he had wound around my wrists.

I struggled not to look to my right to search for Evelyn, her muffled cries riddling the air in her fear. I had to keep him focused on me.

Before I could process it, he was in front of me, kneeling on one knee. He pressed the tip of the knife to my neck. With his other hand, he'd fisted my hair and yanked back my head, exposing my throat.

Terror shocked through my senses.

"Nate," I begged. "Why are you doing this? I thought we were friends."

He only tightened his hold on my hair. "You're a slut and a tease just like her, aren't you? You all are. Pretending like you're interested then spreading your legs for someone else."

Panic surged and the confusion flared, and my lungs squeezed so tight that I couldn't breathe. I angled back, needing to get away from the blade trembling in his hand.

His fury distinct.

"I don't know what you're talking about, Nate."

"Kimberly, that whore." Delirious rage poured from his mouth. "After I offered to give her everything, she said she didn't want anything to do with me, Paisley. She lied and said Evelyn wasn't mine. Can you believe it? My own daughter?"

My head spun. What was he saying?

"She fucked those guys at work. She thought I wouldn't know. That I wouldn't see. But I was watching, Paisley. For four years they kept me locked up. Did she really think I would have forgotten when I got out? I had to teach her a lesson for what she did, and those men deserved it for touching what was mine. But when I showed her what her actions had caused, gave her the chance for atonement, she started screaming. After everything she'd done, she was going to blame me?"

Holy shit.

Holy shit.

His confession careened through my consciousness.

Kimberly hadn't been killed out of retaliation toward Caleb.

Nate had killed Kimberly and the men he knew she'd slept with.

"Then that piece of shit Greyson took my daughter, and he tried to take you, too. He'll pay for it. I have to punish him, just like I had to punish Kimberly. Punish her for being a slut. Tell me I don't have to punish you, too."

Frantic, I shook my head. "No. You don't. I'm right here."

He laughed an ominous sound. "You know, Caleb Greyson actually thought he was going to find me. Pathetic. I was here the whole time. Watching. Waiting. Everyone thinks I'm the fool, but I know everything. I know who deserves to live and die. And I'll make him pay for trying to take my daughter away."

Oh my God. I tried to breathe through it, to figure out how to make him believe that I was on his side.

"He is a total jerk, isn't he? Let's go. You, Evelyn, and me. Right now. Let's go. Leave this place." I tried to smile, to nod in encouragement, to push the words out around the clot of horror that locked my throat.

Fear potent.

Greater than anything I'd ever felt.

I just had to get us out of here, and I'd figure the rest out later.

He stroked the pad of his thumb along the angle of my cheek. "Okay. We're gonna have to take care of Greyson first, though."

Sickness clawed at my stomach, then one second later, the door burst open. Dust flew through the tumultuous air.

Caleb stood in the doorway when it cleared, lit by the light that streamed in behind him.

In a flash, Nate was on his feet, and he yanked me to mine and pulled me in front of him, pinning my back to his chest while he kept the knife pressed to my throat.

Terror ripped through my consciousness, while all those blips of memories you see before you die flashed through my mind.

The things that meant the most. The things that counted. The love and the laughter you shared.

But in the end, right that second?

It all amounted to one thing.

One thing that mattered.

A promise of hope that spilled from my mouth and sealed my fate.

"Caleb, get Evelyn and run!"

Chapter Forty-Eight

Caleb

THREE HOURS HAD PASSED SINCE EZRA AND HIS TEAM HAD shown. Three hours since Ryder had called. Three hours since terror had blotted out hope.

Everyone I knew had descended on the ranch, Ryder and Cody and a bunch of their friends. Six more officers had arrived from the next county over.

We'd embarked on searching every inch of the ranch, scouring for a trace, a clue, anything that would indicate where Nate had gone.

An APB had been put out on Nate's truck, plus Paisley's and Evelyn's faces had been broadcast on every news channel and social media outlet, asking for any information.

Dakota and their friends were out talking to everyone in the town, showing pictures, begging everyone to keep an eye out and to report anything suspicious.

More officers had been sent to Paisley's grandfather's house. There was no evidence of an altercation. The only thing of note was her phone that Ryder had found on the sidewalk. It'd likely slipped from her hand or had been tossed out the window.

Because Nate had been there.

He'd been.

I knew it.

Knew it to my soul.

And Paisley wouldn't have been skeptical of him showing, either. She would have trusted him. She would have climbed right into his truck, lured by a monster who'd hidden in broad daylight.

I wracked my brain for any hint of recognition. Where I knew him from. How we were connected. What I had done to him that made him believe warranted the vile depravity.

There was nothing there. No recollection of his face or his family name.

There had to be a reason.

A tie.

I couldn't fucking believe he'd been right here, under my nose the whole goddamn time. He had passed my rigid background check. Had slithered around like the scum that he was while wearing that smug smirk on his face.

He'd been the one in control. The one manipulating this fucked up, twisted match. Toying with me, biding his time while he had me in knots, spinning me in fucking circles while he'd been pulling the strings.

Lurking.

Taunting.

Waiting to strike.

Horror curled through me in a snarl of sickness. I just prayed to God we'd get to him in time. That he wouldn't harm them before we found him.

Because everything about this felt different.

Before he hadn't left a trace, and now, it seemed he wanted me to know his face.

And somehow—somehow, I knew they were near. Could feel their hearts bounding in my veins. Could sense their spirits. Could almost hear them calling my name.

I'd just finished going back through the barn when my cell rang.

"Mert," I answered, desperate for news.

He cleared his throat. "There are some fresh tire tracks leading out to pasture three. Fence is clipped again in the same spot as last month. Not sure how long it's been that way, but gauging by the dirt, looks recent to me."

My mind raced, hopelessly searching for a connection, for anything that would draw someone out that way.

"The cabin." I wheezed it when it hit me, remembering Paisley and Evelyn telling me about the dilapidated cabin they had found on one of their rides out in that direction. "The cabin."

I ended the call without saying anything else, immediately dialing Ezra who was searching the next property over. "Did you find something?" he asked when he answered.

"Think I know where they are. There is an old cabin to the northeast of my property. Paisley and Evelyn found it on one of their rides. Mert found some tracks that led that direction."

"Stay where you are, I'll be right there." He ended the call.

That was not going to happen. Every second that passed lessened the chance that they would be found alive.

I didn't hesitate, I ran from the barn and toward one of the hands who'd returned after searching on horseback. "I need your horse."

I mounted it, taking the reins, kicking my heels into its flanks and sending it bolting across the ranch. My gun burned where I had it tucked in the holster at my side.

A thunder of hooves pounded below me as we blew out of the main area of the ranch and into the fields, rushing over the land.

Here, the grasses were knee-high.

We barreled through the disorder.

I felt it.

The mayhem that whipped through the hot air that blew against my face.

Chaos.

She was near.

I felt her like a reckless dream that electrified my soul.

A thrumming call in the distance.

The horse must have felt it, too, the urgency in his stride as we raced over the hills. We followed along about two hundred yards from the river, taking a scant path that drove us east.

My chest squeezed as we made it over a hill. There was a thicker section of trees tucked close to the river, but what seized my heart was the sight of the pickup truck sitting a ways back from them, as if it couldn't go any farther and had been abandoned.

The closer I came, I could see the doors sat open.

I flew past it, jerking the horse to a stop when the terrain became too rough, and I'd be faster on foot.

I jumped off, racing for the trees, finding a path that ran the edge of the river where the trees had become a narrow wood.

Dense and thick.

Massive branches stretched out in a vast canopy, shrouding the rays of sunlight and creating a lush garden below.

I fumbled along beneath them to the sound of the rushing river, the chirping of birds, and the thunder of my heart that beat like a war drum in my ears.

Pulsing and banging as I tore through the green grasses and wiry brush.

Intensity swelled.

That feeling I'd thought I could never recognize. The one I'd wanted to shake.

It possessed me then. Overflowed. Became the life beat in my soul.

I slowed when I was impaled by the aura.

Menacing and cruel.

A frenzy was in the middle of it. Fear so thick it coated my tongue, filled my lungs with their desperation.

Wrath rushed through my veins, a stampede that trampled all reason and sight.

I quieted my steps as I pushed through the disturbance that clotted the air, crouching lower as I came upon an area that was more overgrown than the others. Shrubs rose up to create what looked to be an unkempt fence line.

The beats of my heart turned jagged.

Spikes of frenetic energy that pumped.

There was an opening where a gate had likely once stood, and all the oxygen fled from my lungs when I peered inside to the flattened plot of ground.

In the middle of it was a tattered shack, long deserted, the roof caved in on one side and the railings of the porch splintered and sagging. The glass was shattered from one window.

Small cries emanated out.

Clawing through the thickened air in a despairing plea.

Voices intoned beneath Evelyn's whimpers, hushed, painted in their own oppression, though wisped in a faulty hopefulness.

Feigned.

Paisley.

"He is a total jerk, isn't he? Let's go. You, Evelyn, and me. Right now. Let's go. Leave this place."

I could feel the way every word shook from her tongue.

I pulled my gun from the holster, inhaling as I flicked off the safety then cocked it. I edged through the break in the foliage, gun in two hands, each step careful and quieted. I tried to control my breaths that hacked in and out, cleaving gasps that sent shockwaves of fury palpitating ahead of me.

I eased closer, trying to conceal my footsteps as I stepped onto the crumbling porch and to the door.

I inclined my ear to the wood.

"Okay. We're gonna have to take care of Greyson first, though."

Fear saturated through.

And I knew I couldn't sit idle. Every second that passed only put them at greater risk.

I reared back and kicked it in.

It clattered open. Dust billowed, kicking up a grimy haze. Through it, my eyes darted, calculating everything.

Evelyn was on the left. Bound and facing the opposite wall.

Paisley and Nate were on the right. He'd been crouched in front of her, but in a flash, they both were standing, the fucker using Paisley as a shield as he jerked her back to his chest.

A blade was pressed to her throat.

Relief gushed out of Paisley when she saw me.

And for the flash of a second we were held.

Held in understanding.

Then she shouted, "Caleb, get Evelyn and run!"

"Knew you'd come," Nate snarled from behind her in some kind of twisted triumph, ignoring Paisley's shout.

"I'm right here," I told him.

My gun was angled down toward the floor, ready to take the shot when he gave me the opportunity.

Tears tracked down Paisley's face, those mossy eyes dampening in a plea.

Go.

She was willing to sacrifice herself for Evelyn.

My perfect, reckless angel.

My chest tightened, words grinding out as I forced myself to look at Nate. "You were waiting on me? So why don't we hash this out? Man to man. Only a pussy would draw women into it."

I refused the flash of my sister's face, refused the agony, focused on taunting this bastard into doing what I needed him to do.

Because I needed him to let my girls go.

They had to be safe.

They had to be.

His laughter was riddled with disbelief. "You thought you were just going to take her from me?"

He'd wanted Paisley.

I'd known it.

I just hadn't known there was a psychopath behind it.

"Paisley doesn't have anything to do with this."

Incredulity dripped from his snort. "I'm not talking about Paisley, though it's clear you wanted her, too. I'm talking about Evelyn."

Evelyn?

At the sound of her name, Evelyn whimpered.

I wanted to run to her.

Cover her ears.

Shield her from the fear and pain.

"Your sister tried to keep her from me, now you. You Greysons think you get to run the world, don't you? Keep a man from his child? She paid for it, too. Now you're going to."

Chaos whipped.

A storm through my mind.

What was he talking about?

What was he saying?

"She didn't even tell you who Evelyn's father was, did she? Bitch thought she could keep me a secret except for when I found her running back to your office that night like you were going to protect her from the fate she earned. She wasn't going to get away with it, and neither are you. I've come to take back what's rightfully mine."

That time Paisley whimpered, and she mouthed, *Get Evelyn.*

While the mayhem spun. Spun and spun through my mind.

The realization catching up.

He'd killed my sister because he was Evelyn's father.

But why my Director of Project Management? Why my corporate attorney?

"Kimberly was nothing but a slut, and I sure was hoping Paisley here wasn't, but it looks like it to me. Did you fuck him?"

He shook her violently then.

Delirium oozed from his pores, insanity in the tip of the blade piercing her flesh.

Paisley cried out, whimpering as she succumbed, fully leaning back against him as tears tracked down her face.

I scoffed, even though it was choked. "I haven't touched her. This is between you and me."

"Well, we already know you die today. The question is, if Paisley here is gonna die, too. Seems to me, you changed your tune as soon as pretty boy showed up here." He hissed it at her ear.

Frantically, she shook her head against his chest. "No, I haven't. I'm right here. Let's go. You and me."

"Liar."

He dragged the blade across her throat.

"No!" I shouted.

Blood spilled out, and he shoved her forward. Her hands went to her throat as she dropped to her knees.

"Paisley!" I screamed. Agony cut me in two. "Paisley!"

"Go," she gurgled.

Horror sheared through me, my entire body in turmoil, in this rage and desperation.

I lifted my gun to Nate, but he'd produced his own, and I knew I only had one second, and I had to make a choice.

A choice I never wanted to make.

I fired a shot at him.

I didn't wait to see if it'd struck. I rushed for Evelyn and scooped her into my arms. I had to get her out of this cabin, to Ezra who should be here any second, then I would return for Paisley.

The perfect weight of the child almost made me stumble. The relief of having her in my arms. The truth that she was breathing and whole.

I darted back to the doorway to the shouts of the monster behind me, "You piece of shit. You were always gonna die, but now it's gonna be painful."

Protecting Evelyn against my chest, I shifted enough that I could fire a wayward shot in his direction, hoping to divert him.

I just had to get her through the fence line, and she would be safe.

I flew through the opening, rounding to the path that ran the river.

Two officers were running our way, their guns drawn.

Relief blazed, mixed with the shearing torment that burned me through.

Paisley. Paisley. Wait for me. Wait for me. I silently begged it, screamed it, compelled her spirit to listen.

To hang on.

Not to let go.

"You bastard. I will peel the skin from your body," the voice hurled from behind.

I could feel the heat of his poison seeping out, the malignancy, an infection that threatened to overwhelm.

"Get down!" Ezra was suddenly there, coming up to the side of the other officers, his gun drawn.

346 | A.L. JACKSON

I dove to the ground, protecting Evelyn the best I could as we hit the thick grasses below. My body covered hers.

Armor.

A shield.

My life I would gladly give.

Gunshots rang out. Piercing the air.

Shouts and roars.

I covered Evelyn's head, held her against me while I peered out to the mayhem that went down beside us.

Nate was struck again and again, his body riddled with bullets. He stumbled back and to the side before he tripped into the river.

Gone.

A roar of something unintelligible ripped out of me, and I hugged Evelyn to me for a second, whispering, "You're safe. You're safe. I have to get Paisley. Stay right here."

I tried to keep the tremoring out of my voice, the misery that wailed.

I jumped to my feet.

"Get an ambulance out here!" I shouted as I ran back for the cabin, fucking hating with every step that I'd left her, but I knew putting Evelyn first was what Paisley and I both had to do.

Because she was our meaning.

The purpose we had found.

One we had found together without having any clue of its significance. The way one little girl would change us.

I blew back through the doorway and dropped to my knees at her side. She was face down on the hard plank floors.

Blood pooled around her.

"Paisley." It left me as a prayer. "Paisley."

I touched the side of her neck. Her pulse point beat weak. So weak. A bare intonation that still blustered through my veins and poured into my soul.

I slowly rolled her over. Her face was ashen, her lips so pale, her neck gaping where he'd slashed it open.

Ripping off my shirt, I balled it up and pressed it firmly to the wound. "Paisley."

"Oh, fuck." Ezra gasped it behind me.

"Get an ambulance!" I screamed it that time. "Get an ambulance right now!"

I turned back to her, leaning over her, begging her, "Stay with me. Stay with us. We need you. Today, baby. We need you today. Now and forever."

Because I didn't know how to do this without her.

The one who'd come into my world and shaken it to its foundation.

Changed everything that I knew.

This chaotic, wild girl.

My beautiful, reckless angel.

Chapter Forty-Nine

Caleb

I SAT SLUMPED IN THE CHAIR OF THE SMALL ROOM, HELD IN THE silence that droned with tragedy. A television hung on the wall, muted with captions running along the bottom of the screen.

The news channel replaying and replaying the headline that the Seattle Slayer had been killed during an abduction/hostage situation in Colorado.

I wanted to ram my fist through the fucking screen, hating the way they repeated his atrocities, that they gave him a name as if he'd earned a title.

His real name had yet to be announced publicly, though Ezra had called and given it to me, saying his family would also be informed. Cowan Gringling. A man with a long history of mental illness, psychiatric admissions for homicidal delusions, someone my sister had somehow fallen in with before she'd realized the demon hiding underneath.

Five years ago, he'd been convicted of attacking his mother in her kitchen. She'd survived, and a year ago, he'd been released.

A year ago when he'd killed Raffi and Miles.

A year ago when he'd killed my sister.

I blew out a strained sigh and sat forward, resting my elbows on my thighs as I scrubbed my palms over my face like it could break up the thousand pounds of exhaustion that weighed me down.

So heavy I could hardly breathe, the oxygen squeezing in and out, each a prayer issued to the heavens.

I'd been in this room for the last three hours.

Paisley had been AirVac'd to Denver to a level 1 trauma center. I'd forced my way onto the helicopter, refusing to leave her side.

She'd coded on the way here, suffering hemorrhagic shock.

Because she'd lost too much blood.

Too much fucking blood that I was covered in.

The only solace in this was that Evelyn was safe.

Forever.

There would no longer be a threat lurking in the shadows.

I sniffed, not realizing moisture blurred my eyes until I heard the commotion at the door. I looked up to find Ryder, Ezra, Dakota, and Paisley's grandfather rushing in.

All the kids were staying with Dakota's mother, including Evelyn. Ezra had seen to it that she was cared for, checked out that she had no injuries, before he'd taken her to Pat's house so everyone could make the drive to Denver.

At least I knew she was safe.

Surrounded by people she knew until I could get back to her.

And I prayed she'd find comfort in it, in the new friends she'd gone on about, in her family that she was just getting to know.

I thanked God she'd come to identify this place as her home.

That we could stay here now.

We didn't have to run any longer.

My chest constricted and my heart wobbled. But at what cost?

"Oh my God, Caleb, have you heard anything else?" Dakota rushed forward. Her face was a mess, splotched with red, her eyes so swollen it seemed impossible she could see through the slits.

I forced myself to stand on my weakened legs. "No. Not since we got here."

"Oh, God." She wrung her hands, and tears slipped from the corners of her eyes. "Please let her be okay."

Ryder wound his arm around her waist to support her. "She's going to be. She has to be."

He met my gaze, pain in his, for Paisley, for Dakota, for me.

"Are you okay?" he asked.

My head shook, and I tried to swallow around the splintered razors that had gathered in my throat.

Ezra stepped forward and pulled me into a hug. "It's okay, man. It's going to be okay. Evelyn is safe, and that fucker is dead. Rest in that for now."

"There's no resting until I get to look into Paisley's eyes."

Tightening his arms, he nodded in understanding, murmured, "You will."

When he pulled away, I turned to Paisley's grandfather who loitered just inside the room, the old man fidgeting with the cap he'd pulled from his head and fighting the tears that brimmed in his eyes.

I moved to him, forcing my voice to cooperate when I stood in front of him. "There are not enough apologies to make up for what happened today."

Each word curdled on my tongue.

Sorrow rippled through his aged features, his voice craggy when he spoke. "And not one you owe. She loves that little girl like her own, and I think both you and I understand the willingness to die for the ones we love. Paisley would. I know she would. But it's not gonna come to that. I feel it. Right here."

He knocked his fist against his heart. "She's too strong for that. Has too much life inside her. Too much to give. Probably a bit of trouble to get herself into, too."

I choked on a soggy laugh. "I'm sure there is a bit of that left inside her."

"You gonna be waiting for her when she wakes up?"

"Yes."

He gave me a clipped nod. "Good. Then after that, you promise me you won't ever leave her side."

"I won't."

Sniffling, he wiped his nose with a handkerchief.

"You should sit down and rest. I was told it might be a while," I told him, but we didn't have a chance before a woman opened the waiting room door and poked her head in.

"Paisley Dae's family?"

"That's us."

She slipped in, and I fucking hated the grim expression she wore, the way her jaw was long and dread pooled in the depths of her brown eyes. "I'm Dr. Laconie. Paisley is out of surgery and in intensive care recovery."

A collective breath was released, the air lightening by a lifetime of sorrow.

Everyone reached out, grabbing onto each other. Hands twined. Fingers squeezing with all the power our souls possessed. Like with the connection, we could breathe hope and belief into existence, and by extension, it would be poured into Paisley.

The doctor's attention jumped around to each of us, care in her voice when she continued, "She is stable at this time…" She slowed, carefully phrasing her next sentence.

"But she did code again during surgery."

I nearly buckled, the air ripped from my lungs. On my left, Dakota tightened her hand on mine and her grandfather clamped down on my forearm as both of us nearly dropped to our knees.

"We were able to get her back quickly, so she wasn't without oxygen for long, so we are hopeful there is no brain injury. But she did lose a lot of blood. The good news is the cut was at an angle and missed her trachea and jugular, saving her from bleeding into her lungs, but her carotid artery on the right was nicked. We were able to repair the injuries, and she received a massive blood transfusion. Now we have to wait to see how her body repairs itself. We should know more in the next twelve hours."

"Thank you," I forced out.

She gave a soft nod. "It's going to be a long road. You might want to get showers and some rest. I understand the extreme duress of the situation earlier today."

She looked at me when she said it.

But I wasn't going anywhere.

Because as soon as they let me in her room, I sat vigil.

Her hand held in both of mine, her knuckles to my lips, the machines beeping quietly in the background while that energy whirred.

Twelve hours passed.

Then twenty-four.

Two days.

It was close to three days before she finally opened those mossy eyes.

Sparks of emerald.

Glimmers of life.

"Reckless Angel," I whispered at her knuckles, my heart crashing in my chest, battering at my ribs to get to her.

The storm I never expected.

My sweet, perfect chaos.

Chapter Fifty

Paisley

CALEB ANGLED INTO THE PASSENGER SIDE OF HIS RANGE Rover, slipping one arm around my back and the other beneath my knees.

"What are you doing?" I asked as he picked me up and into his arms. "I can walk, you know."

Except the words came out hoarse, my throat still sore and making it hard to speak.

It only made that stony jaw lock tight as he knocked the door shut with his hip. "What does it look like I'm doing, Paisley? I'm carrying you inside."

He began up the walkway toward the house.

This house that the last time I left, I'd despaired I'd never see again.

My home that I'd ached for because of the people inside.

This man who was all harsh, rigid lines and steeled, controlled ferocity and the little girl who'd written herself on me in permanent ink.

Evelyn had spent the last two weeks with Dakota and other times with Pat when Dakota was needed at the café. Caring for her. Loving her.

This patchwork family coming together to care for the child who'd come to mean the most.

I'd been hospitalized that entire time, mostly sedated because of the severity of the pain and to help me heal faster, then I'd been asked to speak as little as possible once I'd been well enough that they hadn't kept me under.

The whole time, Caleb had never left my side other than to go to a hotel to take a shower or to run downstairs to grab food.

This morning, I'd been discharged on heavy meds and instructions that I would start therapy next week. Instructions that I needed to continue to take it easy and rest.

Instructions that Caleb had clearly taken to heart.

He carried me through the door and upstairs to my room while I clung to him.

He set me on the edge of the bed, then he climbed down onto his knees in front of me, the man between my legs as he took both my hands between his.

"Caleb."

His head shook as he tightened his hold. "You're supposed to talk as little as possible, Paisley, so please let me be the one who speaks."

Part of me wanted to roll my eyes and accuse him of being bossy, but I couldn't with the swell of intensity that blazed around him. Severity binding the muscles of his arms.

The ice of his eyes molten.

Blue fire.

We'd spoken so little during my stay at the hospital. His only concern had been my getting well, his whispered prayers as he'd clung to my hands filling me full of belief.

I'd asked only of Evelyn, and he'd promised me she was safe and staying with Dakota and her mother.

That she was alive and whole because of me.

But the truth was, we were both alive because of him.

Because he'd fought the only way he knew how to.

Now, he knelt on his knees at my feet like an offering. Like he still didn't understand the way I saw him. As if he hadn't already been absolved.

He curled both hands around mine, and he pressed my knuckles to his lips, staring up at me when he began to speak. "Now that you're home, I need to say a few things."

I pulled my hand away and brushed my fingertips through his hair, silently encouraging him to continue.

His eyes dropped closed for a moment, like he was gathering himself.

Then he opened them and stared up at me with that potent gaze, his voice rough and raw when he began to speak. "The day everything went bad, you asked me to love you, Paisley. To trust you to stand beside me and Evelyn. You'd promised we could do it together. But I pushed you away because I thought it was the answer. I thought having you in my life would only bring you danger, and I was terrified of it. So fucking terrified of you being hurt that I *hurt* you."

Pain filled his raspy words. "I said things that were lies to drive you away. And still, you ended up right back with us, anyway."

A choked sound locked in my throat. I ran my fingertips down the sharp edge of his gorgeous face.

Electricity hummed at the connection.

Affection spun through his features, and he reached up, fluttering his fingers over the bandage on my throat without touching it. "You protected her, Paisley, protected this child that was committed to my care. Protected this child the way a mother would."

Moisture gathered in my eyes, and Caleb pushed up higher on his knees. Running his fingers through my hair, his head angled in emphasis. "You protected her the way I want to forever protect you. The way I should have in the first place. By keeping you close, right beside me where you belong, but I was the fool who thought you'd be better off with me pushing you away."

He swallowed hard, his throat bobbing with emotion. "But pushing you away only hurt us. And I know I have warned you that I've done horrible things in this life, and I have. Any number of them could have made someone hate me enough that they were willing to commit these atrocious acts to get back at me. That's not going to go away, Paisley, but I can promise you that I will be a better man than the one I was. I'll fight to be worthy of you and Evelyn."

"Caleb." Emotion curled through his name.

He shook his head. "Please let me finish."

I dipped my chin in a soft nod, my insides shaking with his confession, and he only held onto me tighter as he continued, his thumb brushing over the tears that kept tracking down my cheeks. "I'd only allowed myself to love one person in my life because I never thought I had the right, and maybe I don't, but it doesn't matter."

He took me by both sides of the face, framing it in his big hands, the burn of his eyes meeting mine. "Because there is not one thing in this fucking world that could stop me from loving you, Paisley Dae. Not one thing. Because I love you. I love you today, and I'll love you tomorrow, and I'll love you forever. And I'm kneeling here, at your feet, begging you to forgive me. Begging you to love me back."

Everything I thought I'd lost swelled in anticipation, and I pushed out quieted words around my sore throat, unable to keep from speaking. "You think I stopped loving you? Do you think I didn't understand? That I didn't know?"

"I hate that I hurt you. That I did it wrong."

I nodded through the blur of tears. "You did do it wrong, but then we finally did it together, and that's what matters."

Air puffed from his nose, and he nodded. "Together."

"*Together,*" I mouthed.

He dropped his forehead to mine. "I love you, Paisley. I love you in a way I didn't know existed. In a way that I feel in every beat of my heart. With every breath that I take. You consume every minute. Every second. You and Evelyn? You're my life now. In every way."

Joy bound me in intricate knots, my voice rasping with the truth. "And I love you. Every day. Now and forever."

Torment continued to roil in his eyes. His regrets. The sins. Everything he'd done wrong. I touched the hollow beneath his eye. "Are you upset that you weren't the one to end him?"

I remembered…remembered how vehemently he'd wanted to be. The vengeance that had pounded through his bloodstream, driving him to animosity and hate. He'd thought he'd succumb to it.

His head shook, and his voice deepened in emphasis. "I wanted revenge, Paisley. I'd wanted to hurt the man who'd hurt my sister, somehow thinking it might make up for the things that I'd done. But in the end, it didn't matter—it didn't matter because the only thing that mattered was you and Evelyn."

He inhaled then rushed. "I realized I didn't need revenge. I needed my family."

Emotion tightened my chest, and I traced my fingers over his face. His brow and his cheeks and his lips.

Overwhelmed.

Overcome.

Complete.

A riot of knocking suddenly echoed from downstairs. Dakota's voice carried on the air. "Hello, we're here."

"Upstairs," Caleb shouted back. He pushed to standing, though he didn't move from my side.

A thunder of footsteps clattered on the wood, banging up the stairs and down the hall until Evelyn was standing in the doorway.

All messy brown hair and wide brown eyes and adorable dimpled chin.

Wearing shorts and a pink tee and her bedazzled boots.

The beat of my heart and the story of my soul.

She raced in, and she threw her arms around my waist and buried her face in my stomach. "It's my very favorite day in the whole world because you got home, and I love you to the moon and all the way back again."

I smoothed my hand down the back of her head, and I turned my gaze up to the man who was staring down at us.

Yeah, it was my very favorite day, too. Every single one I got to spend with them.

Chapter Fifty-One

Caleb

THE NEXT MORNING, I STEPPED OUT THE FRONT DOOR WITH Evelyn's hand in mine. The sun was a white orb where it blazed in the endless blue of the Colorado sky, and the child trotted along at my side as we headed down the path in the direction of the barn.

Paisley was resting.

Recuperating.

And I wasn't sure I'd ever been so grateful for anything in my life.

That and the little girl who kept beaming up at me as she skipped along, radiating excitement.

But it was the scars beneath that had me clinging tightly to her as I led her down the path. What had everything locked tight as I thought of what I would say to her.

I hadn't gotten the chance to talk to her much during the time Paisley had been in the hospital. Our hopes and worries wrapped up in her care.

But now—now I prayed it was a time to move on.

That it was a time for peace.

A time for healing.

"I think it's really good that you want to go to the barn with me to see Mazzy. She's going to be so excited to see me because I haven't seen her in so many days, and she definitely missed me a whole lot, as much as I missed her, because I love her so much and she loves me right back." The ramble of words fell from her as she kept grinning up at me.

Each glance tightened my chest in a way that I'd once been terrified to contemplate.

"I know she is definitely going to be excited to see you."

We rounded through the double doors that stood open. Mert gave me a nod as we passed. There was a reticence to the vibe of the crew. No doubt, what had happened here had affected them. Left them unsettled and questioning everything since they'd considered Nate one of their own.

No one had guessed or known.

A man named Cowan who had changed his name when he'd last been released from the correctional facility where he'd been kept in the psychiatric ward. When he'd found where we were living, he'd learned everything he could about ranching, a fraud who'd pretended to be someone he was not.

A chameleon who'd slipped in unnoticed.

It still made me sick, but I'd also come to understand I couldn't continue to live in the past.

In the mistakes.

In the fears and regrets and shame.

Mazzy whinnied when we came near, and Evelyn let go of my hand, bouncing on her boots and clapping her hands as she squealed, "See! I told you she missed me. Do you hear her telling me how happy she is to see me?"

She raced for the stall gate, hiking up on her toes, singing, "I love you, too, Mazzy! I came back, and now I'm home, and I get to stay with you forever!"

Forever.

It sounded about right.

I held her back so I could unlatch the gate, and I stepped inside, running my hand up the horse's neck, somehow knowing she would never hurt Evelyn.

That she and I were now kindred spirits.

A team that got lucky enough to be a part of Evelyn's life.

Evelyn came forward, using the skills Paisley had taught her, still cautious as she approached. Mazzy pressed her muzzle into Evelyn's face.

Giggling, Evelyn threw her arms around the horse's neck. "You are the best horse in the whole world."

I leaned back against the stall and just watched her for a bit, as she took the brush out of her small tack box and began to brush Mazzy, her sweet voice filling the air as she rambled to her horse, telling her about how much fun she had with her cousins and Kayden while she'd been at her long sleepover.

My throat thickened, and I knew it was time for me to push into the subject of why I'd brought her out here. "I'm really glad to hear you had a good time with Ms. Dakota and Ms. Pat."

"It was a really good time, but I missed you and my Ms. Dae the most."

I eased forward, choosing my words carefully. "We missed you a lot, too, and I thought about you the entire time while we were at the hospital."

"So Ms. Dae would get all better?"

"That's right. Because she went through something really scary and bad, but now she's going to get better. It's something you went through, too, Evelyn."

I could almost see the way her little spirit flailed in the memories. Palpable.

Battering against me and making me want to wrap her in my arms. She quieted her voice. "I didn't get hurt even a little bit, so it's okay."

I came to kneel in front of her, turning her to face me. "But I bet you were scared."

Hesitation filled her before she gave me a timid nod. "I was really very scared, but you came on a horse even when you don't even like to ride on them, and you took me and Ms. Dae away from the bad man."

She said it like I was their hero.

But I was no knight.

I was just a *bad man* who'd learned what was good.

I brushed a lock of brown hair from her face and tucked it behind her ear, keeping my voice soft. "And now he's gone forever, and he can't hurt you anymore, but sometimes just thinking about it—remembering it—can make us scared again. But I want you to remember that I'm always right here, watching over you. And if you're feeling scared, you can come to me, okay? You're never alone."

"I like that."

"I like it, too." I tipped up her chin. "I like it because I love you, Evelyn. I love you so much, and I need you to know that you and Ms. Dae are the two most important things to me in this world."

And that feeling that I'd fought for all these months swelled, breaking free of its confines.

Flooding.

Washing.

Infiltrating every crack.

Her smile was shy, and her shoulders went up to her ears. "Because we're your favorite day?"

"Yeah, you're my favorite day."

"Good because I already love you to the moon and back again."

Emotion crested. So fucking thick I could hardly speak. "And I know I can never replace your mother, Evelyn, and I know you miss her, but I want you to know you're my family now, and I will always stand for you and fight for you and support you, and I'd like to be your dad if that's alright with you."

"Well, I already got enough uncles, and I never had a dad, so I think that would be a really good idea."

A choked laugh scraped free, and I pulled her into my chest and hugged her tight.

She wrapped her little arms around my neck.

Devotion thrummed. A thunder of this love that I'd refused.

And I'd thought in one moment my heart had gone dead.

A moment in time marked with my end.

I was wrong.

I'd just needed a reason for it to beat again.

Epilogues

Paisley

I CUT THROUGH THE BIG RED RIBBON ON THE BARN DOOR. A barn that had been built about an acre up from the main one. A barn with stables inside and new pens out back. A barn built on the land that had stolen my breath when I'd come over the hill to find the beauty waiting below.

But it was the people I hadn't known were waiting for me that had changed everything.

A round of cheers went up as the ribbon fell to the ground, and Evelyn jumped at my side, clapping her hands like crazy as she shouted, "You did it, Ms. Dae. You did it!"

My spirit kicked, and I swept my hand down the back of her head as she beamed up at me. "We did it. I couldn't have done it without my favorite business partner, now could I?"

"We're a really good team, right?"

"That's right, we are."

Strong arms wrapped around me from behind, and Caleb leaned in and pressed a kiss to my cheek, his voice a low scrape that never failed to make my belly flip. "I'm so proud of you, Paisley."

Everything hummed. "Thank you for helping me reclaim this dream."

I looked up at the sign over the doors.

Our Favorite Day Equestrian Care Center.

"It's all you. I'm just glad to get to be here to witness it."

Dakota stepped into our line of sight, grinning that smirk she liked to wear. "Well, I think congratulations are in order. Good job, Paisley-Cakes. I knew you'd find exactly what you were looking for."

My heart expanded, and I glanced at the two people at my side who had filled every recess of my heart, made me realize what I wanted in my life and who I wanted to live it for. Then I looked at my grandfather who was looking at me with that soft belief and pride he'd always watched me with, and my heart expanded that I got to have it all. Be with Caleb and Evelyn, plus my grandfather now lived with us, taking one of the rooms on the bottom floor of the house. I couldn't describe the joy it brought me that I could still fully be there for him, too.

Then my attention drifted to the rest of our friends who'd gathered to celebrate our opening day.

I'd known when I returned to Time River I was returning to where I was meant to be.

Coming home.

And home was what I found in a little girl who was only supposed to have been an easy job to make some extra cash and her grumpy, surly, suit-wearing dad.

Except he didn't wear a suit anymore. He was wearing jeans and a rugged button-down, the sleeves rolled up to expose the ink on his skin. That strong, fierce jaw was coated in stubble that I was constantly scratching my nails into, never able to get enough.

The man the sexiest thing alive.

He'd sold off Greyson Industries, his time now committed to the ranch, committed to us because he no longer wanted to be a part of the world he'd left behind.

And he was tugging at my hand with this expression on his face that had me quirking up a brow. "What are we doing?"

"Come with me."

"Where are we going?"

Evelyn giggled and clapped, and I was just then noticing that Ryder and Ezra were leading our horses over. Calista, the mare I'd claimed as my own because it turned out Caleb really didn't mind a bit if I took one since he had plenty to go around just like Evelyn had said, and the one Caleb used when he rode.

My grandfather led over Mazzy.

All three of them were already saddled.

"Up you go," Caleb said, patting Calista's saddle.

A frown crawled to my face. "What are you up to, Mr. Greyson?"

I only used his last name when I wanted to tease him. He'd make me pay for it later. I couldn't wait.

"Just want to go with my girls on a little ride. Do you have a problem with that?"

"With all our guests here?"

"They'll be waiting for us when we get back."

A low laugh rippled up my throat. "All right, then."

I put my boot in the stirrup and tossed my leg over my gorgeous horse. Evelyn followed suit, just like I'd taught her to do, my little one who was fast becoming a pro. Caleb mounted his.

We took off at a slow canter, hooves kicking up a cloud of dust as we headed to the northeast. It was our favorite direction to explore. The area might have held some awful memories, but we'd set out to making better ones. So Evelyn wouldn't be fearful of the beautiful land and be rest assured that it was her home.

So even when the ugly thoughts crept into her mind, she would have the good ones to combat them.

And she rode without fear at my side.

Her sweet face filled with joy, with that belief and goodness that had always poured out of her.

Caleb was on my opposite side, sneaking peeks at me that throbbed at my center and rushed through my blood.

I didn't think I'd ever felt so right than I did right then.

The cool breeze whipping in my face as we raced over the rolling hills.

Caleb led us in the direction of our favorite spot.

A grand bur oak we'd discovered about a mile up along the river.

Someone had to have planted it more than a hundred years before, its branches thick, twisting high and low, creating a lush canopy overhead and the perfect picnic spot underneath.

We had them often, our bonds strengthening every day.

And today as we came upon it there was already a picnic waiting. A blanket was spread out with a basket sitting on top.

But it was the words that had been formed by a bunch of river rocks in front of it that brought me to a quick stop.

Marry me.

And I realized Caleb was already off his horse and on his knee.

"Paisley Dae, on this day of new beginnings, on this day of chasing your dreams and following your heart, I was hoping your heart might have followed me to this place, too. The second I saw you, you nearly knocked me to my knees. This wild, beautiful, reckless girl who stole my breath and made me crazy. Turned out, you were only making me crazy for you. Wholly and completely. And you're going to have me on my knees for my whole life, and I hope you'd be willing to spend that life with me."

I slipped off the side of my horse, my fingers pressed to my face as tears blurred my eyes.

Evelyn bounced at my side, grabbing for my hand, her face so bright. "Do you love him to the moon, Ms. Dae?"

"Yeah, Evelyn, I love him to the moon. And I love him all the way back."

Caleb

Paisley slowly dropped to her knees in front of me.

A halo of white whipping around her stunning face. Mossy eyes sparking with that emerald green.

A treasure. That chaotic beauty I'd never stood a chance against.

"What do you say?" I murmured as I reached out to trace my thumb along the apple of her cheek.

"Nothing would make me happier than getting to share this wild ride of a life with you." She said it as she glanced at Evelyn with a wistful smile on her face, the woman so in tune with the child who grinned at my side.

My heart drummed a wayward beat as I dug the ring from my pocket and took her trembling hand and slipped it onto her finger.

I never thought my life would come to this. That I'd get a chance at something good and right. That after everything I'd done, two people would look at me like their lives were better with me in it. I thought I'd deserved a world of isolation spent in my penthouse suite in Seattle with the proof of my sins hidden in the shadows below me.

But they'd proven to me I wasn't defined by what I'd done, but instead I was defined by the man I chose to be.

And I'd chosen to be one that lived for them.

Fought for them.

Cared for them.

Supported them as they chased down their dreams.

The greatest gift and honor I could ever receive.

Evelyn leaned in close to my ear, whispering, "Do you think it's okay if Ms. Dae is my mommy now?"

A deep ache stretched across my chest. I would forever miss my sister. Would forever regret the way everything had happened between us.

But in the end, I knew she had trusted me.

She'd trusted me with her daughter.

A child who'd knitted Paisley and I together.

Irrevocably.

Permanently.

Completely.

Tears streaked down Paisley's face. Paisley and I had talked about it at length. We'd decided to give Evelyn the time to make that choice for herself, knowing it would be confusing for her. Paisley never wanted to take Kimberly's place. Never wanted to try to erase her memory.

She just wanted to be there for Evelyn in whatever capacity she needed her.

"If you would like that, Evelyn, then I would very much like it, too."

Evelyn grinned and stuck out her hand. "Then it's a deal."

Paisley choked over a laugh, pulled Evelyn to her chest and hugged her instead, and I wrapped my arms around them both.

Breathed them in.

This gift I'd never expected.

A love I'd never thought I'd possess.

And I'd cherish it.

Today, tomorrow, and forever.

Because in them, time beat again.

About the Author

A.L. Jackson is the *New York Times* & *USA Today* Bestselling author of contemporary romance. She writes emotional, sexy, heart-filled stories about boys who usually like to be a little bit bad.

Her bestselling series include THE REGRET SERIES, CLOSER TO YOU, BLEEDING STARS, FIGHT FOR ME, CONFESSIONS OF THE HEART, and FALLING STARS.

If she's not writing, you can find her hanging out by the pool with her family, sipping cocktails with her friends, or of course with her nose buried in a book.

Be sure not to miss new releases and sales from A.L. Jackson - Sign up to receive her newsletter http://smarturl.it/NewsFromALJackson or text "aljackson" to 33222 to receive short but sweet updates on all the important news.

Connect with A.L. Jackson online:

FB Page https://geni.us/ALJacksonFB
A.L. Jackson Bookclub https://geni.us/ALJacksonBookClub
Angels https://geni.us/AmysAngels
Amazon https://geni.us/ALJacksonAmzn
Book Bub https://geni.us/ALJacksonBookbub

Text "aljackson" to 33222 to receive short but sweet
updates on all the important news.

Made in United States
North Haven, CT
07 July 2024

54501277R00224